Annie S. Swan

The gates of Eden

A story of endeavour

Annie S. Swan

The gates of Eden
A story of endeavour

ISBN/EAN: 9783744748780

Printed in Europe, USA, Canada, Australia, Japan

Cover: Foto ©Andreas Hilbeck / pixelio.de

More available books at **www.hansebooks.com**

THE GATES OF EDEN.

FIVE SHILLING SERIES.

---*---

THE GATES OF EDEN.
A Story of Endeavour. By ANNIE S. SWAN. Large crown 8vo, cloth, with Portrait of the Authoress.

BRIAR AND PALM.
A Study of Circumstance and Influence. By ANNIE S. SWAN. Large crown 8vo, cloth extra, Illustrated.

ONE FALSE STEP.
By ANDREW STEWART. Large crown 8vo, cloth extra, Illustrated.

NOEL CHETWYND'S FALL.
By Mrs. J. H. NEEDELL. Large crown 8vo, cloth extra, Illustrated.

SIR JOHN'S WARD.
By JANE H. JAMIESON. Large crown 8vo, cloth extra, Frontispiece.

ST. VEDA'S; or, The Pearl of Orr's Haven.
By ANNIE S. SWAN. Large crown 8vo, cloth extra, with Frontispiece by ROBERT M'GREGOR.

KILGARVIE.
By ROBINA F. HARDY. With Frontispiece by ROBERT M'GREGOR, R.S.A. Large crown 8vo, cloth extra.

MADELINE POWER.
By ARTHUR W. MARCHMONT. Large crown 8vo, cloth extra.

AFTER TOUCH OF WEDDED HANDS.
By HANNAH B. MACKENZIE. Large crown 8vo, cloth extra.

THE GUINEA STAMP.
A Tale of Modern Glasgow. By ANNIE S. SWAN. Large crown 8vo, cloth extra.

EDINBURGH & LONDON:
OLIPHANT ANDERSON & FERRIER.

THE
GATES OF EDEN

A STORY OF ENDEAVOUR

BY

ANNIE S. SWAN

(MRS. BURNETT-SMITH)

AUTHOR OF 'ALDERSYDE,' 'CARLOWRIE,' ETC. ETC.

' I cannot hide that some have striven,
Achieving calm, to whom was given
The joy that mixes man with heaven:

Who, rowing hard against the stream,
Saw distant gates of Eden gleam,
And did not dream it was a dream.'
—TENNYSON'S *Two Voices.*

NEW EDITION

TORONTO, CANADA

WILLIAM BRIGGS

EDINBURGH & LONDON

OLIPHANT ANDERSON & FERRIER

1893

CONTENTS.

—o—

THE GATES OF EDEN.

CHAPTER I.

THE SHADOW OF DEATH.

'Then fell upon the house a sudden gloom,
  A shadow on these features, fair and thin ;
And softly, from that hushed and darkened room,
  Two angels issued where but one went in.'

LONGFELLOW.

'YE think she'll pu' through, Jenny ?'

'Eh, I dinna ken ! Katie Law never had muckle strength tae come an' gang on, and she's been mair dowie this while nor I likit tae see,' answered Jenny Scott ; and her kind eyes turned with a mournful interest on the neighbouring cottage, about which there was a solemn hush of expectancy that summer afternoon, for there were great issues at stake.

'John Bethune 'll miss Katie, if she be ta'en awa',' said the first speaker, settling herself in the doorway for a comfortable gossip. 'I've often said tae oor Tam that he's faur ower muckle set on her.'

'I wadna say that, Kirsty; she's a winsome, bonnie cratur. I've bidden aside her noo for twa year an' mair, an' I never saw but a smile on her face.'

'Aweel, maybe no; but I like folk that can girn whiles, it shows they hae some gumption,' said Kirsty Paterson. 'But I'se warrant ye John got the wrang side o' her whiles as weel's ither folk's men.'

'I dinna think that, Kirsty,' said Jenny, shaking her head; 'she's fell fond o' him tae. Eh, I houp she'll get through, for his sake as weel's her ain. He's a by-ordinar' fine man. As I say whiles to Sandy, he hasna a brither.'

'Aweel, gie me a man that disna set hissel' up for better nor his neebors,' maintained Kirsty stoutly. 'I'm sure it wasna at Auchtermairnie he got his graun' ideas, for auld John Bethune's a canny man, an' jist like his neebors. He kens the taste o' Jean Brunton's ale, I'll warrant ye, though John in-by pertends that he wadna fyle his lips wi't. But I say,' she added, lowering her voice, 'wha's in-by forby the doctor; onybody frae Auchtermairnie?'

Jenny Scott shook her head.

'Na, it's no Shoosan Bethune that'll come to Katie Law in her trouble. She's never been i' the Star that I ken o' sin Katie cam'.'

'No, she has not,' said Kirsty, with quiet relish. 'An' my guid-brither's sister's man i' Kennoway telt me that Shoosan said she wad never darken their door while she leeved. And when he telt me, I jist says, says I, whaur did thae Bethunes get their pride? Though Katie Law was only a bit servant lassie, was she no' as guid as them? Nae doot they hae been in Auchtermairnie verra near as lang as the Laird's folk hae been in Ba'foor. But what aboot that? They're nae better nor wark folk. I canna bide sic pride.'

'Wheest, Kirst! is that no' a bairn greetin'?' interrupted Jenny in a warning, excited whisper; and immediately they strained their ears, and stretched their necks over the paling towards John Bethune's door. But the dead stillness there remained unbroken by the slightest sound.

'D'ye no' ken wha's in? Is Nanny Broon doon?' asked Kirsty eagerly.

'There's naebody that I ken o' but Jean Cam'll,' answered Kirsty. 'Her an' Kate's aye been thrang, ye ken.'

'Ou ay, faur ower thrang; I've often said to Tam there wad be a grand turn-up among them. Jean 'll be up in the buckle the day then. She likes brawly to be first an' foremost,' said Kirsty Paterson, for she had an old grudge against the mistress of the Knowe. 'For me, I wad think shame to stap my nose into ither folk's business the way she does.'

'John gaed for her, Kirsty, for I saw him mysel' just efter denner-time. Nannie Broon's maybe in tae, for ocht I ken.'

'Wheesht, wummin, there's somebody at the sneck!'

At that moment the two worthies were rewarded by the sight of John Bethune himself on the threshold of his own door. His face was white and haggard, the deep eyes under the rugged brows darkened by a strange agony, his voice when he spoke scarcely rose above a thick, unsteady whisper.

'Get somebody to rin to Auchtermairnie, will ye?' he asked, apparently unconscious of the devouring interest with which they hung upon his looks and words.

'Ay; the skule's oot, I hear the bairns,' answered Jenny at once. 'I'll rin for my Tammy, an' set him aff at aince. Hoo's Katie?'

The man only shook his head, implored her to lose no

time, and again vanished within.   The neighbours looked
at each other a moment, then simultaneously and omi-
nously shook their heads.

'I'll awa' for Tammy,' said Jenny at last, and, march-
ing up the road, she collared the urchin from a band
gathered round the window of the shop, greedily eyeing
the latest thing in 'sugar-bools,' and marched him down
to the house, instructing him concerning his errand all
the while.   At the door she took in the greasy leather
bag which contained his school-books, and, bringing him
instead half a pease-bannock spread with treacle, bade
him be off, and not let the grass grow beneath his feet
till he got to Auchtermairnie.   Tammy retired at a brisk
trot along the dusty road, encumbered by neither shoes
nor stockings, the wide corduroy breeches of his mother's
make flapping like sails about his sunbrowned knees.
After having satisfied herself that Tammy was really off,
Jenny Scott returned to her gossip, and the pair plunged
once more into the luxury of speculation to which Katie
Law's serious illness gave rise.   The whole past, present,
and future of the Bethunes was discussed, and they concluded that if Katie died and left a living bairn, John's
sister Susan would just need to return to her old post of
housekeeper to him, and, as that would leave the old man
and Peter uncared for at Auchtermairnie, they set about
finding a wife for the latter, and so their talk became
a very involved and responsible affair, which it would
not be easy to follow out to any sort of ending whatsoever.

Meanwhile Tammy, having got beyond his mother's
observation, was taking his time over his mission.   The
first interruption occurred at the smithy, which was a
favourite resort of his, and where he would sit for hours
watching John Henderson at his work, thinking him far

more to bo envied than a king. To Tammy it seemed a
beautiful and splendid thing to have nothing to do but
nail shoes on to horses' feet, and blow up the fire till it
glowed again, the latter part of the smith's labours being
especially to be desired in the winter-time. He whisked
round the corner, and, planting himself on the seat of a
reaping-machine awaiting repair, contentedly munched
his treacle bannock, and watched the smith's operations
with devouring interest. They were especially engrossing
at that moment; for one of Carriston men had brought
in an unbroken filly to be shod, before she was put out
to the grass. She was a dainty, high-bred thing, intended
for Mr. Lawson's own riding, and she seemed to have a
curious aversion to standing still. The sweat was pouring
over the smith's face, and the man at her head was red
with his exertion of trying to hold her in. After having
watched the shoeing process to a close, Tammy leisurely
descended from his perch, and crossed the road to the old
quarry to look whether the birds were hatched in a nest
under a whin bush known only to himself. Having
satisfied himself on that point, and carefully handled the
eggs, he bethought himself of his errand, and ran across
the fields like a hare, plunging through hay and corn,
knowing his supple limbs would soon carry him safely
beyond observation or chase. It was after five o'clock,
and Susan Bethune was sitting down to her afternoon
cup of tea, when he arrived breathless at the door of
Auchtermairnie,—a cosy farm-steading standing a little
off the road, within half a mile of Kennoway.

'I'm no' for naething the day; awa' ye go,' she called
out in answer to the knock, but started to her feet when
the urchin answered back shrilly,—

'Ye're to come awa' to the Star as fast's ye like, my
mither says. Katie Law's maist awfu' ill.'

'Oh, it's you, Tammy Scott!' said Susan Bethune un-graciously, when she came out to the door. 'Wha set ye wi' that message then?'

'My mither set me. I think John Bethune bade her,' answered Tammy. 'The doctor's there, because Jock Philp was haudin' his pownie, an' a' the wives is oot, so she maun be gey ill.'

'Weel a weel, tell them I'll come wast when I'm ready,' said Susan Bethune with a peculiar compression of her lips. 'Here, see, there's a piece tae ye, an' see ye dinna stane the jeuks as ye gang by.'

Tammy accepted the burnt end of oatcake offered to him in rather a gingerly fashion, and directly he got past the house he laid it down on the garden dyke, and pro-ceeded to look out for the ducks, which had never been in his thoughts till Miss Bethune herself mentioned them. In a few minutes there was an unusual splash-ing in the mill-dam, and the air filled with a chorus of quacking, while Tammy, having had his sport, and fear-ing the consequences, ran off home as fast as his bare and nimble feet could carry him. Susan Bethune, how-ever, paid no attention to the noise proceeding from the mill-pond, her mind being completely absorbed by the news the boy had brought. It had spoiled her tea, and after taking another mouthful she poured it out, and put the things back in the dresser. Then she set on the pot for the six o'clock porridge, and went out of doors in search of her father. They were all hoeing in the potato field, the old man keeping up his drill with the rest; but when he saw her waving at the gate he put down his hoe and crossed over to speak to her; as he did so he wiped the sweat from his brow, and stretched himself with a sigh. He was very weary, for he was a bent old man, whose days of toil ought to have been past. But so long as Peter Bethune, who was now absolutely master in Auchtermairnie, had his way, there would not be much resting for any within its walls.

'That's a laddie frae the Star, faither,' said Susan, directly he was within hearing. 'John's wife's doon, an' they're seekin' me to come wast.'

Nothing could be more unreadable than her expression of face as she uttered these words; it would have been impossible to tell whether she was well or ill pleased at the summons.

'Ye'll gang then, Shoosan?' said the old man eagerly. 'The puir lassie has nane o' her ain,—ye'll gang to the Star surely noo?'

'I dinna ken,' said Susan, and there was evidently a hard struggle going on in her mind. 'They maun learn that a'body's no' aye at their beck an' bow. John 'll find his error noo, I'm thinking, in mairryin' a cratur wi' nae folk.'

'Wha's laddie was't, an' what did he say?'

'It was that wee deil, Tammy Scott. It's maybe a' a lee, ye ken; but he said the doctor was there, an' of coorse a' the clashin' wives is oot.'

'Then ye should gang awa' the noo, Shoosan,' said the old man anxiously; 'Pete 'll let me lowse, an' I'll yoke Donal' in the milk-cairt for ye.'

''Deed no; I'm no' gaun ridin' through the Star for them or ony ither body. I'll awa' in, an' mak' the par-ritch. It's near six onyway, an' I'll hae my goon an' bannet on gin ye come in,' said Susan. 'Tell Geordie, wull ye, to bid Else come down to the byre at half aicht, for I'll no' be hame.'

So saying, Susan Bethune nodded her head once or twice, and stalked away back to the house.

'What was Shoosan seekin'?' asked Peter, stepping from behind the workers to speak to his father.

'Katie's doon, an' they're for her wast, but she'll no gang or it comes up her ain back,' said the old man, and he looked across the flat fields to the clustering red roofs of the little hamlet, where his favourite son had his home, and there was a wistfulness in his eye which told that all his sympathies were there.

'She's quite richt. There's naething like bein' independent wi' folk,' said Peter with a coarse laugh. 'John should hae been mair canty wi' Shoosan when he had her. Ye canna blame her noo.'

'He never did ocht till her. It wasna a deidly sin to tak' a wife,' said the old man mildly.

'Shoosan thocht it, though,' laughed Pete again. 'Come on, then; we can gang up an' doon the dreel again afore six.'

A rough, uncouth, ill-conditioned fellow was Peter Bethune, and his blustering, domineering disposition was quite in keeping with his outward appearance. He had a tall, slack, ill-knit figure, and a big head adorned by a shock of tawny hair, already thickly mixed with grey. A heavy beard concealed the lower part of his face, but there was nothing attractive in what was visible. The eyes peering out from under the shaggy brows were of a steely blue colour, and his glance, though as keen as that of a fox, seemed restless and shifting, and was never a moment still. Susan Bethune was not greatly beloved, but everybody agreed that she was far preferable to her eldest brother. She had borne a bitter disappointment in her youth, which, coupled with her way of life, had somewhat soured her disposition, which was naturally kind, and even affectionate. She had been in a manner twice disappointed, for, when her lover had proved false, she had turned with all her affection to her brother John; and he also had failed her,—at least he had taken a wife, for which Susan had said she would never forgive him. Old John Bethune had but two sons, and John was the younger. There was little between them in years, but the disparity in other respects was complete and striking. Peter had always been a lout, void of feeling, and inclined to bully anything weaker than himself. He was greedy, as well as masterful, and as the brothers grew up together, John found it impossible to support existence at Auchtermairnie, though there was work to keep both employed. He was by nature quiet, gentle, and reserved, fond of books, and even of the refinements of life, for all of which Peter had the utmost contempt. 'Wark an' siller' was Peter's motto; and after a time things came to such a crisis that John left the farm and went to the Star to live. His father bought him a croft, and after a little time John quite fell in with the ways of the village, and got a loom fitted up in the ben-end, for hand-loom weaving was at that time the staple industry of the place, and the industrious made it pay well. Susan went with John as his housekeeper, and never had man a more faithful, self-denying servant. Nothing in the shape of work came amiss to Susan Bethune. She could just as easily hoe a breadth of potatoes, or gather rack behind the plough, as she could sit by the fireside and wind the pirns for her brother's loom. She was a capable, provident housekeeper indeed, but her effort ended there. No neighbour was ever allowed to cross the threshold of the cotttage; work, work, work was Susan Bethune's creed, and if John ventured to step into a neighbour's house for an hour's friendly chat, she would not speak to him for days. She was verily an Ishmaelite. whose

B

hand was against every man except her brother John, whom she strove to make as comfortable as she could.

In his leisure time John Bethune carefully and methodically perused the productions of the master minds among poets, theologians, and philosophers. Novels were at that day unknown in Star, and if one did happen to be handed from fireside to fireside, though it might be enjoyed in secret, it was outwardly condemned as a parcel 'o' unholy lees.' Then, when busy with his loom in 'the shop,' as the ben-end was always termed, he thought over his reading, carefully digesting and analyzing it all, till his mind became a well-filled storehouse of knowledge such as money could neither buy nor take away. For ten years this monotonous, uneventful, but not unprofitable way of life went on for the brother and sister, until one summer-time a mighty and unlooked-for change took place. John Bethune was an elder in the parish kirk at Kennoway, and in his regular attendance at that place of worship he fell in occasionally by the way with a bright-eyed servant lassie from Newtonhall, whose winning way and modest behaviour, as well as her intelligent and observing mind, interested him not a little. In outward appearance she was as unlike him as could well be imagined, and the disparity in years was not greater than the wide contrast between them. She was an orphan whom the ladies had procured from some institution, and of her antecedents or parentage nothing was known. That in itself was sufficient reason to Susan Bethune why she should not be named in the same breath with John, for if the Bethunes were poor they had aye been respectable, and could count their forebears back to covenanting times, when a Bethune of Auchtermairnie had followed brave Hackstoun of Rathillet through every vicissitude of his stormy career. John Bethune's wooing was of a very matter-of-fact, sensible sort. After having well considered the thing in his own mind, he asked Katie Law a plain, straightforward question, and, having received an honest, maidenly answer, he quietly and without ado informed Susan that, as he was going to be married, it would be better for her to go home to Auchtermairnie, especially as their mother was failing, and would be the better of her help. The time had gone for Susan Bethune to storm or flyte, though in youth her tongue had been the talk of the country side. She made no remark, nor asked any questions whatsoever, but there and then packed up her gear, and went home to the farm. And for many a long day she never suffered her eyes to light on her brother John and his bonnie young wife in Kennoway kirk, nor did she ever darken their door. On the solitary occasion when John, on his father's invitation, brought Katie into Auchtermairnie at tea-time on a Sabbath afternoon, Susan retired out to the stack-yard, and remained there till they went away. Her proceedings did not in the least trouble John, who had done his duty by her over and above, but it weighed on Katie's gentle heart, who, poor lassie, was keenly sensitive to the least slight cast upon her, or upon her husband for her sake. She was very happy with him, for she truly loved him, and for two bright years their cottage was the abode of love and peace ; and those who were privileged to sit down by their ingle-neuk went away saying it was good to be there. Of these old sores Susan Bethune was thinking as she stalked in her upright fashion along the green highway to the Star. She was not a comely person to look at, although in youth she had been a handsome lass whom many admired. But now her face was thin and worn, as if a secret sorrow had eaten into her heart, her brow had many wrinkles on it, and her resolute mouth many a hard line and un-promising curve. Then her scanty hair was quite grey, and was dressed so plainly and severely that it did not in any way soften her rather prominent features. Her attire was a thrifty gingham of a very large pattern, an ample plaid, and a plain, Quaker-like brown bonnet. It was just about half-past six when she passed by the smithy, and of course there had to be half-a-dozen ploughmen to gape at her, and run in to tell the smith that there was Susan Bethune actually on the way to her brother's. Looking neither to the right nor to the left, Susan Bethune walked through the village to her brother's door. There was a group of women still in Jenny Scott's garden, which considerably augmented as word was passed from door to door that Susan Bethune was in sight. She did not even look at them, nor pause to ask a single question, but lifted the sneck of her old home and walked in. At the kitchen door Mrs. Campbell, the motherly mistress of the Knowe, met her with finger uplifted in solemn warning.

Susan pushed her impatiently aside and stalked over to the bed.

Oh, could that white wasted face, with the deep pain-lines upon it, be the winsome face of Katie Law, which had been wont to look so bright and bonnie, like a picture framed by the white lappets of her bridal bonnet? At the foot of the bed sat John, with his head bowed down upon his hands.

'Katie Law's no' deid, is she, Jean Cam'll?' asked Susan Bethune quickly.

'Ay, puir lassie,' said the kind soul with eyes full of tears. 'She has gotten through wi't at last.'

CHAPTER II.

BEREAVED.

'Ah, the dead, the unforgot!
From their solemn homes of thought,
Or in love or sad rebuke,
Back upon the living look.'

WHITTIER.

'AN' whaur's the bairn?' asked Susan in a loud whisper, her expression one of blank consternation. For answer the mistress of the Knowe opened the door of the little back room which had been Susan's own sleeping chamber in days gone by, and motioned her to enter. And there by the little low hearth sat Nannie Brown, with two tiny morsels of humanity lying on her knee.

'Mercy me! is there twa?' asked Susan so shrilly that thoughtful Jean Campbell instantly shut the door between, so that the desolate mourner in the kitchen might not be disturbed.

'Ay, wee twin laddies, puir things!' said the large-hearted woman, her eyes bent in an infinite compassion upon the motherless infants.

Very curious was it to see the expression on Susan Bethune's face as she bent over Nannie Brown, and looked earnestly at the bairns. If there yet remained any soft spot in her heart, surely the sight of the twins in their helplessness might have touched it.

'It's an unco handfu' for John, puir fellow,' she said in a short, quick way. 'Ae wean wadna hae been sae bad ; but twa !'

'Ay, puir man; but the bairns 'll be a comfort tae him, I dinna doot. The verra care they'll be till him will gar him bestir himsel'. But, as ye say, it's a gey handfu' for a weedy man, but we'll just a' need to help to rear Katie's bairns.' Saying which, honest Jean Campbell looked straight and keen into the hard, unsympathetic face of Susan Bethune, and then turned away with a little sigh. There was not much promise of sympathy or help written there.

'We'll need tae gang back to Katie noo, Shoosan,' she said significantly.

'Hae ye gotten a'thing ready ?   Had I kent o' this I could hae brocht things frae Auchtermairnie.'

'A'thing's in the kist in the kitchen ; Katie showed them to me yestreen, when I lookit in to see how the lassie was keepin' up her heart.   Puir wifie, I leuch at her, but there was a solemn and earnest look in her e'e I didna like,' said Jean Campbell sorrowfully.   'There's a lang bedgoon an' a cap the Misses gied her, a' sewed by their ain hands ; but maybe ye hae seen them ? '

'Hoo could I see them ?   Brawly ye ken, Jean Cam'll, that I hae never been in John's hoose sin' his waddin',' answered Susan Bethune harshly, for her conscience was at work remorselessly reproaching her for the part she had acted towards her brother's unoffending wife. She could have wished now that she had been less hard ; but what avails such regret when it comes too late ?   Well for us if we stifle not our finer impulses while opportunity is given for their fulfilment. From the grave none come back to receive atonement from the living.

Gently Jean Campbell opened the door once more, and re-entered the kitchen. All was as they had left it, the pale, sweet, still face on the pillow, and the bent figure of the man at the foot of the bed, sitting so motionless that it might have been thought he too had bidden farewell to life.

'John, my man,' said the tremulous, kind voice of Jean Campbell, while Susan stood awkwardly by, seeing nothing but the dead face of Katie Law, which seemed to wear for her a look of unutterable reproach. 'John, my man,' repeated Jean Campbell, when her first words made no impression, 'ye'll hae to gang into the ither end till we get things dune. Shoosan's here, John, anxious to dae her best to help ye in yer trouble.'

A deep and shuddering sigh shook the stalwart frame, and he rose heavily to his feet. He looked at his sister, who, poor awkward soul, so out of place in the house of sorrow, would have uttered her sympathy had she known how, then walked away to the door, took his hat from its accustomed place, and went out into the still brightness of the summer night. The little knot of gossiping wives, oblivious of everything except this topic of absorbing interest, hushed their whispering voices and fell apart a little at sight of John Bethune. So far as he was concerned, they might have continued their talk, for he saw them not. For the time being John Bethune was possessed by one thought, so deep and awful that it was more than he could bear. The wife whom he had loved, nay, whom he had worshipped with all the rugged strength of his deep, intense nature, lay dead in the house. That fact, like a great black despairing cloud, shut out all else from the man's mind. He walked slowly up the middle of the road till he reached the schoolhouse, and when the schoolmaster, busy among his flowers, saw him, he leaned over the low wall and asked for Mrs. Bethune.

'Katie's deid, Maister,' John answered, and passed on without paying any attention to what the schoolmaster was saying. Mr. Farquhar watched him turn down the footpath to the moss, and when a few minutes later he had occasion to go to the back of the house for his spade he saw a solitary figure sadly wending its way through the green heather tops, in a slow, aimless fashion. Then a look of deep compassion came upon the master's face; he knew by experience how awful is that first lone, silent battle with the sorrow of a life. John Bethune was alone indeed in the solitude of the moss, for the peat-workers were all away home, and there stood the carts, laden and covered, ready to go off in the early morning to Cupar. For a time he wandered up and down the brown, uneven ridges, even looked curiously at the place where the folks had been casting peats that very day, and then, coming all at once to a fresh, green hillock covered with soft turf and budding heather, he sat down and nerved himself to face manfully his bereavement—to look a little ahead into life without Katie. Oh, but it was dreary work! and as he thought of the empty, empty house, great heavy tears gathered in his eyes, and seemed to burn themselves into channels on his cheeks. They were wrung from the very depths of a heart not touched by every passing emotion; they were such tears as men shed only once or twice in a life-time. It was curious, and yet perhaps not to be wondered at, that John Bethune had forgotten all about the bairns,—the helpless little laddies who would never know a mother's care. His thoughts would not go forward at his bidding; they only lingered regretfully with the past, mocking him almost with its precious memories, with the sweetness of its happy, tranquil days. Oh, these two brief, bright years had been like a breath of heaven to him! no man had been more blessed, more utterly content than he! Then something of the stern old creed his grandmother had taught him rose up before him, reminding him how he had sinned and come short. He had not crucified the flesh, nor kept himself from idols; for had not Katie been his idol, whom he had loved and worshipped with a fervour which condemned him now? Ah, it is so much easier to take to our hearts a living, breathing presence that can give love for love, than to yearn for the infinite and unknown, that can only be approached by faith. It seems to me that faith is not a natural impulse to humanity, but rather a plant cultivated in the soil of sorrow and disappointment. By and by there stole into John Bethune's heart a sweeter assurance than that old stern creed; and these words whispered themselves to him in accents of healing: 'Love one another, as I have loved you.' With that deep peace and comforting thought there came to him also, with a sudden sweetness, a consciousness of the exceeding beauty and fulness which encompassed him,—that sunset beauty which Katie had loved to look upon in the long summer evenings from their cottage door. Their common love for the sights and sounds of nature had been a very sweet bond between them. The sun had set over the Lomond Hill, and the sweet gloaming was creeping over the earth, without quenching too suddenly the lingering glory still streaming from the radiant west. The sky was a wonder of loveliness, in its thousand varying hues, soft, indescribable, inimitable tints mingling with clear

azure and brilliant carmine shot with bars of gold.
Right above the little cottage, where kind hands were
preparing Katie for her last sleep, the moon hung clear
and bright, only waiting for the darkness to show her
wondrous power. The pleasant stillness was only broken
by the cheery chirp of the corn-craik, or by the lowing
of the cows in Broomfield Park growing impatient for
the sweet bunch of clover awaiting them in the byre at
milking-time. The fair world was full of promise; haw-
thorn-tree and sweet-brier bush were bursting into bloom,
the graceful ferns were uncurling their delicate fronds in
every shady nook, and in another month the moss would
be a blaze of purple heather bells. John Bethune
wondered at the rapid progress everything had made
since he had been down the moss with Katie a month
ago on a Sabbath evening.

A quick sob broke from his lips as the thought came
home sharply that never again should he walk with
Katie here or anywhere, till perchance they might
together pace the golden streets of that happier home to
which God had already taken her.

He rose up to his feet, uplifted his eyes to the sky
with a passionate, yearning gaze, as if they would fain
penetrate its mysteries, and find Katie beyond.

As he turned to go, there came stealing across the
green fields the note of the cuckoo, calling sweetly and
clearly to its mate: another thing to bring back memories of Katie, for only yesterday she had said the cuckoo
was late this year, and wondered whether he had quitted
his haunt in the Falkland Wood. Ah, well! he had
many sweet memories to live upon, and the hope that was
in him would give strength for each day,—and what
need we more ?

When John Bethune once more entered his own

dwelling, there was nobody in the kitchen, and he was glad of it; for he could look unobserved at the sweet face of the silent sleeper on the bed; and though the murmuring sound of voices in the inner room told that the house was not deserted, he entered so softly that they did not hear him. Very softly, and with reverent hand, did John Bethune lift the pure covering from his wife's face, and let his eyes dwell upon it. Even a little time had wrought a change there, for all the pain-lines were gone, and there had even crept back to the girlish cheek a sweet hint of the bloom of yore. So natural and life-like did she look, indeed, that it was hard to believe that death had claimed the mortal part of Katie Law for ever. Everything about her was spotlessly white and of the finest quality,—gifts from the kind ladies who had been very loth indeed to part with her. Little did they dream how soon, and in what way, their handiwork was to be used. On the little deal table at the side of the bed, Jean Campbell, with one of these finer touches so characteristic of her, had spread a pure linen cloth, and laid Katie's Bible on it, side by side with a little bunch of lily-of-the-valley, which grew so plentifully in a shady nook behind the rain-water barrel at the back of the house. These little things touched and soothed John Bethune, and the look of peace deepened on his face. With a gentle sigh, he let the covering fall lightly over the face again; it did not occur to him to kiss or touch the dead. The Katie he had loved was not lying there, but was even now mingling with the great company of the redeemed. So, lifting Katie's Bible, he sat down by the hearth, and opened it at the Revelation. And there Susan found him, when she came out presently to get something for the infants. She started, not having heard him come in; and then she looked rather helplessly round, as if she felt she ought to say something, but could not find words.

'Is that you, Susan?' said John, and he actually smiled. 'I am glad to see ye. I wish ye had jist come a wee quicker. Katie wearied on ye comin'; but that's past.'

'Had I kent she was that ill, John, I wad hae come,' Susan answered quickly. '·Bide a wee, till I fill the kettle for Nannie, an' I'll sit down aside ye a wee. We maun see what's to be dune wi' the handfu' ben the hoose.'

In her own swift, decided, but rather noisy way, Susan filled the kettle from the water pitcher in the lobby, and took it back to the room fire. Then she returned to the kitchen, shutting the door between, so that Nannie might not hear what they said.

'It is a handfu', John,' she said, sitting down by the fireside, and crossing her hands on her lap. 'I dinna ken in a' the world what ye are to dae wi' the craturs, that's a fact.'

'Is Mistress Cam'll awa', Susan?' asked John quietly.

'Ay, it was byre-time. She's a kind woman, Jean Campbell, an' a prudent as weel. She disna carry clashes ony way frae hoose to hoose.'

'No, she's abune that. Ay, I'll no' forget what Jean Campbell has dune for me and mine, Shoosan. She's been like a mither tae Katie sin' ever she cam' to the Star; and Dauvit's no' ahint her in kindness.'

'Weel, weel, I dinna doot,' said Susan with a note of impatience in her voice. 'But what's to be dune wi' the bairns? that's the question in the meantime.'

'The bairns? I'll get them brocht up some way.

I'll get some decent middle-aged woman to come an' keep the hoose; an' Jean Campbell promised Katie that she wad see that the bairns were weel guided. Nae doot it'll be a battle; but life's a battle at the best.'

'Imphim,' was Susan Bethune's sole comment. Truth to tell, it piqued her to find that John did not count in any way upon her assistance. And yet, what could she expect? What had *her* treatment been of him and his for many a day?

'Ye'll no' hae heard that Peter's gauna tak' a wife,' she said presently.

'Peter!' exclaimed John, looking up in utter surprise. 'Ye dinna mean to say't?'

'Ay, div I,' repeated Susan rather sourly. 'There's nae fules like auld fules; it's Sammy Tamson's weedy in the Windygates he's seekin'.'

'That auld wife!'

'Ay, that auld wife. He's gane to the opposite extreme,' said Susan grimly. 'Of coorse it's her siller an' her gear. There's naething bonnie nor braw aboot her; an' sic a temper. He's bad they say, but she'll kick up bonnie waps in Auchtermairnie, I can tell ye.'

'You an' her'll no' 'gree very sair, I doot, Shoosan,' said John soberly.

'Me an' her gree! we'll no' try't. When she comes in I gang oot. I'm no' that auld nor that failed but I can earn saut to my kail yet.'

There was a short silence, for John Bethune was revolving in his mind whether it would be just to Katie and to Katie's bairns to ask Susan to come back to the Star. He need hardly have hesitated on Katie's account either. Well did he know that she, in her angel compassion and sweet charity would have been the very first to offer poor Susan a home. For she was to be pitied indeed. It seemed as if nobody in the wide earth had need of her; she was a woman who had missed her mark in life.

'Is't to be sune, Shoosan?' he asked at length.

'At Mairtinmas,' was Susan's brief response. 'I daursay it micht be suner were I oot the road; but I canna get a place till the term.'

'What's faither sayin' til't?'

'Oh, naething. He's gettin' into his dotage, puir man, an' he thinks a'thing Pete does is richt. The twa hae gotten completely roond the auld man, an' when Lucky Tamson gets her nose stappit into Auchtermairnie, there'll no' muckle come oot o't for you or me, John.'

'Ye're welcome to come back to yer auld bit, Shoosan, if ye can be fashed wi' the toil o' the bairns,' said John slowly. 'Ye'll no' tak' kindly workin' to the frem at your years. What d'ye say?'

Susan Bethune sat in absolute silence, with her eyes fixed on the smouldering fire. There was a strange softness in them when she raised them to her brother's face.

'If ye wad let me, John,' she said, her hard voice a trifle unsteady, 'I wad toil nicht an' day for you an' for the bairns. I'll seek naething but my bite an' sup, an' I'll guide the bairns as weel as ever I can, for the sake o' her that's awa.'

'Then ye'll come, Shoosan? thank ye,' said John quietly, and for a time there was no more said.

'John,' said Susan at last, her voice sunk almost to a whisper, 'd'ye think Katie forgied me afore she gaed awa'. Oh, if I had only the chance to tell her noo hoo I rue my daein's in the past!'

'There was naething in Katie's heart, Shoosan, but

love an' kindness to every human bein'; she never spak' o' you but wi' respect,' said John; and then he laid down his head on Katie's Bible, wholly overcome.

Unwonted tears stood in Susan Bethune's eyes as she witnessed the tempest of grief which shook the stalwart frame of her brother John. There is something awe-inspiring in the upheaving of a still, self-contained nature; we stand silent before such dear-bought tears.

'Dinna, John, dinna gie way!' pleaded Susan, for she could not bear the sight. Then she rose up and touched him gently on the shoulder; and after a moment their hands met in a fervent clasp. They were very near together in that moment. It was as if the long years had rolled back, and they were boy and girl again, gathering buttercup and gowan by the wayside, with naught but love in their hearts. And so sorrow is infinite in its power, infinite because divine.

CHAPTER III.

ALONE.

'Then turn, and the old duties take,
Alone now—yet with earnest will,
Gathering sweet sacred traces still,
To help thee on.'

A. PROCTER.

EXT morning word was sent to such as had been more intimate neighbours, or had shown any special kindness to the dead, to come and see her as she lay so still and white in the sleep which knows no earthly awakening. It was an old custom peculiar to the place, and though John Bethune did not himself care about it, Susan was very particular that no mark of respect should be wanting, and that the neighbours should not have an opening to say that anything was neglected or passed by. All who were asked came as a matter of course; to stay away would have been taken as a mark of disrespect to the dead. When the wives began to arrive, John retired into the shop and sat down at his loom, for he could not have borne to see so many curious eyes staring at his darling, nor could he have endured to hear the stream of morbid talk at which her death and the circumstances would give rise. He heard, however, the low and continuous hum of conversation, which was only interrupted once by the shrill wail of the infants, doubtless roused from their slumber to be inspected by the throng. Susan Bethune comported herself with dignity through the ceremonies, and in her effective way put her foot on any questions which she deemed the outcome of idle curiosity. Two qualities Susan Bethune possessed beyond a doubt, prudence and reserve concerning herself and the affairs of her own family; and certainly none could accuse her of meddling with other people's business. The neighbours were obliged to retire at last with their curiosity still unsatisfied, for Susan had skilfully parried every question concerning her brother's intentions, and when Kirsty Paterson, more bold in her curiosity than the others, had inquired whether the bairns were to be taken home to Auchtermairnie, she only answered with a fine indifference, ' Maybe, Kirsty,' but even that was sufficient for that worthy's fertile imagination, for she immediately took it upon her to publish abroad the fact that John Bethune's bairns were going home to Auchtermairnie, with the further groundless addition that he was more than likely to leave the loom, and give up the land, though it was paying well enough, just because he could not bear to live in the Star without Katie. So news was spread in the Star by the indefatigable Kirsty, whose sole occupation and interest in life was ' redding up ' her neighbours and their affairs. It was well enough known that the truth was not in her, and yet it was wonderful how her stories spread and were believed in the place; and how those who behind her back applied to her the choice appella-

C

tion of 'an auld lecar,' were the very readiest to stand
open-mouthed while she emptied her repertoire for their
benefit.   In the gloaming that same night one of the
ploughman lads from the Knowe went from door to
door, as was the fashion, bidding the folk turn out to
Katie Law's burying at two o'clock next afternoon.   So
in the sweet, still, drowsy sunshine the mournful proces-
sion set out from John Bethune's door to lay Katie
Law in her last resting-place beside the Bethunes in
Kennoway kirkyard.   At his father's earnest solici-
tation John Bethune went into Auchtermairnie to
his tea on the way home, and to have a talk over
family affairs.

'Shoosan 'll hae tae telt ye, dootless, that Pete's
gaun to get Mag Tamson,' said the old man with a
queer, dry chuckle. 'What think ye o' his bargain,
John ? '

'If Pete is pleased, faither, it's nae business o' mine,'
answered John languidly, for it seemed strange to him
that other men should be thinking of marrying when
such desolation had overtaken him.   'There's naething
against the woman that I ken o'.'

'Na, na, there's naething against her, an' she has a
wecht o' siller, forby sax or seeven hooses east at Enster.
Ay, ay, Pete's a sly dowg.   Ye never was sae wise in
yer ain interest, or ye wad never hae taen her
that's awa, puir lassie,' said the old man. 'Wheesht,
here's Pete !   Dinna let on I was sayin' onything
aboot Mag.'

Peter Bethune, jealous and suspicious lest they should
have been discussing him, had wrenched himself away
from the neighbours discussing 'craps' on the road, and
came hurriedly up to them just as they reached the
door.   It hurt John to see how the old man cowered in

behind him, as if afraid to encounter Peter's evil eye. He knew that his brother was not a pleasant person to live with, but he had no idea of the manner in which he persecuted the old man, until his life had become a miserable burden, which he would gladly lay down.

'I'll jist awa' up an' see if Geordie minded to water the staigs,' he said nervously, hurrying off in his funeral clothes, as if glad to get out of the way.

'What was the auld ane sayin' aboot me?' inquired Peter suspiciously. 'Had he a fine story about the Windygates?'

'No, Shoosan telt me that, Peter,' answered John quietly. 'Ye're no' ill to please wi' a wife.'

'What faut has she? She's maybe no sae young an' weel-faured as yours was,' said Peter with unfeeling candour. 'But she has years upon her heid, an' sense, which few weemin hae.'

'An' siller in her pocket forby, Pete,' added John with the glimmer of a dry smile. 'Weel, if ye be half sae happy as I was, ye'll bless the day ye ever saw her.'

And then his eyes wandered eastward in the direction of the quiet kirkyard, where the sunshine of his life had been buried not an hour ago.

'Shoosan's unco ill at it, John,' said Peter presently. 'But a man canna live single for ever, because he happens to hae a sister at hame. What think ye?'

'I dinna think Shoosan's that ill at it, Pete,' said John gently. 'But ye needna bother yersel' about her. She's comin' back to her auld bit in the Star.'

'Eh, d'ye say sae?' queried Peter with a quick, eager, satisfied grin. 'That's a guid thing for her' ('an' for me,' was on his lips, but with unusual consideration he held his peace).

Then they went into the house, and Peter, casting his black coat, set on the kettle, and proceeded to put the tea-things on the table, for Susan had well schooled the men-folk of the household in the art of doing for themselves. It could not, however, be called a tempting meal, and John ate very sparingly, and spoke but little. He did not know what it was, but in Pete's presence he felt his lips sealed, and could only answer his remarks in the briefest monosyllables.

'I'll need to be stappin',' he said directly the meal was over. 'Shoosan·'ll be wearyin'; an' it's time I was hame.'

'Ye micht sit till I gang up to the field and see what they're aboot. It's near lowsin' time,' said Peter. 'An' syne I'll gang wast the road a bit wi' ye.'

'I'll no' wait, Peter. Faither 'll convoy me a bit. I hae twa-three things to speak about onyway,' said John, rising to his feet.

Peter looked rather annoyed. He was divided be· tween jealousy of what John and his father might say, and distrust of his ploughmen, who, as is often the case with those bound to a hard master, were only eye and lip servants, who only did their duty under that master's supervision.

'Ye're in a fell hurry,' he said sourly. 'Ye'll no' gang faur, faither; there's a heap adae, an' it'll be sax o'clock in a crack.'

'No, I'll no' bide,' said the old man meekly, and walked away very gladly with John, half expecting Peter to call him back every minute. 'Pete's an awfu' billy to work, John,' he said when they were fairly out on the road; and a little sigh followed the words, as if he felt weary at times of his son's industry.

'Let him work as hard as he likes, faither, but dinna you fash,' said John in his kind way. 'Ye hae gane mony a lang, sair yokin' in yer time. Ye should rest noo.'

'Eh, man, Pete wadna let me. He hauds at me mornin', nune, an' nicht. I canna get my twa hoors at denner-time like the men; an' I'm fell wearit for't, I can tell ye. I'm whiles ower tired at nicht to sleep,' said the old man childishly. 'Ye wadna be sae hard on the auld ane, John.'

'Peter has nae richt to gar ye work, faither. Are ye no' the maister? Dinna dae it.'

'It's easy sayin' that, but I'm fear't at Pete, John. He's a wild loon, an' he's gotten the better o' me,' said the old man hopelessly. 'It'll be waur, I doot, when Mag Tamson comes hame. She's no' just wi' greed, they say, an' a tearin' worker as weel. I whiles wish, John, that I was lyin' quate i' the mools, as weel's yer mither an' yer wifie, puir lammie. She had aye a bonnie bit olink for the auld man.'

'Faither,' said John after a pause, 'ye hinna let Pete get his haund on the siller or the deeds o' ony o' the property, hae ye?'

''Deed he's gotten mair nor he should hae gotten. I hav'na the heid I used to hae, John, an' he said he wad manage things for me an' save bother. But I'll hae to gang ower to Cupar, I doot, an' see Wulson the writer. If I could get slippit awa' some Seterday, maybe when Pete's at Kirkcaldy market, ye micht meet me at Markinch, an' we wad gang up thegither.'

'I could dae that, but there's nae reason what way we should dae onything on the sly, faither. I'll come along some nicht sune, an' redd things up wi' Pete. The siller's naething to me, but there's Shoosan. She deserves her share. She has wrocht for it.'

'Verra weel; only dinna roose Pete, or there'll be nae leevin' wi' him,' said the old man rather anxiously. ' I houp, my man, that nane o' your bits o' laddies 'll be as ill to you as Pete's been to me.'

'I houp no', faither,' was John's answer, given in a low, almost stern voice, for his righteous ire was kindled against his brother.

'Weel, I'll awa' hame, John,' said his father when they reached the gate of Newtonhall. 'I'll mebbe come wast an' see the bairns gin Sawbath nicht if you an' Shoosan's no' east. Dinna be lang o' comin', wull ye no'?'

'No, I'll no' be lang, faither,' answered John with a kind smile, and, shaking his father warmly by the hand, he turned and went his way. The old man looked back often ere the curve in the road hid his son from sight, and there was a moisture in his poor dim eyes suspiciously akin to tears.

It seemed to John Bethune, as he entered his own door that night, that he had left the sweetest and best part of his life behind for ever, and that what still remained, whether long or short, would only be a life of duty and conscientious care, unmixed with any brightness whatsoever. That had all been buried that day in Katie's grave. Susan was sitting at the fire with the two infants on her lap, and it was quite wonderful how much at home she looked in that position. They were not asleep, only lying toasting their little pink feet, and blinking at the fire.

'Weel, John, hae ye gotten 'd a' by?' said she very softly for her. 'Ye've surely been in at Auchtermairnic?'

'Ay, faither wadna let me by. I've gotten my tea, Susan,' answered John, and, laying off his black coat, he came over and stood looking with a strange curiosity at the little atoms of humanity on his sister's knee.

'They're sma' but they're fine bairns, John,' said Susan, not without pride. ' A'body says sae.'

'Ay, they're verra sma'. It's queer to think that they'll be men some day. They'll tak' a heap o' growin' afore then.'

'They'll come on. What are ye gaun to ca' them, John?'

'The auldest ane 'll be Alexander, efter faither an' efter godly Alexander Bethune that fell beside Rathillet on Airsmoss,' said John. 'We'll mak' him a minister, Shoosan. Katie aye said that if the bairn was a laddie, she wad mak' him a minister.'

'An' the ither ane?'

'Jeems, I think. Katie had aince a brither, ye ken, an' his name was Jeems. We'll ca' him Jeems Law. I think Katie wad like that.'

'An' what'll ye mak' o' him?'

'I dinna ken. We'll see hoo the laddie turns oot. There's the laund here, ye ken, an' the loom efter I'm dune.'

'I doot if he'll be content to sit at a loom a' his days, puir man,' said Susan. 'Wha'll ye get to carry them to the kirk, John.'

'Naebody. Maister Bell 'll jist come oot an' christen them in the hoose. He disna care aboot it, I ken; but in the circumstances he'll come.'

'Surely,' answered Susan. 'I wish I had the next three year by, John. Did ye say onything to Pete aboot Mag Tamson?'

'No' me; he spak aboot her first. ' I think the auld man has a puir time o't wi' Pete. He's a graspin', hard-hearted lump.'

'Ay is he,' answered Susan with extreme emphasis. 'Mag Tamson maybe thinks she's gotten a bargain, but she'll find oot her mistak'. If she has a' they say, she's a fule to tak' oor Pete. The twasome 'll fecht like cat an' dowg.'

'We hae naething adae wi' that, Shoosan; but we'll hae to see that faither gets justice atween them,' answered John rather wearily, as if the discussion saddened and annoyed him. 'But I'll hae to get awa' to the loom. This kind o' wark 'll no' fill thae twa mooths,' he said with a mournful smile, and touching with tender, almost reverent finger the soft faces of the bairns. 'I'm like you, Shoosan; I could wish the next three year, ay, an' the next twenty year by, or I see the craturs stannin' on their ain legs.'

'I dinna ken, maybe they'll be a greater care then nor the noo,' answered Susan.

'Ye're richt. We can but houp an' pray that they may grow up wi' the grace o' God in their hearts, an' then there'll be nae fear o' them,' said John as he turned away to resume his work, which had been laid aside since Katie's death.

It was dreary work for a few days, ay, for weeks at first, and yet it was wonderful how the interest of the bairns kept his thoughts from dwelling too much and too painfully on his loss. It is a merciful provision God makes oftentimes for the bereaved. He knows so well just what we need, and how much we can endure.

The twins were just like other children, more fretful than they might have been, perhaps, under their mother's care. For Susan, poor body, though so willing, was of necessity awkward in handling them, and made many a queer and laughable mistake. But she did her duty by them faithfully, as any mother could have done, bearing patiently their fretfulness, and never uttering a word of grumbling or complaint. Even those who disliked her most could not say otherwise than that she had done well. The first year was one of toil more unremitting and wearing than even John Bethune dreamed of. But by and by, when they were past the most trying period of child-life, and began to toddle on their own little legs, and utter these uncertain sounds which fall so sweetly from baby lips trying the mysteries of speech, they became a constant source of interest and diversion to their father and their aunt. They made for both the very sunshine of life, and often John Bethune's eyes would fill with unbidden tears at the thought of the joy it would have been to Katie to have watched with him the gradual and exquisite unfolding of their infant powers.

Before the twins were six months old, Peter Bethune's wife entered upon her reign at Auchtermairnie. She was a widow, with a married daughter, and three grown-up sons, who, however, were all in the way of doing for themselves. She was a managing, clever woman, and for the first time in his life Peter Bethune tasted the luxury of being thwarted and set aside. His wife had been accustomed to rule all her days, and it was not easy for her to obey now. Both being obstinate, they speedily disagreed; and it appeared as if Susan's prediction was likely to be fulfilled.

She was avaricious as her husband, but she had finer feelings, and a higher sense of right and wrong. Therefore she upheld John in his desire to have the property equally divided, and she also shielded the old man from Peter's petty tyranny; and, indeed, tried to do her duty at Auchtermairnie. But there could never be happiness there, for there was neither grace nor love to sweeten life's daily toil. But there was love and peace in the little cottage at the Star, and Katie's bairns grew apace, until they left their childhood behind.

CHAPTER IV.

TWO SONS.

'The deep, sad yearnings of an earnest soul.'

IT was the third week in September, and the folk were all 'leading in' round about the Star an early and abundant harvest. The days were shortening fast; the mistress had to take a lantern to the milking at nights, and the early mornings were beginning to be very cold and grey. But it was a busy, happy, cheerful time, and when it was well over, folk were ready to prepare themselves for the lighter labours and more abundant leisure of the winter.

The harvest moon was at its full on the night when David Campbell was building the last stack in the corn yard; it was his custom, and had been his father's before him, to build the first and the last stack every year. The mistress paused for a moment when she left the byre to watch the stir in the yard, and then hurried down to the house with her pails, to find the usual little knot of customers clustered at the door discussing the homely gossip of the day.

'Ye're a' there that's onything worth, I see,' she said in her cheery way. 'I'm late the nicht, for baith Mary and me's been oot the best pairt o' the day. The thrang 'll wear by, though, an' then we'll get a breath.'

'Your thrang's seldom by, Mistress Cam'll,' said Kirsty Paterson with a kind of girn, just as if she grudged the mistress her busy, happy life.

'Aweel, Kirsty, if it never wear by, we maun jist fecht on till we maun lie doon,' she said, as she measured out the milk with swift, unerring hand.

Kirsty took her milk and retired, but hung on the doorstep a minute to hear a neighbour make some remark about some strangers who had come to Carriston by the afternoon train. Mrs. Campbell was civil and attentive to them, but she did not encourage them to stand, for her hands were so full of work she hardly knew where to turn. When she went ben to the kitchen, she started to see a figure sitting on her husband's chair, apparently deep in thought.

'Oh, it's you, Jamie Bethune?' she said pleasantly 'A' weel the nicht? Is yer auntie better?'

'Yes, she's better,' answered the lad briefly.

'Yer faither an' Sandy's back frae St. Andrews. Mary saw them gang yont the road i' the darkenin',' she said, as she proceeded to light the lamp. 'Is onything settled?'

'Yes, it's a' settled,' answered the lad in the same still, quiet way. 'Sandy gangs awa' to the college Monday eight days.'

'Aweel, I wish him weel,' said the mistress; and for a little there was no more said. Although she was silent, she was keenly watching the lad as she went busily about preparing supper for the men; and she saw

well enough that there was something amiss. Jamie
Bethune, the younger of poor Katie Law's twins, had
grown to be a tall, slender stripling, of build and appearance
more resembling a city boy than one reared in the Star.
He stood already five feet nine in his stockings, but his
figure was loose and unformed; his pale face, with its
large, irregular features, very thin and haggard. It was
not a handsome, scarcely a good-looking face, but it was
redeemed from plainness by the earnest, speaking dark
eyes, which shone like stars under a broad, open brow,
indicative of ability and thought. Jamie Bethune was not
of much account in the Star, being spoken of mostly as
Sandy's brother. It was Sandy, bright, clever, rattling
Sandy, who won everybody's heart, and made his mark
wherever he went. Few loved the shy, awkward
younger brother, because he was really known to very
few.

'What's your trouble, Jamie, my man?' said Jean
Campbell kindly; for, in spite of all, Jamie was her
favourite, because he reminded her of the poor young
mother she had loved so well.

'Naething. I was only thinking; that's a',' answered
the lad with a heavy sigh, which escaped him against
his will or inclination.

'Ay,' was the mistress's reply, but that dry mono-
syllable implied a great deal. 'Tell yer faither, Jamie,
that we'll be at his barley the morn. The last sheaf 'll be
in aff Edom's land by this time, I expeck. Ye've a guid
crap the maister tells me!'

'Ay, it's no' bad,' said Jamie, rousing himself with an
effort. 'They've graund stuff on Auchtermairnie this
year, Mrs. Campbell. Uncle Peter was tellin' 's on
Sawbath that he has some oats very near six feet high.'

'That'll please yer Uncle Peter, laddie,' said the

mistress with a laugh ; 'he likes by-ordinar' things. Oh, here's Mary.   Mysie's surely ta'en an unco' strippin' the nicht, lassie ! '

The young girl, who at that moment entered the kitchen, turned her back to hide the deep blush which overspread her bonnie face, but she had never a word to say.   A sweet and winsome lassie was Mary Campbell, the orphan daughter of David Campbell's brother, who had come to them when she was a little toddling thing, scarcely able to walk or talk.   She had been in all respects like a child of their own to the childless couple at the Knowe, and the love between them was almost as strong as that between parent and child.   She was only sixteen, a year younger than the Bethunes, whose companion and playmate she had been since ever she had come to the Star.

She was not only bonnie, but her bright and happy disposition made her beloved by both young and old. No harvest maiden or other merrymaking was complete without her, and at the dancing when the market came round she had more partners than any of her companions. But though she was such a favourite she disarmed all envy and jealousy by her own sweet gentleness, and there was not a particle of coquetry in Mary Campbell's disposition. Her aunt had brought her up to work early and late, but she was wonderfully indulgent, and did not try her strength too far.   When she had somewhat recovered herself she nodded to Jamie Bethune, and, taking off the big apron tied above her dainty print dress, she smoothed her shining fair hair before the little glass.   It was a bonnie, rosy, healthy-hued face reflected there, lit by a pair of deep grey eyes, capable of many varying expres- sions ; it was curious that when in repose these eyes gave to Mary Campbell's face a somewhat sad cast, which would have surprised those who knew her only in her merrier moods.

'Can I gang oot a wee, Auntie Jean?' she asked. 'Or will I bide to wash the dishes?'

'Whaur d'ye want to be trailin' to the nicht, lassie?' asked Auntie Jean rather slily. 'Ye should bide an' wash the dishes, ye ken brawly, but awa' ye go. Dinna bide late, an' dinna gang faur.'

Mary nodded, her face radiant, and, casting a shawl about her head and shoulders, she said good-night to Jamie, and disappeared.

'Sandy 'll be waitin' to gie her the news, readilys, said the mistress with a comical smile. 'It's a kind o' divert to see the craturs. They're faur ower young, I tell them, to be thinkin' on sic a thing; but I needna speak, I was makin' my providin' when I was Mary's age. Ay, that's a gey while syne.'

The mistress's keen eyes dwelt most searchingly on the lad's face as she spoke, and he smiled as if he rather enjoyed what she was saying. Evidently Mary was not connected with his despondency. In a moment, however, the pleasing brightness disappeared from his face, and it resumed its downcast and even sad expression.

'Ye'll miss Sandy when he gangs to the toon, Jamie,' said the mistress kindly.

'Ay, I'll miss him,' Jamie assented. 'Mair, likely, nor he'll miss me.'

'But it's a guid thing, as I said to Dauvit, that ye arena baith gaun thegither. Yer faither couldna weel want ye baith, an' there's plenty for you to dae at hame.'

'Ay, there's plenty, sure enough,' said Jamie, speaking with a strange bitterness. 'There's no' muckle time for naething but wark doon by.'

Mrs. Campbell lifted her head from her work, and

looked with a strange swiftness into the lad's face. In a moment the whole thing was made plain to her, and she wondered at her own blindness.

'Wark's guid for folk, laddie; it has cured mony a sorrow,' she said softly. 'We dinna aye like it, my man, an' whiles we think we could carve oot a better way for oorsel's, but when ye've lived as lang as me, ye'll hae learned, I dinna doot, that the Lord's ways are the best. ay, the best for a' in the end,' she added, more to herself than to him.

'D'ye think He tak's as muckle interest in's as that, Mrs. Campbell?' inquired Jamie. 'There's that mony things gae wrang, that a body can hardly think it.'

'It's when oor veesion's dim wi' oor ain troubles, maistly o' oor ain makin' tae, that we begin to herbour sic thochts. It'll a' come richt by and by, if we wad but hae patience to wait and see,' said the mistress quietly. 'Aweel, here they come to their supper; I hear the maister speaking. Will ye no' bide an' tak' a bite wi' them?'

'No thenk ye, I've bidden ower lang a'ready,' said the lad, rising to his feet. Mrs. Campbell accompanied him to the door, and as he turned to go she laid her hand on his shoulder, and looked with kindly sympathy into his face. 'Jamie, my man, wad ye like to fill a poopit tae?'

'No, I wadna; but I wad gie my richt hand, Mrs. Campbell, for Sandy's chance,' said the lad with a strange passion. 'No' that I grudge him it, mind ye, but it's an awfu' thing to be tied doon to wark ye dinna like.'

'Ye mauna gie way to sic thochts, Jamie; yer wark's honest and honourable, an' if ye stick in, ye're bound to dae weel,' said the good woman, wisely putting a curb on her own sympathies, which were all with him. 'There's an auld proverb, laddie, that says, " Ilka dowg has its day." Yer day 'll come in guid time. Till then content yersel', an' be as happy as ye can, like a man.'

There was no time to answer, for just then the maister and the men came round the corner, and the guidwife ran in to see that everything was ready for them.

James Bethune returned the farmer's cheery guid e'en, and walked away down the road with his hands in his pockets and his eyes fixed on the ground. There was the usual group of loungers gathered about the door of Andrew Aitken's shop, mostly lads of Jamie's own age, and they laughed to each other as they saw him go by. He never forgathered with them, and so they disliked and made fun of him just because they knew so little of him. Sandy, on the contrary, was a prime favourite with them all; he had a fine, open, happy-go-lucky way with him which took the edge off the patronizing airs he had adopted towards the village lads since he had gone to teach in the Markinch school. The lamp was lighted in John Bethune's kitchen, and the light shone steadily through the white blind, and made a bright pathway across the garden. But somehow Jamie felt no inclination to go in; he knew very well he should find his father and aunt discussing Sandy's future, and he did not feel that interest in it which he told himself he ought to feel. So he stole quietly round the end of the cottage, and, walking to the foot of the yard, leaned up against the dyke, and looked away across the moss, which lay bathed in the glory of the harvest moon. It was a night of rare beauty, and the air, without being cold, was keen and bracing and deliciously refreshing. James Bethune had inherited from his mother a passionate love for nature, and at times the moonlight loveliness of a harvest night had power to move him to the inmost soul. Not

D

so to-night. He was wretched, and his heart was filled with thoughts for which he hated himself. It was no new thing for him to long for the advantages so freely bestowed on Sandy. It was very long since he had first envied him his book-learning, but somehow these longings had never reached such a climax before. These moments of bitter discontent, of passionate kicking against our destiny, are common to humanity; but it is a surprising thing how little sympathy one shows to another in such circumstances. In finely-strung natures, these longings become a living pain, none the less keen and unendurable because it is dumb. They do not suffer least who never give their woes a voice. From his very infancy James Bethune had been set aside, and placed second to his brother. Sandy had early exhibited that precocious cleverness and smartness which in a young child is so delightful and fascinating, especially in the eyes of an indulgent and partial parent. John Bethune watched the rapid development of his boy's powers, with a slow, quiet joy he could not have expressed in words. The child, destined from birth' for the ministry, was likely to have a bright career before him. He was first at school; learning was no trouble to him, and he was reading in the 'threepenny' before Jamie had mastered the alphabet. The younger was slower in movement, in speech, in comprehension; in fact, he was a tortoise beside his clever brother. Sandy was forward with his ability, and pushed himself into notice everywhere. When the minister made his periodical visitation, it was Sandy who went glibly through the Catechism for his benefit, while Jamie would hang shyly back, biting his finger, and refusing to utter a word. And so he was set down as stupid,— 'dull i' the uptak',' as Star folk had it,—and John Bethune was persuaded that ability to read, write, and count

was education sufficient for him. He was removed from
the village school before he was twelve, just when his
mind was waking up into greater activity, while Sandy
remained to attain still greater proficiency in the common
subjects, and to receive the rudiments of Latin and
mathematics from Mr. Farquhar. When he was thirteen,
he went down to teach the younger classes in the Markinch school, receiving, in return, instruction in all the
higher branches, and thus laying a good foundation for
his college life. And while Sandy, well dressed and
cared for, went like a gentleman to his light labour, and
had liberty to study all evening if he liked, Jamie was
kept hard at work on the land in the summer-time, and
at the loom every spare moment. His reading was
taken on the sly. Many a time had he carried a book
with him to the field when he was supposed to be hoeing,
and steal an hour for which he had to make up by
working after-hours. Against his way of life Jamie
Bethune never dreamed of complaining. He was one
of these still, reserved natures which live within themselves, and are only revealed to a very few, sometimes
to none. But his heart knew its own bitterness, and
there were wells of feeling and possibilities in the lad
undreamed of by those among whom he lived. In all
this John Bethune had no thought of wronging his
younger son. He simply saw in him a commonplace
lad, who could work with his hands, and who showed no
decided bent in any direction. And since Sandy was so
undoubtedly a scholar, he thought he was doing his
duty by both. Sandy should be fitted to make his
mark in a higher walk in life, while Jamie should be
left with the land and the loom, at which he could make
a good livelihood; probably the Star would hold him all
his days. Such was the good man's idea, and he placidly

made his plans, and strove to execute them, only asking that he might be spared · to see his sons come to man's estate, and occupying, each in his own sphere, honourable positions in life. Such unconscious wrongs are often done under a strong sense of duty. But their results are not the less grievous, because the motive which prompts them happens to be generous and pure.

With his elbows leaning on the mossy wall, James Bethune wrestled with the first problem life had presented to him. He felt within him the stirrings of manhood, and there whispered to him visions of great achievements, of noble aims, and vague but loveliest possibilities which the lad himself could scarcely understand. Only he knew that he was miserable in the Star, and that his mind dwelt continually upon the wider sphere which he knew was to be found in the world beyond the quiet hamlet which was supposed to be large enough for him. He had read again and again in his father's books of men who had risen from the veriest obscurity, and had been enabled, by their own sheer industry and force of character, to shape the destinies of nations.

The majority of these great minds, both in his own and other times, had struggled with early disadvantages, and in that very struggle had won their mightiest power. Why should not he put his hand to the plough, and make a desperate effort after something beyond the meagre trammels of his existence?

'I'm a fule!' he muttered, in very scorn of himself. 'I'll think nae mair aboot it. The mistress is maybe richt. Maybe this *is* the place for me after a'.'

Looking across the moss again he saw two figures coming leisurely up the path. In the glorious light it was easy to distinguish them as his brother and Mary Campbell. He could even see that Sandy had his arm round the girl's waist, and that their heads were very close together. A slight bitterness dwelt for a moment in his eyes, as the thought came that everything seemed to be given to Sandy, without any trouble on his part to obtain it. Not that he was in the remotest degree jealous, or interested beyond ordinary in Mary Campbell, only it seemed to fit in with the rest of his thoughts.

'Were I Sandy,' he said to himself as he went away to the house, 'I wadna hae naething to dae wi' lassies for ten year to come. Hoo can he ken his ain mind at seeventeen? He'll change fifty times afore he's thirty.'

Nine was striking as he went into the house, and he found his father waiting with the Bible in his hand, his aunt having evidently gone to bed.

'Whaur's Sandy?' asked his father rather sternly. 'It's efter nine—time we were a' in oor beds.'

'He'll be here the noo, likely,' answered Jamie, sitting down at the fire. 'I've been at the Knowe. Dauvit's to be at the barley the morn.'

'Ay, that's weel. Is he a' in?'

'Ay, a' in,' was Jamie's answer; then the twain relapsed into silence. Seventeen years had wrought a great change in John Bethune; his face was deeply furrowed, his hair and beard almost white, his figure much bent at the shoulders. But the keen eye had lost none of its old steady light, nor were his forces abated. He was still able for a good day's work, though it told upon him more severely than when he was in his prime. He turned over the leaves to the 119th Psalm, and sat with the book open, waiting for Sandy. Strict discipline was maintained in John Bethune's household, and though Sandy was indulged in some things, there were others in which he dared not disobey. It was a grave offence to be out after nine. In about five minutes they heard the garden gate swing, and next moment Sandy dashed into the house in his usual noisy fashion, banging the door behind him.

. 'Less din, Sandy; yer auntie's in her bed. It's twenty meenits past nine,' said John Bethune sternly; and then, without waiting for an explanation or excuse, began to read from the ninth verse of the psalm. When the reading was finished he offered up his usual solemn prayer, every word of which the boys knew by heart. Many a time in their younger days they had puzzled themselves over his mysterious utterances, some of which they scarcely understood yet.

Directly they rose from their knees the brothers took their candle and went away up the trap-stair to the garret which had been fitted up for them when they grew too big to sleep beside their father. Aunt Susan, as of yore, occupied the little chamber opening off the kitchen. Directly they were in their own humble room, Jamie began to undress; he did not feel in a mood for talking. But Sandy was in great spirits, and rattled on about St. Andrews, and about the college, and his future, till Jamie could have prayed him to hold his tongue.

'My word, Jamie, it'll be a fine difference to me living at St. Andrews. It's very slow for a fellow here when he kens as much as me,' he said in his boastful way. 'Some day when you're no' busy ye must get father to let you come to St. Andrews, and I'll show ye the sights. It's a bonnie toon. D'ye no wish ye were me?'

'No. I'm sleepy. Be quiet,' said Jamie rather sourly. 'You havena to rise at five. Blaw oot the caun'le.'

Not for worlds would Jamie have admitted to his brother that he envied him his privileges, and that he found it so hard to wish him well. The lad had two enemies to contend with—his own discontent and his bitterness against his brother, who he knew regarded him with a species of good-natured contempt. Sandy blew out the candle and discreetly crept into bed. When he saw Jamie vexed he always held his peace, because he knew that something serious was at the bottom of it.

'I'm vext I was sae short, Sandy,' said Jamie by and by, after a brief, sharp struggle with himself. 'I houp ye'll get on, an' win a lot o' prizes at St. Andrews, an' get a graund kirk efter ye're through.'

'I'll try, man; an' of course, whatever happens, you an' me'll aye be the same. An' ye'll come an' bide wi' me at my manse, maybe, when somebody ye ken's a minister's wife,' said Sandy in an unusual burst of confidence.

'We'll see,' said Jamie with a laugh. So, friends once more, they turned over and fell asleep.

CHAPTER V.

SYMPATHY.

'A hand was laid
In tenderness on his sore heart;
A voice said, Courage take !
The world is wide. There may be room for thee.'

HAT'S Sandy sayin' til't the day ?' inquired Susan Bethune one fine summer morning, when her brother entered the house with his student son's weekly letter in his hand. The old man's face was so radiant, his manner so excited and eager, that involuntarily Susan put more interest than usual into her question.

'Graund news, Shoosan. He's gotten a bursary worth thirty pound a year for twa year. I kent it was in the laddie. I wadna wunner to see him principal o' St. Mary's himsel' yet !' exclaimed John Bethune, and, reaching his spectacles, he proceeded to read out the letter to his sister, pausing every moment or so to call her attention to the beautiful flourishes in the handwriting and the fine construction of the letter. It was a touching and beautiful thing to see the old man's pride in his boy's accomplishments and success; there were actually tears in ‚his eyes as he read and reread the precious epistle; and, seeing that, Susan Bethune was struck to the heart by a strange sense of uneasiness which was almost pain.

'Eh, but ye are bound up in Sandy, John,' she said, and almost unconsciously she shook her head as she spoke.

'It's no' a sinfu' pride, Shoosan. I dinna pit him afore his Maker,' said John Bethune, half arrested by her words. 'An' I hae reason to be prood; d'ye no' think it?'

'Ay. He's a wunnerfu' chiel' for heid wark,' Susan admitted, and her eyes wandered to the window, from which she could see Jamie with his scythe in the grass field. The thought in her mind at the moment was whether Jamie might not have done as well had he had his brother's chance. Susan Bethune was a woman who kept her own counsel, and never spoke unless with good reason, but for all that she had observed and resented the distinction her brother had made between his boys all their lives. She supposed Sandy lay nearest his father's heart because of his close resemblance to Katie, and she did not blame him for that. Susan Bethune was very tender now in all her thoughts of her brother's dead wife. But she did wonder that a Christian man, and an elder in the kirk, should be so indulgent to the one and so hard upon the other, who, like the elder brother of Holy Writ, was always with him, labouring for his good early and late. Not that Sandy could be compared to the prodigal by any means, only he had always been more of a care and trouble to his folk;

falling far short of Jamie in obedience and willingness to do what was required of him. Jamie was Aunt Susan's favourite, and out of her deep love she watched him when he thought he was least observed, until she had arrived at a pretty correct conclusion concerning him. She saw him restless and discontented even when he made least sign; she watched the gradual decay of interest in the croft, the loss of that cheerful readiness to perform and even to anticipate all his father's desires, and her heart grew very heavy about the lad. She never dreamed of uttering her sympathy, or of seeking to win his confidence; she belonged to a stern, undemonstrative race, who deemed any exhibition of the finer feelings a sign of weakness; nevertheless her dumb compassion and silent sympathy found vent in ways of their own, such as little attentions paid to his creature comforts, and little gifts now and again, which rather surprised Jamie, though he did not in the least understand the motive which prompted his aunt to bestow them.

'He'll be hame next week, he says, for twa-three days,' said John Bethune presently. 'There's mair news even than the bursary in't. He's gotten what he ca's a holiday engagement to gang to the Heelan's to tutor a gentleman's twa sons. They're at the schule in St. Andrews, an' their faither disna want them to forget a' their lessons in the holidays, so he has hired Sandy to keep them at them, an' gang aboot wi' them in the holidays. It'll be a fine thing for him, but I was coontin' on haein' him at hame for twa month at least.'

'Ay,' said Susan; for somehow she felt relieved to hear that Sandy was not to spend the long vacation at home. For he would go about like a gentleman, giving himself doubtless many airs on account of his success, while Jamie would be in the throng of the harvest. In her jealous love for her favourite, Susan Bethune was perhaps a trifle hard upon Sandy.

'I'll awa' an' tell Jamie. He'll be as prood as a prince,' said John Bethune, rising; and Susan watched him go down the fields, and saw Jamie leaning on his scythe, while his father imparted his grand news of Sandy's success. Then, suddenly recollecting how she was putting off her time, she began to prepare the vegetables for the broth in rather an abstracted fashion, for the interests clustering about her brother's sons were very absorbing that morning. While she was thus engaged, John returned, not looking quite so well pleased as when he went out.

'Jamie's a queer stick, Shoosan,' he said rather drily. 'Gie him wark, an' it's a' he cares about. He had hardly a word to say ower Sandy's fortune. My! but there's a bonnie difference atween them.'

'No! sae muckle as ye think, John,' Susan was tempted to say. 'Dinna let yer pride in the ane blind ye to ony guid in the ither.'

'No, no; Jamie's a guid, honest, hard-workin' chield. Puir chap, it's no' his faut he hasna a heid like his brither,' said John Bethune placidly. 'It's a wise ordination o' Providence that there should be folk for a'thing. Jamie 'll mak' a gey canty bit leevin' here, as I've dune afore him. But I'll awa up an' tell Dauvit Cam'll. They'll be as pleased as oorsel's.'

So saying, the old man put his letter and his spectacles in his breast pocket, and went away to get the kindly neighbours at the Knowe to share in his joy. Very often that forenoon did Susan Bethune look through the little window and across the fields to the park where Jamie was employed. She saw that he was making little speed, and that very often he stood quite still, as if absorbed in thought. And her heart grew heavier still about the lad. When he came in to his dinner, she looked kindly at him, but did not mention the bursary to him; but it was the old man's whole talk during the dinner hour, and again at tea-time, and Susan Bethune saw that Jamie's interest in the matter was forced.

'Whaur are ye gaun, Jamie?' she asked, when he was leaving the house again after work hours. 'I was wunnerin' if ye wadna gang east to Auchtermairnie wi' me the nicht. Robert Tullis, the baker, brocht word that yer uncle Peter's wife's geyan ill. I'd need to gang an' speer for her.'

'I'll no' gang the nicht, auntie, unless ye want me very muckle,' said Jamie, who was always kind and considerate to his aunt.

'Are ye no' weel, my man?' she asked kindly.

'I'm quite weel. I'm gaun ower the moss, maybe as far as Kirkforthar,' answered Jamie. 'But if ye want me to gang east, I'll gang.'

'I'm no' parteeklar, but I dinna like ye to gang about sae dowie-like yer lane. Ye're no' half sae cheery as ye used to be.'

He smiled a dreary smile and vanished, knowing that in another moment he would forget his eighteen years, and give way to tears. We have all known such weak moments, have felt at times that the four walls of a house could not hold us. We have had experiences in which uttered sympathy could not reach us, when we have only found strength in the wideness of the pitying skies, comfort in the dumb sympathy of the stars.

James Bethune took his favourite way to the peat-moss, walking on quickly until he reached a little wooded hillock, among whose hospitable trees the cuckoo had sought her nest for the first time within his knowledge. He threw himself face downwards on the turf, and there lay, battling dumbly with the passionate, miserable yearnings of his soul. He felt amazed and terrified at the wildness of his own imaginings, at the darkness of the thoughts whirling in his brain. He was at war with all the world, and felt himself an Ishmaelite, whom every man's hand was against. Nobody cared for him, nobody would mourn him though he were dead and buried; they might miss his labour, as they would miss that of any of the animals on the farm, but that would be all. That was one of the darkest hours in James Bethune's life, upon which he never afterwards cared to reflect. He hated himself for his hard, unholy thoughts, for his bitterness against his father and his brother, but he felt powerless to curb them. All kindlier feelings seemed to have died within his breast. But it was not so. A step sounded behind him, a kind hand fell on his shoulder, a familiar voice called him by name. It was the touch and the voice of Mr. Farquhar, the schoolmaster.

' Look at this plant, Jamie. I have been in search of it since ever I came to Star. Isn't it strange that I should have found it to-night, when I was not particularly anxious about it ? '

Jamie, who had not yet quite lost his old respect and wholesome awe of the schoolmaster, picked himself up, and touched his cap. Mr. Farquhar sat down on the bank, and motioned the lad to a place beside him. He was keenly observant of his pale face and clouded eyes, but he made no sign that he saw anything amiss.

'This is an insectivorous plant, James,' said Mr.

Farquhar, touching the leaves with caressing finger. 'It eats insects. Flies and such like alight on it, and are instantly sucked into this hollow, see! When the leaves expand again the insect is dead, and the greedy plant ready for another. Curious, isn't it? I knew it was to be found on the moss, and I came on it to-night quite by accident.'

'I've seen that growin' often. I could hae showed it to you, but I didna ken it ate flees,' said Jamie with interest. 'I can show you where the bonniest ferns grow tae, if ye like.'

'Thank you, I shall be glad to take advantage of your offer. I have often wanted a crack with you since you left school, but you are like another kind of plant, called the sensitive plant, which curls up at a touch,' said the master with a quiet laugh. 'What have you been doing all these years since you left school? not keeping up your lessons, I suppose?'

'I read as muckle as I can, but I havena muckle time, ye ken,' answered Jamie, the master's interested voice and kindly eye winning his confidence at once.

'No, I see you on the fields early and late,' said the master. 'But in winter you will have some time to yourself in the evenings, surely?'

'Ay, when I'm no' at the loom,' answered Jamie. 'But it's slow wark gettin' on yersel'.'

'Your brother is doing great things at college, I was very pleased to hear to-day,' said the master. 'Has he never helped you on?'

'Oh no! I wadna ask him,' said Jamie hastily, and a quick flush sprang to his cheek, as he remembered how Sandy had laughed and scoffed once when he asked him to teach him Latin. 'What does a plooman or a farmer want wi' Latin?' he had said; 'if ye maun read ye should get agricultural books, Jamie, an' no' fash yer heid wi' Latin. Ye wadna be lang o' tirin' o'd onyway.'

'Would you like to learn Latin, Jamie?'

'What wad I no' like to learn, sir?' fell involuntarily from Jamie's lips, and a light sprang into his eyes, which made the master look at him with a deeper interest. When he had had him in the school, he had obtained occasional glimpses of a brighter intelligence, which had made him think the boy might turn out better than was expected. But when he left school, and seemed content to plod on at manual labour, the master concluded that he had no higher aims.

'Has your brother's success emulated you with a desire after his scholarship?' he asked, more to draw the lad out than from any idea that such a thing seemed probable.

'No. I wad hae bidden at the schule, Mr. Farquhar, if I could. I canna bear workin' on the laund nor at the loom. It mak's me feel that wild and wicked whiles, I'm feart at mysel'.'

'That's bad. Are you sure it is not just that restlessness which comes to most of us at one period of our lives, that desire for change, no matter what form it takes?' asked the master kindly.

'I dinna think it's that. I wadna leave the Star to work at onything else if I couldna get to books,' answered Jamie, eager to vindicate himself, and forgetting in this new joy of confidence that he was making known his most cherished and secret dreams.

'Does your father know of this, Jamie?'

'No; an' he wadna believe it though he was telt. He thinks Sandy's gotten a' the brains, an' that I'm only fit

for the harrows or the loom,' said Jamie, not bitterly,
but with a kind of sad conviction which touched the
heart of the master not a little. 'I *am* stupider than
Sandy, sir; but if aince I get a grip o' a thing I never
let it go. It micht tak' me langer to be a scholar,
but I believe I wad succeed in the end.'

'And what bent does your inclination take? Would
you follow the vocation Sandy has chosen?'

'Oh no, I couldna be a minister; I think a man
maun be by-ordinar' in a'thing afore he tak's *that* upon
him,' was the lad's answer. 'I dinna ken exactly what
I wad dae; I whiles think I'—

But here he paused abruptly, and his face flushed
again. He had curbed himself just in time, for *that*
fond dream was too wild and presumptuous to be
breathed to mortal. The schoolmaster, with that rare
delicacy characteristic of his fine nature, did not
press the question, understanding perfectly the lad's
reticence. To say he was amazed at the revela-
tions of Jamie Bethune's nature scarcely describes his
feelings.

'Suppose we make a bargain, Jamie,' he said; 'you
will help me in my botanizing and fern-hunting, and
I'll help you with your lessons. Could you come an hour
two or three times a week, and we'll try our hand at
Latin and whatever else we may fancy, eh?'

The lad's face flushed deep crimson, and the master
saw his sunbrowned hands tremble.

'Nay, don't say a word. It will be a mutual benefit,
for I am getting rusty myself,' said the schoolmaster,
smiling. 'Is it a bargain, then?'

'If ye like, sir,' said Jamie quietly.

It might be a poor way of expressing his grateful
appreciation of the master's offer, but these two, I think,

began to understand each other that summer night on the Star moss.

'Are you going home now? I am, and we may as well walk together,' said the master. 'This is a glorious night, man. Just look at Orion and the Pleiades. Do you know anything of astronomy, Jamie?'

'Some. I ken the big planets. My father has a book on't, I whiles read,' answered the lad. 'I aye think, Mr. Farquhar, that there couldna be a bonnier picter than the sun settin on' the Lomond Hill, in the simmer when the heather's oot.'

'I agree with you. When Mrs. Farquhar and I came first to Star, Jamie, we wondered how we could live in such a bleak, unlovely country; but it was in winter; you will not remember, it was two years before you were born. Your father and I were married within a week of each other; but his wife was spared a little longer than mine,' said the master, and he took off his hat and pushed back his grey hair from his brow. 'It is wonderful how we get used to things, my lad, and how unbearable agonies become gentlest memories upon which we love to dwell. My wife learned to love the Star, and because of that I have never cared to leave it. People wonder that I have never sought a wider sphere, but I have found it wide enough for me, and I sometimes think that, though I have fallen so far short of what I might have been, the place will not be any the worse though I have lived in it so long.'

'I'm sure no',' said Jamie fervently, looking with a strange new reverence at the fine face of the master, which was now furrowed deep by the hand of time, while his hair and beard were whitening fast. He wondered that the master should talk so unreservedly to him about that sorrow which had sapped the springs of hope in the

very prime of his days, and made it a common saying
that the schoolmaster had never held up his head since
his wife's death.

'Well, we have got quite friendly over the insectivora,
haven't we?' said the master pleasantly when they
reached the schoolhouse gate. 'When will you come
and get your first lesson? Not till your brother is
away again, I suppose. Your father told me he would
only be at home for a few days. Come in whenever
you like. I am always at liberty, you know, between
six and ten.'

'I'll be sure to come, sir, thank ye,' said Jamie gratefully; then with a warm hand-clasp they parted, friends
for life. As the schoolmaster entered his lowly dwelling,
he felt that glow in his heart which is the reward of
doing good. Apart from the blessing a generous action
may confer on others, it gives to him who is its author a
sense of sweet satisfaction, which compensates for any
sacrifice he may have made, and the man whose life is
spent in the planning and execution of such deeds lives
perpetually among the fragrant odours of heaven.

It had not cost Gilbert Farquhar much to express a
kindly interest in his old pupil, and to offer to help him
in so far as lay in his power; but it meant a great deal
to Jamie Bethune. He did not go into the house just
at once that night; but strolled through the village,
along the quiet path by the burnside, and up as far as
Carriston gate, just to be alone for a little with the
sweet hopes which had begun to blossom in his heart.
The future was no longer dark and gloomy, but a fair
horizon, bright with promise, illumined by the sunshine
a good man and a true friend had cast upon it.

In a day or two Sandy came home from college,
flushed with his success, and full of airs and conceits

such as country lads are wont to affect after a brief term
of town life. In Susan's eyes this conscious and open
pride spoiled Sandy altogether, but his doting father saw
no flaw in the lad, and would listen by the hour to his
stories of St. Andrews life. Sometimes, in his desire to
create an impression, and to glorify himself, Sandy was
apt to colour his statements just a little, and, while those
at home implicitly believed that he was the chief centre
of interest at St. Mary's College, the fact was, he was of
very little account, and occupied a very obscure position
there. As to the bursary, it was too common an honour
to be thought much of, for the University was so richly
endowed that those who did *not* receive a bursary were
in the minority. But Sandy took care not to communi-
cate that item to the Star folk.

Susan Bethune was both surprised and relieved to see
how very little effect 'Sandy's blawin',' as she termed it,
had on Jamie. He listened to him with as much
patience and interest as his father did, and did not
appear in the least envious or jealous. It seemed to
Aunt Susan as if he had become the possessor of some
happy secret, which had imparted to him a lightness of
heart she had never seen in him before. His smile and
laugh were not now so rare, and he had never been more
cheerful in his life. Altogether that week of Sandy's
vacation was a pleasant time for them all; nothing whatever happened to mar its harmony, or to leave a sting
behind.

One thing shrewd Aunt Susan, as well as Jamie,
observed, that Sandy did not spend much of his time
at the Knowe. Aunt Susan had never at any time
entertained the idea that there could be anything serious
between Sandy and Mary Campbell, they being but
bairns in her eyes; but Jamie knew that his brother

had talked a great deal of nonsense to the girl, and, as it was evident Sandy was already evincing signs of changeableness, it was to be hoped Mary would have sufficient sense just to accept it, and laugh over that old-time nonsense.

Ah, poor Mary! it had not been nonsense to her; and, young though she was, her heart had already awakened to a woman's love.

CHAPTER VI.

A WOMAN'S HEART.

'Love, art thou sweet? Then bitter death must be.'

TENNYSON.

ET on yer hat, see, Mary, an' gang doon wi' the maister to the schule,' said Jean Campbell to her niece.

'No, auntie, I'm no' gaun,' answered Mary in a low voice, and she bent her head over the flowers in the window to hide her wet eyes and her quivering lips.

'What for no'? It's an unco' like thing if ye'll no' gang to hear Sandy Bethune preach. My certy! I've seen the day ye wad hae walkit to Cupar an' back for less,' said the mistress with good-natured sarcasm.

'I canna help it, auntie; I'm no' gaun,' answered the girl in a low voice, but firmly as before.

'Aweel, ye're maybe richt. It's aicht days past on Friday since he cam' hame, an' he's never lookit yer airt. My lassie, ye're quite richt to bide at

hame; an' when he does condescend to speak to ye,
jist you lat him see the wrang side o' yer face for
a change.'

Mary made no response, but, with her eyes still down-
bent, she absently picked the dead leaves from the
geraniums and laid them in a little heap on the table.
Perhaps they were emblematical of her withered hopes.
It was now five years since Sandy Bethune had left the
Star, and, after an eminently successful college career, he
had entered on his final term of theological study at the
Divinity Hall in Edinburgh.   During these years he had
been comparatively little at home.   Visits to college
friends or holiday engagements filled up his summer
vacation, and in winter he pleaded press of study as an
excuse for his neglect of the Star.   His father, who
implicitly believed in him still, submitted without a
murmur, though his heart often ached.   Yet, since he had
consecrated his first-born son to the Church and her
ministry, he must bear the pain which at times the
surrender cost.   He had not thought he would have been
called upon to give him up so entirely.   He was getting
very old now, and in his age felt a greater need of
affection than in the days of his manhood's strength.
Yet, though Jamie was still at home, taking entire
management of all home affairs, and relieving his father
in every possible way, there was not that full confidence
between them which might have been a joy to them both.
John Bethune knew nothing of his second son's inner
self ; he was never admitted to the secret recesses of a
noble soul, preparing itself to do battle with the world
by and by.   He had himself to blame.   He had not
only preferred the elder in every way, but he had mis-
judged Jamie, and kept him, in a manner, shut out of
his heart.   The lad's sensitive heart had been early

wounded, and had grown a little hard perhaps where his
father was concerned. It contained wells of affection
never yet opened, and which were undreamed of by
Jamie himself. But though his father was neither
his confidant nor his friend, he´ never failed in duty
towards him; nay, it was that strong sense of duty,
which was the chief part of James Bethune's religion,
which still kept him in the Star. He saw his father
failing, and knew that if he were bereft of both his
sons, he would go down, like Israel of old, in sorrow
to the grave. For in all temporal affairs the old man
leaned upon him; he had given up the work of life
into his hands.

That true friend and good man, Gilbert Farquhar, the
schoolmaster, was now dead; none but James Bethune
himself knew how great and irreparable was his loss. He
had done what he could to help the lad in his struggle,
and had put him on the path of knowledge, and only
left him when he was able to walk through its mazes
unaided. Not a living soul knew of James Bethune's
attainments and proficiency as a scholar. He was
respected in the Star as a steady, well-behaved young
man, who would rather sit at the fireside with a
book, or in the summer - time take lonely walks,
than join the jovial crew who were to be found any
and every night, Sunday excepted, in Jean Brunton's.
He was altogether lost sight of in the splendours of
Sandy's genius, but it was a common saying in the
place that 'John Bethune was by-ordinar' weel aff wi'
his laddies.'

There was great excitement in the Star when it was
announced that Sandy Bethune would conduct a 'preaching' in the school the second Sunday after his return
home for the holidays. Mr. Bell announced it from his

pulpit, and it was a moment or two before his hearers could think who Mr. Alexander Bethune could be. In the summer evenings the preachings held periodically in the Star school were very meagrely attended, the young folks preferring walking or lounging about the roads. But both old and young turned out to hear Sandy Bethune preach, for he was one of themselves.

'Weel, I maun gang, Mary,' said the mistress. 'I wad gang faurer than the schule to hear John Bethune's son preach. Had his mother lived, she wad hae been a prood wummin the day. But I dinna ken either,' she added with an involuntary sigh; 'it has its draw-backs to hae a by-ordinar' bairn. I wadna be sur-prised, noo, to be telt that Sandy thinks shame o' his ain folk.'

'We'll hae to be stappin', then, guidwife,' said the master, coming in from the door. 'The hale wast end's awa' by. The lad's mettle 'll be tried the nicht. What! Is Mary no' gaun?'

'No, she's no' gaun, Dauvit. Awa' an' get on your black coat, see. Ye're no' gaun doon wi' that auld jaicket,' said the mistress, diverting his attention at once from Mary. 'For the auld man's sake, we maun pay the chield every respeck.'

In a few minutes the worthy couple left Mary to her own meditations, and the first thing she did was to put the bar in the door, and then, sitting down in her uncle's chair, she laid her bonnie head down on the table, and began to cry quietly to herself, for her heart was very sore.

Her aunt had unconsciously given her a cruel stab, for until to-night she had tried to find every excuse for Sandy, and had buoyed herself up with hopes which her aunt's blunt words had rudely dispelled. If Sandy

were ashamed of his own people, then doubtless he must
be ashamed of her. With the pain such a conviction
could not fail to bring, there was no bitterness or resentment commingled, for with that humility peculiar to
sweet, rare natures such as hers, she placed herself on a
very low level in comparison with him who had been her
lover so long. She knew she was no fit companion for
one so great and grand and clever, and she had never
dared to think of herself as a minister's wife; there was
presumption in the very thought. But he had said so
often that she was dear to him, that no other should
ever share his future, that she could not just at once
relinquish all thought of him, all claim upon him. She
had not hid her heart from him; he knew she loved him,
and she had never thought shame of it till now. Poor
Mary! It was a hard cross laid upon her, and she was
glad of the deep stillness and solitude in the house
(there were so few quiet hours at the Knowe), so that
she might face this sorrow which had come into her
young life, and if possible nerve herself for the future,
robbed of all the sweetness of the past. For nearly
an hour she sat in the same position, and then she rose
quietly, and began to busy herself about the house.
Once, as she went to get something out of the dresser,
she took a glance into the little looking-glass against the
wall, and started a little at her own paleness. She
rubbed her cheeks to try and bring back their colour,
but in vain; then she hoped nobody would notice anything amiss in her appearance. The worst of all would
be if anybody suspected she was fretting because Sandy
Bethune had slighted her; her maidenly pride and
dignity rose at the very suggestion of such a thing.
It was a very sweet winning face reflected in the
little mirror, and the sunny hair arranged in smooth

womanly braids was most becoming to the neat little head.   Then her figure had lost all the angular curves of earlier years; and altogether Mary Campbell was a sweet and attractive young woman, and many as good a man would have given half his possessions for Sandy Bethune's chance.   But Mary had neither looked nor listened to any wooing save his alone; she had been absolutely and devotedly true.

At seven she took the milk-pails and went up to the byre.   It took her about an hour generally to milk the five cows, and she was just finishing the last when she heard voices and footsteps approaching, and then half-a-dozen folk burst into the byre, eager to be the first to give the news.

'Eh, but we had a graund discoorse, Mary!   Ye missed a heap,' cried one.

'Eh, thon's a deep lad.   It's just exterordinar' to see him stannin' up an' settin't aff wi' his haunds better than Maister Bell hissel',' said another.

''Deed he mak's a show, an' sets aff a heap o' braw words, but there's no muckle in't for common folk,' said Kirsty the malcontent, edging in her adverse criticism just for contrariness.   'For my pairt, I canna but think that, had as muckle been spent on oor eddication, we micht hae dune mair.'

'It wad be a braw sicht to see you haudin' forth in the schule, Kirst,' laughed the master, whose portly presence at that moment filled up the doorway.

'Was there mony there?' Mary forced herself to ask, in case her silence should be remarked on by the argus-eyed throng.

'Ay, it was crammed to the door; a heap o' Kennoway an' Markinch folk there as weel's oor ain,' answered the maister.   'Are ye dune, Mary?   Awa doon then, bodies, an' get yer milk, till I get the kye putten out.'

'Ye've been braw smairt, Mary,' said Mrs. Campbell, meeting her at the door. 'But it's aicht o'clock. He keepit us geyan lang, but we never wearit. Thon's a star, lassie,' she added, lowering her voice, so that only Mary heard. 'If only he has grace to guide his gifts.'

Mary set down her pails, and, after washing her hands and unpinning her skirt, she put her little shawl about her head, and stole out by the front door, to be away from all the talk about the preaching. She was in that half trembling, excited state, in which a very little would break her down. It was not dark yet; the pleasant sunlight seemed loth to give way to the darkness, and so lingered, even when the stars were peeping in the sky. It was a peaceful and beautiful night, and there was that stillness in the air peculiar to the Sabbath day. It is a blessed thing when the human heart beats in unison with that holy calm. She wandered up to the cornyard, and, leaning up against one of the sweet-smelling haystacks, folded her arms, and stood still. She felt soothed by the solitude and by the hush of the deepening night, and a strength came to her which relieved her burdened heart. Mary Campbell knew nothing of doctrinal points such as Sandy Bethune had been wrestling with in his discourse, but there was in her heart a confidence and faith in God which would have put his Christianity to shame. She firmly believed that this trial would not be beyond her endurance; and, without uttering any formal petition, she mutely sought and received strength from above. In this better frame of mind she turned to go back to the house, but, ere she had gone many steps, she saw a figure coming up the garden path, whose tall outline was too familiar to be mistaken.

'Why do you hurry past me, Mary?' said a deep, manly voice, with an assumption of playfulness. 'Have you not a word to say to an old friend?'

Mary stood still, but said nothing. If she had spoken, a little natural indignation must have displayed itself, and she was determined that Sandy Bethune should not see that she was in the least affected by his indifference.

'Why didn't you come and hear me, Mary? That was shabby. You promised to come long ago.'

'We couldna a' get,' Mary answered quietly, and beginning to move on to the house.

'Don't go in yet, Mary. I've been in, and your aunt was very dry to me. Have I offended her, do you know?'

'I canna say,' was Mary's brief answer.

'Won't you walk up the old road with me? I have ever so many things to tell you and to explain. Come on,' he added coaxingly, touching her arm as he spoke.

Mary hesitated; she was strongly tempted. Ah, the familiar voice and winning way had not yet lost their charm! Sandy noted the hesitation, and immediately took her hand on his arm, with the air of proprietorship she had been wont to find so sweet. So Mary turned with him; perhaps it might be as well to understand each other once for all.

'Of course you've wondered why I've never been up since I came home,' he began. 'But the fact is, a fellow has hardly a minute to himself. I've been twice to tea at the Manse, and of course I've had to go down and see old Robertson. But I haven't sinned beyond all pardon, have I, Mary? If I hadn't known you to be so good and forgiving, you see, I wouldn't have dared to do it, so you have yourself to blame.'

'That's a queer way to put it, Sandy. If you had wanted to come, you would have found the time, easy enough,' said Mary quietly.

'Now don't be hard upon me, Mary, when I'm so penitent. I *was* disappointed when you didn't come to the school to-night. Why, I looked all over the place directly I came in.'

'I dinna ken hoo ye had time to think aboot me ava',' said Mary. 'Was ye no' shakin' wi' nervousness?'

Sandy laughed. 'Not likely. When a fellow has to hold forth before the professors and all the students, it isn't a few Star folk that'll disconcert him. Did they think I did well, Mary?'

'Yes, they a' seemed weel pleased.'

'Is that all you'll say to me, Mary? Now you *are* offended, though you say you're not. Why, what'll you do when you're a minister's wife? I can tell you a public man's wife sees very little of him. He must be at everybody's beck and bow.'

'I'll never be a minister's wife, so I needna fash,' said Mary in the same quiet, aggravating sort of way.

'Dear me! are you going to throw me off after all this time, and after the way I've cared about you, and trusted you since ever we were anything?' exclaimed Sandy incredulously.

Mary withdrew her hand from his arm and stood still on the grassy path. They were quite alone, and would not likely be disturbed, for the old road through the Knowe fields was but little used, especially on the Sabbath day. It was quite dark now, but as they stood in silence a moment, the moon suddenly rose from behind a cloud, and shone full upon them both. It touched Mary's sweet, serious face with a tender light, and revealed plainly her companion's tall, well-built figure and handsome, clear-cut face. Sandy Bethune had improved greatly in personal appearance, and had quite lost all the awkwardness of his earlier years, and which still characterized Jamie. Sandy, among other things, had quickly picked up city polish and city ways. His ministerial garb became him well, too, and he was a lover of whom any girl might be proud.

'I want to speak to you, Sandy,' she said, looking away beyond him, and speaking in low, clear, firm tones. 'Things have been long in my mind, and it's time they were said. I think you an' me's made a mistake. I've seen this long time that you've no' been the same, an' I want to tell you that I dinna and wadna seek to keep ye bound. Let me speak,' she said, raising a deprecating hand, when he would have interrupted her, 'an' syne I'll haud my tongue. I ken brawly that I could never be a minister's wife, nor a fit companion for you. I ken naething, nor I couldna conduct mysel' to your likin'; ye wad sune be ashamed o' me, an' wish ye hadna ta'en me, an' I couldna bear *that*. So I think we'll pairt. Mind, I dinna blame ye; I ken it's me that's daein't, an' should ye get anither mair like ye, I'll wish her an' you weel. Ye maun ken in yer ain mind that I'm richt,' she said more hurriedly, for the strain upon her was very great. 'An' now I'll awa' in. Guid-nicht.'

'Not so fast, my lady; there must be two to that bargain,' said Sandy Bethune, for never had the girl before him seemed so sweet and dear as now, when she was seeking to break the bonds between them. For the

moment he forgot how often he had been ashamed
of her, how often he had wished himself free from
the tie which had become irksome to him, how often
he had blamed the folly which would give him a
wife who would *not* grace her position; and all the
old love came uppermost, sweeping everything before
it. He folded his arms about the slight figure,
and drew her to his heart; and she sobbed there,
not seeking to draw herself away. The effort she had
made had bereft her of her strength, and she could
not keep calm.

'So you thought you had no more ado than speak the
word and I was off?' he said tenderly. 'My dear, you do
not know Sandy Bethune yet. I won't give you up,
unless you say you don't like me, for you are the sweetest
lassie in the world.'

Poor Mary! She loved him well, and these words fell
upon her ears like sweetest music, and for the moment
every fear, every misgiving, was set at rest.

'So you thought that because I was getting on I wanted
to throw you over? What an idea!' he said grandly, and
almost convincing himself that she had wronged him by
the thought. 'Why, Mary, half the pleasure of looking
forward is that you will share the future with me. Only
two years more, and then I'll show you whether I'm
ashamed of you or not. But I'll tell you what. I'll lend
you books, and in two years you'll can crow over me.
And if you'd only not speak the horrid Star Scotch, not
one of the fine ladies I've seen could hold a candle to you.
Couldn't you try, Mary?'

'What would folk say?' asked Mary with a very
doubtful smile.

'You mustn't mind what folk say. I consider you,
and you must consider me,' said Sandy calmly. 'You

have such a sweet voice, that if you just talked a little more refined, you would be quite a lady.'

'I'll try to improve myself for your sake, Sandy,' said Mary with a slight sigh. ' But if I'm slow and stupid ye mauna be vexed wi' me, and aye mind that if ye think I wad be a hindrance or a drawback to you, I'll never haud ye bound.'

'Now don't begin that kind of nonsense again, Mary,' said the young man, laying his hand on her lips. ' You are my own dear lassie, and I won't give you up, not likely; that would be a pretty mean thing to do.'

' Well, if ye like me as weel's ye did, Sandy, I'll say nae mair,' said Mary with a half sob in her voice. ' It's whiles no' easy kennin' the richt thing to dae.'

' It's easy enough in this instance : you must just wait till I get a kirk, and then everything 'll be right. And when I'm in Edinburgh, Mary, if you don't hear regularly from me, you needn't begin to think I'm forgetting you, or any other absurd notions into your foolish little head. Because I shall have to study hard, you know, and I'll have less time than ever, if I'm to do any good.'

' A' richt,' answered Mary. ' I'll mind what ye say.'

' And I'll send you some books directly I get to town, and you must read every word, mind, and anything you don't understand you must write to me about. If you write often, you know, you'll improve both in composition and handwriting, and we'll have you an accomplished little lady in no time.'

Mary smiled. If she had been less meek and humble by nature she would have resented the patronizing tone of her lover's remarks. But what was in reality a species of shame at her scanty accomplishments, she took for loving interest in herself. For his sake she would apply herself, and faithfully follow out his behests, in order that she might not be a shame to him in that strange, wonderful life which one day they were to share together.

CHAPTER VII.

CHANGE.

'A meek quiet soul that bore its burden silently.'

TWO more years slipped quietly away, marked by only one event of family interest to the Bethunes, the death of Peter's wife at Auchtermairnie. She had been in feeble health for many months, and the end was not unlooked for. Her last years had been embittered by her husband's irritability of temper and extreme niggardliness, which had increased with age. They said she was not sorry to slip away from life and its many cares. After his wife's death Peter Bethune continued to live alone at the farm, doing his own turn, and cooking his own bite, such as it was,—a drink of milk and a piece of the coarsest bread sufficed him at any time. His out-door servants would not stay with him, he was such a hard taskmaster, and would have them up by daybreak, and working till dark. Then he was always at their heels, watching them with his evil,

distrustful eye, and nagging at them till service became
irksome and unbearable. He had no intercourse with
his neighbours, and seldom went near his own kin at the
Star. Neither did he trouble the kirk much, and, as to
giving aught away, the very beggars avoided Auchtermairnie as if it had been plague-stricken. Yet still he
prospered in the acquisition of worldly wealth, and his
hoard of gold grew bigger every day. Few loved, yet
many pitied Peter Bethune, for he was that melancholy
spectacle of an old man tottering on the brink of the
grave, his whole heart and soul bound up in the affairs
of this world. He was fast journeying towards an
eternity of which he knew nothing, and for which he was
making no preparation. How different with his brother,
who was like a stook of corn fully ripe, ready to be taken
at the Master's will. As John Bethune grew older, his
fine character received many a mellowing touch which
added to its beauty. He grew less stern towards evil-
doers, and had a word of kindly charity and pity for the
most erring. His manner even acquired a more kindly
and gentle tone, and he made life sweet indeed for those
of his own household. Susan, growing frail too, could
not but think sometimes that John was getting very ripe
for heaven. One thing pleased and satisfied her, that a
more perfect confidence began to rise, slowly but surely,
between Jamie and his father. Gradually John Bethune
got a deeper insight into the mind and heart of his
second son, and found there much that surprised him.
He marvelled at the store of knowledge the lad had
made his own, and it was of a more solid and lasting nature
than that which Sandy had acquired at the college. For
Jamie had not only read intelligently, but he had
brooded and pondered over his reading until he had
sifted the wheat from the chaff, and filled the garner of

his mind with choicest seed, which would one day bear its rich harvest.

'Man, Jamie,' his father would say to him at times, when perhaps in the course of earnest talk he had let out more than usual, 'whaur did ye learn a' that? It's a perfect mystification to me. Ye're like Burns, surely, ye've pickit it up at the ploo an' the harries. Ye've no' haen that muckle time o' yer ain.'

'I've aye had as muckle as dae me, faither,' Jamie would reply, and then skilfully change the subject. In his utter unselfishness, he tried even to prevent his father from imagining that he chafed sometimes over the monotony of his daily toil, for James Bethune was more than ever resolved never to leave the old man while he lived. He had ceased to fret over the harshness of his destiny, though at times a wave of the old longing would sweep over him, and he would feel like a bird beating his wings against prison bars, and panting to be free. There was in his heart a deep conviction that his time would come; and more, that the future would demand all the preparation and discipline of the present. So, while he diligently prepared the soil for the fruits of the earth, a somewhat similar process was going on in his own mind. One winter evening the little household was gathered about the hearth, making a truly pleasant picture. In his own chair sat the old man, with his elbows leaning on the arms and his fingers meeting together at the tips. His eyes were fixed on Jamie, who was reading aloud from Mill. On the other side of the hearth sat Aunt Susan, busy with the 'rig and fur' of a pair of socks for Sandy (little did she dream, honest woman, that, though Sandy might and would probably accept them, he would never wear such homely hose).

Susan Bethune was now within one year of the allotted

span, but her figure still retained the straightness of youth. Her face, however, was weather - beaten and deeply wrinkled, and her hair was very grey. She was knitting busily, but ever and anon she paused and looked over her spectacles from father to son, and then, giving a satisfied nod, would go at it again with redoubled energy. She did not pretend to be edified by what Jamie was reading, or even to understand it, but it was enough for her to see that it interested them. There was a striking resemblance between John Bethune and his son; both were fine-looking men. Jamie had not, indeed, that refinement of appearance so characteristic of Sandy, but he had a powerful, well-knit frame, a grand head, and an open, honest face, lit by an earnest eye, which mirrored a pure and noble soul. There was a gentleness in its gleam when he glanced up from his book at times, to ask his father's opinion on what he was reading, or perhaps to make a comment of his own, which told of a warm and sympathetic heart. About seven o'clock they heard the garden-gate shut with a bang, and next moment somebody opened the door and came in. Jamie sprang up and threw open the kitchen-door, and there was · Sandy standing in the little lobby coolly shaking the snow from his overcoat and hat.

'Bless me, laddie, is't you?' cried the old man, jumping up, while a rare light of joy illumined his face. 'What way did ye no' send word, and Jamie wad hae been doon meetin' ye?'

''Deed ay. It seems stormy, tae,' said Jamie, shaking his brother warmly by the hand. 'Have ye gotten yer Christmas holidays?'

'Not yet. I've come to tell you some news; guess what?' asked Sandy with a smile. 'Well, Aunt Susan, always at the old thing, eh?'

'Aye at it, Sandy, my man. Eh, ye're a great muckle chield; isn't he, John?'

'He is that,' said John Bethune delightedly, for his heart had filled at the sight of his boy. 'Sit doon, man, an' gie's yer news. Pit on the kettle, Shoosan.'

'I don't need anything; I dined just before I left town,' said Sandy quickly. 'Well, my news is that Mr. Alexander Bethune, probationer, has been elected minister of Lochbroom.'

'Eh, that's graund news! But whaur's Lochbroom? Tell's a' aboot it, quick, man!' said his father excitedly.

'Lochbroom is in Dumfriesshire, five miles from Lockerbie,' Sandy hastened to explain. 'I preached there twice in the vacancy, though I wasn't a candidate; you see I thought I had no chance.'

'Is't a parish?' Jamie asked.

'Yes, a parish church. A fine living it is, and a beautiful place, and not too far from Edinburgh.'

'What's the steepend?' inquired Aunt Susan anxiously. and, smiling, she pointed to the old man, whose eyes were closed and his lips moving. They knew he was returning thanks to the Lord for His goodness to him and his.

'The stipend is not so big as it should be—only two hundred,' said Sandy discontentedly. 'But there's a fine manse and a good glebe. It'll do till something better turns up.'

'Mercy me! hear till him!' exclaimed Aunt Susan in dismay. 'My certy, Sandy Bethune! ye're no blate, turnin' up yer nose at twa hunder.'

John Bethune opened his eyes, and looked at his son wistfully and searchingly, as if he would read his inmost soul. It was not the first time Jamie had seen such a look on his father's face in relation to Sandy. Right well did he know the vague feeling of sadness and disappointment which prompted it. 'Hae ye accepted the ca', then, Sandy?' he asked after a little.

'Not yet, but I mean to,' answered Sandy. 'Half the fellows are wild with envy. It's not every one who steps in so easily in these hard times. But I thought I made a good impression when I was down last; they were all so civil to me. It seems a nice congregation—very select.'

'What micht ye mean by select, my man?' asked the old man mildly.

'Oh, well, they're mostly superior folk—gentleman farmers and such like; and then there are three heritors, Sir John Bruce of Cairniehall and Colonel Lewis. They and their families, of course, only attend for a month or two in the summer, when they are not in London or abroad. The other heritor, Mr. Lorraine of Nethercleugh, attends regularly, I was told.'

'Oo ay, they'll be the kind o' folk that'll need a corner o' heevin to theirsel's,' said Aunt Susan brusquely, for she was inwardly disgusted at the way in which Sandy spoke. 'It's a guid thing for you if there's no mony puir folk there.'

'Why, Aunt Susan?' asked Sandy quickly, for he detected well enough the sarcasm underneath her words.

'Oh, jist because puir folk an' you dinna 'gree noo, Sandy, sin' ye've gotten to be sic a great big man in your ain opeenion. There noo! ye can chow that at yer leisure; an' ye needna girn at yer auld auntie, for she's no' carin' a peen's heid for ye,' said Aunt Susan calmly. 'I'm no verra religious, Sandy, but I ken that when the Lord was upo' the earth, He didna fash whether folk was

" seleck " or no.　He likit the common folk, an' He's the
common folk's freen' to this day.　Weel, I'll awa' to
the byre.'

So saying, and having relieved her mind, Aunt Susan
bounced out of the kitchen, and left the three to themselves.　Jamie was unable to repress a smile at his
aunt's unwonted eloquence, but the sad look still lingered
on the old man's face, and Sandy's was flushed with
indignation.

'She's a frightful old dragon that!' he exclaimed.
'How you ever put up with her tongue passes my
comprehension.'

'She's maybe no' that faur frae the bit, my son,' said
John Bethune; then, leaning forward, he looked with a
great and solemn earnestness into Sandy's handsome face.
'Sandy, my man, if I thocht ye were to enter on the
preachin' o' the word, an' a' the solemn duties an'
responsibilities o' a minister in ony but the richt speerit,
I wad for ever rue the day I dedicated ye to the Kirk.
Mind ye, ye'll hae to gie an accoont o' yer talents to Him
that judges the heart an' no' the ootward action.　Think
on that, Sandy, and pray withoot ceasin' to be keepit
back frae presumptuous sins.　Him wha's servant
ye are was meek and lowly, an' Paul, that graund
disciple, was never withoot the fear that while preachin'
to ithers he micht be a castaway.　It's in that
speerit, Sandy, ye maun enter on yer wark, else ye
canna prosper.'

An awkward, almost painful silence followed upon the
old man's solemn warning.　Jamie turned to his book
again, while Sandy sat twirling his thumbs, and looking
moodily into the fire.　He felt himself aggrieved, after
having rushed home to tell them the news, that they
should receive him with such cold congratulations.　At

that moment Sandy Bethune felt further off than ever from his own folk. They would never understand nor appreciate him, and it was hardly possible to put up with their ignorant, old-world notions.

'Don't be so hard on me, father,' he said, feeling that some remark was expected of him. 'Of course I mean to work hard, and do as much good as I can. It wasn't fair of Aunt Susan to come down so hard upon me. What does she know about it any way?'

'She means weel,' said the old man, and then a silence fell upon them again.

'Well, I'll away up to the Knowe, and tell them the news,' said Sandy, jumping up. 'What are you reading, Jamie? Mill's *System of Logic?* Upon my word, you are going in for philosophy with a vengeance. But do you understand it?' he added curiously, and the tone of the question brought the ready flush to his brother's cheek. At four-and-twenty he was as sensitive on some points as a child.

'Understand it! Ay, does he, an' a hantle mair than me, or even you, Sandy, wi' a' yer college lare,' said the old man, with a certain deep satisfaction and pride which astonished Sandy as much as the fact of Jamie reading Mill.

He smiled, just a trifle incredulously, and went away out of the house. Knowing that Mrs. Campbell's milk customers would be about the kitchen entrance at the Knowe, he took the trouble to go up the old road a bit, and then through the stackyard to the front door. The snow had ceased to fall, and the sky was breaking up, and revealing, here and there, blue patches set with stars. The frost was intense, and already the snow-covered paths were growing crisp and slippery. David Campbell himself answered the low knock, and peered out curiously

when he opened the door, wondering what front-door
visitor could be so late on a stormy night.

'Maister Bell!' he exclaimed when he saw the figure
in clerical garb. 'Na; oh, is't you, Sandy Bethune?
Come in. Naebody was expeckin' you.'

'I won't come in, thanks. Is Mary in the house, Mr.
Campbell? I want to see her for a little.'

'She's no' in. She's at Markinch, speerin' for her
Auntie Katie that's doon wi' the cauld. Come in an'
gie's yer crack till she comes back.'

'I think I'll go and meet her. She'll be sure to come
over the Cunan Hill, I suppose?'

'Oh, sure! it's the nearest way frae Northhall,
ye ken, an' the best, especially on a snawy nicht.
But what's brocht ye to the Star a' on a sudden
the nicht?'

'I'll tell you when I come back. It's good news,'
said Sandy with a laugh. "Is there a stick in the
lobby? Hand it out, please. The roads are very
slippery.'

'There's my faither's tree till ye,' said David Campbell,
handing out the stout crook which had stood for fifty years
and more in the lobby at the Knowe. Thus equipped,
Sandy trudged off. Directly he was beyond the houses
he lit a cigar and walked on quickly, pondering certain
things in his mind. He felt a vague dissatisfaction, an
uneasy consciousness that his relations with the Star
were not quite what they should be. Every step he took
was bringing him nearer Mary Campbell, but the thought
had not power to thrill his pulses, or make his heart
beat faster; and yet he had not seen her for nearly four
months.

The sky gradually cleared as the wind rose, and when
he passed through the wickets into the path which led

over the hill, he could see Mary coming over the brow of the slope; at least, there was a woman's figure standing out clearly against the deep blue of the sky, and which would in all probability be Mary. He walked more leisurely now, and just met her at the base of the hill.

'Oh, Sandy! she exclaimed breathlessly, and yet somehow she did not exhibit that surprise he expected. The explanation was that he was so continually in her thoughts that it could not have seemed very strange though he should appear sometimes at her side.

'How are you, Mary?' he asked; and after holding her hand a moment he stooped and kissed her. As he did so he saw her eyes fill with tears.

'They didna ken ye was comin', surely. At least I saw Jamie yestreen, an' he said naething aboot it.'

'No, they didn't know; I didn't know myself,' said Sandy rather shortly; for the broad Scotch, even when uttered in so sweet a tone, jarred upon him and vexed him.

'I hope there's naething wrang,' she said rather timidly.

'No. I've got a church, Mary; that's what brought me to Star to-night,' he said. 'We need not stand here. Let us walk on.'

'A church! Oh, Sandy, where?'

'At Lochbroom, near Lockerbie. They have elected me unanimously. I am told there was not one dissentient voice,' said Sandy with his grandest air.

'Near Lockerbie; where's that, Sandy?'

'In Dumfriesshire, you little goose. Have you forgotten all your geography already?'

'I think I have. An' when do ye gang, Sandy?'

'As soon as I can; of course, now it will be after the

New Year; but you're never asking about the stipend or the manse, Mary.'

'But you'll tell me a' aboot it, Sandy,' said Mary with a fleeting upward smile, which had a touch of wistfulness in it. Mary Campbell's love was more a pain than a joy; there was a strange uncertainty and fear mingling with it, and an utter absence of that perfect trust and freedom which makes love's young dream so sweet.

'The stipend is two hundred, besides the glebe, and the manse has ten rooms in it, Mary; different from anything you've been accustomed to.'

'Ten rooms, Sandy!' echoed Mary in a whisper. 'That's mair nor they have at Carriston; as mony nearly, I believe, as what's at Brunton.'

'It's bigger than the Knowe, any way,' said Sandy, without drawing any comparison between it and his own humble home. 'There'll be a dining-room and a drawing-room and a study, then bedrooms of course. It'll take a lot of money to furnish it, but my father must just advance the cash. I must make a good appearance at first, you know; so much depends on that.'

'But sic a hoose is by faur ower big for you, Sandy,' Mary ventured to say, but did not say 'for us,' as most girls would have done.

'Not a bit of it. I've been a great deal in fine houses, and you'll soon grow accustomed. You'll need to pull up, though, Mary, and learn a great deal within the next twelve months, before you come to the manse of Lochbroom.'

Mary sighed. She felt very ignorant and weak and unfitted for the position of which her lover spoke. The burden of the future sometimes weighed very heavily on her, and Sandy was not so helpful as he might have been. He was always readier to find fault than to notice improvements or commend her for doing well.

'Did you read the books I sent to you, Mary?'

'Yes, I read them; but I didna ken the meanin' o' the half in Bacon's *Essays*. I likit some o' the poetry books best,' said Mary. 'I dinna think I'm clever enough to read your fine books, Sandy; it would be better to let me be. I'd rather learn a' ye want me to learn just by listenin' to you. An' I've sae muckle adae that when I sit doon whiles at nicht to a book I fa' asleep.'

Sandy Bethune bit his lip, but when he felt the light hand tremble on his arm, his heart smote him. After all he was a little hard on the poor little girl, who had never had a chance.

'Never mind, my pet. Don't bother your little head any more over Bacon. I daresay he's rather a dry old chap. I daresay you'll do splendidly when you're away from the drudgery of the Knowe,' said Sandy; and as they were in the deep shadow of the malt barns, and nobody was in sight, he stooped down, and kissed her again. Her humility touched him, and he was very fond of her in his own way. And if only she would not speak so broad, she was very pretty, and when properly dressed would look as like a lady as many he knew.

'So you'll need to be getting your things ready, Mary. Women always get a lot of stuff, don't they, when they're going to be married? Of course it won't be for a while yet, till I get settled a while, and am all ready for you. Won't you be glad to come?'

'Ay, if only I can please ye, and mak' ye a guid wife,' said Mary with a sob in her voice. 'But oh, Sandy, mind that if ye think ye wad be better wi' somebody else, I'm quite willin' to gie ye up. I dinna ken what I wad dae if ye thocht ye had made a mistake when it was ower late to mend it.'

'If we weren't so near the Knowe, you little monkey, I'd punish you for such a speech,' said Sandy playfully. Then a smile stole through her tears again, and for the moment the girl's anxious heart was set at rest.

CHAPTER VIII.

SPELLBOUND.

IN the study at the manse of Lochbroom sat
the newly-elected minister on a Friday
morning, trying to collect his thoughts,
in order to prepare his discourse for the
Sabbath day. He found it a difficult task,
for the week had been one of excitement and
event, and it was not easy to compose the
mind and banish all disturbing elements from his
thoughts. Everything was so new and strange; the
very furniture in the room was discomposing, it was
so unfamiliar. John Bethune had told his son to obtain
suitable furnishings for his manse, and send in the bills
to him, little dreaming, honest man, what he would be
called upon to pay.

The Reverend Alexander Bethune had a refined taste,
and liked everything of the best quality. Those who
had already seen the interior of the manse had come
away in ecstasies over the beauty and solid elegance
to be found there. The dining-room was substantially
and chastely furnished in oak and crocodile leather; the

study in mahogany and Utrecht velvet, the drawing-room in ebony and silk tapestry. The young minister knew his father was possessed of ample means, and so took advantage to the uttermost of his permission to please himself. What would the Star folk have said could they have had but one peep into the manse of Lochbroom ? and what would be gentle Mary Campbell's awe and astonishment when she looked upon her future home ?

Such thoughts as these, I fear, occupied the mind of the young minister, and proved more alluring and engrossing than the words of the text he had chosen : 'Whatsoever a man soweth, that shall he also reap.'

He had, however, at length managed in a manner to concentrate his thoughts upon his subject, when his housekeeper knocked at the door.

'There is a gentleman in the dining-room, sir,—Mr Lorraine of Nethercleugh,' she said. 'If you are not too busy he would be glad to see you for a few minutes.'

The minister rose at once, well pleased to hear the name of one of the heritors. It augured well that they should begin so soon to show him neighbourly kindness. He walked into the dining-room and greeted his visitor without the slightest restraint or shyness; the new minister of Lochbroom had the utmost confidence in himself.

'Good morning, Mr. Bethune,' said the stranger with a strong English accent. 'I must apologize for this early call, and also for my unconventional attire. I ride into the village for my letters every morning, and I merely looked in to see whether it would suit you to dine with us to-night. My daughter and I will be quite alone; but it may help to pass an hour or two, and we will be delighted to see you.'

'Thank you, I shall be most happy to accept of your invitation, and to make the acquaintance of Miss Lorraine,' said the minister a little less effusively, for he felt as if that keen, deep-set eye were reading his inmost soul. He had seen Mr. Lorraine at the ordination dinner the previous evening, but had not been so struck by his appearance then as now. He was a man considerably past his prime, with a tall, well-knit figure, and a face which must once have been handsome, though it looked now as if some terrible blast of sorrow had swept over it, scaring a line here and another there, until its contour was marred. The mouth under the heavy grey moustache was grave and stern, and, though he spoke pleasantly and cordially enough, no smile ever came upon his face. He wore riding garb, and looked every inch a gentleman ; somehow Alexander Bethune felt himself miserably conscious of his own insignificance.

'Have you recovered from the ordeal you underwent last night ?' asked Mr. Lorraine. 'I felt very much for you. It seems to me always that the great mistake made at these sort of gatherings is talking too much of and at the guest of the evening. But I must say you took it all very coolly.'

'I tried to do so ; but, as you say, perhaps there was just a little too much said.'

'Well, they have given us cause to expect a great deal from you, Mr. Bethune ; I hope you will be very happy and comfortable among us. I must say I have found the people of Lochbroom and the neighbourhood most kind and courteous, since I came to make my dwelling among them.'

'Have you not always resided at Nethercleugh then ?' asked the minister involuntarily.

G

'No; we only came a year ago, when I bought the
place from the Earl,' said Mr. Lorraine. 'So we are not
county people. I was a merchant in London before I
retired from business. Well, may we expect you at
seven, Mr. Bethune?' he broke off with strange abrupt-
ness, and the minister wondered to see a deep shadow
steal darkly across his face.

'Thanks, I shall not fail.'

'That's right. If you walk out (it is only three miles
following the burn which flows past your own garden
wall), my man shall drive you back in the evening.
Good morning.'

So, in the same gravely courteous manner, he shook
hands, and took his leave. The minister watched him
ride away up the street, admiring the beautiful chestnut
mare, and filled with the liveliest interest and curiosity
concerning him and his daughter. There was very little
progress made with the sermon that day, there were many
interruptions, and when evening came he felt a trifle
alarmed lest he should not be able to do himself justice
on the Sabbath day.

Shortly after six he set out to walk by way of the
winding stream to Nethercleugh. It was only the third
week in January, but the air was mild and pleasant, and
a new year's spring had made the hedgerows bud and
some green blades peep above ground. The Cleugh road,
as it was called, was a favourite walk with Lochbroom
folk, and the new proprietor of Nethercleugh had won
golden opinions for himself by giving them the privilege
of extending their walk through his grounds, and out
by the north lodge into the Lockerbie road. He saw
that the path was kept in order also, and it was safe
footing even in the darkest night. It was not dark
to-night, however, for the moon was high in the heavens

and objects at a distance were clearly discernible. The path took many a curious winding curve, crossing and recrossing the stream several times, and sometimes losing sight of it altogether.

It is a poor soul that is not impressed by its surroundings, and that does not feel itself uplifted by that solemnity with which nature often seeks to commune with earth's children.

When the human heart is in unison with nature's harmonies, then is it very near to nature's God. The young minister stood still on one of the rustic bridges which spanned the stream, and gave himself up for a moment to the softening influences of the place. No sound broke the stillness but the solemn rustling of the fir tops, and the gentle murmur of the stream as it gurgled and splashed in its pebbly bed. The moonlight was gloriously bright, and through a gap in the trees he could look up to the village clustering on its gentle slope, guarded by the spire of the grey old church,— his own church, where, on the Sabbath day, he must begin his life work, and sow the seed which should bear an immortal harvest. It was a solemn, almost a chastening thought, and at that moment all that was noblest and best in the man was called into being. He forgot all the outward dignity and honour of his position, which, not an hour ago, had been uppermost in his mind. The thoughts which came to him there were almost a prayer, and, for the first time since he had had the ministry in view, he obtained a glimpse of its solemn responsibilities and high privileges. Oh that the influences of that holy hour had but remained! then indeed life would not have been saddened by vain regrets which would go with him to the grave.

Out of a deep, thickly-wooded glade, into which the

moonbeams could not gain admittance, he came suddenly into the park, with its noble trees and soft sward gleaming white under the clear sky. He saw the house in the near distance, a venerable pile, built of the red sandstone common to the district, but which the storms and suns of many, many years had softened and changed so that it would scarcely have been recognised. Ivy clung to its turrets, and the tender mosses crept about its lower walls as if they loved it.

A wide sweep of gravel lay in front, bounded by the soft, well-kept turf of a beautiful lawn, in the middle of which stood one hoary chestnut tree. There were no flowers to be seen; the whole appearance of the place was plain and severe, but beautiful and grand in its simplicity.

As the minister gazed upon the imposing dwelling, and recalled the humble cottage in which he had been reared, his heart swelled with pride, that, through his own industry and merit, he should have raised himself to be received as an equal by its possessor. Perhaps in youth such a thought was natural. The servant who took his hat and coat immediately ushered him up the wide staircase, and, opening the drawing-room door, announced him by name.

'Good evening, Mr. Bethune,' said the now familiar voice of his host; 'you are in good time. Had you a pleasant walk?'

'Very; it is a lovely evening, and the path is quite picturesque,' answered the minister; and, as his eyes grew accustomed to the subdued light in the room, he glanced curiously, almost eagerly round in search of Miss Lorraine.

'My daughter will be down presently,' said Mr. Lorraine, understanding the glance. 'She was in

Lockerbie spending the day, and only returned about half an hour ago. She is usually first. This, of course, is your first visit to Nethercleugh?'

'Yes; it seems a fine residence.'

'It suits us, and in summer it is very pleasant. Beatrice and I are very quiet folk, and are generally content with each other,' said Mr. Lorraine, and a deep, exquisite tenderness relieved for a moment the sternness of his face.

'Surely she must be old and uninteresting,' thought the minister. 'No young girl would be content to be buried in such a quiet country place.'

And yet there was grace and beauty in her very name. The twain relapsed into silence then, and the host stood leaning his elbow on the broad marble mantel, looking almost gloomily into the fire. The guest wondered what kept that perpetual shadow on his face. The stillness in the house oppressed him, and the room, though magnificently beautiful, was sombre and gloomy, rendered even more so by the subdued light from the solitary reading-lamp burning on the table. At last, to the minister's relief, the door opened, and involuntarily he rose to his feet. He could not have described the strange feeling which took possession of him; he felt as if some crisis in his life were at hand.

'My daughter, Mr. Bethune. Beatrice, my dear, you have not been in haste,' he said, looking at her with critical approval. 'Mr. Bethune will soon learn to depend on you for entertainment when he comes to Nethercleugh. I am the most miserable of hosts.'

'Mr. Bethune must not believe that, else he and I shall never agree,' said Beatrice with a slight smile; then she turned to the minister with exquisite grace. 'May I bid you welcome to Lochbroom and to Nethercleugh, and express the wish that you will be very happy with us ?'

'Thank you, Miss Lorraine,' said the minister with an awkwardness altogether new to him; and his face flushed, he could not tell why.

'It is scarcely half-past seven,' she said, moving over to a beautiful azalea on a jardinière near the centre table, and touching it with caressing fingers. 'This plant is beginning to droop, papa; I must have Glover in to look at it.'

'They are best in the greenhouse, my dear; I have often said so,' he replied, and the minister saw with what love and pride he watched her every movement. He had reason to be proud of the queenly figure, whose grace was enhanced by the rich simplicity of her attire. It fell in sheeny folds about her, and the glowing scarlet geranium against the black lace at her throat seemed to impart a reflection of its colour to the pale face. It was a striking face, not so much on account of its beauty, but because it was indicative of character, and seemed to have a story to tell. That it was a sad story the grave, womanly mouth and wistful eyes proved beyond a doubt. They were lovely eyes, deep and unfathomable, and capable of a hundred varying expressions. The lashes and eyebrows were dark, but the abundant hair coiled about the stately head had a sheen upon it which neither painter's brush nor poet's fancy could ever reproduce. It rippled back from a broad, thoughtful brow, which had some deep lines on it, which made it difficult to define her age. In all his life the minister of Lochbroom had seen no woman in the least like Beatrice Lorraine; in her presence he felt as if under the influence of some spell.

'You will be charmed with Lochbroom a month hence,

Mr. Bethune,' she said, turning her deep eyes on the minister's face again. 'It is loveliest in spring.'

'I should think it would lend itself well also to the beauty of the autumn. The surrounding country is so richly wooded,' he answered. 'Do you not admire the colouring of the autumn woods?'

'No, if I had my way there should be no autumn season. It is a sad and miserable time,' she said with a strange passion. 'For me the summer is always shadowed by the thought of the fall of the leaf. I know not how any one can see aught of beauty in the precursors of decay.'

At that moment the gong sounded, and they adjourned to the dining-room. Dinner was a pleasant meal, for Mr. Lorraine made an evident effort to entertain his guest, and there were few subjects on which he could not talk with that fluency born of confidence in his own knowledge. Beatrice also joined in the conversation with easy frankness. She looked well, too, at the head of her father's well-appointed table, and performed her duties with an exquisite grace. The minister felt sorry when dessert was over, and she left the room.

'Do you smoke, Mr. Bethune?' asked his host when they were alone.

'A cigar occasionally.'

'I can suit you. There are some fine Manillas in my sanctum. I shall just get them, if you will excuse me a moment. It is mild enough for us to enjoy a puff outside. Then Beatrice will give us some tea and a song. She sings well.'

'I am sure of it. Miss Lorraine must excel in whatever she does,' said the minister. He was perfectly sincere in his remark, yet it was received by Mr. Lorraine with a swift, curious glance, and a curve of the lips which might have passed for a smile.

'Let me give you a word, Mr. Bethune. If you wish to keep on good terms with my daughter, don't attempt to flatter her; she will resent it at once,' he said. 'The wind is westerly, I see; we had better turn our faces to it. It will refresh us after the closeness of the dining-room.'

In courtesy to his guest, Mr. Lorraine lit a cigar also, but made little progress with it. He talked kindly and quietly to the young minister, chiefly about Lochbroom and the state of the church, but he made no personal remarks, and did not ask a single question concerning the antecedents or past career of his guest. After a ten minutes' stroll to and fro on the gravelled sweep in front of the house, they went indoors, and up to the drawing-room. Tea was in, and a few minutes were spent over it, then at her father's request Beatrice opened the piano.

'Do you sing, Mr. Bethune?' she asked, as she turned over the music sheets. 'Could I not find something here for you?'

'I would rather have the pleasure of hearing you, Miss Lorraine, if you please.'

'Very well,' she said quietly, and, running her fingers over the keys, she began at once, without any of that hesitancy and playful affectation which so many musicians exhibit. Her voice, low and tremulous at first, gained strength as she sang, until a rich, sweet volume of sound seemed to fill the whole room. The familiar but ever beautiful 'Flowers o' the Forest' was rendered with an exquisite and thrilling pathos which almost made the minister hold his breath. She had a magnificent and powerful voice, well under control; and would soften it to the pathetic melody, till it seemed like the voice of tears. Her face flushed as she sang, and he saw the deep eyes glittering, telling how the power of music stirred her to the very depths. When she ceased there was a moment's deep silence.

'Something more, if you please,' he pleaded earnestly, but she slightly shook her head, and at once rose from the piano.

'No more to-night. Please don't insist. I could not,' she said, and, moving over to where her father sat with his face buried in his hand, she touched his grey head as if to comfort him.

'Why *will* you sing these mournful ditties, Beatrice ?' he asked, looking up at length with the faintest smile. 'You know how I dislike them.'

'Shall I give you something merrier, papa ?'

'Never mind. Sit down and let us talk. Come, Mr. Bethune. I fear you find us but indifferent company. I shall be sorry if you find your first visit to Nethercleugh too depressing to care to repeat it.'

'That is not likely, Mr. Lorraine,' said the minister sincerely. But after that the conversation seemed to flag. It was as if some chill shadow rested on the family hearth, intruding itself unasked and marring the harmony and pleasure of the hour. The minister felt it, and after a time he rose and said it was time for him to go. They did not demur nor press him to stay, and the order was given to bring the carriage to the door.

'Come again soon. Although we cannot offer you many inducements, we shall be glad to see you at any time,' said the master of Nethercleugh as he bade him good-night. 'Perhaps you will not always find us very cheerful, but we will do the best we can.'

The minister thanked him, and, as he was being driven rapidly home, occupied his mind with speculations regarding those he had left. That some great sorrow had recently overshadowed Nethercleugh he could not but conclude. What, then, could it be ? Evidences of wealth were there in plenty, but that peace of mind which money cannot buy seemed lacking. Henceforth Nethercleugh would not only be full of interest for him, but it would be a magnet, because it held Beatrice Lorraine.

When the carriage drove away, Mr. Lorraine returned to the drawing-room and threw himself with a deep, heavy sigh into a chair. Then Beatrice rose from hers, and, kneeling by his side, clasped her hands upon his arm.

'Papa, I know you could not bear it to-night. Was it because he reminded you of what Willie might have been ?' said the sweet, pitiful voice. 'Dear papa, your heart is full of anguish. Love is struggling hard to win. Don't be angry. I must speak, or I shall die. I lie awake at nights thinking of him, picturing him a wretched outcast in the streets of London. He did very wrong. You know I do not seek to condone or excuse his offence; only he was very young, and he had nowhere to go when *we* cast him off. Oh, think of him as he was at the best, papa! Remember how you loved him! He was very dear to you.'

'Dear! Ay, too dear! I loved him, God help me! better than my own soul. I made an idol of the boy from his birth, Beatrice, and left you, my poor daughter, to the love and care of strangers. But I have been punished for my sin; my eyes have been opened, and you, my darling, are my all to-night.'

'Oh, do not say that, papa! so long as Willie lives, he *is* your son, you cannot sever the tie,' said Beatrice brokenly. '*I* was always happy; you were kind to me too. Do not imagine I felt hurt or jealous; how could I be jealous of my own dear brother? you had room in your heart for us both. Papa, I feel it very deep in my heart; I brood over it night and day. Oh, is it not a wrong and wicked thing to leave him to his own devices? What if it should accomplish his destruction? Would we not be answerable?' she asked with a shudder.

'Beatrice!' His tone was cold and stern, and she crept away from him, as if stung to the heart. 'I have forbidden you to speak of this. I forbid you again. He has chosen his own path, the path of dishonour and disgrace, where we will not follow him. Henceforth I have only you. May God forgive me if I am harsh to you, my darling!' he said with a burst of passionate fondness. 'I do not mean to be, but you must understand I am to be obeyed in this.' He rose from his chair, as if unable to bear his own thoughts, and went out of the room. A few minutes later she heard the library door close, and the key turned in the lock.

CHAPTER IX.

AN UNGRATEFUL HEART.

'How sharper than a serpent's tooth it is,
To have a thankless child.'

SHAKESPEARE.

IS there nae letter the day yet, John?'

'Nane yet, Shoosan. I wonder, can there be onything wrang wi' Sandy?' said the old man wearily, both his look and tone telling of an anxious heart.

'Hoots no!' answered Susan in her brisk, cheerful fashion. 'Ye maunna get ony sic thocht intae yer heid. It's near the Assembly time, ye ken, an' dootless he'll be busy; but for a' that he micht hae written.'

'He's never been sae reg'lar since he gaed tae Lochbroom,' said John Bethune. 'An' we hinna seen him sin' Februar'. It's a lang time.'

Susan Bethune looked at her brother with a deep compassion, for he seemed to her that morning very old and very frail. Of late his cheek had lost its ruddiness, his eye its wonted clearness; and he looked his seventy-five years to the full. There was a childishness about him at times, too, shown in little bursts of petulance and waywardness which she could not but heed, it was so different from the self-control and calmness of demeanour to which she had been so long accustomed. There is a deep pathos in such changes as these. We do not like to see the fall of a goodly tree, nor the breaking up of a fine constitution; but least of all can we brook signs of failing powers in those we love. To be compelled to watch such sad decay, I think, is one of the chief sorrows of life. And yet it has its bright side, too, if we only care to look at it; for there is another and a brighter sphere where these faculties, worn out by the toil of earth, will be restored to their pristine freshness and vigour.

'I'll tell ye what, Shoosan,' he said, suddenly starting to his feet; 'I'll get ready an' gang awa' to Edinburgh wi' the eleeven train, an' syne on tae Lochbroom in the efternune.'

'Ye'll dae a hantle less,' said Susan calmly. 'What for wad ye flee awa' till Lochbroom the day?'

'To see Sandy. I maun gang, Shoosan; dinna hinder me. Get oot my claes, like a wummin.'

'An' what'll Jamie say when he comes hame frae Cupar?' asked Susan, without making any motion to grant his request.

'He has nae business wi' me. Can I no' gang whaur I like for you or him either?' asked the old man testily; for the moment the idea to pay a visit to Lochbroom entered his head, there and then did he resolve to put it into immediate execution.

'Man, John, be reasonable. Jamie 'll tak' my heid aff if I let ye awa' on sic a jaunt. Ye ken he's that fear't aboot ye,' pleaded Susan, really alarmed when she saw how determined he was. 'Bide or next week, when the thrang o' the land 'll be by, an' Jamie 'll gang wi' ye.'

'I'm gaun the day, an' the noo,' said the old man doggedly, and, opening the kist lid, began to lay out his black clothes, the broadcloth suit he had bought for his wedding so long ago.

'As sure's I live, I dinna ken what tae dae!' said Susan, almost in tears. 'Hoo can ye gang to Lochbroom withoot siller? Ye ken brawly that's mainly what took Jamie to Cupar the day,' she added triumphantly. 'Ye'll hae to bide or the morn, onyway.'

'Na, na; I hae as muckle as tak' me there an' back,' said the old man quietly. 'Whaur's my new neepkin? this ane's a' torn at the edge.'

'If ye're gaun, ye're gaun wi' what ye can get for yersel'. I'll no' tak' it on mysel' to help ye, John Bethune,' said Susan shortly. 'Hoo d'ye think an auld cratur like you will ever find yer way awa' sae faur? Ye're waur than a bairn, I declare.'

'I'm no' that faur through but what I can gang there and back, Shoosan,' answered the old man, proceeding rapidly with his dressing, Susan watching him all the while with anything but a kindly eye. She could hardly believe he would really persist in his determination until he bade her 'guid mornin',' and, taking his stout stick in his hand, turned to go.

'Ye're a bonnie-like sicht to gang awa' to the manse,' she said, jumping up then. 'Let me brush yer coat; an' see, there's yer ither neepkin, ye can tie't about yer neck on the road or i' the train, an' if ye're killed, dinna blame me.'

'Nae fear; dinna pit yersel' aboot for me. I'll be back safe and soond the morn,' he said cheerily, pleased as a child to get his own way. 'Tell Jamie

he can haud in or I come hame, an' syne break oot
on me.'

Susan Bethune shook her head. She was very
uneasy and troubled in her mind; but, as she said to
Jamie when he came home, 'Ye micht as weel
attempt to gar the sun stand still as pit yer faither
past a thing when he's set on't. He's a perfect deil
wi' thrawnness.'

Jamie said very little, but he was not the less anxious
about his father; indeed, he had it in his mind once or
twice to go after him and bring him safely home. However, he tried to reassure himself with the thought that
his father was not so very frail yet, and that he had all
his faculties about him. Surely if he arrived all right at
Lochbroom, Sandy would see to it that he would get
safely back.

He could not but wonder how his brother would take
the visit, for he had never once invited any of them to
come and see him, and Jamie himself was too proud to
go unasked. It was long since he had become convinced
that Sandy was ashamed of his relations; his habit of
deep study and pondering thought had given him a keen,
unerring insight into human nature, and he could read
his brother's character like an open book. He regarded
him with a strange commingling of feeling, half wondering, half sad, but he was too generous to judge him
harshly, and could find many excuses for the weakness
he only half understood. I fear Sandy was not always
so generous where Jamie was concerned, but that is a
common failing. It is so easy to pick faults, so hard for
the most of us to acknowledge good in others. And yet,
when we so strive at times, and succeed in conquering
our meaner impulses, is not the sweet satisfaction which
follows a reward sufficient for the struggle?

In due time the old man arrived in Edinburgh, and on inquiry learned that he would get a train for the south early in the afternoon. He was just like a child in his delight at finding himself amid the stir and charm of new scenes; his spirit was still young, and in his exuberance he forgot the frailty of his bodily frame. As the train sped past the shores of Cobbinshaw Loch, through among the bleak solitudes of the Lanarkshire hills, and entered the greener and more abundant beauty of the southern counties, he began to think, for the first time since he started on his sudden journey, on the object he had in view. What if he arrived in a strange place so far from home to find Sandy away? It was quite possible that such might be the case; however, he tried to banish such a thought, and tried to interest himself again in the scenery through which he was being so rapidly whirled. They passed Lockerbie, and when the train steamed into a little station about three miles farther on, he jumped up and peered eagerly out, sure they had arrived at Lochbroom.

'Lochbroom!' re-echoed the guard, in his sharp, brusque fashion. 'You should have changed at Lockerbie for Lochbroom. You had better get out here and wait for the next train coming from the south.'

'When'll that be, though, my man?'

'Six o'clock. Come, get out, or you'll be carried a few miles farther out of your way.'

'Hoo faur is't frae here to Lochbroom?' asked John Bethune, stepping out to the platform.

'About six miles. Rather far for an old fellow like you. You'd better wait for the train,' said the guard, and next minute he sounded his whistle, and the train steamed away.

'Six o'clock! that's verra near twa hoors yet. I'll

walk,' said the old man. ' I'm fair sair sittin' onyway. Eh me ! I dinna care about thae railway trains.'

He made some inquiry at the station-house, and set out manfully on his walk. Oh, could Susan Bethune but have seen the old man toiling along the dusty road, with his black coat over his arm and his bare head exposed to the sun! words would not have been adequate to express her righteous ire. Somehow the surrounding country no longer had charm or interest for John Bethune, and he began to wish he had not been quite so headstrong in the morning. It was one of the loveliest of May days. The sky was brilliantly clear, the sunshine radiant, the west wind soft and caressing in its touch. Then the whole earth was clothed in green ; the corn was a foot above ground now, and on the earlier lands potato and turnip tops were visible on the furrows. The air was full of melody, and of that happy promise which seems to come home to us more in May than at any other time. There was not much bloom yet, but buds were plentiful, both in hedge and tree, and on the undulating banks which rose on either side of the road. Time was when these things would have touched and filled the heart of John Bethune, but to-day he had no glad eye for them, but thought rather of his cosy corner by the fireside at home, with a great longing to stretch his limbs in his own arm-chair. The old man was weary, and in need of rest. He sat down once or twice on the way, hot and tired as he was, and took no thought of putting on hat or coat ; then when he was cool again he would trudge on again, straining his eye over every little eminence to catch a glimpse of the spire of Sandy's kirk. They were six long, long miles to him, and when at last he saw clustering on the brow of a little hill the houses of the village, he

H

was too tired to strain his eyes any longer in search
of the manse or the kirk.   Both were hidden from
his point of view, however, by the old elms in the
kirkyard.

'Is thon Lochbroom, lassie ?' he asked a field-worker,
who came out, hoe in hand, from a potato field.   .

'Ay, that's Lochbroom,' she answered.   'It's a fine
nicht.'

'Ay, lassie.   An' whaur micht the manse be, my
wummin ? if ye could direck me the nearest road, I wad
be muckle obleeged.'

'D'ye see the brig ower the burn,' she said, pointing
along the road.   'Weel, gae doon by the side o't, an'
follow the fit-path richt alang tae yon clump o' trees.
Thon's the kirkyaird, an' the manse gairden's jist beside
it.   Ye'll get in by the gairden gate, an' up to the back
door.'

'Thenk ye, my lassie; I'll be fain to see't, I can tell
ye, for I'm fell tired,' said the old man; then, putting on
his coat and hat, for the cool evening shadows were
beginning to fall, he trudged on to his destination.
When he reached the trees, he saw the spire of the
church peeping through the green boughs, and involuntarily he stood still and took off his hat.   It was a
sweet spot; surely the heart of man could desire no
more, he thought, than to be permitted to break the bread
of life within these walls.   A high wall enclosed the
manse garden, with the topmost branches of the fruit
trees only visible above it.   The old man's heart began
to beat a little quicker, as he ascended from the burn
to the door, and turned its handle.   Once within the
garden, he could see the picturesque church, and also
the substantial, handsome house which was now Sandy's
home.   The garden was richly stocked and well kept;

apple, pear, and plum trees against the walls were a
mass of pink and white blossom, and all the spring
flowers were blooming in the trim parterres. What a
pride glowed in the old man's heart as he looked upon
the goodly heritage which was now Sandy's and involuntarily he added that his lines had fall n in pleasant
places.

The garden rose in a gentle ascent, and then there
was a flight of stone steps which went down to the
clean, cool stone court at the kitchen door. It was wide
open, and he could hear the indistinct murmur of voices
within, also his nostrils were greeted by a very rich and
savoury odour, which made him remember how very
lightly he had fared since morning. He knocked on
the door with the head of his staff, and, after a considerable time, he heard a hurried footstep, and then a
middle-aged woman, very smartly dressed, answered the
summons.

'Is the minister at hame, ma'am?' he asked, respect-
fully, for he could not think that this fine lady could be
Sandy's servant.

'Yes, he's at home, but he is engaged. We have a
dinner-party to-night. It would be more convenient if
you could call to-morrow, unless it is anything very
particular.'

'I'll see him the nicht raither, if ye please,' said the
old man. 'Tell him I've come a faur road to see him,
wull ye?'

'If that is the case you had better step this way,'
she said in no very well-pleased way. 'Please make
haste; I am waiting the table, and can scarcely be
wanted.'

'Very well, my wummin, lead on,' he said, and
followed her through the kitchen, and up-stairs to the

dining-room flat.   Then she showed him into the study, and shut the door.

With what deep interest did John Bethune look round the luxurious, well-furnished room; he had never been in so fine a room before; it far excelled Mr. Bell's study at Kennoway Manse.   He was standing looking at the books in the well-lined shelves, when the door was hastily opened; and he turned swiftly round.

'Weel, Sandy,' he said joyfully.   'Here I am.   Ye wadna be expeckin' me, eh ? '

'Indeed I was not, father,' said Sandy, and his face reddened, whether with surprise or annoyance it was difficult to tell.   But he shook hands cordially enough, and bade him sit down.

'What tempted you to come off in such a hurry ? You should have written first.'

'I couldna, man.   I didna ken mysel', till ten o'clock this mornin', that I was comin'.   What way hae ye never written ?   I was fear't something was wrang.'

'Oh, I've been busy arranging for supply, and so on,' said the minister briefly.   'I wish I had known you were coming, father.   It is most unfortunate, but I have some of my leading members to dinner to-night.   They have been very kind to me, and I had to make them some sort of return.'

'Ye're gey sune begun wi' denner-parties, my man,' said John Bethune with a curious smile.   'Weel, if I had my face an' hands gien a bit wash, I'll just come in an' get a bite wi' ye to save bother.   Yon's a gey saucy-like quean ye hae doon the stair.'

The minister looked at his father almost in dismay. Never had the old-fashioned, faded blacks looked so ill, he thought; they no longer fitted the figure which had shrunk so sadly since they were made. How could he take the antiquated, awkward-looking figure into the next room, and introduce him to his guests? He fancied he saw the start of surprise, the ill-concealed amusement, with which he would be received. No, he dared not face such humiliation.

For once in his life Sandy Bethune was entirely wrong. His poor, mean, paltry pride made him misjudge others, for there was not one of his guests who would not have honoured him and joined him in showing respect to the good old man, who, whatever his appearance or attire, was more of a gentleman than his handsome son would ever be.

'I don't think you would enjoy yourself, father. They are all strangers to you, as well as to me,' said Sandy awkwardly. 'I think you would be much more comfortable here; and Christina will bring you up some dinner. They won't stay late. By eight o'clock I'll be ready to have a long chat with you.'

'Verra weel, Sandy my man; if ye think yer braw freen's wad think shame o' yer auld faither, I'll bide here,' said John Bethune with a twitch of his lips, for Sandy's words went straight as an arrow to the mark, and wounded him, how keenly Sandy would never know.

'Now don't run away with that idea. Come away to the dining-room if you wish,' said Sandy quickly. 'I was only thinking of your comfort. Are you coming, then, for I must go back to my guests?'

'No, I'll bide here. Awa' ye go, and dinna fash aboot me,' said the old man, striving to speak more cheerfully. 'If yer servant wummin 'll bring me a bite, I'll tak' a stretch on the sofa, for I'm sair tired. I've seen the day when sax miles wadna hae garred me turn a hair. I gaed past Lockerbie, ye ken,' he added, in answer to Sandy's astonished look, 'an' as there wasna a train for twa hoors, I jist walkit on.'

'That's worse and worse,' said Sandy. 'Well, Christina shall bring you a glass of sherry immediately; and after your dinner you can rest here. Nobody 'll disturb you.'

So saying, the minister left the room to rejoin his guests, but for him the evening's pleasure was spoiled. He courteously apologized to them for his absence, and again took part in the conversation with his usual brilliancy, but his heart was not at rest. Conscience smote him, and he despised himself. Yet he had not the courage to still that accusing voice by obeying its warning dictates. He did not know that in steeling himself at that moment he was making it easier to repeat the experience; he did not think that by this weak surrender to as poor and despicable an idea as ever took possession of a man, he had lowered himself, and taken the edge off the finest fibres of his being. Those seated at his board were all men of substance and worldly estate, some had birth and family heritage to boast of, and he could not bring before them the old man whose life had been spent on the fields and at the loom, and who had none of the polish of the outside world. It was a great effort to him to sustain the semblance of good spirits and cheerfulness. However, he succeeded well, and his guests assured him they had spent a happy and profitable evening. Directly they were gone, he hurried into the study. His entrance did not disturb the old man, who was lying on the sofa sound asleep; his grey hair lying out on the pillow, his wrinkled and weather-beaten face wearing the peaceful expression of deep repose. As Sandy looked, his heart yearned over him, and he wished he had overcome that foolish pride, and introduced him to his guests, when he was so willing to come. Ah, vain regret! that hour's weakness must henceforth be a bitter memory through life to the minister of Lochbroom. He drew a rug over the recumbent figure, and then, seeing that the window was open, he stepped lightly across the floor to shut it. The creaking of the rope awoke the sleeper, and he started up.

'Is't sax o'clock, Shoosan?' he said drowsily, imagining himself at home. 'Oh, it's you, Sandy! I mind whaur I am noo. Is yer folk awa'?'

'Yes, they're all away, and I'm at your service, father,' said Sandy cheerfully. 'Have you had a good rest?'

'No' bad; but, man, every bane in my body's sair. I doot I've gotten the cauld wi' the heat I got on the road. I couldna get hame the nicht noo, I suppose?'

'Not likely. Do you think I would allow you, even though it were possible?' exclaimed the minister. 'No, no; here you are, and here you must stay for a day or two at least.'

'Na, na, I maun gang the morn. I couldna be at hame here; it's ower braw,' said the old man, shaking his head. 'Ay, man, ye've a fell fine hoose; I houp ye may hae grace to guid it a'.'

'I hope so, father,' said Sandy quietly, for he felt uncomfortable and miserable, he could not tell why.

'I'm jist feart, laddie, that ye'll be carried awa' wi' the snares o' the warld,' continued his father, looking at him with a penetrating, wistful eye. ' I've wairned ye afore, an' I wairn ye again, that ye'll bo ca'ed to accoont for a'thing the Lord's gien ye.   It's accordin' as we hae opportunity, ye ken, that we'll be judged.   Keep an e'e, Sandy my man, on the opportunities; they slip by unco fast, an' we canna get grup o' them when they're aince by.   Man, I'm jist by-ordinar' tired.   I'll gang tae my bed if ye like. I'll look roond aboot the morn a wee afore I gang awa'.'

The minister, anxious to make amends for past short-comings, gave orders to his housekeeper to set the guest-chamber in order for the stranger, and went up himself afterwards to see that everything was right.   Long after his father went up-stairs, he heard him praying in the deep, solemn tones he remembered so well, and well did he know what was the burden of that prayer.

The old man's heart was heavy and anxious about the son who had been the child of his many prayers, and the dearest object of his love and hope for many a year.   He said he was well in the morning, though he spoke with a slight hoarseness, the result, no doubt, of the draught from the open window in the study while he slept.   After breakfast he took a hurried walk through the churchyard, saw the interior of the church and the manse, but seemed fearful lest he should lose the morning train.   Nothing would induce him to remain at Lochbroom another hour.   Seeing his persistence, Sandy forbore to press him, and went as far as Lockerbie with him to see him safe'y into the Edinburgh train.

' Weel, Sandy, I'm glad I've seen yer pairt,' he said at parting.   ' I'll maybe be mair content at hame noo. Look weel after it, my man, an' dinna forget that it's the Lord's vineyaird, an' that ye maun dress it for Him. May He bless ye, my son, for ever and ever.'

The solemn words were . almost like a benediction, and a vague, indefinable sadness took possession of the young minister as the train slowly steamed out of the station, and he looked his last on his father's face. Most of us have experienced a similar premonition, when the dark shadow of a final parting has first whispered itself to our hearts.

At home, James Bethune had found it difficult to concentrate his attention on his work. Soon after dinner-time he dressed himself and went away down to Markinch to be in time for the afternoon train, saying to his aunt that, if his father did not come with it, he would wait in the town till six o'clock. It was by the latter train that the old man arrived. Jamie saw him the moment he alighted, and thought he looked better than when he went away, he had such a fine ruddy colour on his cheek.

'Weel, ye loon, hae ye gotten back again?' he said with a smile, when the old man came up the steps. 'Ye've lost half a day's wark to me as weel's yer ain wi' yer stravagin'.'

A bright light sprang into the old man's face, and he laid his hand on his son's strong young arm, and looked up into his face with an expression which Jamie never forgot. It was absolute in its trust and confidence and love.

'Eh, Jamie, I'm gled to see ye, an' I'm fain to be at hame again,' he said; 'I'll no' seek to gang sae faur frae hame my lane again.'

'I think no'; but Sandy wad be prood to see you?'

'Oo ay, but there's nae place like hame. Man, thae railway trains tires an auld body when they're no' accustomed to them. I think I've gotten the cauld, tae; I dinna feel weel.'

'I'm vext to hear that,' said Jamie in his quiet, kind way. 'Here's Balfour, see; we'll hae a hurl hame.'

And before the old man could demur, the order was given, and in a few minutes one of the inn cabs was carrying them easily and quickly up the brae to the Star. The flush still remained on the old man's cheek, and once when Jamie touched his hand, it was burning, and there was a feverishness in the very brightness of his eye which he did not like.

Jamie dismissed the cab at the wickets, in order that Aunt Susan might not be alarmed to see them drive up to the door. But directly she got them in she saw that there was something amiss, and, without ado or remark, she ordered the old man to his bed, first making him bathe his feet and drink a bowl of gruel.

'Ye've surely gotten eneuch jauntin' to serve ye a while,' was her sole comment on the affair. But after he fell asleep, she confided her fears to Jamie.

'He's gotten an awfu' cauld. If he's no' better in the mornin', ye maun get Dr. Hay ower frae Leslie. It's no' a canny thing to let a cauld get sutten doon on an auld body.'

'What can hae gien him the cauld? I'm sure baith yesterday and the day hae been warm.'

'Oh, he'll hae been in a damp bed! They hizzies o' servants, deil tak' them, dinna care where they pit folk.'

'But surely Sandy would look after that, auntie?'

'Sandy!' echoed Aunt Susan in grim scorn. 'He hasna as muckle gumption as a taed, or he wadna hae let him awa' wi' sic a cauld on him. But I'se warrant ye, yer faither bides at hame efter this, or I'm cheatit.'

Aunt Susan was right. The old man went no more from home; for next time he crossed the threshold of his own door, he was carried by loving, tender, reverent hands to his last rest beside his wife in Kennoway kirkyard.

His illness was brief, but fatal in its issue. He had not strength to struggle with the weakness consequent upon severe congestion of the lungs, and succumbed exactly a week from the day when he had set out so full of hope to visit Sandy at Lochbroom. All he loved were by him when he died, but he was unconscious of their presence. His talk was all of Katie; he seemed to think she was at his side.

And so he died—a good man, full of years, whose place would never be filled to the many who had long loved and honoured him in the Star. He had lived knowing he must die, and so, when it came, death was to him great gain.

CHAPTER X.

SANDY'S WORD.

ON a little hillock among the heather and bracken on the moss sat the brothers, now orphaned, on the evening of their father's burying. They had much to say to each other, and the neighbours, with their usual officious kindness, had taken possession of the house, and there was not a quiet corner in it. Susan Bethune, grown garrulous in her age, was more tolerant of their intrusion, and was even glad of their company. John's death had given her a great shock, from which it was predicted by the wives that she would never recover. Perhaps Sandy's grief was the most poignant, at least it was more demonstrative, possibly because it was commingled with remorse, of which the others knew nothing. John Bethune had prudently kept his own counsel, and, though he had told them all about Lochbroom, he said nothing of the cool reception he had received. But Sandy could not forget. He was too miserable to think of anything but the events of the past week. The Assembly had now met, but he felt no desire to go, though he had looked forward with pleasurable anticipation to making his first appearance there as a placed minister. Jamie had little to say ; he could not vent his feelings in tears or in many words ; only he knew that to him his father's death would be a life-long sorrow.

'The Star's fast changin', Sandy,' said Jamie. 'The auld folk's slippin' awa' by degrees. This'll mak' a difference to us baith.'

'Not very much. You'll miss him most, of course, —you and Aunt Susan,' said Sandy with a gulp. 'It'll be easier for me, I daresay ; my work is more engrossing than yours. Head work always is.'

Jamie sat silent a moment, watching the red sunset glowing behind the Lomond Hill, with a strange, far-off look in his eyes. It was a bright, still, beautiful evening, calculated to soothe and comfort the most troubled spirit. The air was full of low twitterings, for the birds were all busy and happy, knowing the glad, bright summer was come at last. The soft evening breeze was laden with those delicious scents to which we cannot give a name— the tribute of the wayside blossoms to the wealth of summer sweets. The cows were already out on the young grass, and were dotted here and there over the fields, lending a pleasant variety to the scene.

'When are ye gaun to be married, Sandy ?' asked Jamie quite suddenly, after following the flight of a swallow till it was lost in the blue expanse above the Knowe.

'Married! What a thing to speak about to-night,' said Sandy quickly. 'I don't know when I shall be married; perhaps never!'

'An' what about Mary Campbell?' asked Jamie quietly, feeling impelled to continue the subject, though he saw from Sandy's face that it was not altogether pleasant to him.

Sandy sat silent for a moment; his brother's words had diverted his thoughts into an entirely new channel.

'She must just wait my time!' he said rather crossly. 'Women are such a bother, Jamie. They're always so much in earnest, and so anxious to get through with things.'

'But you will marry her some day?'

'Oh, I suppose so. I don't know what you will think of me, Jamie; but, between ourselves, it was a great mistake of me to engage with Mary Campbell.'

'I aye thocht ye was ower sune begun, but efter ye grew older, an' aye gaed aboot her, I thocht it was a' richt. But, Sandy, ye maun gang through wi't noo. It wad be a great sin to leave her, an' she's a bonnie, sweet, winsome lassie, if ever there was ane.'

'She wad be the very wife for you, Jamie,' said Sandy quickly; but Jamie just shook his head.

'I'll never marry, Sandy. To me what folks ca' love's a great mystery. A' weemin's alike to me.'

'If you could just be in my shoes for a week down yonder, Jamie, it would convince you more than my speaking for a week that I have made a mistake, a great mistake! Why, Mary could no more hold her own in the manse of Lochbroom or mix with the ladies yonder than she could fly in the air. She would be like the lady Tennyson writes of, Lord Burleigh's wife, who was bowed down with a weight of honour unto which she was not born. I wish I knew what to do,' said Sandy, picking the green tops from the heather and tossing them impatiently aside. 'I sometimes get sick tired of life, Jamie. Things go so contrary always.'

'It's jist as ye look at life, I think. I aince thocht that tae, but when I got a clear glimpse o' my duty, I did it, an' a' thing cam' richt.'

'Well, what would you say was my duty in this case ?' asked Sandy eagerly.

'To marry Mary Campbell as sune as ye can, and mak' up yer mind to mak' her as happy as ye can. She's a quick, clever lassie, an' she'll pick up fine ways in nae time. She hasna a chance in the Star. She'll win them a' wi' her blithe winsomeness. Nae fear o' them wonderin' at her. I suppose they a' ken *you* belang to workin' folk. If ye like her as weel as ye did, ye'll be as happy as the day's lang.'

'But that's exactly where it lies, Jamie. Supposing, now, that there was another whom I liked ten thousand times better than Mary Campbell, what would my duty be ?' asked Sandy eagerly.

Jamie turned his head, and looked his brother straight in the face.

'Is that hoo it is, Sandy ?' he asked gravely.

'Yes; and, man, if you saw *her*, Beatrice Lorraine, you would not be astonished at me even for a moment. She is like some queen or princess, whom everybody must fall down and worship. Beside her Mary Campbell would look something like what yon evening star will look by and by when the moon is up,' said Sandy in a quick, impassioned voice. 'I tell you, you know nothing about it. Yon's the kind of woman to take possession of a man's whole soul, and make him feel that he could do or dare anything to win her.'

Jamie Bethune looked at his brother with a kind of strange, sad wonder. There was something almost fearsome in such a passion; surely it could not be a good thing for any man to be so set upon a creature of clay like himself.

'I dinna ken what to say, Sandy. Ye are beyond me a' thegither.'

'Think what a help such a woman would be to a man. Why, with Beatrice Lorraine at my side, I could rise in the world as high as it is possible in my profession. She would open the door of any society, and I can tell you there is more in a woman's tact and ability than in a man's genius to raise him in the world. Why, with a right wife, there is nothing a man may not aspire to and attain. Mary Campbell is a sweet, nice country girl, I grant you; but she would simply be a drag on me all my days, and I would need to be content in Lochbroom to the end of the chapter.'

'If that be the case, the suner ye tell her sae the better, Sandy; but I wadna like yer job,' said Jamie in a quiet, cold, stern voice. 'Is she a foreigner, this woman?'

'No; her father is English, a retired merchant who bought the estate of Nethercleugh from the Earl of Lockerbie.'

'So they're gentry,' said Jamie, and he dropped his head on his hand and sat silent again. Somehow he felt himself estranged from his brother more than he had ever been, for there was something within him which told him Sandy was far, far wrong. Oh, was this to be the end of the old man's prayers? Better, then, that he was away before he saw his son wholly given up to the world.

'Of course you think I'm a perfect wretch,' said

Sandy at length; 'but, as I said, you know nothing about
it. After all, I don't think it's advisable to bring up
children above their station as I have been; it only
makes them discontented. I often envy you, Jamie,
quite content as you are with the land and the loom
and your book of an evening. You can't have any idea
of the struggle a fellow has in the outside world, fighting
against the disadvantages of birth and upbringing. They
clog his footsteps all his days.'

Jamie sat silent still. He felt no desire to confide
aught of his own battle to his brother; it would lie for
ever between himself and God.

'Then you mean to marry this lady?' he said at
length.

'I wish I thought I had a chance,' said Sandy, his
breath coming quick and fast again. 'She is such a calm,
still, unfathomable creature, that it is impossible to guess
at her feelings. That's what makes her so desirable.
Most women are ready to be made love to at any time,
but you never get any nearer to Beatrice Lorraine.'

'But ye're gaun to try onyway?'

'Yes; I am trying now.'

'Well, ye'll tell Mary Campbell afore ye gang awa',
an' ye'll be honest wi' her, or I'll tell her mysel',' said
Jamie almost passionately, for he felt for Mary almost
as if she had been his own sister.

'I'll not promise to see her; I can't stand a woman's
tears and that kind of thing. But I'll explain it all in a
letter, and I'm sure she'll thank me for it some day. She
will be far happier with some one else.'

'It's weel ye can comfort yersel' wi' that,' said Jamie.
'I dinna ken muckle aboot sic things, Sandy, but it
seems to me that ye are actin' the part o' a mean
scoondrel, an' if I were Mary Campbell's brother,

ɪ

I'd break a stick ower yer back, minister though ye be.'

'Oh, come now! there's no use speaking like that, you know,' said Sandy, his face reddening. 'Not a minute ago you said it was my duty to give up Mary if I liked another better. It's the best kindness I can do her.'

Jamie was miserably vexed and distressed. This was a strange, sad ending to their father's funeral day.

'I think we'll better slip awa' hame, Sandy,' he said, rising to his feet. 'This is neither a pleasant nor a profitable conversation.'

'You are not much help or comfort to a fellow, Jamie. I'd do more for you,' said Sandy reproachfully. 'I'm sure I mean to do right, and I try hard enough, I can tell you. If you knew more about it, you wouldn't be so hard on me.'

'I dinna mean to be hard on ye, Sandy. We've need to be freen's noo, for there's only us twa,' said Jamie, for all at once a sense of his own utter desolation swept over him, and nearly unmanned him. 'It's my turn to speak noo. I'm no' gaun to bide in the Star, Sandy.'

'Not bide in the Star? Then where on earth are you going?' asked Sandy in the purest amazement.

'I dinna ken yet, but as sune as I get things settled I'm gaun awa'. My wark here's through noo, an' there's nae use for me to bide.'

'But what do you mean? What are you going to do?'

'I'm gaun into a newspaper office in the toon, an' I'll work my way up,' said Jamie briefly, for it was a trial of no ordinary kind for him to subject himself and his life-dreams to Sandy's cold, critical, contemptuous opinion.

'A newspaper office! Are you daft, Jamie Bethune? What would a fellow like you do there? What has put such a thing into your head?'

'It's been in my heid for ten or eleeven years; it's no' a new freit,' said Jamie quietly. 'I've been workin' an' gettin' mysel' ready when folk kent naething aboot it. I'm no' askin' naething frae you, Sandy; but I wadna dae sic a thing withoot tellin' you, because there's only you an' me left.'

'It is well you don't expect anything from me,' said Sandy loftily, 'because you won't get it. I'll never give my countenance to such a thing, and if you persist in your idiotic determination, you must just bear the brunt of it. You can make a good thing of it here, and there's nothing to hinder you from taking a farm, and making a good position for yourself in that way. But a year or two in the city will soon convince you of your folly, and you'll remember my warning when your money's all spent, and you find yourself only an atom in that miserable stream of humanity which folk call the poor.'

Sandy was the fine, highly-educated gentleman now, talking in his most offensive and grandiloquent strain; his brother felt it, but kept his natural resentment to himself.

'I've coontit the cost, an' I ken what I'm daein',' he said firmly. 'If I fail, I'll no' trouble you, Sandy; ye'll never need to think shame o' me.'

'Fact is, you've read those humbugging and sentimental biographies and autobiographies till you've got the length of imagining yourself a genius,' said Sandy scathingly. 'I tell you it won't do. Hundreds besides you have allowed themselves to be led away by a similar idea, and lived to rue it bitterly. I assure you there's no room for you, and if you go into a newspaper office, it'll just be to set up types all your days.'

'Ye seem to hae judged my capabilities wi' wunnerfu' exactness,' said Jamie with a touch of bitter humour. 'Weel, we'll drap the subject. I'm no' a bairn noo, ye maun mind, but a man, wha kens what's what as weel's yersel'. I'll gang my way, an' you can gang yours, an' we'll no fash ane anither mair nor we can help.'

'All right. This is your doing, not mine, remember,' said Sandy shortly, and turning upon his heel he left his brother to finish his walk alone.

Jamie returned slowly to the house, thinking over many things. He was grieved and hurt at the way in which Sandy had received his confidence, yet not surprised. There was a soreness in his heart which was almost anger, for when had he denied his help or sympathy any time when Sandy had seemed to need it ? Henceforth he must walk life's way alone; there was something in the very thought which made his heart swell with a new resolution, and stirred his pulses. In the house he found his aunt alone, sitting close to the fire although the warm, genial sunshine was playing about her feet. As he looked at the grey, weather-beaten old woman, a deep, peculiar tenderness took possession of him, for she loved him; had she not given proof of it through these many years of faithful, untiring service ?

'Are ye a' yer lane, auntie ?' he said gently; and she looked up at him with an affectionate smile.

'I was thinkin' aboot ye, laddie. Sandy 'll be awa' to the Knowe, I suppose ? Sit doon an' let's hae a crack.'

Jamie drew in his chair, and Aunt Susan leaned her

elbows on her knees, and, with her chin in her hand,
looked at him with a mingling of keen interest and deep
affection. 'D'ye ken what I was thinkin', Jamie, as I
sat my lane?' she asked. 'I was thinking that yer
wark's by in the Star, an' that there'll be naething to
hinder ye frae gaun awa' noo, whaur yer heart's been
for mony a day.'

Jamie started in the greatness of his surprise.

'Ay, ye thocht yer auld auntie saw naething, though
she keepit quiet. My man, I likit ye ower weel no tae
be concerned in what concerned you,' she said with a
shrewd smile. 'Brawly did I ken whaur a' yer book
lare an' readin' was takin' ye, an' noo I'm gaun to say
my say, an' syne you can say yours. Ye've bidden here,
I ken, for yer faither's sake, an' I ken it's in ye to bide
for mine; a'body afore yersel' wi' you, Jamie, an' has aye
been; but I wadna thole that. So I've gotten't a' redd
up in my ain mind. Ye'll gang awa' to the toon, an'
I'll bide an' keep the place for ye; I'm no' that failed
yet but what I can dae my turn. An' there's Dauvit
Cam'll, ye ken, aye ready to help; ay, an' there's twa
three mair that'll dae me a guid turn for your sake,
laddie, an' for the sake o' them that's awa'. Wheesht! let
me say my say. I'll keep a hame for ye, my laddie, so
that ye'll no' feel yersel' an orphan a' thegither, an' the
gear 'll aye be getherin', ye ken, an' ye'll maybe need it a'.
Jist ae thing mair: ye need want for naething, Jamie,
for a' I hae is yours. Sandy's faur abune the likes o'
me noo, an' wad likely be abune my siller tae. No' a
word noo. I've settled it a'; an', Jamie, ye hae yer
faither's blessin', for I telt him no' lang syne what I
thocht ye was efter, an' he said— But there, I'll keep
that wee bit or some day when ye're dowie an' need
something to cheer ye on.'

James Bethune sat silent a moment, for his thoughts
lay upon him like a great deep flood, which could find no
vent.   Then Aunt Susan reached out one withered hand,
and Jamie took it in both his own, and after a moment
raised it to his lips.   The impulse would not be set
aside, and the little graceful act was only the due
reverence to the woman who had been to him a mother
indeed.

'I'll never forget, auntie,' he said huskily; 'an' if
I ever think lichtly o' a' ye hae been an' dune for me,
then may God punish me as I shall deserve.'

Susan Bethune wiped her eyes, but there was a smile
upon her lips.   Oh, was not this one hour of deep satisfaction compensation indeed for all her anxiety and
toil?   She had redeemed her vow to Katie Law, and,
even if she was summoned to meet her now, she need
not be ashamed.

It was late at night when Sandy came in, and he left
by the early train in the morning.   The parting between
the brothers was brief and constrained, and Jamie did
not as usual convoy him part of the way to the station.

'If you think better of your foolish project, I shall be
glad to hear from you,' was all Sandy said; but Jamie
answered never a word.   He was too deeply hurt to
forget all in a moment.   Sensitive, long-suffering natures
take long to recover from a wound which a shallower
spirit could cast flippantly aside.   His mind was made
up to remain in Star till the harvest was past, so that
there would be as little as possible requiring his aunt's
supervision at the farm.   Through the summer he confided his plans and hopes to David Campbell, from whom
he received such kindly encouragement and good-will as
did his heart good.

'I dinna pretend to understaun' what ye're efter, Jamie;

but this I ken, that whatever ye dae ye'll dae weel; an' yer faither often said lately that the Star wad never haud ye. An' I dinna think ye'll ever think shame o' the Star like some we could name,' said the honest man; and Jamie saw the dark shadow cross the open, cheerful countenance, and felt a pang at his own heart. 'It'll never be noo, Jamie,' said the maister, lowering his voice. 'Mary hersel' kens that, an' Jean was tellin' me she had lockit a' the bits o' things she had been sewin' at awa' in her box. Forgie me sayin't, Jamie, but he'll never prosper, minister though he be, an', God forgie me, I can hardly wush him weel. He may get a brawer, but he'll ne'er get a better nor oor Mary.'

'Dauvit, I wad gie my richt hand if Sandy hadna dune't,' said Jamie, the veins in his forehead starting in his deep feeling. 'Ye ken my opeenion o' his conduct, I am sure.'

'Ay, ay, ye are a different make. Weel, my man, as lang as yer auntie bides doon the road, I'll gie an e'e till the place, ye ken that. Is't newspaper writin' ye're gaun in for, or what?'

'Whatever I can get to dae at first,' answered Jamie; 'whatever comes readiest to my hand. Maybe I'll be able to write something some day.'

'Aweel, it's extraordinar' to think the twasome o' ye should be seekin' the same gate. Sandy's a clever loon, but he hasna balance. Keep yer balance, Jamie, whatever success ye hae,—a man's naething withoot balance, —an' I wush ye weel.'

Peter Bethune was in a furious rage when he learned of his nephew's intention. He would not even listen to any explanation whatsoever, but swore that he could go where he liked, but that he would never finger a copper of his money, or again darken his door. He also flatly refused to give Susan a helping hand with the land, at which neither Jamie nor his aunt were greatly put about. They were better without his interference, and there were plenty willing hearts and hands in the Star.

CHAPTER XI.

TRIED.

'Young dreamer, God is great!
'Tis glorious to suffer,
'Tis majesty to wait.'

HEN we are meditating some great change in our lives, or are about to take some important step, upon which may hinge the very issues of our destiny, we seem to live in a strange, unreal world, which possesses terrors as well as charms for us. We have proved the past by experience; the present is still with us; it is the future we yearn over and yet dread. All change involves more possibilities than certainties, and so naturally we hesitate a little, almost fearing to go forward. But when we are convinced of the wisdom of our choice, and the final resolve taken, then half the vague terrors which oppressed us seem to fade away. Resolution is the parent of calmness and strength, and with these two we are well equipped for the battle of life. James Bethune was grateful for the kind wishes and good will which he knew would follow

him into his new life, their memory would somewhat
sweeten the anxious toil of the future. He would be
utterly alone and unaided, for none of those who wished
him well could help him, save by their prayers. As he
made his preparations a calmness of spirit, unlike anything he had previously experienced, gave him new
strength and courage to go forward. The die was cast ;
he had revealed his aim and purpose, and now it
remained for him to prove upon what ground he had
dared so to aspire. Should he fail—but what young,
strong, passionate heart ever admitted the possibility of
failure in its ardent undertakings ? It were a poor
world but for the perpetual dayspring of hope in the
human heart. He had only one acquaintance in Edinburgh, one Adam Farquhar, cousin to his friend the
schoolmaster ; who had been wont to spend every
holiday he could spare at the Star. James Bethune
had met and grown very friendly with him at the
schoolhouse, and had received many a hearty invitation
to pay a visit to him in Edinburgh. Adam Farquhar
had a bookseller's shop in Bank Street, and did a steady
if somewhat slow business among the lovers of old and
rare books. James Bethune had often thought of
writing to him and laying before him his desires and
aims, but, feeling that a meeting face to face would be
more effectual and satisfactory, he went away over to
Edinburgh one grey October day to ask his advice.
The nature of his business would probably bring him
into contact with literary and newspaper folk, and
perhaps he might be able to procure an opening for
the lad in whom his cousin had taken such a deep
interest. In thus seeking the advice of the bookseller,
James Bethune showed his wisdom. He was no idle
dreamer, who imagined the world an El Dorado, where

fame and fortune awaited the adventurer at every turn, but only an earnest soul, seeking his life work, prepared to endure hardship and privation if only some of life's grand possibilities might become realities to him.

It had been a grey, misty morning when he left the shores of Fife, but in Edinburgh the mist was charged with a thick, drizzling rain, which greatly obscured the beauty of the city. It was not James Bethune's first visit, however, and he was, besides, too much occupied in thinking of how Adam Farquhar would receive him to pay much heed to his outer surroundings. When he reached Bank Street a great shyness took possession of him, and made him feel as if he could never venture into the shop, a dingy, insignificant little place enough, although a very considerable competence had been amassed there. He stood at the window for a while looking at the books, but seeing them not; until, with a broad smile at his own foolishness, he summoned up his courage, and boldly walked in. The gas was lighted within, and shone on the musty rows of books, and illumined, too, the yellow, shrivelled face of the little antiquated old man behind the counter. He was writing with a very large quill pen in a very large ledger, but looked up very briskly when the young man entered, and came forward with a cheerful smile on his face.

'Rather a disagreeable morning, sir, but we must look for this sort of thing in its season. What can I do for you? I've just picked up a very rare copy of Burns, the original edition—almost priceless. Will you look at it, sir?'

'Don't you know me, Mr. Farquhar?' asked James Bethune with a smile.

'Know you? can't say I do,' said the bookseller, tapping his bald head with his quill. 'But let me see. Yes, I *do* know you. I remember your face quite well. But what's your name?'

'James Bethune, sir, from Star; perhaps you'll mind me now?'

'Yes, I do. Glad to see you; come in,' said the old man, shaking his hand with extreme heartiness. 'So you've really looked me up at last. And how are all the Star folk—the denizens of that celestial sphere? ha, ha! I must have my little joke, you know. Ah, poor Gilbert! these were happy days I used to spend with him, and yet they saddened me too. I never saw a man with so light a hold on life, nor I never knew of a more touching case. His life was a kind of dedication to his wife's memory. I never saw such devotion between two; but she was a very exceptional woman. I've never been in the bonds myself, so I don't understand it, you know. But there! I'm forgetting myself as usual. Come away in. We can have a nice long chat to-day, for there won't be much business doing.'

So saying, the garrulous and kindly old man led the way past the well-lined book-shelves into a little inner chamber where there was a bright fire burning, and a comfortable arm-chair on each side of the hearth.

'Take off your overcoat, and your boots, too, if you like, and make yourself comfortable,' said the old man. 'How's your folks? father well, eh?'

'My father has been dead since the month of May, Mr. Farquhar,' said James Bethune quietly, but the bookseller saw the firm under-lip quiver, and knew he had touched a sore point.

'Eh, you don't say so? well, well, he was a hale, hearty old man when I saw him last; but all flesh is grass,' he said, pressing his finger-tips together and looking meditatively into the fire. 'So you'll be pretty much alone at the Star now. Your brother has scored a success in life, if I may so put it. He is very acceptable to his people, I am told.'

'I am glad to hear it,' said Jamie sincerely, and there was a moment's silence.

'And are you taking a little holiday to yourself?' asked the old man at length. 'Now that I get a better look at you, I see how much you seem to need it. Why, man, you look quite old. What is your age, if I may be so bold as to ask?'

'I was five-and-twenty on the eighteenth of last June, Mr. Farquhar, but I feel a bit older than that.'

'Ay, you were always of a serious, advanced turn; my cousin always said so. Well, are you going to make a stay for a day or two? I'll be glad to keep you if you like. I live across the Meadows, and my housekeeper, honest woman, will make you very comfortable.'

'Thank you very kindly, Mr. Farquhar, but I'm not for staying the day. I've made bold to come and ask your advice about something I'm thinking of doing.'

The bookseller pricked up his ears, and an interested, pleased look came upon his face.

'Well, I'm sure I'll be glad to listen and to help you too if I can; my cousin did think a lot of you, and so do I for that matter. But there, what were you going to say?'

'I'm thinking of leaving the Star, Mr. Farquhar, and coming to push my way in the town. Had my father lived, I would not have been here to-day, but now that he is away there's no duty to keep me from trying to better myself.'

The bookseller nodded.

'It's all right. *I* understand all about it. Young ardent spirit, adverse circumstances, hopes, aims, ambi- tions, opportunity come at last. Glad of it. Well, *what* are you going to do?'

During these disjointed remarks Adam Farquhar did not look at his visitor's face, but kept his eyes steadily on the fire, and rubbed his hands together, nodding all the while. He was deeply interested, and much pleased at the confidence reposed in him. He was one of these rare souls, which would never grow too old to share the joys and hopes and aspirations of youth. James Bethune had wisely chosen his friend and counsellor at this important crisis in his life.

'It's a newspaper office I would like to get into, Mr. Farquhar,' said James Bethune, sitting forward and fixing his deep, earnest eyes on the old man's face. 'But I hardly know how to set about it. It's not easy, I am told, to get into such places.'

'No, my lad, it's not easy; and, if you'll excuse me saying it, it'll be doubly difficult for you. You see, you are pretty old to begin with, and you've had no experience of anything in that line. You see, one needs to be apprenticed in these kinds of places from boyhood. But now, tell me frankly what you expect to do after you are in, suppose you should be so fortunate.'

'Well, I thought I might get a place as a reporter at first. I've learned shorthand, and I know it pretty well, and I can put a thing together pretty fairly,' said James Bethune with slightly flushing cheek, for it was difficult for him to speak of his own capabilities. 'And from that I might rise by degrees,' he added with kindling eye. 'If they saw I could do my work well, they might advance me a little. I believe I could write, Mr. Farquhar.'

'Well, we'll see,' said Mr. Farquhar, rubbing his hands more slowly and thoughtfully together. 'You see, the thing is this. Everything is overrun now-a-days. Why, the way the book business even is cut up is really heart-rending; indeed it is. If I hadn't turned my penny years ago, when times were better, it's not now that I'd make anything to keep me in my old age. But that isn't much to the point. You're a thoughtful lad, and you should be able to see for yourself that it's only the best that can come to the front. There's no room, as it were, for mediocrity, especially in the literary business, which is just a business like anything else, though higher, of course. Do you think you have *that* in you which will force you to the front, eh?'

'I don't know, Mr. Farquhar,' said James Bethune, rising, and beginning to pace up and down the narrow room. 'I cannot understand myself. I seem to be aye struggling, struggling after I hardly know what. Thoughts come to me which I think sometimes are worth writing down, and then I feel as if I had a lifework somewhere to do, and must go in search of it. But I do not know how or where to begin. It is very hard to find the right way. I get desponding over it whiles, too, and think that life must just be one long struggle after what we can never attain.'

'So it is, my boy, so it is, to such spirits as yours,' said the old man; and he shook his head as he looked on the flushed face, the glowing eye, and ill-suppressed excitement in the young man's every movement.

'What does your brother advise?' he asked presently, and in an instant James Bethune's whole manner changed.

It was as if some chill shadow had suddenly fallen darkly across his heart.

'My brother and I are not at one about it, Mr. Farquhar. He thinks I am a mad dreamer, and he has cast me off. I shall never speak to him about myself any more.'

'Well, well, often our own folk understand us least; familiarity, as it were, blinds them. Don't be downcast about that,' said the old man cheerily. 'If you succeed, he'll be the very first one to say you've done well. I've seen the same thing hundreds of times in my life. Ay, ay, there's nothing succeeds like success, but in the meantime it's to get a beginning for you. Are you ready to come to Edinburgh just now?'

'Yes, I'm all ready.'

'Then suppose you come here to me for a little. I've nobody in the shop, and you could help me with cataloguing and all sorts of things; of course I'll pay you a wage for your work, which won't oppress you. You'll have plenty leisure for study and self - improvement. Then we can keep our eyes open, and be ready to grasp the very first chance. Would that do, eh?'

'It would do very well, Mr. Farquhar; but I didn't mean anything like this when I came to see you. I never thought of your helping me in *that* way,' said Jamie, almost in distress. 'I could never think of being a burden on you. I'll come and be in your shop, and help you as much as I can, but I won't take a halfpenny from you. I don't need it. I am well provided for, Mr. Farquhar, and the land brings something every year, you know. So if you'll let me come on these terms, I'll be glad and grateful, sir.'

'Well, well, I admire an independent spirit when I see it; so we won't say anything about terms just now,' said the old man, laughing. 'You'll go into lodgings of course. I know of a very decent widow woman across the street there who could give you a very comfortable room. I know she has been looking out for a lodger, but *that* is overrun like all the rest. It will be fine and near the shop, and central for everything else, and I can thoroughly recommend her, as she has cleaned my shop for the last five years.'

'Very well, sir, that'll do fine, and I'll come as soon as I can,' said James Bethune, with a joyousness of look and manner which made him look years younger. The old man could not but observe the change in him, but he had no idea of the deep, hopeful satisfaction in his heart. He felt indeed as if he had got his foot on the first step of the ladder, and that his ascent, though it might be slow, was assured.

'Some of my best customers won't be back to town till the end of the month; and, who knows, one or other of them may know of some opening. We'll keep our eyes open; and the most of them would put themselves about to oblige me. You see, I do the right thing by them, for I don't mind telling you that there's no class of people more imposed on in this wicked world than the book hunters,' said Adam Farquhar. 'Perhaps you may have to take something very small—menial even—at first, but I don't think you'll mind that.'

'No, indeed. I don't mind how hard I have to work at first, if only I could get a beginning,' said James Bethune with great earnestness. 'I don't know what to say to you, Mr. Farquhar, for your great kindness to one you know so little about.'

'Tut, tut, man,' said the bookseller hastily. 'Not a word. Some day, maybe, I'll reckon it a great honour and pleasure to be able to look back upon this day.

K

I'm doing nothing to deserve thanks. I'm not a very religious man,—that, is I can't talk much about it,—but I count it a duty and privilege to help any struggling in life. I was once a poor boy myself, and, bless you! I've nothing else to occupy me.'

So a kindly, helpful word once more smoothed the way for James Bethune, and he returned to his home in the afternoon with a hopeful and happy heart. He found Aunt Susan ready as ever to rejoice with him, and she urged him to lose no time, although she knew right well what a blank there would be in the little house after he was gone.

A week later James Bethune bade farewell to the Star, not without deep regret, nay, keenest pain, for it was his home, and many memories would hallow it to him for ever. Aunt Susan bade him farewell bravely, without a tear; but after he was gone, and the door shut upon her, she tottered to her chair, and shook like an aspen leaf. She had given him up to that great unknown world, and felt just as a mother might, who has watched her boy go forth to battle, scarcely hoping or expecting to see him in life again.

He found his lodging ready for him, a comfortable place enough, in which he thought he could make himself at home. And then he unpacked his books, and laid his clothes in the drawers, wondering at himself all the while; it seemed so like a dream. Then began a strange new life, almost like a dream too in its complete contrast to the old.

By eight o'clock every morning he was in the little shop, busy among the dusty old books, which were a very dear part of Adam Farquhar's life; and the old man found him a willing and capable assistant. Never had the shop been so thoroughly overhauled and put in such perfect order. Dust became a thing unknown, and the place assumed a trim and bright appearance it had not worn for many years. But, though James Bethune thus conscientiously and willingly made himself useful to his kind friend, his heart was not greatly in his occupation. He could not understand the old man's bibliomania, and the longing for a wider sphere still pursued and tormented him as of yore. It was the world of men and things he wanted to study now; he had dwelt long enough among written lives and dumb companions.

His evenings were entirely his own, and he availed himself to the full of the many intellectual advantages the city offered; and so his mind expanded, and the confidence of knowledge grew upon him, until in a half-trembling way he began to use his pen; to give a voice to the thoughts which thronged upon him like the waves of a great sea. He was not unhappy; but his life was narrow and confined, utterly devoid of any sweetening influence whatsoever, and possessing nothing to draw him away from self. So a great shyness and constraint hedged him in, and he became so silent and self-contained, that Adam Farquhar wondered sometimes whether he were unhappy, and rued the step he had taken. From the first time of his coming to Edinburgh, he became a regular attender of St. Giles, and never did scholar sit more humbly at the feet of a master than did he at the feet of the cultured and eloquent preacher who so faithfully broke the bread of life within its ancient walls.

The Sabbath mornings were gleams of brightest sunshine to James Bethune, and it was under the pillars of St. Giles that he felt more happy and content than anywhere else. It was a relief to him to get rid for a

little of all the perplexing and engrossing interests of the
week, and give himself up to the sweet, holy influences
of the hour and the place. He loved and reverenced
Dr. Kinross long before the Doctor knew of his existence; but at length he began to take note of the
pale, earnest-eyed, solitary being who was never absent
from his place, and who hung upon his words with
such breathless and deep attention. But it was some
time before he succeeded in discovering his name and
place of abode.

Immediately after his early dinner on the Sabbath
day, James Bethune took his solitary walk into the
country, returning sometimes long after the early
darkness had fallen upon the city. The Pentland
Hills was his favourite resort; he found a deep delight
and companionship in the stillness and solitude which
seemed to refresh and invigorate him. There the air
was pure and sweet; he loved to inhale it, for he
often felt depressed and out of sorts with the closeness of the atmosphere in which the greater part of his
time was spent. Often as he walked his eyes would
turn with deep longing across the grey waters of the
Forth, to where the little hamlet on the edge of the moss
lay under the shadow of the Lomond Hills. Sometimes
he felt that he had made a mistake in leaving it, and
could almost have resolved to go back to the old ways
and the old folk who had long loved him. For he
was terribly alone in the wide and busy city; the human
soul cannot brook such desolation, and will not be stilled
in its yearning for human sympathy and love. It was
nearing Christmas, and he had never heard a word from
or of Sandy, who had evidently cast him off for ever.
Aunt Susan remembered him every week in the letter
which Mary Campbell wrote for her every Thursday

night. In other ways, too, she gave evidence of her love and care, for many a basket of good things found their way from the Star to the little dingy room in the Old Town. But for these little things, James Bethune had hardly been able to bear up against the monotony and loveless solitude of these first months in Edinburgh. He felt as if he were making no progress whatsoever, and that any action would be preferable to the enforced idleness of his days. Adam Farquhar's customers did not seem to be able to help in any way, for, though the few he appealed to on Jamie's behalf were willing enough, they had not the power to get an opening for him. And so the dreary, uneventful days went by. New Year came and went, and still there was no change. One mild, soft January evening, when he returned after dark from his usual Sabbath walk, his landlady opened the door to him with visible excitement in her manner and appearance.

'A gentleman called upon ye sin' ye gaed oot,' said she, following him into his room. 'Wha d'ye think, but Dr. Kinross of St. Giles himsel'? An' he was rale disappinted like that ye wasna in, and bade me tell ye, gin ye wasna ower late o' bein' back, to gang ower to his hoose in George Square an' see him.'

'Dr. Kinross!' exclaimed Jamie. 'I wonder how he found me out?'

'Trust him; he'll find a'body oot if he wants to. Ye'll gang, wull ye no'? He was fell anxious like that ye should.'

James Bethune hesitated only a moment. The little dingy room did not look particularly inviting at that moment, he felt no desire to read, and he had been so dull and miserable all day that anything in the way of a change was welcome. He forgot his shyness, his shrinking from strangers, and, turning about, he went down the stair and out once more into the busy streets. There was a gathering in front of St. Giles, listening to the fervent exhortations of a street preacher. When first he came to Edinburgh, Jamie had been both astonished and interested in these street preachings, but now he never paid any attention to them, but walked on his way as absorbed and unheeding as if he had been wandering across the ridges of the Star Moss.

How soothing and grateful the quiet of the pleasant place where the minister dwelt! He could hear the echo of his own footsteps on the pavement, and the tree-tops in the gardens rustled with a solemn and familiar sound which reminded him of home. His heart was sore and empty somehow; all day he had felt as if there was not much good in anything, and had almost been convinced that life was scarcely worth living at all. Before he had time to think, he had rung the bell at the minister's door, and it was answered immediately by a maid, who ushered him straight into the study, as if she knew who he was, and had been fully expecting him. There was no one in the room, but the easy-chair drawn up to the fire, and the open Bible on the table, indicated that it had not been long unoccupied. He was standing rather awkwardly by the table when the door opened and the Doctor entered. How reverend and noble he looked! Never had his fine presence seemed so striking or his face so winning and attractive. That rare, kindly smile won every heart.

'I am glad you have come. We have known each other a long time, I think,' he said, as they shook hands. 'Come, sit down. As we are friends, we must proceed to learn a little more about one another.'

In a moment James Bethune's awkwardness and shyness was gone; melted away for ever in the radiance of that kindly smile. They sat down together near to the fire, and ere many minutes the lonely heart was unburdened, all its secret care poured into a sympathizing and understanding ear. Dr. Kinross possessed that rare gift, so invaluable to a minister, of being at once able to touch the heart and command the confidence of those with whom he came in contact.

'Now that we have had a talk, suppose we go and see Mrs. Kinross and my girls,' said the minister, rising at length. 'Nay, you must not refuse. You will like my wife, and there is a small maiden of the name of Minnie who will soon pull you out. Her sister Dora is quieter, as is to be expected of a young lady. I have only the two, and they are dear, good children, and a great blessing to their father and mother.'

'But I am not fit for ladies' society, sir,' said James Bethune with an anxious smile. 'I have never met any ladies. How can I talk to them?'

'Oh, don't fear! they'll talk to you,' said the Doctor with a twinkle in his eye, and led the way up the wide staircase to the drawing-room door. It was a little ajar, and the Doctor, with a smile, motioned his companion to look in before they entered. It was a pretty picture, the long, low room, lit by the bright red glow of the firelight, which lent a deeper tint to the warm crimson of the carpet and the rich hangings at the opposite window. In a low chair by the hearth sat a lady of delicate and fragile appearance, with a face so sweet and beautiful, that James Bethune thought it like the face of a saint. It was the face of a woman who had known sorrow, and whose heart was a wellspring of love and sympathy for all humanity. Her hands—very white and fragile hands they were—lay lightly across each other on her lap, and she was listening while her daughter read aloud from a ponderous volume on her knee. Dora Kinross was a tall, pale, self-possessed young lady, very gentle and ladylike in all her movements, a very different being from the blue-eyed, golden-haired little maiden sitting on the rug at her mother's knee.

'All in darkness yet, dears?' said the Doctor's sonorous voice in the doorway. 'Jump, Minnie, and light the candles. Mamma, here is our friend of whom we were speaking to-day.'

In a moment Minnie was on her feet scrambling for the match-case on the mantelshelf, while Mrs. Kinross, rising, took a step across the room, and held out her hand.

'How do you do? I am very glad to see you,' she said, and she spoke as if she meant it, and her hand-clasp was hearty and sincere.

'Thank you, ma'am,' said James Bethune shyly, and yet his earnest eye met her kind glance without hesitation, for its sweet motherliness filled his heart to the brim.

Then Dora came forward and shook hands in her demure, gentle fashion, and Minnie, having managed to light the candles, turned about, and with her two round blue eyes took a deliberate survey of the stranger.

'Oh, I know you; you sit in the corner behind the middle pillar in church,' she said candidly. 'I often look at you to see if you look away from papa while he is preaching, but you never do.'

'Ha, ha! that shows how closely you attend upon your father's ministrations, pussy-cat,' said the Doctor with his hearty laugh. 'I believe you know every face in church, child.'

To his surprise, Minnie had not her usual ready answer at hand. She had resumed her seat at her mother's feet, and sat there quietly listening, while the others talked, but studying intently all the while the stranger's face.

'Come, Dora, let us have "Lux Benigna,"' said the Doctor, at length pausing in his walk and opening the organ. 'You will like the musical part of our service at St. Giles, Mr. Bethune ; I consider it very fine.'

'I like it very much now, sir. At first it seemed strange, and I could not join in it, but I am getting better acquainted with the tunes now.'

'So you will. Come then, my dear,' said the Doctor, and in a few seconds the sweet strain of 'Lux Benigna,' in which the Doctor's voice and his daughter's blended beautifully, rang through the room. When it was over they began to sing another, and Mrs. Kinross turned to the young man at her side, and began to talk in that sweet, motherly way which went straight to the heart. James Bethune could not but feel at his ease with her ; nay, it was a joy and a pleasure, none the less keen that it was so new, to feel himself of interest to some one in the great city, which had been so long a barren wilderness to him. When he took his leave at length, it was upon the understanding that he must come again soon, and often, a promise he had been very ready to give. Very sweet to him was the Doctor's warm hand-clasp and deep 'God bless you.' Very sweet, too, was his wife's smile, and gently-expressed hope to see him soon again. But perhaps sweeter than all was the clasp of the child Minnie's two hands on his, when she uplifted her wide blue eyes to his face.

'Do come again soon,' she said coaxingly, for her heart had warmed to him. 'Come on a day not Sunday, and I'll show you the doll Uncle Lorraine brought me from Germany on my birthday. It has a thing in its back you screw, and it walks across the floor just like i do, only funnier; there, ask papa if it isn't true!'

CHAPTER XII.

THE MANSE OF ST. GILES.

'Nothing comes free cost here; Jove will not let
His gifts go from him, if not bought with sweat.'

HERRICK.

S was to be expected, Doctor Kinross was
anxious to forward James Bethune in his
desires and aims, and to procure for him
some opening which would really be a beginning to his lifework.   But that was no
easy task.   In a great city there are few
unfilled spaces ; it is the sad truth that in most
walks of life the·supply of labourers far exceeds the
demand.   He had considerable influence with those
connected with the press, and received promises from
several that his protégé would be kept in mind.   So
through the spring months James Bethune plodded on,
helping Adam Farquhar in the day-time, and studying
or writing in the evenings.   So deep a hold had Doctor
Kinross taken of his heart, that he even brought
himself to show him some of his pieces, both poetry
and prose, rightly believing that he would be both a

competent judge and a kindly though keen critic of their merits. They were not perfect,—what early work is?—but they were full of promise, and had the true ring about them. The Doctor saw at once, nor, indeed, was he surprised thereat, that the young man had an original and cultured mind, and would never number among those scribblers who mistake an imitative faculty for literary genius. He strongly advised him to send something to *Chambers's Journal,* and even offered to take it himself to the editor; but James Bethune said he would prefer to send it from his own obscurity, and allow what he wrote to stand or fall by its own merit. In which decision he showed the wisdom and manliness of his spirit. He was willing, nay, deeply grateful, to accept help and advice in some things, but there were others upon which he had his own deep convictions, which nothing would set aside. It was more to please his friend than of his own will that he complied with his request, for he had none of a new writer's ardent desire to rush into print, but was rather held back and kept down by a miserable consciousness of his own shortcomings. His power of expression was not yet equal to his high ideal, and he sometimes despaired of ever being able to clothe his thoughts in suitable words. It was a healthy and wholesome doubt, of which he was yet to receive the benefit. He had many long flights of imagination in these early struggling days; many aspirations which it seemed impossible he should ever reach; many sweet, great thoughts which could scarcely hope to find any vent.

His soul was stirred within him often by his great longing and desire to do some worthy thing; to be able to write something of which not only himself, but others in the world, would be the better. Such longings are

not to be despised or scornfully cast aside as idle
dreamings; it is always a worthy and an ennobling thing to
look up. We can never look too high in that good way ;
the fault most common to us being the ease with which
we stoop to what is lower than the noblest in our
nature. The little prose sketch—which was in truth a
poem in its beautiful and simple wording—was accepted
by the editor, and appeared in due course. With his first
modest literary gains James Bethune bought a gift for
his aunt, and sent with it the magazine, with a broad
red line drawn round his own article, which had no name
attached. He did not send a copy, however, to Sandy,
for even yet he could not forget the sting of his quick, contemptuous words. He had seen him in Edinburgh once,
walking in the street with another minister ; and, as he
had never come near the shop in Bank Street, though he
knew well enough from Aunt Susan where his brother
was, it was evident to Jamie that he meant to sever all
connection. In his intercourse with Doctor Kinross,
James Bethune never mentioned his brother's name, and
it never occurred to the Doctor to associate the popular
young minister, whom he had inducted to his charge at
Lochbroom, with the struggling aspirant for literary
fame. It was with deep, genuine interest the large-
hearted minister watched the growth and development of
James Bethune's powers; and he made him truly and
heartily welcome to the manse. James Bethune found it
so pleasant a place that he came sometimes unasked,
which always pleased the Doctor and his wife. Minnie
elected to make him her especial friend, and in her own
sweet, childish way did him boundless good. But, though
life was not utterly devoid of sweetening influences, he
had much to try and discourage him. His spirit constantly chafed, because he was making so little apparent

headway, and it became impossible to him to remain any longer in Adam Farquhar's shop.

Out of his perplexity and anxiety a resolve began to shape itself, and to demand fulfilment. He applied for every likely post advertised; how often he tasted the heart-sickness of disappointment and hope deferred was only once revealed to another, and that was years after. Doctor' Kinross was in his study one Friday evening early in the month of May, when the servant brought James Bethune's name, with the request for five minutes' conversation.

'Come away, James; good evening,' he said, shaking hands with him when he entered his presence. ' I don't allow much disturbance on a Friday evening, but I was thinking of you a little ago, and I supposed you would be here. Has anything turned up ?'

'Something has turned up, sir ; but whether anything will come of it is another thing,' answered James Bethune with a slight smile. ' Perhaps you noticed an advertisement in Wednesday's *Scotsman* for a reporter for the *Glasgow Journal.* I applied for it at once, and they have written back asking for some reliable reference. It is against me, you see, not having had any previous experience, but they seemed pleased with my letter. Will you read what they say, sir ?'

'Certainly.' The Doctor pushed back his chair, and perused the open letter handed to him.

'Well, that is good so far. But do you think this kind of work will suit you? It is awful drudgery. Have you any idea of what a reporter for such a paper has to do ? "

'Yes, I know all about it. I don't expect I shall like it particularly ; but it isn't what we like, but what we can get to do now, Doctor Kinross,' said James Bethune with a slight bitterness. ' I can't go on like this much longer. Anything—sweeping the streets, I think sometimes, would be preferable to this stagnation.'

' You are quite right. I only said it to try you,' said the Doctor with his kindly smile. ' Well, do you wish me to give you a reference ? '

' If you would be so kind, sir. I know of no one else.'

' I will do so gladly. I wish I could do more. If I had my way, James, there would be few difficulties in your way. I am afraid life is going to be a harder struggle for you than for most men ; but you must not lose heart. There is One who knows all, and who will never fail.'

' Ay, I know ; but I *shall* succeed, Doctor Kinross. If I had not known that, do you think I could have supported the misery of the last six months ?' said James Bethune passionately. 'I know of nothing harder in this world—and there are many hard things in it, sir—than to be willing to work, and yet have no opportunity.'

' Ay, there are many hard things in life, very many,' said the Doctor musingly, as he walked slowly to and fro the room. ' Great are its mysteries, and the older we grow we feel less inclined, I think, to question or seek to unravel them. Perhaps we grow tired, and are too glad just to leave it all with Him. But well do I understand your struggle. Take care, my friend, lest in these tumults you miss the way. There is a verse of one of Faber's hymns which is often with me, and which seems to contain the sweet germ of the whole matter. It is this—

" Ill that He blesses is our good,
    And unblessed good is ill ;
And all is right that seems most wrong,
    If it be His sweet will."

Whatever may be your lot in life, James, you know that we wish you well.'

'Yes, sir; but for you, and for the privilege of coming here, I could not have lived the past six months.'

'Ah, well! some day, looking back, you may be able to say they were part of that needed discipline which we must all undergo in some form,' said the Doctor. 'I am just afraid that the poor drudgery of this reporting work, should you succeed in being appointed to it, may blunt your taste for higher things. And yet I need not fear. If your ambition is indeed that divine spark of genius, it will survive and grow stronger because of adverse surroundings. If not, well, perhaps you will be as well to be rid of it, and devote yourself to the more prosaic work of life. And now I must send you away. I shall write that letter at once, and you will let me hear the result as soon as you know it yourself?'

'Yes, sir. Good-night!'

As the Doctor held the hand a moment at parting, he looked into the pale, earnest face with something of love and compassion in his own. That look went to James Bethune's heart, and his eyes filled with tears.

'God bless you, my friend,' said the doctor huskily. 'Such sharp stings are the price which must be paid for the higher gifts; but your joys, when they come, will be no mean recompense. Good-night!'

'Won't you come into the drawing-room, Mr. Bethune?' said a coaxing voice, and a bright face, framed in gold, peeped over the balustrade as he went out into the hall. 'Mamma knows you are here, and would like you to stay a little. Dora has a lovely new song. Wouldn't you like to hear it now?'

'Not to-night, Miss Minnie, if you please,' said James Bethune, looking up at the smiling face. 'Say to Mrs.

Kinross that I am vexed and troubled about something, and no fit company for any one to-night.'

'Vexed and troubled! Oh, I am so sorry! Do tell me about it!' and in a moment the slim figure was downstairs, and two white hands were clasped on his arm, while the young face looked up into the grave, stern one with real solicitude.

'How could I tell you, Miss Minnie? No trouble or vexation should ever come near one so bright as you,' he said with a strange, caressing fondness in his look and tone. Between James Bethune and Doctor Kinross's young daughter there existed a deep, warm affection, such as is sometimes seen in a brother and sister between whom there is considerable disparity in years.

'Come now, *don't* say that. Papa calls me Pussy-cat and Sunbeam, and says I will be an ornament to society some day, when he wants to tease me very badly. But I am not all nonsense, please. Do tell me. I can be so sorry for any one I love. Do you know it was me told mamma you had come, and I've watched on the stairs for you all the time you were with papa. Is it a very bad trouble?'

'Not very, Miss Minnie. It will wear by.'

'"Wear by"? What a nice expression! Nobody can say things just like you. So you won't tell me?'

'You wouldn't understand. It would only puzzle your little head trying to think it out.'

'Well—oh, there's papa! I should be at my lessons, you know. Yes, papa, I'm at them,' she cried, darting up-stairs two steps at a time, while a peal of merry laughter sent its sweet echoes through the house.

'You elf, I'll punish you!' said the Doctor, shaking his fist at her.

She threw him a kiss over the stairs, and ran off singing to the schoolroom.

'I believe Minnie knows by instinct when you are in the house,' said the Doctor, smiling. 'I forgot something I intended to ask you, James. The Assembly opens next Thursday, and we have a few friends to dinner that evening. Will you come along later, say about eight? I should like you to meet one or two who will be there. Nay, don't refuse. You know it is imperative that you should see something of society. So we will expect you about eight.' And, without waiting for an answer, the Doctor nodded and hastily withdrew into the study.

The next few days were full of deep anxiety, not only for James Bethune, but for those who were interested in him. Adam Farquhar especially could not rest or attend to his work, he was so anxious that his protégé should obtain the situation. Not that he thought it by any means worthy of him, but he saw very well that the lad was growing hopeless, and feared lest he should become so thoroughly disheartened as to throw up his city life altogether. That, he was sure, would be a mistaken step.

'For who knows, my man?' he would say in his facetious way. 'Perhaps about the end of the twentieth century somebody will be selling rare copies of Bethune's works in this very shop. Ha, ha! wouldn't that be a joke, if only we could live to see it?'

On the opening night of the Assembly, James Bethune dressed himself in his best, and went out to George Square. Only that day he had heard definitely regarding the situation in Glasgow, and after a week's delay he was somewhat surprised to receive notice of his appointment, coupled with the request that he would enter on his duties at once if possible. He was in good spirits, for, though the work might not be such as he would have chosen, still it was work, and might be the stepping-stone to something higher. It is the spirit in which we accept our lot in life which lowers or ennobles it; in very lowly places there are to be found examples of heroism, of noble self-sacrifice, which make the angels rejoice.

James Bethune's friendly intercourse with Doctor Kinross and his family had done him boundless good in many ways. Perhaps not the least of these was that the occasional companionship of refined gentlewomen had taught him many of those little courtesies of life which are not to be despised. James Bethune had never lacked the instincts of a gentleman, and now he had acquired that ease of manner and complete self-possession which had been wanting when he first came to the town. When he mounted the steps to the minister's door that night, he heard the sound of singing come floating down through the open windows of the drawing-room, which held him for a moment spellbound. It was a wondrous voice, deep, rich, and exquisitely sweet. He leaned up against the pillared doorway and listened breathlessly, but there came to him no whisper of warning; he did not dream that he was approaching another and a greater crisis in his life. When the singing ceased he rung the bell, and was at once admitted. Just as he hung up his hat, Minnie Kinross, in a white dress, with her fair curls lying round her like a halo, came dancing down the wide staircase, her face radiant with welcome.

'Why are you so late? Do you know it is nearly nine?' she said, folding her two hands over his.

'There are so many nice, nice people here! I am sure you will like them. Come, and I will take you to the drawing-room under my wing.'

So saying, she slipped her hand through his arm, and led him away up-stairs. The drawing-room door was a little ajar, but just as they reached the landing Doctor Kinross opened it and looked out.

'How are you, James? You know we are glad to see you. I guessed what Minnie was after when I heard the bell ring, and saw her disappear.'

'I received a letter from Glasgow by the evening post, sir, and I had to answer it at once. I am sorry if I am late,' answered James Bethune, and as he spoke they entered the room.

It was full of people, and, without looking round, James Bethune went straight to Mrs. Kinross's chair, and sat down by her side. She greeted him with a warm, bright smile, and told him in a word how glad she was to see him. Minnie, who had followed him closely across the room, sat down on a little stool at his side, and almost unconsciously he laid his broad hand on the sunny head with a lingering and caressing touch The child's love for him was a very bright thing in James Bethune's life.

'Have you heard anything from Glasgow yet?' asked Mrs. Kinross kindly. 'The Doctor and I were talking of it this morning.'

'Yes, ma'am; the letter came this evening, and'— He came to an abrupt stop, and his listener looked at him in questioning surprise. His eyes were fixed on a group at the other side of the room; his face wore an expression of absolute surprise.

'That is Mr. Bethune, the minister of Lochbroom, standing by my niece,' said Mrs. Kinross. 'You seem

to recognise each other. Of course, it is the same name!
Can it be possible that you are related ?'

'He is my twin brother, Mrs. Kinross,' said James
Bethune slowly and heavily, for the look in Sandy's eyes
was not one of welcome, and smote him chilly to the heart.

'Impossible! How is it we have never heard you
speak of him ? Doctor Kinross inducted him. You know
he is a native of the district, and his brother-in-law,
Mr. Lorraine, is one of the heritors of Lochbroom.'

James Bethune bent down his head a moment, and
shaded his troubled eyes with his hand. Mrs. Kinross
saw there was something far amiss, and the child
Minnie looked at her friend with all her childish heart
in her eyes. And just then the minister of Lochbroom crossed the room and stood before them.

'I was so astonished when I saw you come into the
room, Jamie, that I could hardly believe the evidence of
my own eyes,' he said, speaking as if with an effort.
'How are you ?'

'I am very well,' answered Jamie, and they shook
hands, but not with the warm grip of mutual satisfaction and love.

'You must have a great deal to say to each other,' said
Mrs. Kinross, rising. 'Come, Minnie, you must give Mr.
Bethune some peace, you know.'

Minnie rose obediently, only to retire to another
corner and watch her friend, who she saw was vexed
and troubled, for love had taught her to read every
expression of his face. The minister of Lochbroom
took the chair Mrs. Kinross had vacated, and for a
moment the twain sat in absolute silence.

'How did you ever manage to get in *here?*' said
Sandy at length, with significant emphasis on the last
word.

'It is easily enough explained. I go to St Giles, and Doctor Kinross has been very kind to me, that is all,' answered James almost coldly, for his brother's look and tone were not less bitter to him than of yore. 'But if I had known I was to meet you here, I would not have come. It is rather awkward for us both.'

'You are right. But what have you been doing to yourself? You look quite different. I declare I would hardly have known you. But there, I must go,' Sandy broke off suddenly. 'We can have a talk again.'

So saying, he rapidly crossed the room, and James Bethune saw the explanation at once. Some one was going to sing, and it seemed to be Sandy's place to set the piano-stool, and arrange the music on the stand. He could not see the face of the singer,. but he noted the graceful curves of the slight figure, and the wondrous sheen of the bright hair worn like a coronet above her brow.

'Here I am again, Mr. Bethune,' whispered Minnie Kinross at his side. 'I may sit by you, mayn't I? You see there's nobody to speak to me to-night except you.'

He nodded, and laid his hand lightly on hers, as if to enforce silence, for the singer had begun. As that grand voice rose and swelled in richest melody through the room, James Bethune felt his heart first stirred and touched, and then it was as if a strange, abiding peace stole upon him, making him feel as if no trouble or care could come very near him any more.

'Are you going to cry, Mr. Bethune, you look so solemn?' whispered Minnie. 'Doesn't Beatrice sing splendidly? She is my cousin, you know, Beatrice Lorraine, and that is Uncle Lorraine sitting beside the ministers quite at the other side of the room.'

James Bethune started at the name, and looked with deeper interest towards the piano. The singer had risen, and he could see her well. Even as he looked at the sad, pale face, lit by the soul-speaking eyes, there came to him no prevision of the future. His chief interest at that moment was to see the woman who had eclipsed Mary Campbell, and whom his brother would give so much to win. She was beautiful, but her face was unutterably sad. It looked as if some sorrowful life-history had been long written upon it; and these deep eyes had · wells of suffering and pathos in their depths. He saw Sandy bend low over her and whisper something in an impassioned voice, but she only smiled very faintly and slightly shook her head.

'I do love my Cousin Beatrice!' continued Minnie confidentially; 'only she is so quiet and sad. Of course she is very sorry about Willie. I never saw Willie, but he did something very bad, and nearly broke poor Uncle Lorraine's heart. Oh, here is papa bringing Uncle Lorraine to speak to you, so I'll run away.'

So saying, the light-hearted child skipped away once more; and James Bethune rose as the two gentlemen approached him. Doctor Kinross briefly introduced them, and with a nod and a smile returned to the discussion of church matters which the song had momentarily interrupted.

'I was getting beyond my depth over yonder,' said Mr. Lorraine as he sat down; 'I am quite a novice in the history of the Established Church. And how are you liking your city life?'

His tone and manner were so kind that James Bethune for the moment was taken by surprise, and did not at once reply.

'I see you wonder at my question. Doctor Kinross

has spoken to me about you, and I was anxious to have a little talk with you.   You came to town in exceptional circumstances, I understand,' continued Mr. Lorraine in the same interested, kindly manner.   'You must have found it a great change.'

'I did.   It has taught me a good few things, sir.'

'Ay, necessarily.   Take care lest it teach you what you may have cause to regret.   Keep your principles untarnished, I entreat you.   City life has had too many victims already ; do not add to the number.'

James Bethune could not but look at the man in astonishment, he spoke with such impassioned earnestness; but suddenly he remembered Minnie Kinross's confidence concerning her relatives, which gave him all the explanation he required.

'I will try, sir,' he answered quite simply and earnestly ; and he looked with something of compassion at the sad, proud face, which bore so evident an impress of no ordinary sorrow.

'You are just beginning life, and if you only remain true to yourself, there is no fear of you,' said Mr. Lorraine.   'You will find it a hard battle, but life at the best is that; and you have the look of one who will struggle manfully, and do your best to make it noble and true.   I wish you well.'

'I thank you, sir.'

'And if you ever come to visit your brother at Lochbroom (I was astonished to find our minister was your brother), we will be glad to see you at Nethercleugh. I should like to introduce my daughter to you, but I see they are asking her to sing again.   Perhaps I shall have an opportunity before the evening is over.'

CHAPTER XIII.

BEATRICE.

'Hers is a spirit deep and crystal clear,
Calmly beneath her earnest face it lies,
Free without boldness, meek without a fear,
Quicker to look than speak its sympathies.'

LOWELL.

IN a corner of Mrs. Kinross's drawing-room
sat the minister of Lochbroom, somewhat
gloomily regarding his surroundings. No
one was paying any heed to him at that
moment. In the oriel window a clerical
clique was discussing the Disestablishment
Question, and the ladies had gathered about
Dora's tea-table to talk over a forthcoming fancy
fair.

Beatrice Lorraine was not among them, nor the child
Minnie.

In a far corner of the room, half hidden by the
folding leaf of a draught-screen, James Bethune and
Beatrice Lorraine were in deep conversation. That the
theme was interesting and engrossing to both was

beyond a doubt. Her beautiful eyes were fixed on the grave, earnest face before her, and her lips parted as if she hung in breathless attention upon his words. Close beside his chair stood Minnie Kinross, with her bare round arm on his shoulder, her eyes fixed in childish love and wonder on his face. These things surprised and annoyed the minister of Lochbroom ; and, unable to bear his own thoughts, he rose at length and joined the group in the window.

· ' Why didn't you tell us you had a brother in town ? ' asked Doctor Kinross, turning to him. ' By the bye, have you seen this month's *Chambers's ?* But of course you are in the secret.'

' What secret ? I do not understand you, Doctor Kinross,' said the minister shortly and coldly.

' Oh, nonsense ! Don't you know who is the writer of that article on " Social Relationships " in the *Journal* for this month ? '

' Indeed, I do not.'

' Then I have the privilege of being able to give you a very gratifying surprise. It is from your brother's pen ; and with such rare promise we shall all have occasion to be very proud of him, perhaps at no distant date.'

Alexander Bethune preserved a cold silence. The Doctor eyed him a moment with his keen, deep, searching gaze, and then glanced involuntarily across the room. There was little resemblance between the brothers, and the casual observer would not have hesitated a moment as to which was the more striking and attractive. The minister of Lochbroom was undoubtedly a handsome man. His features were regular and refined ; his whole physique and appearance that of a polished gentleman. His clerical attire became him well. and seemed to show his fine figure to the utmost advantage. The other had a powerful, well-knit frame, but it was certainly not enhanced by his attire, which had not been cut by a city tailor. His face had lost the ruddy country hue, and his features seemed large and prominent, while his thick dark hair lay in careless masses on his brow, which was beginning to wear the lines of deep care and thought.

His hands were large, and still marked with the hue and the coarseness of his early toil. But as the Doctor looked, his heart warmed to the one as it had never warmed to the other, because he knew that that plain casket held a noble and beautiful soul. The elder brother was one of those who would dwell at ease, and make life's pathway as gentle and sweet as possible, who would step aside from toil and unpleasantness, preferring ever the path of flowers and sunshine to the steep ascent among the stones and briers. About the younger there was a suggestion of strength and manliness which would have its fulfilment in a life of self-sacrifice and noble deeds. He was one who would seek for life's grandest meanings, and, having found them, would seek to make others partakers in his rich heritage. Such was the resolve written on his brow, and flashing in every glance of his deep and earnest eyes. Dr. Kinross could not but wonder what was the theme which so engrossed James Bethune and his niece, and a rare tenderness came into his face as he watched the unutterable sympathy plainly written upon Beatrice's beautiful face. What were they talking of? Not very much after all. Their conversation had been a little constrained and disjointed at first, because, when Mr. Lorraine brought his daughter to James Bethune's side, and left her there, a great shyness and reserve came upon him. He could talk without restraint to volatile Minnie, or to the sweet, womanly elder sister, or the gentle mother, but this beautiful creature filled him with awe and reverence, and he felt himself robbed of his usual self-possession. She had had a great sorrow, which still overshadowed her, and he looked at her with an infinitude of compassion, not the less deep and sincere because it was and must be dumb. She was so utterly unlike any woman he had ever met before, and when her eyes, like stars, looked into his, it was as if all power of thought and speech fled for ever. This strange silence and reserve, however, was speedily broken, when she spoke, in that sweet, mellow undertone we look for sometimes in vain in those who possess the gift of song.

'You have not been very long in Edinburgh. It is a beautiful city, is it not? I have seen none like it anywhere.'

'Have you visited many cities, Miss Lorraine?'

'Yes, my father took me abroad two years ago, and we visited every capital in Europe.'

'That would be a rare enjoyment indeed!' exclaimed James Bethune involuntarily,—'almost an education in itself.'

'It would be to you, or to any other whose mind and heart were free and open to receive every impression,' she answered with a somewhat sad smile. 'We travelled under peculiar circumstances, and a great sorrow made all the world look dark to us. Though it had been the dream of my life to travel, when the time came it surprised and grieved me to find how little I enjoyed it. Pleasure and happiness depend so much more upon our inner selves than on any outward surroundings or influences; do you not think so?'

'Undoubtedly, and life is very much as we make it for ourselves. Yet I often wonder if it is possible to reach that state of which Paul speaks when he writes that he had learned to be content in whatsoever estate he found himself.'

'There are different kinds of contentment, I think,' said Beatrice Lorraine. 'There is the slothful content of indolence and stagnation; then there is that false contentment which those affect who profess to have gone to the very foundation of things, and to find no good in anything ; then that noble and true contentment to which a human soul can resign itself, even when it sees that duty forbids the exercise or fulfilment of its highest desires.'

'That is the true contentment indeed, Miss Lorraine, but it is purchased sometimes at a fearful cost. Duty is often a relentless and cruel taskmistress.'

'Only until the task is learned,' said Beatrice softly, and a sweet smile parted her lips as she spoke. 'But pardon me, I have no right to speak so to you who have suffered just there. It is so easy for those who have not borne the burden to wonder that others should complain. I spoke without thinking, as I too often do.'

'But you are right. Let me tell you a little about myself, Miss Lorraine,' said James Bethune, for the soul looking out from these starry eyes was full of that sympathy which breaks down the barriers of reserve and forges the first links of all friendship. 'When I was a boy at home, I had many a conflict between duty and inclination, which grew stronger and more difficult to overcome as I grew older, and the desire for some wider sphere and greater knowledge increased. I did not grudge my brother his advantages, but only rebelled because I could not share them. My father had no knowledge of these rebellings, and kept me closely at

work, thinking he was doing best for me.   Then he
was growing old, and without one son at home would
have been lonely, so for his sake I stayed.'

'But not without reward ; that would come, did it not?'
asked Beatrice, leaning forward a little in her earnestness.

'It did in many ways, for I became necessary to him
in his old age ; and I thank God now that strength was
given me to fulfil my duty to him.   He knew nothing of
my struggles.   If he had, he would have been the first
to bid me go.'

'Then he is gone now ?'

'He died last spring, just after he visited Lochbroom.
I am surprised that you did not know.'

'So recently as that !' she exclaimed in surprise.
'No, we did not know ; your brother is reserved
concerning himself.   I did not know you and he were
related till an hour ago, when Minnie whispered it to
me.   Is your mother alive ?'

'Oh no ; she died when we were born.   Sandy and I
are twins.   We have never known a mother's love,
but since Dr. Kinross has admitted me to his home,
I have known what it is to long for it.   Mrs.
Kinross comes very near my ideal of a saint, Miss
Lorraine.'

'Yes, Aunt Dora is very good,' said Beatrice, and her
eyes filled with tears.   'I too am motherless ; her
memory is very shadowy now, but Aunt Dora has filled
the blank in my heart.   Human relationships are very
sweet, are they not ?   They give us sometimes foretastes
of heaven.'

'I have only known enough to long for more,' said
James Bethune involuntarily.

'But you must be a great deal to your brother, and he

to you,' she said, glancing across the room to where he stood moodily watching them both.

James Bethune observed her glance, and saw how her eyes were quickly down-dropped, and how the colour heightened in her delicate cheek, and thought he could read these signs aright. Sandy was to be successful in his wooing, then, and poor Mary Campbell must just try to drink the waters of forgetfulness. Although he could not approve of his brother's doings, he no longer marvelled that he should have swerved from his allegiance to his first love for the sake of Beatrice Lorraine.

'We were as boys all in all to each other,' he said evasively, for he could not tell an untruth even to spare Sandy in the eyes of the woman he loved. 'He did not approve of me giving up the work of the farm, and perhaps I was a little headstrong, and we were both hasty. But it will all come right by and by.'

'But you do not regret leaving now?'

'No, although I have had a trial of enforced idleness which was very hard to bear. I have no time to lose, for I am no longer a boy. I have been successful in obtaining an opening in Glasgow, and if unremitting toil and fervent resolve can win for a man any of life's prizes, they shall be mine.'

'What is your ambition?' she asked eagerly. 'Do not think me curious; I am deeply interested, and I have always thought with reverence of those who aspire, and set themselves to win what is noble and worthy of possessing.'

'I do not know that I could put it in words. It is many-sided: only if God has given me the gift of a writer, and I sometimes think He has, I should like to use it for good; to write what would help others as well as myself in the higher life.'

' With such an ambition you must and will succeed,
said Beatrice, and the petals of the yellow rose at her
throat stirred with the heaving of her breast.   She was
deeply moved, indeed, her nature was quick, ardent, deeply
sympathetic, full of great possibilities if only it had
wider scope.   Life for her had long been narrowed and
confined ; first by a father's carelessness and indifference,
then by his great and absorbing need of all her love and
care.

James Bethune slightly shook his head, and the light
in his eyes somewhat paled.

' It is only sometimes that hope whispers of such
a joy.   Oftener I am depressed by my own weakness,
and overwhelmed by perplexities and thoughts which I
can neither understand nor fathom.'

' But these will be swallowed up in the wisdom of experience,' she said earnestly.   ' There is confidence in
knowledge, and when you get to the foundation of things
all perplexities will disappear.'

' As the waves and their restless tossings are
lost in the calmness of the ocean depths,' he added
with a rare smile.   ' That is a great thought, Miss
Lorraine, and full of comfort.   I shall remember it
all my life.'

' But there will always be something—we must leave
something which even knowledge cannot explain away.
Were all life's mysteries revealed here, what would
remain for us to learn yonder ?' she said softly.   ' I have
a vast pity for those who have made scientific knowledge
clear up all heavenly mysteries ; for the joy of trust
is denied them.   In their innermost hearts I am sure
they must often be very miserable.'

' Beatrice, my dear, I am sorry to disturb you,' said
the deep, rich voice of Doctor Kinross behind them.

But they are growing impatient to hear you sing again. Will you give us "The Lost Chord" now?'

'Yes, uncle.'

She rose at once, smiled, and crossed the room. James Bethune, forgetful for a moment where he was, leaned his elbows on his knees and followed her every movement with his eyes. His heart was stirred within him; he could have gone away out into the stillness of the night to ponder over the revelation she had been to him. For it is a great revelation to an earnest soul to find another as earnest, and to know himself not alone in his strivings after what is great. But suddenly the room filled with song once more—such song as James Bethune had never before heard, and did not dream had any existence in the world. It was the deepest yearnings that can enter a human soul finding vent in fittest melody, and its tribute was a deep and sacred silence which seemed to fall on the assembled company like a benediction. When she ceased there was no applause, for pleasure, like all other emotions, is deepest and keenest when it finds no voice.

Then some one said it would be well to leave with such a softening memory of a happy evening, and so the guests began slowly to disperse.

'Where do you lodge?' asked the minister of Lochbroom briefly, stepping across to his brother's side.

'In Bank Street; will you come and share it with me?' asked Jamie eagerly, for somehow his heart yearned over his brother; he felt himself so destitute of these sweet human ties of which Beatrice Lorraine had spoken.

'Oh no; I have rooms at the Windsor Hotel. You might walk down with me. We may as well have a chat when we can.'

M

'Very well,' said Jamie quietly; but he could scarcely help turning a little away from his brother, he spoke in such a cold, commonplace, distant way.

Just then Minnie Kinross slipped up to his side, and looked up at him with her innocent, childish eyes.

'Well, Miss Minnie?'

'You have never told me that story you promised, and you talked all the time to Beatrice and never to me,' she said reproachfully. 'Will you take me up Arthur's Seat on Saturday, Mr. Bethune?'

'Yes; and I'll tell you two stories to make up,' he said, smiling now, for the child's sunshine was irresistible.

'You should beware of what promises you make to Minnie, Mr. Bethune,' said Miss Kinross, laughing. 'She will plague your life out now.'

'It will not be for long, Miss Kinross; I leave Edin-burgh next week.'

'Indeed? I am very sorry; we will all miss you,' said Dora Kinross with genuine regret in her tone. 'But Glasgow is not a thousand miles away; we shall see you often, I hope, else Minnie will be inconsolable. We shall miss you on Sabbath evenings most of all.'

Dora Kinross was quite sincere in all she said, but she purposely spoke with greater warmth because the minister of Lochbroom was within hearing. She had been puzzled as well as surprised that they should never have been made aware of the relationship between the brothers, but after a little thought her shrewd per-ceptions had assisted her to a correct conclusion, and the Rev. Alexander Bethune fell accordingly in her estima-tion. It was a harmless delight to her to show him how very highly the brother whose existence he had thought it better to ignore was esteemed and honoured among them.

Although Doctor Kinross's drawing-room held Beatrice Lorraine, Sandy Bethune was glad to leave it that night. He was neither happy nor comfortable in his mind.

At the corner of Lauriston those who were walking home separated, and the two brothers pursued their way together along George IV. Bridge towards the New Town. Jamie was determined not to be the first to speak; unless in answer to questions, he would give no information regarding his way of life or future prospects.

'Well, how are you getting on? Well, I suppose, or you wouldn't be as you are. I must say you are wonderfully improved,' said Sandy when they had gone some distance in silence.

'In what way?'

'In every way; you don't look so countrified, and you speak much more correctly. But how have you managed to lay aside the old Star dialect so quickly? You spoke broadly enough the last time I saw you; and now there is only a slight accent which betrays your Fife origin.'

'I could have spoken English correctly enough long ago, if I had seen the need,' said Jamie quietly. 'I like the broad Scotch best yet; but it doesn't do for all company.'

'I see. I heard you say to Miss Kinross you were going to leave Edinburgh. Where are you going?'

'To Glasgow.'

'What to do?'

'Work as a reporter.'

'Is that all? Why, from your airs one would think you were going as editor of the *Herald*, or to fill some other equally responsible position. How on earth have you ever managed to get so intimate at St. Giles ? '

' I told you already,' answered James Bethune briefly, for Sandy's sneering tone wounded him as of yore.

' So you wrote that article in *Chambers's* ? They were praising it inordinately. Mr. Brown of Greyfriars predicts for you a grand career. Well, I never thought it was in you.'

' Are you sure of it now ? '

Sandy laughed, and swung his cane backwards and forwards by his side. ' Well, I suppose I must admit it now. I'm sure I wish you well. When did you see Aunt Susan ? '

' A fortnight ago, I was over.'

' Who else did you see in Star ? '

' All the folk. They are quite well at the Knowe.'

' Is Mary quite well ? '

' She seems to be.'

' They wouldn't ask for me, I suppose.'

' No, they never mention your name.'

' I suppose they regard me in a very black light. What do you think of Miss Lorraine ? '

' She is very beautiful. I had no idea she would be such a beautiful woman.'

' Don't you remember me telling you that before ? '

' Yes, but I allowed something for your imagination. Are you engaged to her ? '

' I wish I was. I am just where I was when I saw you last. Do you know, I can hardly preach or attend to my work for thinking about her.'

' Then the sooner you get the question settled the better for yourself and your people.'

' But, man, I'm afraid to venture. If I lose her I don't know what I shall do.'

James Bethune could have smiled, even in the middle of his brother's impassioned speaking. To hear the cool, calculating, confident Sandy speak so humbly was wonderful indeed, and an abiding proof of the levelling power of love.

'What were you speaking about over in yon corner? You seemed to be deeply engrossed.'

'I could not tell you all we said. She is a noble, good woman, Sandy. If you win her, I hope you will make her happy.'

'Do you think I have any chance? Did you speak about me at all? Of course she knows you are my brother now. I hope you didn't give her all the particulars of our early life. You'll soon learn now, Jamie, that it will be to your advantage to bury it in oblivion.'

'Why?'

'Oh, because people in good society lay great stress on a man's antecedents. He is seldom judged on his own merits.'

'Would you call the Kinrosses good society?'

'Certainly. Doctor Kinross's forebears have been ministers in Lockerbie for generations, and his brother, who is minister there now, is on intimate terms with all the county people.'

'They don't seem to me to take up their heads much with folk's antecedents, and I have seen a good deal of them.'

'Oh, well, perhaps they are exceptions, but they don't prove the rule. You'll soon see I am right. Well, here's my hotel. Are you coming in?'

'No, it is after eleven; it is time I was away home. I am always in after six in the evening, if you care to look me up.'

'Well, if there's nothing of particular interest at the Assembly, I'll look in to-morrow evening.   Good-night.'

'Good-night.'

'I hope you don't bear me any grudge for what I said last time we met,' said Sandy, the clasp of his brother's hand touching a tender chord in his heart. 'I did not mean to hurt you.'

'It *did* hurt me, but I'll forget it now.   I'm glad I've seen you again, Sandy.   I have been lonely enough all winter.'

So they parted with something of the old glow of brotherly affection in their hearts.   Jamie wended his way slowly along Princes Street, which was almost deserted now, save by the waifs and wanderers who frequent the streets of a city by night.   The soft, star-gemmed sky beamed down in benignant pity on these poor wanderers ; and the pure radiance of the young May moon lay like a veil of mystery over all.   The breath of summer was in the mild and balmy air, and the first blossoms of the mignonette sent up its sweet tribute to the midnight air.   James Bethune crossed to the garden side, and walked slowly with his head bent, taking no heed of anything around him, for many thoughts oppressed him.   He felt as if every step in life brought him face to face with new mysteries, with things hard to understand and harder to bear.   That night he had obtained a glimpse of something which had hitherto had no place in his thoughts.   It had dawned upon him that there were other things more desirable than fame or fortune, things which neither of these could buy.   He had read much about the influence of women upon the conduct and affairs of men's lives ; how the weak and erring had been raised, and the noble made nobler and better by a woman's love.   The deepest feelings of his heart were stirred, and there came to him in the midnight stillness unutterable yearnings for some sweet influence which would satisfy the impulses of affection, now for the first time called into being. It would be too much to say he had learned to love Beatrice Lorraine in the brief hour of their acquaintance, only in her he had met the first woman who had the power to interest him. What influence was she to have upon his future life ?

CHAPTER XIV.

DESOLATE AGE.

'My way is fallen into the sear and yellow leaf,
    The fruit, the flowers of life are gone,
The cankerworm and the grief—
    Are mine alone.'

BYRON.

ILL ye come east, Miss Bethune? The maister's awfu' no' weel, an' there's no' a cratur to dae a hand's turn for him.'

'Oh, it's you, Wull,' said Susan Bethune, peering out into the darkness, and discerning the figure of the foreman at Auchtermairnie standing by a horse and trap outside the garden gate. 'What way hae ye brocht the beast? Is he that ill that I maun gang east the nicht?'

''Deed is he. He's been compleenin', ye ken, sin' afore hervest; but it was staunin' in the tattie dreels yesterday in the weet that did for him. It rained a' efternune, an' he was that anxious to get them a' up that he wadna let's lowse.'

'Deil tak' the body! he's wark daft,' said Susan
Bethune a trifle testily, for she was by no means inclined
to leave her own cosy fireside so late on a raw November
night to share the cold comfort of Auchtermairnie. 'Is
he in his bed ? '

'Ay, noo. He had bit to lie doon, for he couldna.
staund. He's a' pains, an' he has an' unco like hoast. I
doot he's by wi't this time.'

'Aweel, he's an auld carle noo, an' he hasna been
guidit since Marget dee'd,' said Susan in a matter-of-fact
way. 'Bide a wee or I rake oot my fire an' pit twa-
three things thegither, for I'll likely hae to bide or the
morn, onyway. Wull the beast no' let ye in to the
fire a wee? it's a cauld nicht.'

'Na, she'll no' staund. I'll jist wait,' said the man;
and Susan Bethune with a nod disappeared indoors. Still
active despite her seventy-three years, she made herself
ready in an incredibly short time, and, well wrapped up,
took her place in the dilapidated milk-cart, which still
did duty as a gig at Auchtermairnie. The animal, a
fresh young filly of Peter Bethune's own rearing, rattled
them rapidly over the ground, and in less than half an hour
they were at Auchtermairnie. A feeble light flickered
through the dirty panes of the kitchen window, the only
sign of life about the dreary house. Susan Bethune got
out cautiously, and, grasping her carpet-bag, marched
into the house, sniffing as she went, for the close,
musty smell seemed to catch her breath on the very
threshold.

'Weel, I'm here, Peter,' she said as she entered the
kitchen. Receiving no answer, she set down her bag
and approached the bed.

'Are ye sleepin', Peter ? '

'Na; I wish I was,' came in a feeble voice from under

the clothes, then a violent fit of coughing shook his exhausted frame, and made him almost gasp for breath.

'Mercy me, that's a dreidfu' hoast! What d'ye mean, ye auld gomeril, staunin' in weet tattie dreels till ye get yer death? I'm sure ye hae plenty o' this warld's gear to serve ye a' your time, noo. Ye micht let the thing abee. Is there ony caun'les in the hoose?'

'Na; but there's the stable lamp ahint the door; but if ye pit on a bit stick it'll mak' licht enough.'

Susan Bethune paid no attention to his suggestion, but took down the stable lamp, lit it, and brought it to bear on the sick man's face. She was touched by his haggard and miserable appearance, but her pity turned to indignation as her eyes lighted on the grimy sheets and blankets which covered him. She was a sworn foe to dirt in every shape or form.

'Weel, jist lie still or I get the kettle biled, an' I'll gie ye a warm drink, an' pit a poultice on for that hoast, an' the time the kettle's bilin' I'll get clean things for the bed, if there's sic a thing i' the hoose. The doctor 'll be here the morn, an' it wad be a disgrace if he saw ye as ye are.'

'I'm no' needin' a doctor, Shoosan. It's only a cauld.'

'Wull 'll ride that young beast ower to Leslie first thing i' the mornin',' continued Susan, just as if she had not heard his feeble remonstrance. 'Noo ye may as weel keep quate, because if I'm to be here ava', I'll dae as I like. Eh, certy, sic a hoose!'

It was no wonder that Susan Bethune heaved a prodigious sigh as she gazed round the kitchen, which was wont to be so clean and snug and cosy, both in her own and Marget's time. It was a dirty, dingy, smoke-discoloured place now, with cobwebs hanging here and there and everywhere, and the dust lying thick on every-

thing which was not in daily use. Taking the lamp in
her hand, she went away to the room end to seek some
clean bed-linen, and she shivered as she entered the close,
damp-smelling place, which was in worse condition than
the other end. She had difficulty in opening the
drawers, as they were swollen with the damp; but at
length she succeeded, and, finding what she sought,
returned to the kitchen, and piled up peats and coals on
the fire till her brother turned uneasily in his bed and
asked why she was so lavish with the fuel. But she
paid no heed to him, only hung up the sheets close to
the cheerful, strong heat, and proceeded to prepare some
peculiar kind of gruel, for which she was famous in the
Star. It had never been known to fail to relieve cold.
When the wretched old man was made warm and comfortable, and had drank a bowl of the gruel, he felt
much relieved, and fell into a sleep, which was only
disturbed at times by his cough. Susan Bethune, after
considerable trouble, managed to push the old sofa from
the room to the kitchen, and, throwing off her dress,
wrapped herself in a warm shawl and lay down in front
of the fire. But she could not sleep, it was so strange
to be once more at the old fireside, and the place seemed
to be peopled with memories and phantoms of the past.
They were not all sad memories, and yet the old stock
was getting far reduced, and the chances were that very
soon there would be another family in Auchtermairnie,
and the name of Bethune would soon be forgotten in the
place. It was a matter of regret at times to Susan
Bethune that neither of her brother's sons had elected to
follow in the way of their forebears, and yet she knew
that they were better to follow after their own inclina-
tions than to take up an occupation for which they had
no love. Then her thoughts centred upon her own boy,

as she always thought of Jamie in her heart, and she
gave herself up to visions of his future, which was to be
great and grand far beyond her comprehension; for
there was nothing to which Jamie might not aspire to
and attain. Her love and pride and faith in him were
what made life sweet to her now; indeed, she had nothing
else to live for. His constant thought of and consideration for her were also things passing sweet, for, though
he was busy in his new way of life, he was never too
busy to write his weekly letter on the appointed day,
and he never forgot to send her the earliest copy of anything of his own which had found its way into print.
It would be impossible for me to attempt to analyze or
describe the strange commingling of reverence, love, and
wonder with which the old woman regarded these
printed pieces. They were carefully read and re-read
by herself, lent for one night to the kind, interested
friends at the Knowe, then wrapped in a silk handker-
chief and laid beside the lavender-scented linen in her
own kist. A wonderful place was Susan Bethune's kist;
its whole contents, of no mean value, were intended for
Jamie's wife, should he ever take one. She was thinking
of old times, reviewing her own life and its changes since
she had gone for the second time to make her home in
the Star, when her brother woke up and asked what
o'clock it was.

'Near twal',' she answered without rising. 'D'ye
want onything?'

'A drink o' water. Eh, wummin, it's like there was a
burnin' fire in me! There's something awfu' wrang!'
he said uneasily. 'Tak' aff some o' they sticks an' cool
the place.'

'It's no' het ava, man; it's you that's fevered,' said
Susan, bringing him the water, which he drank feverishly,

and asked for more; but she refused to give it until the doctor should come. 'I doot it's gaun to gang hard wi' ye this time, Pete!'

'My time's maybe come; an' yet I'm no' that auld, only seeventy-seeven. Marget's first man was ninety when he dee'd, an' auld Saunders Law in the Star eichty-six.'

'Ay, but, lad, they took care o' theirsel's,' said Susan briefly. 'Hoo aften hae I wairned ye no' to tear yersel' dune as ye've been daein' a' yer days.'

'Weel, weel, I had to work or the place wadna pay,' said the old man, playing restlessly with the fringes of the counterpane. 'What aboot John's sons? When did ye see that silly cratur, Jamie? Is he in the puirs-hoose yet?'

'No, he's in Glesca, gettin' twa pound a-week as a reporter, an' money for ither things forby,' answered Aunt Susan with quiet pride.

'Weel, I'm sure he's no' worth it. It wad set him better to drive a pair on Auchtermairnie yet. It'll be an unco-like thing when there's no' a Bethune in Auchtermairnie.'

'Ay, but we canna help it. The laddies hae ither wark to dae,' said Susan with a little sigh.

'Weel, ye'll write, or get somebody to write to Sandy the morn. He'll better come through an' see efter things. The feck o't 'll gang to him.'

'Is yer wull made, Peter?'

'Oh ay, it's made.'

'An' does the minister get a'?'

'Ay. I telt Jamie that unless he bade at hame he wadna see a hapney o' my siller, an' I'll keep my word.'

'But what aboot Marget's laddies?'

'They've gotten a' they're gaun to get,' replied the old man with a girn. 'They got the Enster property divided when Marget dee'd, an' there's nae mair fo them.'

'But her dochter, puir lassie, her that's a weedy at Leven—ye micht dae waur than leave her a hundred or twa. Marget didna come to ye empty-handit onyway. Ye got a hantle mair than the Enster hooses.'

'Maybe; but I deserved something for takin' her. She wasna weel-faured,' said the old man with a wretched attempt at a smile. 'I'm wearit noo, Shoosan. Eh, I wish it was the mornin'! If ye wad gae 'wa' an' no' speak sae muckle till a body, he micht get a sleep.'

'Ye're aye the auld carle yet, Pete; as thrawn as a ravelled wab,' she answered. 'Noo, see, keep the claes aboot ye. If ye dinna dae as I bid ye, I'll gang back tae the Star wi' the daylicht, as sure's I'm here.'

So saying, Susan Bethune turned down the lamp, and laid herself down again gladly, for she was missing her accustomed night's rest. For some hours there was silence in the kitchen, broken only by the sick man's cough and hurried breathing, and the occasional falling of the ashes from the grate as the fire settled itself to burn more slowly and steadily till the morning. Before five Susan was astir again, and by the half-hour the foreman was speeding over the road to Leslie to summon the doctor. The forenoon was well through, however, before he put in an appearance, and after his brief examination of the old man, he had little to say. Susan Bethune, who had met him often by sick and dying beds, knew his opinion by the expression in his face just as well as if he had put it in words. Peter was dying.

She followed him out to the door, and stood in silence while he mounted his horse.

'He is an old man, Miss Bethune ; over seventy, is he not ? '

'Ay, he's seeventy-seeven.'

'Ah, well ! he has passed the span, and he's had a long and healthy life.'

'Then he hasna lang ? '

'A few days ; a week at the most. You may apply the remedies I have recommended, but I fear they will not avail much. Both lungs are seriously congested.'

'That's jist as John was, ye'll mind, Doctor Hay ? '

'Yes, I remember quite well. It is a curious coincidence. You are standing out well. How are these clever nephews of yours getting on ? '

'Brawly. Did ye see Jamie's last paper intae *Chaumers's ?* '

'Yes, I saw it. He will make his mark yet. Well, I must go. If I am passing, I'll look in to-morrow morning.'

'A' richt ! Guid mornin', sir,' said Susan Bethune. and re-entered the house.

'What are ye claverin' an' whisperin' there sae lang at ? ' asked Peter querulously. 'What did he say ? Am I gaun to dee or no', that what's I want to ken ? '

'Ye are verra seriously ill, Pete,' she answered, look-ing with deep compassion at the withered face and the restless eye, gleaming under the shaggy brows with an unnatural brilliance. His unkempt grey hair hung over his brow, and gave to him a wild appearance—how different, she could not help thinking, from John in his last illness ! She wondered at her own callousness concerning Peter, remembering how her heart had been wrung when she was told that there was no hope for John. Ties of blood are strong, no doubt; but they can be robbed of strength and sweetness alike by indifference and neglect. Peter Bethune had lived for himself and selfish ends all his days, and not many regrets would follow him to the grave.

'Weel, if I maun dee, I maun, I suppose ; but I'm no' that auld,' he said in the same fretful, querulous tone. 'Marget's first man was faur frailer nor me, an' he leeved till he was ninety.'

'Dinna fash yer heid aboot Sammy Tamson, Pete. If yer time's come, ye needna mind; an' if no', ye maun seek for grace noo.'

'Grace! I've never dune onybody ony herm, I'm sure. I've neither been a drucken nor a dishonest man; I've aye paid my way. What mair can a cratur dae ?'

'That'll no' open the door to the kingdom o' heevin, Pete. Ye maun ask the Lord to forgie ye yer sin for the Saviour's sake, or ye canna win there.'

'Aweel, I'm sure He micht forgie me, for I've aye paid my way. Maybe I've never gien that muckle to the kirk, but a body canna gie to a'thing; an' as for gaun every Sawbath, I was gled to get a rest, especially as ye didna get muckle whiles when ye gaed.'

'Aweel, Pete, I canna arguefy wi' ye, my man; only I houp and pray that the Lord 'll hae mercy on yer soul,' said Susan Bethune sorrowfully. 'Sandy 'll maybe be able to mak' the thing plain till ye. I askit Doctor Hay to telegram to him, an' he'll maybe be here the nicht.'

'Aweel, I'll be gled to see him,' said the sick man drowsily, and turning over he fell asleep again; but it was a troubled, uneasy slumber, broken by many a start and moan of pain. Susan Bethune's heart yearned over him unspeakably, but she did not know how to speak or prepare him for the last great change, and could only pray for him in her heart.

The day wore on slowly, but the old man seemed to grow more uneasy and restless, and was never a moment in the same position. It was a wild, wintry day; rain fell in gusty torrents, and the wind howled and whistled through the dreary house with many an uncanny sound, which made Susan Bethune feel eerie and melancholy, and wish for something to divert her thoughts. About the darkening there came a timid knock to the door, and when Susan Bethune opened it she saw a woman standing there, with a little boy clinging to her skirts.

'Weel, my wummin, what d'ye want?' she asked, holding the candle higher, so that she might see the stranger's face.

'I'm Mistress Galbraith—Jeanie Tamson that was,' she said meekly and humbly. 'I was up at the Windygates the day, an' they telt me the maister was awfu' ill. I cam' to speer for him.'

'Come in. Ye was surely fell anxious when ye stravaged the road wi' that bairn on sic a nicht. Come in,' said Susan Bethune drily, and yet her glance was kind and compassionate, and she took the little boy by the hand, and led him into the warm, well-lighted kitchen, the mother following behind.

'Sit ye doon; ye are a puir, jimpy thing, Hae ye no' been weel?' asked Susan abruptly. 'Dinna speak abune yer breath; he's sleepin', ye see, an' he's sair needin't.'

'I've been gey silly sin' my man dee'd; I've haen

N

ower muckle adae,' said the widow. 'It's a sair fecht for a weedy wummin, Miss Bethune.'

'Ay, is it. I was speakin' till him aboot ye the day. He canna mend, the doctor says, an' I wad fain see justice dune afore he dees,' said Susan Bethune in her stern, matter-of-fact way. 'Ye'll no' hae gotten muckle frae him readilys ?'

'No' a bawbee, an' when I made bold to come and speer for my mither's claes an' things efter she dee'd, he cursed and swore at me like a' that,' said the widow. 'D'ye no' think it but richt that I should get something for my bairns ? He got a guid pickle gear and siller wi' my mither.'

'I ken that, lassie, an' I certainly think ye should get whatever was yer mither's, baith claes and siller,' said Susan Bethune decidedly. 'It was a stupid marriage for them baith, I think.'

'Wha's that clashing wi' ye there ?' cried the old man shrilly, waking up out of his sleep, and raising himself on his elbow. 'It's you, Jean Tamson, sittin' at my fireside ! Ye may clear oot, you an' yer bairn, for ye'll no' get naething here. Are ye jist waitin' or I'm a corp tae tak' a big haul ? but ye'll find ye're mista'en, my leddy. Ye marriet a ne'er-do-weel, wha spent a' ye got, and ye maun jist lie on the bed ye hae made. Pit her oot, Shoosan, or I'll rise an' dae't mysel'.'

The little boy, who had been warming himself at the fire, looked in silent terror at the wild old man, glaring at them from between the curtains of the bed, and then set up a shrill scream.

'Gae 'wa' into the ither end, my wummin, whispered Susan Bethune hastily. 'I'll kindle a fire for ye, an' ye can sleep there a' nicht. Awa', see, or he'll be in a perfect fury.' So saying, she lifted the candle, and hurried them away to the other end, and bade them keep quiet there till she had quietened the furious old man.

'Nae suner is a body laid doon wi' a gliff o' cauld even, than there's twa or three, or half a dizzen, sittin' roond like corbies, waitin' or he dee,' he said fumingly. 'Ye'll better get awa' back to the Star, Shoosan; ye're in league wi' thae Tamsons, an' they're a greedy, ill set, that leeve for ever aff ither folk.'

'Wheesht, see, this meenit, or I'll gie ye a fricht, my man,' said Susan Bethune quietly. 'Lie doon, see, an' keep the claes on yersel'. Eh, but ye're a thrawn deil.'

The old man tossed and struggled with the bed-clothes, throwing them off as fast as his sister put them on, until, thoroughly exhausted, he sank back almost gasping for breath.

Then Susan Bethune carefully covered him with the clothes, and turned away with a sore heart. It was a pitiful sight to see the old man struggling on the very brink of the grave, so loth to leave the world, because its gear and concerns were still his only gods. Oh, how different from the calm, beautiful peace with which John had waited his summons home to dwell for ever with the God he had so faithfully served through all his blameless life! She wiped her eyes as she looked into the dancing fire, and prayed that her last end might be like John's. She carried a shovelful of blazing coal into the other end, and built up a roaring fire for the widow and her boy. But she dared not talk to her, lest Peter, hearing their voices, should get into a passion again. About seven o'clock, as she was making a spoonful of porridge for the bairn, the door opened, and the minister of Lochbroom stalked in.

'Eh, man, I'm fell gled to see ye! An' hoo are ye?' she said, shaking him heartily by the hand, and looking with interest into his handsome face, which had a fine ruddy colour just then, owing to the exertion of walking through wind and rain.

'I am very well, thank you, Aunt Susan ; and how are you?' he asked. 'I got Hay's telegram about half-past one, just in time to catch the two express, or I wouldn't have been here to-night. How is he?'

'Faur through. He's sleepin' again, an' nae wunner, efter the ferment he's been in. Eh, he's an awfu' auld cratur! I houp, Sandy, ye'll be able to pit him in a better frame o' mind. He's faur frae bein' ready to dee. But ye'll be a' weet?'

'Oh no, it is more wind than rain. When did you come from Star?'

'Only yestreen. He's no' been lang ill, but he canna lest. Eh, man, ye're growin' an awfu' wise-like chield!'

'Wasn't I always that, Aunt Susan?' he asked with a smile. 'When did you hear from Jamie?'

'Yesterday. He never misses his day,' said the old woman with happy pride. 'Isn't he a wunnerfu' chap?'

'He's going to succeed after all. There's a terrible resolution in him,' said the minister, drawing in his chair to the fire. 'Why, what's that?' he added with a start, for the sound of a child's prattle fell upon his ears.

'That's puir Jean Tamson, yer Auntie Marget's lassie, that was left a weedy intae Leven, ye ken,' whispered Aunt Susan. 'She's come ower, nae doot, to see what she can get for hersel' an' her bairns, an' I canna blame her. If ye get ony crack wi' yer uncle ava', ye maun try an' show him his duty. That puir cratur has mair need o' a pickle siller than either you or Jamie.'

'Has he made a will?' asked the minister musingly.

'Ay, so he says, but what'll be in't dear only kens. We can hardly expeck it to be just. He disna ken the meanin' o' the word. Eh, man, I canna but think on the difference between his last days an' yer faither's. Thon was an end we a' may envy.'

'They were always very different,' said the minister rather abruptly, for memory had a sting; then he changed the subject, and led her on to talk of other things.

'You look as if you needed a rest, Aunt Susan. I'll sit up with Uncle Peter to-night,' he said at length. 'And I'll promise to wake you when he needs anything.'

'Very weel; I'm no' sweer, for I'm fell tired. He's soon' yet, an' it's a peety to wauken him. I'll lie doon in the front o' the bed beside Jeanie, an' ye can gie's a cry when he waukens. Here's the sofa for ye.'

The minister threw off his boots, and, covering himself with the old plaid, lay down, but not to sleep. Thought was busy within, and memory was at work. The present, with all its absorbing, passionate interests, its hopes, fears, and indescribable yearnings, was absorbed in contemplation of the past. A voice seemed to arise out of that dead past, asking him warningly whether he was redeeming the speeding time; whether he had aught to show for all that had been given to him; whether, in the sphere of life whither he had been called, he had conscientiously and unselfishly done what he could. We do not often welcome such thoughts. He is a happy man who can look within without fear, who can think with calm satisfaction of duty well done; who has no accusing voice to whisper, 'Thou art the man.' Self in a selfish man is its own avenger.

'Shoosan, gie me a drink!' The feeble, faltering request broke Sandy Bethune's reverie, and he leaped to his feet.

'Wha are you?' asked the sick man wonderingly. 'Oh, it's you, Sandy! When did ye come?'

'An hour or two ago. I am sorry to see you so poorly, Uncle Peter,' he said, laying his firm, strong hand on the poor nerveless fingers. 'Are you feeling very weak?'

'Oo ay, I'm clean dune. Are you come to look efter the bawbees tae?'

Sandy Bethune's face flushed, for no such thought had as yet presented itself to his mind.

'Ye dinna like that,' chuckled the old man. 'Aweel, I canna blame ye. Set up Shoosan, wull ye? I canna get breath.'

The minister went out into the lobby, gently called to his aunt, and then returned to the bedside. Seeing the difficulty the old man felt in breathing, he put his arm round his shoulder, and raised him up among the pillows. The fast glazing eyes looked up into his with a look of strange questioning, which was painful in its intensity.

'Ye're a minister, Sandy. Whaur d'ye think I'll gang in the ither warld?

'If you trust in God's promises, Uncle Peter, you will go to heaven.'

'Ay, but what's the promises? I canna mind them. I wish I had leeved a different life. The wull's i' the drawer up the stair; ye'll get the key in my breek pooch. I'm no' able to alter 't noo, but ye'll see Jean Tamson disna want, an' share the rest wi' Jamie; I was maybe ower hard on him.   Is that you, Shoosan?'

'Ay, it's me, Peter, my man; ye're slippin' awa',' said Susan Bethune with her apron to her eyes.   'Pray for yer uncle, Sandy.'

'Never heed noo,' said the old man in a drowsy whisper.   'He'll maybe lat me in, for I've aye—paid— my—way.'

CHAPTER XV.

RETRIBUTION.

'For her sweet sake he sinned, and she would
Have none of him. He paid the price, and went
Forth to the night alone.'

At the old-fashioned bureau in the best room at Auchtermairnie sat the minister of Lochbroom, the flickering candlelight gleaming fitfully on his face, which wore an expression of perplexity almost amounting to bewilderment. It was about five o'clock in the morning. Susan Bethune and Jeanie Thomson, after having performed the last offices for the dead, had laid themselves down again to snatch an hour or two's repose. There was no need to watch any more by Peter Bethune now. Sandy had lain down, too, on the sofa in the kitchen, but, though he was no coward, he could not close his eyes and the dead so near. It is a strange mystery—the awe and dread with which mortal clay can fill the living; the bravest of us quail at the touch of the unseen. So the minister had been glad to escape from the kitchen, and now, in his absorbing interest in the papers before him, he had forgotten his natural shrinking.

It was the last will and testament of Peter Bethune, farmer in Auchtermairnie, and its contents were brief enough, yet wholly satisfactory to Sandy Bethune. For it made him sole and absolute heir to everything that had pertained to his dead uncle; and when he opened the bank-book lying in one of the pigeon-holes, he started in surprise at the substantial balance lying to his account in the Commercial Bank at Leven.

It came within a few shillings of three thousand pounds; and, when the stock and crop and implements were sold, would make a very snug little fortune. And it was all his, left to him absolutely and entirely in the document before him, which none dared dispute. The minister of Lochbroom was not a mercenary man,—that is, he had not Peter Bethune's love of gold for its own sake,—but he was keenly alive to the influence and import-ance it could confer upon its possessor. As he sat there in the dim stillness of the early morning, new hopes and loveliest dreams sprang in his heart, dreams and hopes which had but one centre—Beatrice Lorraine. With what confidence could he ask her from her father now when he had something more than his meagre stipend to offer! His heart bounded, his pulses leaped at the thought. But there was Jamie, and his uncle's step-daughter down-stairs, the old man's dying charge. Was it not as sacred and binding as any written words? He rose, pushed back his hair from his brow, and, walking over to the unshuttered window, looked out upon the dawning day. Strange thoughts chased each other through his brain, his heart beat almost to suffocation, his brow reddened, his hand upon the window-sill trembled as if with ague. Temptation had him in its fiercest thrall. With a deep, heavy sigh, which was almost a groan, he turned about at length, and, stealing softly downstairs, went out of doors. It was a calm, quiet morning, with a strange, grey stillness lying over all, as if the earth were weary after the beating of the storm. One long yellow line away to eastward gave promise of the wintry sunrise, the only break in the grey expanse of sky. He stood only a moment on the threshold, and then turned away through the corn-yard, where the busy poultry were already enjoying their morning meal. The ground was wet and sodden, and covered with the last autumn leaves which the night wind had whirled from the chestnut trees. They rustled under his feet as he walked, but he paid no heed; his own thoughts were all-absorbing. He clasped his hands behind his back, and walked slowly, with his eyes bent on the ground, following unconsciously the pathway which led up to the higher fields. The light broadened as he went, and the misty shadows began to rise from the uplands as the new day stole upon the earth. He stood still at length at a little stile, and, folding his arms on its mossy rail, looked about him curiously, almost as a stranger might have looked at what was unfamiliar. Yet he knew every rood and pole, every stone and land-mark for miles around; no scenery in the world would ever be more familiar than what was spread before him at that moment. It had a dreary and desolate look in the chill morning light,—the barren stubble fields; the potato fields, with only heaps of sodden shaws and the long, newly-filled pits to tell of what had been; the bare pasture-lands, bleached and sodden with the rains; the swollen burns and leafless trees, all seemed to say sadly and pitifully that the reign of winter had begun. Yet there were some comforting things too in that wide prospect; each homestead had its well-filled stackyard, and on the earlier lands the lea had its long regular furrows already upturned for winter wheat. He turned his face towards the Star, with its background of purple-brown moss, framed by the graceful peaks of the Lomonds. He could see the thatched roof of his father's house; how long it seemed since he had been wont to call it home! He could see the Knowe too, and could even discern some figures moving about the out-buildings, the ploughmen, probably, beginning the labour of another day. As is often the case in moments of strong feeling, he was keenly observant of every minute detail, even when his mind was fully occupied by something else. Alexander Bethune had a battle to fight that winter's day; a grand opportunity offered itself for him to obtain a signal victory over himself. But he did not face it yet. He preferred rather to hover about the temptation, to try and parry a little with an evil thought, picturing to himself all it would involve and all it would give, although assuring himself all the while that he would never do the wrong with which he was tempted. Still thinking, still picturing all the advantages which might be his if he allowed his uncle's will to stand, he began slowly to retrace his steps to the house. The inmates were now astir, Aunt Susan busying herself with the breakfast, and inclined to grumble because she had allowed the day to get so far ahead of her.

'Come awa' an' get yer bite, Sandy,' she said when she heard him come in. 'I saw ye awa' up the Whummle Brae. It's near eicht a'ready; I declare there's nae day the noo. Wull ye can bide or the funeral's ower?'

'Yes; I'll go to Edinburgh to-morrow, and see

about supply.   I think I'll walk down to Leven this morning.'

'Are ye gaun to get a'thing frae Leven?   Yer uncle said the meer wad jist tak' him in, an' a'thing could be dune as cheap's possible.   Puir cratur, he bothered hissel' aboot siller to the hinder-end.'

'That's nonsense, Aunt Susan.   He must have a proper funeral,' said the minister testily.   'I'll need to telegraph to Jamie too.'

'Eh, I houp he'll can get, for I'm fain to see him,' said Aunt Susan with a tremor in her voice.   'It'll need ye baith onyway, for there'll be a heap adae. There'll hae to be a roup in Auchtermairnie at last.'

'I suppose so.   It is a pity Jamie had not been at home to step into Uncle Peter's shoes.   It would have suited him very well, if only he could have brought himself to think it.'

Aunt Susan shook her head.

'The laddie kent his ain ken best.   The way fermin' is noo, he's better whaur he is.   But this'll be a windfa' for you, Sandy.   Yer uncle telt me yestreen that ye get a'.   But ye'll mind Jamie, an' that puir cratur ben the hoose onyway.'

'Of course, of course!' said the minister hastily, and bent his head low over his cup, for the hot blood rushed to his face and dyed it red.

'I threepit wi' him to be just wi' his gear, but ye micht as weel threep wi' a stane dyke,' said Aunt Susan, not noticing her nephew's slight confusion.   'Aweel, a'thing comes tae an end.   An' hoo are ye comin' on at Lochbroom?   When are ye gaun to bring yer braw wife to the manse?   Jamie telt me aboot her last time he was ower.'

'Jamie is too ready with his tongue, Aunt Susan,' said

the minister shortly. 'It was time enough for him to speak so sure when I am sure myself. I have never asked any woman to come to the manse yet.'

'Aweel, ye needna be sae short. I wasna speerin' an impident question, Sandy,' said the old woman candidly. 'Are ye for awa' to Leven a'ready? Laddie, ye're jist like that kittle mare o' yer uncle's—ye canna rest a meenit. A body disna get muckle crack o' you.'

'I had better go and get everything ready, for if I don't get supply, I'll be obliged to go home and come back in time for the funeral on Monday. I'll telegraph to Jamie at once, and see if he can come.' So saying, Sandy put on his coat, took his hat and umbrella, and set out for Leven.

The message was duly sent, but the answer came back that it would be impossible for Jamie to come, as he was just starting for Inverness to report the proceedings of a Highland Convention which was to last for two or three days. The minister failed in securing supply, and was obliged to go home next day, so that Susan Bethune was left alone at Auchtermairnie over the Sabbath. But she kept Jeanie and the boy with her, and they were nothing loth to stay. On Monday forenoon Sandy returned, and followed his Uncle Peter's remains to the grave. He was the only near relative, for none of the old man's step-sons attended, though they were all within easy distance. They had always been at war, and would not put themselves about to pay any respect to him now. These things of course occasioned plenty of talk both in Windygates and the Star, and the Bethunes and their affairs at that time got an extra redd-up. The roup would be the next excitement, followed by the entrance of a new tenant to Auchtermairnie. During the next few weeks the minister of Lochbroom had a busy time of it, running between Auchtermairnie and his own parish. Everybody agreed that he had been very generous to Jeanie Thomson; for he had not only given her everything that had been her mother's, but made her a present of ten pounds and all the gear left in the house after Aunt Susan had taken away such things as were valuable in her eyes because of their old associations.

While all this was going on, Jamie was working hard at Glasgow, and never giving a thought to his Uncle Peter's money or gear. He was kept busy late and early, for the season had begun in Glasgow, and he had so many meetings to attend that he sometimes hardly knew how to manage them all. There would be no holiday for him, he wrote his aunt, until winter was past. He had very little leisure for his own special work, yet time was far from being lost to him. His employers, speedily recognising in him a mind above the average, and being willing to help him as far as lay in their power, in return for his conscientious and unremitting attention to their business, made a point of sending him to all the best meetings, where he could hear men of culture and experience lecture or speak; and so a new and valuable field was opened up to him. Apart from his duties as a reporter, he was asked sometimes to contribute articles on social or literary topics for the weekly issue of the *Journal*, for which he was handsomely paid. Altogether it looked as if he had reached that tide in his affairs which, if taken at the flood, would lead him on to fortune. Martinmas saw great changes at Auchtermairnie. The roup was a great success, and brought in a clear thousand to the lucky minister of Lochbroom. There had been keen competition among the bidders, and the new tenant, a Kirkcaldy grocer, with plenty of means but little skill in farming, was made to pay very sweetly for what stock and implements he purchased. When it was all over, and everything turned into hard cash, Sandy wrote to his brother, telling him about his uncle's will, and offering to help him with some money, which he might regard as a loan if he liked. But Jamie wrote back at once, congratulating him upon his good fortune, and thanking him for his offer, which, however, he declined. His salary was sufficient for his needs, and he was saving money fast. In the last sentence he threw out a hint about Beatrice Lorraine, and expressed the hope that he would hear something definite concerning her at no distant date. It did not cost James Bethune any sting to write in such a strain, for, though he had been deeply interested in the woman Sandy had so long loved, it had been a strange, distant kind of interest, which one might feel in some object dazzling and desirable, perhaps, but far out of reach. He looked back upon that evening spent at the manse of St. Giles as a bright spot in his existence which he would never forget. The face of Beatrice Lorraine was engraven on his heart; he could recall every changing expression, every flash of light in the magnificent eyes, every sweet intonation of her voice ; but he believed that when she became his brother's wife he should be able to regard her as a sister, whom it was a privilege and an honour to love with a brother's love. And so his memory of her was no disturbing element, but rather a sweet, ennobling thought, urging him on towards everything good.

Jamie's letter set the minister of Lochbroom a-thinking that December evening when it came. He had been so much from home of late that he had seen very little of the Lorraines. Why should he wait any longer ? He had no hope of ever being sure of her answer to the question which would make him a happy or a miserable man. No woman had ever so puzzled him before; her very indifference to him rendered her doubly desirable in his eyes. He was not altogether without hope; the flattery and attention to which he had long been accustomed from other women made him inclined to believe that this one would not refuse.

As he sat there in the stillness, heart and mind filled with thoughts of her, there came to him a great yearning to look upon her face, to hear from her lips the words which would make for him weal or woe. There was no reason why he should not see her within that very hour, so he rose, and, following his own impulse, left the house, and turned along the now familiar Cleugh road.

It was a bright, clear, frosty night, with a brilliant moon at its full. There were white caps on the Lanark hills, and the north wind was biting enough to hint at a promise of more snow. There were no leaves in the Nethercleugh woods now, and on the burn path it was almost as clear as day. But the minister of Lochbroom could have walked that way blindfolded, he knew every step by heart. He walked quickly, for the air was bitterly cold, and his whole appearance was that of a man who had an end in view. In little more than half an hour he stood on the stone steps of the house, ringing for admittance.

'Mr. Lorraine is not at home, sir, but Miss Lorraine is,' said the servant who answered his summons.

'I will see Miss Lorraine, if you please,' he replied abruptly, and the girl looked at him in slight surprise, missing the accustomed pleasant word which made him so popular with his parishioners.

'Very well, sir,' she said, and shut the door, while he took off his hat and coat. Then she opened the library

door and announced him by name. As he entered he
heard the rustle of a silken robe, and in the dim firelight saw Beatrice Lorraine rise from her low chair on
the hearth.

'How do you do, Mr. Bethune? I am all alone and in
darkness, you see,' she said, and he fancied her voice a
little unsteady. 'Please let us have candles at once,
Kitty,' she added to the servant. 'Papa is not at home,
Mr. Bethune.'

'But he will return to-night?'

'Oh yes. Uncle John and Aunt Dora are at Lockerbie Manse, and papa has gone to dine with them. I
was disappointed that I could not accompany him, but
I have had a cold for some days, and papa would not
allow me to go out,' she answered, and as the maid
lighted the candles in the silver sconces on the mantel,
she averted her face a little, half shading it with her
hand. The gesture caused the lace at her sleeves to fall
back to the elbow, revealing the exquisite contour of the
round white arm,—the most beautiful arm the minister
of Lochbroom had ever seen. The maid stirred up the
fire and left the room, then a constrained silence fell
upon its occupants.

'When did you hear from your brother? He is well,
I hope?' said Beatrice at length, but still her eyes were
averted, as if she could not meet his gaze.

'I do not hear from him very often, but I believe he
is well; and I know he is very busy. He was always
a plodder.'

'He will succeed, I am sure. When will he pay a
visit to Lochbroom?'

'I can't tell. He seems to have no time for anything
but work. Life is hardly worth living at the price he
pays for it.'

o

'I would not say that. Work is a noble and ennobling thing. I sometimes wish I had not such an idle life. It is not easy to know just what is one's duty,' she said musingly, and her hand fell from her cheek, and then he saw traces of tears in the magnificent eyes; they moved him to the very depths.

'It is a quiet life you lead here, Miss Lorraine. Not many like you would be so content.'

'It is easy to be content beside those we love, is it not?' she asked with a swift, bright smile. 'It is only at times I fret when I see what good others do while I live at ease here. Perhaps my opportunity will come some day; at present my duty is to my father, and nothing must interfere with it.'

'Would you never leave him?'

'Not while he needs me,' she answered, and her colour rose, for there was deep significance in his tone.

There was a moment's intense silence, then the minister rose to his feet. His face paled, his eyes shone, his lips trembled a little when he spoke.

'Then there would be no hope for any who might seek your love?' he said almost hoarsely. 'Beatrice, I stand before you to-night an unworthy suppliant, with nothing but my love to recommend me. That is earnest and true, it will make or mar my life. What have you to say?'

She raised her hand almost in pleading, the red dyed her cheek, and then left it very pale, her voice fell almost to a whisper.

'Oh, hush! Do not say that; I cannot listen. I believe what you say, but it can never be.'

'Because of your duty to your father?' he asked, taking a step nearer to where she stood, in her great beauty, the woman for whose sake he had laid a sin upon his conscience, perhaps in vain.

'I could not leave him, but it is not that. I'—

'In other circumstances,' he interrupted, with the painful, eager intensity of a man speaking of a vital matter. 'If I wait—if I prove to you by years of devotion the sincerity and depth of my love—would there still be no hope?'

He was making her suffer keenly; to a sensitive, deepfeeling nature it is always a terrible thing to inflict pain upon another.

'It would be wrong—unkind—to mislead you,' she said hurriedly. 'It could never be. I could never be worthy of the love you offer. I am deeply grateful, but I could never be your wife.'

'Never?' he repeated, and there was a ring of despair in his voice. 'Miss Lorraine, I have been and am a weak, faulty, erring man. You would help me to a better life. Without you I dare not think of what the future will be. You have become a part of myself; I cannot give you up.'

'Oh, hush! To-morrow you will regret these wild words. I cannot think that life does not hold many dearer interests,' she said, and laid her white hand on the mantel as if seeking some support. 'May I ask you to go now? I cannot bear any more.'

'Is your decision final and unalterable, Miss Lorraine?' he asked in a low voice, though his eyes still gleamed with passionate feeling.

'Yes, yes; final and unalterable,' she answered brokenly. 'I am very sorry. Life is full of hard things, and we have all sorrow to endure. Forgive me if I have caused you pain; I would not do so willingly.'

He spoke no word in reply, but, turning upon his heel, quitted the room and the house. That was a dark hour indeed for the minister of Lochbroom; the light of hope

was quenched for ever in his aching heart. He had loved
and lost; was there not a grim justice in his pain? At
the Knowe, Mary Campbell endured her own heart-sickness, hiding it from the prying world, and feeling that
for her all interest in life had fled. What saith the
Scriptures? 'With what measure ye mete, it shall be
measured to you again.'

CHAPTER XVI.

SHADOWED LIVES.

'Oh, memories! oh, past that is!'

GEO. ELIOT.

'MY daughter, are you not in bed yet? Do you know it is nearly midnight?'

'Yes, papa; but I wanted to wait for you. Had you a pleasant evening?'

'Very, but we missed you.'

Mr. Lorraine wheeled in his favourite chair to the fire, and stretched out his hands to the cheerful blaze with a sigh of content.

'There is no place like home, Beatrice, and home is the best place for me now. I sometimes feel that I am a shadow on the cheerfulness of others. Not that I grudge them their enjoyment, only I cannot share it.'

'You only imagine it, dear papa. You are not so gloomy as you think,' said Beatrice affectionately. 'I am so glad you had a pleasant evening. How are Uncle John and Aunt Dora?'

'Very well indeed. They intended going home to-morrow, but will come up here and spend the day instead. They were so disappointed at not seeing you. You are very dear to them, Beatrice, and I do not wonder at it. My darling, every day I live I wonder more and more at my own blindness and at your beautiful unselfishness.'

'Hush, papa! I have only done my duty, nothing more, and love has always made it sweet,' said Beatrice, rising from her chair and sitting on a low stool at her father's knee.

He laid his thin white hand on her head with a touch full of love,—a touch which thrilled her through and through. There was an element of remorse in his love which gave it a strange intensity; every caressing touch and tender glance seemed laden with a prayer for forgiveness. The foundation upon which he had first built all his paternal hopes and love had failed him, and in his desolation he had turned to the daughter whose existence had till then scarcely cost him a moment's thought. In a careless fashion he had seen that she was provided with all she required; he had sent her to the best schools at home and abroad, but he had made no effort to win her confidence, or to still the hunger of her motherless heart. And so she had grown up still, reserved, self-contained, an enigma to those who knew her best.

But when the blow fell on her father's heart, when the son he had idolized and indulged paid him back in the bitter coin of ingratitude and shame, she revealed herself, and, stepping into the gap, laid a tender hand on the gaping wound, softening and healing it with a matchless tenderness and unselfishness, and making her love a shelter and solace upon which he learned to lean with an intensity which surprised himself.

'But what kind of an evening had you, my dear? Did you not find it very dull? You are paler than when I went away. If you have not improved to-morrow we must have the doctor up.'

'Oh no, I am all right,' she said quickly, and averted her face a moment from the keen, tender eyes bent so searchingly upon it. 'Mr. Bethune was here to-night, papa.'

'I am glad to hear it; he would help to pass an hour pleasantly. And what has become of him lately? we seem to have seen so little of him.'

'Papa, may I tell you something?' Beatrice asked, with an exquisite gesture of trust and hesitation.

Her father gave a great start: there was something in the rising colour, in the lowered voice and hesitating manner, which sent a sudden fear to his heart. Was his 'one ewe lamb' about to be taken, when he had but newly learned its priceless value?

'What is it, my dear? Do not keep me in suspense.'

'I do not know whether I ought to tell you, papa, but it weighs so heavily on my heart that I must,' she said in a low voice. 'He asked me to be his wife, and I was afraid lest I had unconsciously encouraged him to expect a different answer.'

'Then you have refused him, my darling?' and suddenly she felt her father's arms round her, and he drew her very close to his heart.

For a moment there was nothing said, but that embrace was full of sweetness to the heart of Beatrice Lorraine, for it said more strongly than words how dear and necessary she had become to her father's happiness.

'But, Beatrice, it was not on my account?' he added

suddenly. ' You are not sacrificing your own happiness out of your love for me ? '

' Oh no, papa ! I could never marry him. I like him very well as an acquaintance, but I could never marry him.'

' I am glad of it.'

' Why, papa ? '

' Because he is not worthy of you. He is an eloquent preacher and a clever young man, but there is a something about him which makes me doubt him. May I be forgiven my harsh judgment, but I do not think him either manly or sincere.'

' I have had something of the same doubt, papa, though I have always tried to banish it. It seems to me almost as if he had two personalities, only one of which is revealed to the world. And he is too conscious of himself, as if self were the centre of his ideas and the mainspring of his actions.'

' You have a keen and observant eye, my darling. Our minister is a thoroughly selfish man. I have watched him keenly, especially since I feared lest he should rob me of yourself. His brother, now, whom we met in Edinburgh, is a very different sort. Do you remember him ? '

Beatrice smiled, and made no answer.

Did she remember him ? How often had the earnest face of James Bethune risen up before her ! How often had she recalled his grave, heartfelt words,—the words of a man to whom life was serious and true, and whose idea of its mystery and meaning was wholly noble ! Ay, she remembered him, perhaps too well.

' There is another thing, Beatrice, which makes me glad that you have not accepted him,' said her father presently. ' I am told he was engaged for a number of years—almost since boyhood, I believe—to a young girl in his native place. They say that since he succeeded in life he has become ashamed of her. Is that manly, Beatrice?'

'No; if it is true, it is cowardly and shameful,' said Beatrice with flashing eye. 'Oh, papa, I sometimes think that the less we know about our neighbours the better. There is so much which hurts and jars upon us, and of course it must be the same with those who know us. We do not always do our duty, even though we know it. If I had cared for Mr. Bethune, *that* would have been a very bitter thing to know.'

There was a moment's silence, broken at length by a sudden gust of wind and the rattle of hailstones on the panes.

'The storm is rising, surely, papa. It was a lovely evening when I looked out just before you came in!' exclaimed Beatrice.

'I saw the north clouds spreading over the sky as we drove over the hill,' answered Mr. Lorraine. 'We must look for storms now, I suppose; winter is fairly upon us.'

'Papa!' The girl's voice fell almost to a whisper, and her fingers closed over his with a pleading touch. 'When I hear the wind and the rain raging outside, I cannot sleep. I seem to see Willie always a miserable outcast, with no shelter to go to. I see him so often in my thoughts and dreams,' she added with a bursting sob, 'that I think it must be true. Has he not been punished enough, papa? Let us go away back to London and seek him out. I am sure he would be good now, and he may have suffered, we do not know how keenly. I feel as if I should die sometimes living here in idle affluence, when he may be perishing for lack of the necessaries of life. Listen, papa,' she continued when he would have interrupted her : 'you know how difficult it is even for the deserving to get work in London ; what chance is there for those who have no character or recommendation ? Papa, we may be doing a great sin in thus leaving him, perhaps to sink into deeper crime.'

The beautiful face, pale in its passionate pleading, the yearning eyes fixed on his face, the pleading touch, might have moved him to compassion ; but his heart was steeled against the boy who had disgraced him, and he would not listen. The tenderness died out of his face, and it became set in the old stern mould, which, as a child, Beatrice Lorraine had been wont to dread.

'No, no ; he deserves it all. Whatever he may suffer, he deserves it all. He will never suffer as I have done ; it is not in him ; he is a heartless, selfish boy,' he said, rising to his feet, as if to escape from these speaking eyes and that pleading tongue. 'Beatrice, how often have I forbidden this subject ? Why *will* you intrude it in the few moments of peace and happiness I enjoy ?'

'It was because I thought your heart was softened that I spoke, papa,' said Beatrice with a sob. 'I cannot promise to be silent. Something makes me speak. I believe some day I shall go away myself and seek him out. I do not think it right to let him sink. Christ came to seek and to save the lost.'

Darker still grew the dark brow of William Lorraine, his lips twitched, his hands nervously clenched ; his whole appearance was that of a man labouring under the strongest emotion. He seemed about to speak, but restrained himself, and without a word walked slowly out of the room.

'Christ came to seek and to save the lost.' These words rang their haunting changes in his ears through the long hours of a sleepless night. Beatrice heard him walking to and fro his room, and, guessing something of the conflict raging in his heart, prayed that he might be softened.

She was early down-stairs next morning, anxious to know whether these prayers were to have the answer for which she longed. But the moment she saw her father's face her hope fell; it was calm, stern, immovable, and, though he spoke to her kindly and affectionately as usual, she felt distant from him, as if some barrier had sprung up between them. A little longer yet she must taste the heart-sickness of hope deferred.

As the winter wore on, a feeling of dissatisfaction with the minister began to get abroad in the church of Loch-broom. His sermons were neither so well prepared nor so eloquently delivered, and he 'fell away' in his visitation and other outdoor work. A lukewarmness crept into the pews, and the pulpit was blamed for it. The people began to restrain themselves in giving, and Lochbroom no longer enjoyed the reputation it had gained during the earlier days of Mr. Bethune's ministry, of being one of the most liberal and prosperous parishes in the south of Scotland. The older men in the church shook their heads, and said that they had feared the result of being carried away by flowery eloquence and outward show, and that they were not surprised. The minister not only grew careless in the performance of his duties, but he made no secret of his desire for a change; and was a great deal away from home, preaching on trial in vacant kirks. The good people of Lochbroom were puzzled to account for all this, but it never occurred even to the busybodies to connect the change in their minister with a woman, least of all with Miss Lorraine. The household at Nethercleugh lived in such seclusion and retirement, and mingled themselves so little with county folk or county affairs, that there was very little to be said about them. Then the minister wisely made no change in his demeanour towards them, neither did he cease visiting at Nethercleugh, as many in the circumstances would have done.

James Bethune was still working hard in Glasgow, and had never been able to spare a holiday to visit Lochbroom. Letters passed occasionally between the brothers, and, as Sandy never said anything about Beatrice Lorraine, Jamie concluded that things were just as they had been a year ago, and he had an occasional smile over his brother's dilatoriness in this particular matter. It was so unlike his usual rapid, impulsive way of rushing at things, and getting them settled one way or other without delay. Very steadily, and with rapid strides considering all things, James Bethune cleared his way before him, and gradually approached the realization of his life-dream. From writing occasional bits for the weekly issue of the *Glasgow Journal*, he was promoted to the writing of leading articles for the daily issue, for which his clear, concise literary style was peculiarly suited ; and it did the *Journal* good, for his views of the burning questions of the day were wise, moderate, and liberal, and insensibly his articles improved the tone of the paper. Consequently he had very little reporting work to do; for his employers said that he would prove a distinct acquisition to them, and that if they could retain him it would pay them to give him every encouragement. He still devoted part of his scanty leisure to self-improvement and purely literary work, but what he wrote did not find its way into print, but was locked in his desk for future reference or use. There was no need for him to write just because his wares could find a market; he hoped the time would come when he would be able to give to the world a piece of literary work which would be worthy to be read, and to which all these little bits would contribute. He studied life under the many aspects the great city offered, he invaded its lowest parts, and took mental portraits of its denizens and surroundings, which were a great revelation and a vast sorrow to him too. How little he had dreamed of such depths of destitution and crime and misery in the old quiet days at the Star, where there might be decent poverty, but nothing so debasing and terrible as he found in the east end of Glasgow! The state of the masses became a problem to him which occupied every free moment of his waking hours, and became the haunting spectre of his dreams.

It weighed upon his heart, he took things still so terribly in earnest, but it seemed to be a hopeless, in-solvable problem, for when could one man hope to make any difference or improvement among so many thousands? His effort, however strenuous and well-directed, would be in very truth only a drop in the ocean. He lived a very isolated life in Glasgow, for, though he visited occasion-ally at his employer's abode, and also at the residence of his minister, he had found no second manse of St. Giles. The memories circling round that dear home were fresh and beautiful and sweet, shut in that corner of his heart to which he came when weary or oppressed with heart-ache and loneliness. For such moments came, ay, very often, to the strong man wrestling in the forefront of life's battle; he had still many a bitter yearning after the hidden sweetness involved in the words love and home. The old Star home yet remained unchanged for him so

far as Aunt Susan was concerned, but she was growing
very old and very frail, though she would not admit it.
He had seen the change when he went over at the New
Year holidays, and that, too, vexed and troubled him, for
it was a sad sight to see an aged person alone, with none
to bestow that care and kindly attention which age so
peculiarly requires.

It was the early summer before he could pay a second
visit to the Star, and then it was only to convey the
news of a great change about to take place in his life.
Aunt Susan was slowly and laboriously hoeing her potato
patch one June evening, thinking of him as usual, and
troubling herself because his weekly letter had not come
that morning, when Jamie himself came down the Lang
Raw, and swung open the garden gate. She could not see
him, of course, being in the park at the back of the house,
but he had caught sight of her the moment he reached
the top of the Cunan Hill on his way from Markinch.
His keen, far-reaching eye would have recognised her
tall figure and her red and yellow sun - bonnet at a
greater distance.   He stood a moment just inside the
garden gate, looking at the little flower-plots, which were
quite overgrown with yellow hollyhocks and pink and white
phloxes and garden poppies.   It was a curious medley of
form and colour, but as the beds of thyme and clumps of
peppermint and balsam sent up their strong perfume, his
heart filled somehow ; these very odours were redolent
of memories bitter and sweet.   He turned about, and,
lifting the sneck, went into the kitchen.   It was a low-
roofed, close place that summer evening, filled with the
smell and the vapour of the peat-reek.   How quaint and
strange it all looked,—the primitive, whitewashed fireside
with the bars to keep in the peats ; the heavy, old-
fashioned chairs ; the high, narrow box beds ; the little

deal table; the 'wag-at-the wa',' whose face was yellow with age, its brilliant-hued roses dimmed with the peat-reek of years. It was strange, and yet how familiar! As James Bethune sat down in his father's arm-chair, it almost seemed as if the last two years of his life were a dream, and he was only resting after a day at the harrows or the reaper, he felt so much at home. He was sitting thus, with his arms folded across his breast, his face wearing a far-off, dreamy look, when Aunt Susan suddenly appeared on the scene.

'Mercy upon us!' she exclaimed, half in terror, half in surprise at sight of the stranger at her fireside.

'How are you, Aunt Susan? Not know me, eh? It was a shame to come upon you unawares,' said Jamie, jumping up and gripping both her hands. Then, to his great amazement, she burst into tears. He could not but feel moved at that sight, for when had he seen Aunt Susan weep? Surely she must be frailer and weaker even than he had dreamed.

'Wheesht, auntie,' he said tenderly, and guided the faltering steps to a chair, placing her in it very gently, and then patting her shoulder as he might have done to a child.

'Eh, but I'm a silly cratur,' she said presently, looking up at him with a smile. 'But my heart's been a kind o' grit a' day, because yer letter didna come. Little did I ken what e'enin' was to bring. An' hoo are ye, my ain bairn? Hae ye gotten yer tea?'

It was comical and yet pathetic to hear her call the great broad-shouldered man her 'ain bairn,' but he would always be that to her.

'Yes, but I'll take another cup wi' you, auntie,' he said cheerily. 'I can tell ye I was mad when I saw ye frae the tap o' the Cunan Hill wi' a hoe in yer hand.

What did ye promise me when I was here at New Year?
I aye thocht ye a woman o' yer word.'

It came very naturally to him to speak in the old
Scotch way, and Aunt Susan listened as if it was the
sweetest music she had ever heard in her life.

'Hoots, I wasna daein' muckle, only playin' mysel', an'
the tatties are gaun ower's a' thegither. Dauvit Cam'll
canna win at them or Monday. This heat's brocht
a'thing on at aince. Ye needna fash yer heid, Jamie,
my man. I'll no' hurt mysel' wi' wark. When I sit
doon wi' my haunds fauldit, laddie, I'll just fa' in like a
gysened tub. But what's brocht ye here sae sudden?
Is't yer holidays, or what?'

'No, auntie, there are not going to be many holidays
for me this year,' answered Jamie. 'I've come to tell
you about another shift I am going to make.'

'Anither shift! Tak' care, laddie; ye ken the rowin'
stane gethers nae moss. Are ye for awa' frae Glesca
a'ready?'

'It is to be a change for the better, auntie, and it has
come to me without my seeking. I have got the offer of
a situation in London, and I thought it my duty to accept
it; indeed, it was a very gratifying surprise. Many men
have worked harder and longer than I without ever
getting such a chance.'

'Tae Lunnon!' repeated Aunt Susan slowly, and her
poor old eyes uplifted themselves to the face of her
laddie with a pathetic wistfulness which nearly broke
him down. 'Aweel, laddie, ye ken best. When I gied
ye up, I gied ye up, an' if it's for yer betterment, I
mauna complain. But Lunnon's a faur road, an' an ill
place for a young chield. Ye'll need a' yer grace to guide
ye there, Jamie.'

'Aunt Susan, do you know what I was wondering, as

I came up the road from Markinch? I was wondering whether you wouldn't come with me. I could get a little house with a garden a little way out of London, and we might be very comfortable together. Would you not think it over?'

Aunt Susan lifted her hands in sheer horror at the thought.

'Me gang to Lunnon! Laddie, ye are haverin' noo. I've never sleepit a nicht ooten Fife i' my life! Hoo cud ye think I wad live in Lunnon? Na, na; ye maun gang yer way yersel' or ye get a wife, an' canty wad I be to see the day, if she was worthy o' ye. No' but what I'm prood o' yer offer, my man; an' I'll never forget that ye was wullint tae tak' yer auld Star auntie wi' ye; but I'll dee at hame. An' if ye mind me as weel in Lunnon as ye've mindit me in Glesca, I'll hae nae reason to complain.'

'I am loth to leave you, auntie. It is hard that you should have nobody to take care of you now when you need it most.'

'Dinna you fash yer thoomb aboot me, Jamie. I'm no' ill aff as lang's Dauvit an' Jean Cam'll's at the Knowe,' said Aunt Susan cheerfully. 'An' Mary's a perfeck godsend to me. She comes doon every ither nicht or twa wi' her stockin' or her seam. Thon's a jewel, Jamie. Sandy stood in his ain licht when he slichted her.'

'How *is* Mary Campbell, Aunt Susan? It seems a long time since I saw her.'

'She's weel eneuch in body, but the heart's geyan wae. The cratur kens, I think, that I ken what she's come through. 'Deed I telt her my ain auld story, laddie, an', wad ye believe it? my auld heart grows grit ower't yet. Ay, Sandy Bethune may hae a graund kirk an' a braw

P

manse, an' a leddy wife, but the Lord 'll mind him·aboot Mary Cam'll maybe when he least expecks it. When did ye see or hear frae Sandy, though ?'

'I hear from him whiles. He seems to be gettin' on fine; but there is no word of the wife. Does he ever write to you ?'

'No' him. He sends me a Dumfries paper whiles, if there's ony blawin' aboot himsel' or his kirk in't. But come an' tell me mair aboot yer new scetuation. What is't to dae ?'

'A variety of things, Aunt Susan,' answered Jamie with a smile. 'It's to the office of the *St. Paul's Gazette* I'm going. One of the proprietors is a brother-in-law of Mr. Maclean, my present master. I think he must have spoken to him about me. I am to report, if necessary, and to write articles for the paper. In fact, I think I'm to be a kind of sub-editor.'

'An' what kind o' wage do they gie ye for a' that ?'

'Two hundred pounds, and extra pay for extra work. It isn't a great salary, but the opening itself is worth a small fortune to me. London is the place for a literary man.'

'Ay, maybe. I dinna understand thae things. It's just extraordinar' to hear ye, laddie, when no' twa year syne ye were workin' at the land an' the loom. Ye hae stuck in weel.'

'No man can say I have not wrought hard, at any rate. I've taken it out of myself this winter. Don't you see how thin I am ?'

'Ay, ye are no' fat; but ye're a gentlemanlike chap, my man,' said Aunt Susan with great pride. 'Sandy 'll no' can haud a caun'le till ye noo. An' when are ye gaun awa' to Lunnon ?'

'On Friday night. They are in desperation for a man

to come at once. The one whose place I am to fill died suddenly, and they had no one ready. So I'm going south to Lochbroom to-morrow, and I'll get the London train at Lockerbie on Saturday morning.'

' Od, ye speak aboot fleein' to Lunnon as if it was naething ava'. I wush Star folk heard ye. Ye'll be gaun to bide the morn's nicht wi' Sandy,' said Aunt Susan, and just then the door was softly opened, and who should come in but Mary Campbell, with her stocking in her hand. She started at sight of the stranger, but a bright smile overspread her sweet face when she recognised him as Jamie Bethune. He sprang up, and took her hand in his warm, kindly clasp; but somehow he could think of nothing to say, for there was a change in her which made a strange, bitter feeling against his brother rise in his breast.

' Ye wasna expectin' Jamie, surely, auntie,' she said, and the colour receded from her face and left it as pale as the collar at her throat. ' No, I'll no' sit; ye maun hae a lot to say. Wull ye can gie a look up-by this time, Jamie ? '

' I'll try, Mary,' answered Jamie, and for the life of him he could say no more.

His aunt had said Mary was well in body, but her looks belied the words. She seemed smaller and more fragile, as if she had crept down, and her face was thin and worn; its ruddy bloom and sweet round fulness had both disappeared. The bright, bonnie eyes were deep and sad-looking, the sorrow of a life was plainly written in their depths. And this was Sandy's doing! How could he prosper, how could any blessing ever rest on himself or his work ?

' He's only come to bid us a' guid-bye, Mary. He's for Lunnon noo,' said Aunt Susan. ' Weel, if ye're for

awa', I'll set him up by an' by to gie ye the news.
We're jist in the middle o' oor crack.'

Mary nodded and slipped away.   She was glad to go,
for when she got to the door her eyes were wet with
tears, brought there by the look of deep sympathy in
James Bethune's eyes. She could hide her pain from
the world, but scarcely from those who loved her, and
there was more than one heart in the Star who hoped a
day of reckoning would come for the minister of Lochbroom.

CHAPTER XVII.

SWEET MOMENTS.

'O Love, so hallowing every soil
Which gives thy sweet flower room,
Wherever nursed by ease or toil
The human heart takes bloom.'

WHITTIER.

'A GENTLEMAN to see you, sir. I have just brought him in.'

So said the housekeeper at the manse of Lochbroom, opening the study door on a Friday afternoon, just as the minister had got to the third head of his discourse. He rose with a quick gesture of annoyance, and turned inquiringly to the door.

'Bless me, Jamie, is it you?'

'Yes, it's me. Have I interrupted your meditations? because I can go out for a walk till you are ready to speak to me,' said James Bethune with a smile.

'Not likely. Come in. Man, I'm glad to see you!'

Not for many years had James Bethune heard Sandy speak in such a tone. The look and the warm, fervent grip said more forcibly than his words that he *was* glad to see him.   Was Sandy being taught by slow degrees that the ties of kinship are sweeter than any on earth, and that no other love can so well stand the test of time and of adversity ?

'Why didn't you send word, and I'd have had my sermon written and been at the station meeting you ?'

'I couldn't, because I didn't know myself.   I've come from Fife to-day.'

'From Star ?   Then you are having your holidays ?'

'No, I'm on my way to London; but if you'll give me something to eat I'll speak better.   1 have had nothing since Aunt Susan gave me a seven o'clock breakfast.'

'You're just in time; my dinner will be served in about ten minutes.   Can you wait ?'

'Oh, of course; I'm not just famishing,' answered Jamie, walking over to the window, and looking down the village street, and then across the fertile landscape to the blue ridges of the Lanark hills.   'You have a lovely spot here.'

'Do you think so ?   I'm sick of the place myself. But come, tell me about yourself.   I'm consumed with curiosity.'

'Which, I suppose, I must satisfy,' said Jamie with a smile, and, sitting down in the window, he briefly recounted to his brother the circumstances of the change he was about to make.

'Man, you're a lucky fellow.   You are going to beat me altogether, — a clear case of the hare and the tortoise,' said the minister with a half sigh.   'I suppose you won't be content till you get to the top of the tree now.'

'I'll certainly climb as high as I can. I'm going to write a book after I get to London, Sandy. It will either be the making or the marring of me.'

'It'll be the making, no doubt. I know now it is in you. I say, Jamie, I sometimes wonder why you didn't kick me in the old days. What a conceited ass I was!'

'I knew you would gather sense,' laughed Jamie, out of the gladness of his heart. 'But how are you getting on yourself? I fancy you look rather out of sorts.'

'So I am. I'm about tired of the thing, Jamie.'

'What thing?'

'This,' he said with a comprehensive wave of his hand. 'I'm losing influence in the place; the church is falling off; and, in short, it's time I had a change. I wish I was anything but a minister.'

James Bethune sat silent a moment, and a grave, troubled look came into his face.

'I don't like to hear you say that, Sandy. It is a noble profession, *the* noblest, I think, if it is undertaken with a right heart. You'—

'That's where it is! I haven't the right heart, you see,' interrupted Sandy almost passionately. 'Man, if you knew how I hate and despise myself, standing up there Sunday after Sunday making a hypocrite of myself,—for it is nothing else!—telling people what their duty is, trying to fit them for the kingdom of heaven, when I'm further off from it than the worst sinner among them.'

James Bethune sat round in his chair and looked with deep anxiety into his brother's face. It wore an expression of settled gloom, his eye gleamed with a strange bitterness, his whole appearance was that of a man at war with himself and the world.

'Let me say my say. It'll do me good. I've to keep
so quiet here, and go about so smoothly and circum-
spectly to keep up my dignity, you know, and otherwise
deceive the world,' he said, as if in very scorn of
himself. 'Don't look at me with such pitying eyes.
I don't deserve your pity, for I have wronged even you,
who have always been ten thousand times better to me
than I deserve. Haven't I laughed at and despised you
and tried to keep you down all my life? But I've done
more than that. Uncle Peter charged me on his death-
bed to share his money with you; and did I do it?
No; I let them prove the written will and took it all,
and yet you never grumbled, but only rejoiced in my
good luck. Did you know that that was the surest and
the keenest way to punish me? Man, the memory of
all your goodness has been like a fierce scorpion stinging
me night and day. You'—

James Bethune rose from his chair; he laid his firm,
gentle hand on his brother's shoulder, and looked him
full in the face.

'Sandy, if you don't hold your tongue I'll go away out
of the house this very minute, and you'll never see me
again. You have worked yourself into such a state of
excitement that I'm afraid to see you. What are you
talking about? Aren't you making mountains out
of molehills? What do I care for Uncle Peter's money?
Don't let's have another word. Isn't that the dinner-
bell? Am I to get anything to eat, or am I not?'

His bantering words provoked a trembling smile on
Sandy's lips, but it passed, and unwonted tears stood
in his eyes. Then their hands met in a grip which
hurt, and they looked into each other's eyes with
a long look which revealed to each the other's
heart

'We're chums again, aren't we?' said Jamie cheerily, and his broad hand fell with a hearty clap on his brother's back. 'We'll have a quiet crack ower auld lang syne over our pipes to-night; did you know I had learned to smoke? There's that woman ringing the bell again!'

'Well, I suppose we had better go, as you are so hungry, but I'd rather finish the crack just now,' said the minister, as he opened the study door and led the way to the dining-room.

'I think you are a little dyspeptic, Sandy,' said James Bethune jokingly, as he noticed how very little his brother ate. 'I believe you need a change of some sort. Couldn't you get some one to fill your place for a Sunday or two, and come away up to London with me? I'll be lonely enough anyway till I get shaken down into my new place.'

'I couldn't get away just now. You see I've been absent from my own pulpit a good few Sabbaths lately, preaching on trial in vacant churches. They'll begin to grumble,—indeed, they are grumbling already. Adam Gray, my beadle, gives me many a hint, honest man, thinking that a quiet word from him may induce me to mend my ways, and look better after the parish.'

'Well, the first holiday I get we must have a run on the Continent together,' said Jamie cheerily. 'You mustn't get down-hearted. Don't I know all about what it is to feel one's self falling behind? Man, when I look back on yon dreary six months in Edinburgh, I wonder now I ever held out. We have all these bits of worry to try us, just to show what grit is in us, I think. By the bye, is there no word of a wife to the manse yet?' asked Jamie carelessly, but he kept his eyes fixed on his plate, and did not look at his brother's face. I think he knew very well what the answer would be, for it had just flashed upon him all at once, that Beatrice Lorraine might have something to do with Sandy's distaste of Lochbroom and weariness of life in general.

'There will never be a wife in the manse of Lochbroom so long as I am in it,' said Sandy quietly. After a moment Jamie raised his head and looked at his brother.

'Then she said no?'

'Yes, she said no.'

Sandy pushed aside his unfinished dessert, and, rising from the table, began to walk up and down the room.

'What fools women can make of us, can't they?' he asked with extreme bitterness. 'I despise myself for being so affected by a woman's word, but I can't help it. I don't expect you to understand or sympathize with me. You are lucky in this, as in other things I tell you, whenever a woman comes in between you and your work, you'll stand still for a while.'

'But you are not going to stand still altogether because one woman in the world won't have you,' said Jamie. 'You'll soon get over it. You never used to let anything bother you for a long time.'

'It is easy for you to speak,' said Sandy quietly. 'You needn't wonder now that I would like a change. You can understand what it must be for me to see her so often as I do. Fortunately not a soul in the parish has a suspicion that such a thing has ever happened. Of course she is not a woman to boast of her conquests as I am told some do.'

'No, I should say not,' answered Jamie, for somehow his thoughts had flown back to that evening at the manse of St. Giles, and its undying memories rose up vividly before him.

'Do you know, I often wish I had never been educated for the Church,' said Sandy presently. 'I would have been a better and a happier man living in the Star all my days with Mary Campbell as my wife. Mind, I don't grumble at what has happened to me through Beatrice Lorraine. It is a just punishment for my treatment of Mary. Poor girl! I often think of her. What a sweet, humble, forgiving nature she had! I don't believe she could entertain a hard thought, even of me.'

'You are right. We have not known many women in our lives, Sandy, but they have been all good. We ought to reverence womanhood for their sakes,' said Jamie musingly. 'Do you know I am full of hope for you. I think you are just beginning to get a glimpse of life's meanings. You will do a good work yet in the world.'

Sandy shook his head.

'I don't see how you can make that out. You know what my life has been. I have built from the beginning on a false foundation. How can I ever undo all I have done?'

'Don't you remember Tennyson's lines:—

"That men may rise on stepping-stones
Of their dead selves to higher things"?

They are true, I think, of us all. Life is just a series of fallings and risings, but if we do the best we can, we will be very mercifully judged.'

'I believe God sent you to me to-day, Jamie,' said the minister, pausing by his brother's chair and touching his shoulder with a grateful, lingering hand. 'You have done me great good already. I don't deserve that you should even take the trouble to be interested in my welfare.'

'Wheesht, man! Aren't you my brother? It's just like the old Star days come back. Do you remember how we used to fight each other's battles when we were at the school?'

James Bethune spoke cheerily, with a smile on his lips, but he was very deeply moved. His heart yearned over his brother, and he forgot everything but that he *was* his brother, his only near kin upon the face of the earth. It is a beautiful and a touching thing in our natures, that love can thus smooth away all barriers, and lay a healing finger even on the sorest places, and take the sting even out of very bitter memory. An unselfish heart so soon forgets what has selfishly wounded it, and is ever ready to give love for love. But in this it has its own deep fulness of joy which none else can share.

'Suppose we go out and have a look about us now,' he said presently. 'We have had enough dolorous talk. We'll look ahead now and picture for ourselves a bright future. There's no harm in castle-building, and it helps us over the stony places in our daily toil. Pulling a long face over a trouble never mended it in this world, and never will.'

His sunshine was irresistible, and a glimmer of the old smile dawned on the minister's face. So they went away out arm-in-arm together, just like playmates, talking over their early days, Jamie making a point of calling to his brother's recollection every wild escapade and comical episode of the old Star life.

'Where does Nethercleugh lie?' he asked when they had climbed the inner stair of the church steeple to get a view of the surrounding country.

'That's it down among the trees. You can just see the gables above chestnut tops. It is a beautiful place.'

'It seems to be. I'd like to go up there to-night; Sandy. If you don't like to come, I wouldn't be very long away.'

'Oh, but I will come. I'm not such a coward as all that. I have never made any difference, and have visited them just as regularly. It's the only way to keep the village tongue from wagging. Shall we go now then? They dine at five when they are alone, and we'll be in time to get a cup of tea from Miss Lorraine.'

'Yes, I'm quite ready. I suppose they live very quietly.'

'Very. They mix with none of the society of the countryside. That son who went wrong has cast a shadow over their whole lives.'

'Minnie Kinross told me something about her cousin Willie, as she called him, and Miss Lorraine herself spoke of their sorrow,' said James Bethune as they turned to go. 'How did he go wrong? Was it drink?'

'I don't think so. I rather think he appropriated some money which wasn't his own. But I really cannot speak with any certainty, for nobody seems to know the right way of it. The father is a terribly proud man, and he has never got over it. That's what made him retire from business at the prime of life. It happened in London.'

'They have everything that the world can give, I suppose, but the skeleton is in the cupboard. Every one has something of the sort. I have never met with any exception to the rule.'

'"Man is born unto trouble, as the sparks fly upward,"' quoted the minister. 'That is my text for the Sabbath day.'

'A dolorous one; but you can make it carry a glorious message of hope if you like,' answered Jamie.

'How do we go now? Through the woods? I am glad of that; the roads are very dusty to-day.'

'Yes, we need a shower; see, the very leaves are drooping. What a stillness is in the air! I believe we shall have thunder before morning.'

They talked much as they walked, chiefly of old days and early associations, which were now very precious to them both. Strange how what we thought homely and uninteresting when it was beside us becomes so dear and beautiful when seen through the veil of distance! Memory carries sometimes a magic wand.

Sandy could scarcely understand his brother's deep love and appreciation of Aunt Susan; he had never been able to penetrate beneath the surface, and reach the wealth of love and unselfish care in her heart. He had only known the rugged exterior, which had not greatly recommended itself to him; he had, indeed, thought her coarse and rude, and altogether presumptuous in her dealing with him. Aunt Susan had indeed two personalities, one of which had never been revealed to Sandy. She had closed her heart against him soon after he left his father's house, and had never seen fit to open it again. There was nobody in the world had taken a more shrewd and correct estimate of him than his aunt, and her opinion of him was not very high. Perhaps she was a trifle harsh in her judgment, the fault of her strong, decided nature, which did not admit of a medium in many things. Well or ill was her course; there was no middle state. But their pleasant talk, which, however, was not without its sting for the minister, brought them at last to Nethercleugh, and then James Bethune relapsed into silence. This was her home! How often he had tried to picture it, yet how different the reality! It was in the prime of its beauty now, with the summer leaves upon the fine old trees and the summer freshness over the smooth green turf.

'It is a grand house, Sandy. I had no idea it would be so grand.'

'Yes, it is a fine place. There is Mr. Lorraine at the drawing-room window. I think he sees us.'

James Bethune was conscious that his heart beat a little faster as they mounted the steps to the door, and he forgot to look at Sandy, who doubtless must feel keenly when he entered here.

The maid who admitted them smiled in response to the minister's kindly greeting, and at once ushered them to the drawing-room. The scent of mignonette and roses greeted them on the threshold; the room was a cool, shady, fragrant place—a pleasant retreat from the sultriness without.

'So you have really come at last!' said the deep, rich voice of the master of Nethercleugh, and he greeted James Bethune with a heartiness there was no mistaking. He was really glad to see him.

'I have not lost time, Mr. Lorraine; I only arrived an hour or two ago,' said James Bethune with his rare smile; then he turned to Beatrice, who had risen from her chair. She was speaking to his brother, and, during the brief second ere she turned to him, his eyes took in her whole appearance with a yearning, almost hungering look, such as we bestow on what is unspeakably dear. She was not in any way changed, save that her white dress seemed to make her look younger and more girlish. How beautiful she was! the thoughtful face, with its sweet, womanly mouth, and deep, lustrous eyes, matching the sweet violets at her throat and in the belt about her waist. She stood in the slanting sunlight, which had crept round to the front windows; a broad line of light lay upon her golden head, making yet more wondrous the sheen of the coronet of hair above her brow.

'How are you, Mr. Bethune? I bid you welcome to Nethercleugh,' she said at length, turning to him. Her eyes met his, and a faint colour stole unawares to her cheek. Surely his earnest look had stirred her heart. He took the slim white hand one moment in his own, and felt it thrill him through and through. He thanked her for the word of welcome, and then sat down beside Mr. Lorraine, full of wonder at himself. What did this mean? Why should his pulses beat, the blood rush more quickly in his veins? Why should he feel so yearningly happy in the presence of this woman? Could it be that the love of which he had heard and read had come to him at last, bringing to him only its heritage of pain, for in such love there could be no hope for him? He felt like a man in a dream. To outward seeming he was calm and self-possessed, looking at his ease as a gentleman should; he even spoke and answered intelligently, but he felt like a man in a dream. He saw the graceful figure at the tea-table, the white, beautiful hands touching the delicate china; he caught every varying expression in that exquisite face, every sweet intonation of her voice. He took his cup of tea from her hands, and thanked her with earnest eyes dwelling on her face as if craving a look in return, but she did not give it. One watching closely would have observed a fluttering nervousness in her movements, as if some agitating element had crept into her thoughts. Could it be that in her heart there was any answering chord?

She did not speak at all, only listened with deepest interest, while James Bethune acquainted her father with the change in his prospects. Mr. Lorraine seemed much pleased to hear of it; his eyes dwelt with keen and cordial interest on the young man's fine face, and he nodded occasionally while he was speaking, as if to indicate his satisfaction.

'You'll succeed, I know. We will be expecting to hear great things of you by and by,' he said heartily. 'London is, beyond a doubt, the place for you. You will find there all you need. It will be a great revelation to you. Well, Beatrice, my dear, if the gentlemen have had sufficient tea, we might go out of doors a little. The air of this room, in spite of the open windows, is very stifling.'

'I am ready, papa,' said Beatrice at once. 'If you will just go down-stairs, I will join you in a minute.'

The minister opened the door for her, and as she passed out Jamie looked at him curiously, recollecting for the first time what had passed between him and Beatrice Lorraine. He could not but admire his perfect self-control, his gentlemanly ease and calmness of deport- ment. Whatever he may have felt, he hid it well. None could have detected that he regarded the daughter of the house in anything but an indifferent light. The way in which he had accepted his refusal had gained for him the respect of both father and daughter, and he was made more welcome than before at Nethercleugh.

'You can wait for my daughter, Mr. James,' said Mr. Lorraine when the trio stepped out into the sultry air. 'Come, Mr. Bethune, you are the very man I wanted to see. What do *you* think of the new water scheme for Lochbroom?'

So saying, he took the minister by the arm and led him away in the direction of the shrubbery. They were quite out of sight before Beatrice appeared. She had thrown a lace wrap about her head and shoulders, which

Q

made a delicate and becoming frame for her fair face.
'Are you all alone?' she asked with a swift, bright
smile. 'I am sorry if I have kept you waiting. Where
have the others gone?'

'Along that path. Shall we follow?'

'I suppose so. It is a lovely walk, a continuation of
the path from Lochbroom. Of course you do not
know it?'

'No, I do not know it,' answered James Bethune,
turning to walk by her side.

'So you are going to make your home in London
now,' she said, for the silence was strangely embar-
rassing to her. 'Are you looking forward to it with
great hope?'

'Yes; I ought to be pleased, for it is what I have
wished for long. Few are so fortunate as I have
been.'

'One so much in earnest deserves such reward, I
think,' she said with an upward glance, half smiling, half
serious.

'You speak kindly. I do not know that I can lay
claim to being so much in earnest. I know many who
work as hard, and who need it more perhaps, yet who do
not seem to make any headway in life.'

'That is sad. There are so many such things in the
world. I am weighed down sometimes thinking what
struggles some have, what battles to fight, what burdens
to carry. I fear many must succumb.'

'They do. When I was in Glasgow, Miss Lorraine, I
was often oppressed by such thoughts. It is not known
how many noble hearts have to do grim battle with
poverty, with adverse surroundings, nay, sometimes with
absolute want. It must sadden the very angels in
heaven to see the sights in a great city.'

'In London you will see more, I believe, if you care to seek it,' she said, looking up at him with something of wistfulness in her eyes. He caught that look; it touched his heart, but he did not quite understand it yet.

'Papa and your brother are not in sight,' she said suddenly. 'Possibly they may have crossed the park into the other woods. How shall we go?'

'Are you anxious to join them? If not, let us go on. I have not many such opportunities.'

The words slipped out unawares, and he saw her colour heighten, and the fear oppressed him that he had given offence.

'Pardon me, I ought not to have said that,' he said at once.

'What? There is no offence to pardon,' she answered with a smile. 'This is the gate. This path terminates in a wishing-well. Shall we go and see it?'

'If you please.'

He opened the gate for her to pass through, and in a moment was at her side again.

'You spoke of me making my home in London,' he said presently. 'Do you think it will be a home?'

'I cannot tell; I hope so. Surely some kind influences will gather round you even there,' she said a trifle hurriedly. 'Wherever our work and interests are, is it not home to us?'

'Not always. There are other things necessary; *you* know that as well as I.'

'Mr. Bethune, may I speak to you about something which lies very near my heart?' she said quite suddenly, and in a low, clear, earnest voice.

He turned his head and looked into her face. It was

now quite pale, and her lips were trembling, her breast heaving with emotion.

'If you will do so I shall feel unspeakably honoured,' he said with difficulty, for these were dangerous moments for him.   He felt as if he were playing with edged tools.   'Needless for me to say that any confidence with which you may honour me will be sacred in my eyes.'

'Oh, I know!   Do you think if I did not know I could speak so to you?' she asked hurriedly.   'It is about my brother I wish to speak.   Possibly you may have heard that I have a brother in London, who has been in trouble, who has been, and is, a sorrow to us?'

'Your cousin told me; and you spoke of this sorrow before.   Perhaps you will remember,' he said in tones full of deep sympathy.

'Yes, I remember.   Possibly you do not know the circumstances.   Let me tell you them briefly.   My father was a merchant in London before we came here, and Willie and I were all he had.   He was always a strange, wayward boy, full of whims and fancies and day-dreams; and though papa intended him for a merchant, I, looking on, feared he would never fall in with these plans.   He never cared to work; the drudgery of school was irksome to him.   Give him a book, or a piece of paper and a pencil in a corner, and he was happy; only do not ask him to work. Papa idolized him, indulged him in everything, and yet if he crossed him in any of his wishes he would hardly forgive him.   As he grew older there were often differences between them.   One was that Willie wished to be sent to college instead of to the commercial school where he would receive training for business.   Papa gained the

day, of course, because he left Willie no choice but to
obey. He had set his heart upon seeing him a member
of the firm. Lorraine and Co. was a well-known house
in London, well known and highly honoured. It belonged
first to my grandfather, whose idol it was. Then papa
got the business, and it was his delight to extend it and
make it greater; naturally it was a disappointment to
him when his only son did not share his pride and
interest in it. Things went on in an unsatisfactory kind
of way until the time came for Willie to leave school,
then it was open rebellion. He refused to enter the
office to sit on a stool and add up figures; he wanted to
be an artist or a literary man, or something of that sort.
Poor boy ! he hardly knew his own mind except in one
particular subject—that he would not become a business
man. Papa passed over his entreaties and rebellings with
contempt, and to punish him apprenticed him to another
firm in Fenchurch Street. I tell you all this, Mr. Bethune,
so that you may the better understand what followed,'
said Beatrice, and paused for a moment as if to collect
her self-possession to go on. 'Willie had none of papa's
decision of character. He was weak, easily led, and
could not say no. He was handsome, lovable, winning
in his way. I have never seen any who won such
universal love. Poor Willie !'

A bursting sob choked her utterance a moment, and
James Bethune bit his lip and half turned away. The
sight of her grief unmanned him, and he feared lest he
should say what would be better left unsaid.

'Bound to an occupation he hated, he sought solace
in the company of those who could not do him good but
only harm. He was so entertaining, he had always a
jest and a song ready, and he was much sought after by
those who led him astray. I do not want to blame my

father, for my heart is often wrung for him, but I sometimes think that he erred just at that time. Instead of
trying to wean him away by love from the evil ways into
which he was gradually falling, he sternly reproached
him, and threatened to shut him out of the house.
Perhaps you will not understand papa's harshness so
well as I, who knew what a downfall Willie had given
his hopes, and what a disappointment to his love. For
indeed Willie was always the idol of his heart. He
never had money of his own, papa gave him none, and
the trifle he received from his employers was as nothing
to him, and so he was tempted, I suppose, very fiercely
before he fell. He had learned to gamble, and it
became such a passion with him that he threw off all
restraint and plunged into it headlong. Of course his
employers suffered, but for papa's sake they made no
complaint, passing over unpunctuality, carelessness, and
idleness, until something happened which it was impossible
that they could pass over. It was in the last year of his
apprenticeship, and he was not quite twenty when this
dreadful thing happened. I cannot quite explain to you
what he did, but it was something about a cheque
belonging to his employers, and I know that he could
have been punished heavily for it, even sentenced to
penal servitude, so papa said. But for his sake, because
he was so honoured in the business world, the firm
hushed it up, and Willie was allowed to go unpunished.
But it broke papa's heart, and made him an old man
before his time. Willie was forbidden the house. Papa
disinherited and disowned him, and we have never seen
him since. That is nearly five years ago now, but the
agony is as fresh in my heart as it was then. Papa has
never relented. I have pled with him very often; it is
so awful a thing to allow one's own to drift perhaps to

destruction without stretching out a hand to save. There was good in Willie, Mr. Bethune. He had a warm, loving heart, a sweet, kind disposition, and he was clever, too, in his own way, very clever, if only he had had a chance. How I loved him I cannot tell you. Only I know that I would lay down my life now to save him, and to bring about a reconciliation, for I know that this sorrow will bring papa to the grave. I see it eating into his heart every day, only he will not give in.'

They had reached the wishing-well now—a clear, cool spring flowing into a mossy stone basin in a dim recess, where the sunbeams never shone. The dusky shadows of the deepening night were falling about them, the light was dim and uncertain, and the air was strangely still. She paused there, and, leaning against the trunk of a tall fir tree, lifted her shadowed eyes to the earnest, true face looking down with such deep compassion and sympathy upon her.

'Now I have something to ask; I do not know why I should so presume, unless because you feel some things as I feel them,' she said with a tremulous, uncertain smile. 'If in London you should ever see or hear of Willie, Mr. Bethune, will you do what you can for him? will you speak a kind word, and thus earn the gratitude and prayers of a sister's heart?'

For a moment James Bethune had no answer ready, he was silent in the intensity of the thoughts which lay upon him like a deep flood.

'If I ask too much from one who is almost a stranger, forgive me, and forget what I have told you,' she said at length, with something of sad, proud dignity in her voice. 'Let us go back now. We have been nearly an hour upon the way. They will wonder what has become of us.'

'I did not speak, because I could not find words wherein to express my unutterable sympathy, to thank you for the great honour you have done me,' he said at length. 'I will look upon your request as a sacred charge. If your brother is in London still, Miss Lorraine, I will find him, and, please God, all will come right yet.'

'I would·thank you, only I cannot,' she said simply, and held out her hand. It did not seem presumptuous that he should touch it with his lips; it was the seal of a bond between them,—a bond so sweet to the heart of James Bethune that he could scarcely realize its existence. She had trusted him implicitly, that was sufficient for him yet.

'We must go now, but not until we have drunk of the wishing-well. You are allowed two wishes, one before you drink and one after,' she said, smiling again, and lifting the chain with the cup attached. 'Let me give you the draught.'

'After you, Miss Lorraine, if you please.'

'Oh no! I have .wished times without number always the same thing. Come,' she said, offering the cup.

'Then I wish from the bottom of the heart that your brother may be speedily restored, and that brightest days may dawn for Nethercleugh,' he said, putting the cup to his lips.

'And your second wish, if I may share it too?' she said merrily, for something in the strong, manly presence, and in the resolute yet gentle face, gave her strength and assurance, and it was as if some burden had rolled away from her heart.

'Let me fasten your wrap—see, it has fallen, and the night air is heavy and chill,' he said, and with kind hand drew the lace over her head. As he did so his hand touched hers again, and it thrilled his inmost being.

'Thank you. But your wish?' she said with a gleam of amusement in her speaking eye.

'That I may not tell you,' he answered then, and the quick colour leaped to his cheek, for his tone betrayed more than the words were intended to convey. She gathered the white folds of her gown in her hand, and turned away so quickly that he might have feared he had the second time given offence. Only he saw the answering flush which rose to her brow and dyed it red.

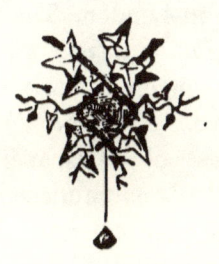

CHAPTER XVIII.

'Heir of the self-same heritage,
Child of the self-same God,
He has but stumbled in the path
Thou hast in weakness trod.'

JAMES BETHUNE found plenty of work awaiting him in London. The post of sub-editor to
the *St. Paul's Gazette* was no sinecure. But
it was congenial work, and he did not find
it oppressive. The *St. Paul's Gazette* was a
different class of newspaper from the *Glasgow*
Journal. It was published in the afternoon,
and, while purveying political and general news for its
readers, aimed at something higher. It was the proprietor's ideal to combine the attributes of an evening
paper and a literary and social review, and to produce
a first-class family journal, full of interesting and wholesome matter. It was an old-established publication
which had seen many vicissitudes, but which had
received a new impetus from its present proprietor, who
was also its editor. He was an able journalist, and the

250

Gazette was rapidly pushing its way into notice. It was a splendid opening for James Bethune, just the field for the exercise of his gifts, where they could be prepared and perfected for even a higher sphere. Mr. Maynard was a reserved and taciturn man, very different from the frank, open-hearted, genial proprietor of the *Glasgow Journal*, and at first James Bethune felt the change keenly. He was received courteously but without warmth; his work was apportioned to him, and he was left to perform it. But there was no interchange of thought, no confidences, no kind links of sympathy between the two. Mr. Maynard did not even inquire whether he had found suitable lodging, or had any place wherein to spend a leisure hour. The relations between them were business-like and purely formal. When Stephen Maynard found a capable servant he was a just master, but no more. James Bethune had been full of hope that perhaps in Mr. Maynard he might find one who would give him substantial aid in his search for Willie Lorraine. He was a London man, and his experience must have familiarized him with almost every form of London life; in all probability he could have named the very spot where such wanderers were to be found, but it was impossible to reach him. As the days went by, James Bethune saw clearly what manner of relations were to exist between them, and relinquished the idea of bestowing his confidence and asking his advice. If Willie Lorraine was to be found, it must be through his own exertions, and it would be no easy task. For the first month or two he attended only to his allotted duties, his own work was neglected. It was not only that his leisure hours were chiefly spent in wandering through the labyrinths of London, vainly seeking for the lost son of the house of Lorraine; there was something else occupying his thoughts. Often Sandy's words recurred to his memory: 'When a woman comes between you and your work, you'll stand still for a while.' So it was with him. And yet I do not know that it was standing still; certainly thought was not stagnant. Nay, he was advancing step by step in the higher life, and love, with matchless though invisible finger, was adding the finest touches to his nature. A pure love is a great educator and an ennobling influence. We cannot love even a worthy pursuit without being the better for it. By and by, out of the sweet new influences at work within, thoughts grew wide and deep and absorbing, demanding at length a voice.

What he wrote in these days had a grace and beauty far exceeding what he had done in the past. The touch of pain, which is the crown of the poet's soul. was not now lacking, for the yearnings in his heart for life's best gifts were full of keenest pain. He knew now beyond a doubt that he loved Beatrice Lorraine with that deep, reverential, yet hopeless love of which Dante sang. He never thought of her as his wife, nor as any nearer than she was now. Between them there was a gulf fixed, that gulf of social position which the longer he lived he saw more clearly defined between class and class. He was one of earth's toilers, dependent upon daily labour for daily bread; while she was a child of ease and affluence, who had never known a moment's anxiety concerning such things.

He was too proud even to think that love could bridge that gulf,—no thought of asking her to share his life of labour and humble endeavour ever presented itself to his mind. He might love her at a distance, he could carry her image with him in his heart, he could ponder her gracious words, and feel them incentives to go forward and upward in life's race, but she must never know.

Sometimes his cheek burned at the memory of that hour by the wishing-well, and he told himself it must not and could not be repeated. Better that they should never meet; he knew he could not always remain master of himself. It must be enough for him to know that she trusted him, and regarded him as worthy a friendly regard. From her own lips he had heard the story of her heart-sorrow; she had given him a sacred charge, which he would strive sacredly to fulfil. That was much —and with that he must be content. Should he succeed in restoring the prodigal to his father's house, he would earn, he knew, a gratitude which would be a sweet solace to him in his loneliness. Their kindly thoughts of him would brighten existence for him, and he looked cheerfully forward to the life of work and struggle and self-denial which he knew lies before all who set themselves to do their God-appointed work. In the scheme of creation there is no place for the idle·dreamer or the slothful dweller at ease; work is the law of the universe, whether we recognise it or not. According as we have fulfilled God's purpose in us here, so will be our rest. Sometimes our eyes are holden, so that we cannot see God's best gifts lying close about our feet, even while we are seeking for some great thing far beyond our reach; but a truly earnest soul, asking and waiting to be guided, will not long be at a loss.

It was a somewhat hopeless task for James Bethune to attempt discovering Willie Lorraine in the mazes of London. Soon after his settlement there came to him, in a letter from Sandy, the photograph of a young, fair-haired, laughing-faced boy, which the minister wrote had been given to him by Miss Lorraine to forward to his brother. Sandy was evidently deeply mystified by this proceeding, but he did not ask any direct question. Jamie merely acknowledged it, not feeling at liberty to reveal the secret, even to his brother. There was a hopeful and manly tone in Sandy's letters now, which was like a refreshing cordial to Jamie, for he could read between the lines, and saw well enough that he was coming out of the waters of Marah not only unscathed, but made nobler and manlier and better in every way. The little items of parish news were cheering, and there were no further hints of a desire for change. It was a healthy sign that Sandy was anxious to redeem himself in his own parish, which had suffered through his backsliding. The photograph, though evidently taken in schoolboy days, would be of use to James Bethune, for though there might be a great change upon the wanderer, the features must be the same.

So he carried it in his pocket-book, and when he was in the streets was constantly on the alert, scanning every passing face in the hope that some day he might have his reward. It was a harassing quest, causing him deep anxiety of mind, and it gradually took possession of him, and became something like a haunting spectre with him both day and night. But it seemed likely to prove hopeless, for winter advanced, and he had not obtained the remotest clue.

Part of the sub-editor's work was to open and look over all the manuscripts sent in, from which he had to select the likeliest, which were then submitted for Mr. Maynard's final decision. At first James Bethune found it an interesting occupation, but it speedily became irksome and even painful. Two-thirds of them were quite unfit for publication, scarcely worth the paper on which they were written. But these meagre productions were often accompanied by pitiful appeals, which contained many a revelation, many a hint of poverty which was almost tragic, against which James Bethune found it hard to steel himself. His great heart had room for all the woes of these unknown scribblers, whom he pitied with a vast compassion. Stephen Maynard was of a different stamp. He looked at everything from a purely business point of view. Would it pay? was the standard by which he judged. He laughed at his subordinate's feeling in such matters, and told him never to read the accompanying letters, but toss them into the waste basket, which was the best place for such rubbish. He was sitting in his dingy little sanctum, from which he could see the dome of St. Paul's, busy with his daily sifting of the manuscripts the morning mail had brought. The gas was lighted, and the fire burning also, for the day was bitterly cold, and a raw heavy fog had the city in its chilling folds. He sighed once or twice as he marked each with the inexorable D. W. T.; it was a dreary task to which he would never grow accustomed. He felt somewhat out of sorts that morning, also the depressing influences of the day and the hour were weighing upon him. He had got about half through with his task when the door opened and Mr. Maynard entered. He was a tall, spare man, with a pale, stern cast of face and a penetrating eye; a man who had been long accustomed to present a hard front to the world.

' Good morning, Mr. Bethune,' he said in his studiously courteous but distant way. ' Disagreeable day, isn't it? Did you read this thing through yesterday?'

He referred to a few sheets of closely-written manuscript he carried in his hand.

'What is it, sir?'

'An article on the housing of the poor.'

'I merely looked at it. I thought it opened well, and

as the subject has been engrossing public attention lately I sent it in to your table,' answered James Bethune.

' It is good. A little wordy perhaps, but it is original in conception. The writer seems to feel keenly on the subject. Where did it come from do you know ? There is no name attached.'

' It was left at the office yesterday afternoon, the boy told me. The person who left it was to call again.'

' Was it a man or woman ? '

' I couldn't say, sir; but we can speedily ascertain,' answered James Bethune, and rising he called down the speaking-trumpet to the office-boy in the counting-house below.

' It was a young man, Hunter says,' said James Bethune after a brief conversation with the boy. ' He seemed to be very eager about it, and said he would call to-day.'

' Well, if he comes you can see him, and return the manuscript. Tell him there is too much theory and too little practical suggestion in it ; and ask him to try again. I like the style of the thing. It is taking, if it was toned down a little. You understand me ? '

' Perfectly, sir.'

' Are you nearly through ? ' he asked then with a careless glance at the litter of papers on the table. ' Toss the rest into the basket and get away to Exeter Hall. The meeting opens at twelve, and it is half-past eleven now.'

So saying, Mr. Maynard laid down the manuscript and retired. James Bethune took it up curiously and looked at it again. The handwriting struck him as it had not done previously, it was so beautifully legible, like the fair round caligraphy of a boy fresh from school. He took a piece of paper and wrote a note to be given to the writer should he call in his absence, and, wrapping up the manuscript, put on hat and coat and went down-stairs.

After giving the boy his instructions, he proceeded to Exeter Hall to report the speech of a great philanthropist on one of the burning questions of the day. It was after two o'clock when he returned to the office. Mr. Maynard had gone out to lunch, and there were some letters lying on the sub-editor's table demanding immediate attention. He was engrossed with these, and had forgotten all about the incident of the morning, when Hunter spoke from down-stairs.

'It's the young man for the manuscript, sir. Shall I give it him, or will you see him ? '

'Bring him up, Hunter,' he called back, and went on with his writing, anxious to have the letters ready for the three o'clock mail.

'Take a seat please, and I will attend to you presently,' he said, glancing hastily at the stranger as he entered the room.

'Hunter, is the bag ready ? '

'Yes, sir, just getting closed.'

'Ask them to wait a moment, I'll be ready presently,' said Mr. Bethune, and with a few rapid strokes he finished the last letter, closed and addressed it, and passed it with the others to the boy.

Then he rose and looked for the first time fully at the stranger who had been ushered into his presence. That glance filled him with pity, but did not strike him in any other way yet. He was a young man, four or five and twenty at most; his appearance and attire betokened extreme poverty. His shabby black coat, long since glazed at the seams and frayed at the sleeves, hung loosely about a thin, slight figure, and his face was

R

sharpened and attenuated, as if he had known what it was to lack many a meal. It was a winning and in some respects a striking face; but it wore an expression of settled melancholy painful to see; and the blue eyes, far sunken under the broad, square forehead, gleamed with a strange bitterness, as if they had been long accustomed to sad scenes. A slight moustache curled on the lip, half hiding the weak, womanish mouth, the most undecided feature in the face. His hair was sunny in hue, and set in close, curling masses about the head, which was well-shaped, but too small to be manly. As James Bethune looked, a strange, wild hope, too improbable to have any foundation in fact, sprang into his heart, agitating him so much that it was with difficulty he controlled himself so as to speak calmly and courteously to the stranger.

'You are the writer of the article on the housing of the poor, I believe?' he said, glancing significantly at the packet in the young man's white, thin fingers.

'Yes, sir.' A light so eager as to be almost wild sprang into the deep blue eyes. 'Will it do? Oh, sir, if you would only take it, and give me a trifle for it! It was written almost with my life's blood.'

'My poor fellow, it is not in my power to accept or reject articles. I am not the principal in this office,' said James Bethune with deep compassion. 'But I am happy to tell you that the editor is much pleased with it, only it is not quite suitable for our columns.'

'Then he will give me nothing,' said the young man with something like a groan. 'My last chance gone! My God! there is nothing left for me now but death.'

'Hush, hush! These are wild, wicked words. My poor fellow! I can see you are in sore straits. Sit down and let us talk over the matter. I have known what it is to struggle for a place in the overcrowded ranks,' said James Bethune with infinite gentleness. ' It isn't quite hopeless. The editor wishes you to rewrite this, and if you can make it suitable he will pay you well for it.'

Again that quick, eager light sprang into the deeply-shadowed eyes.

' What is the matter with it ? It is all true, hideously true. Perhaps I have not minced the matter, nor made it fine enough and sweet enough for the rich people who might deign to read it. But I have done my duty. I have written down what I have seen and known, aye, and what I have suffered. I have been one of the houseless poor.'

' How have you fallen so low ? You were reared in a different atmosphere,' said James Bethune unsteadily, for he had caught a reflection of Beatrice Lorraine in that impassioned face, and hope was changing to conviction in his breast.

' How do you know where I was reared ?' asked the stranger almost fiercely. ' Tell me what I am to do with this paper, and let me go. I am not begging. I don't want your pity. I am willing to work for anything I can get.'

James Bethune restrained himself with an effort, and, taking the sheets from the stranger's hand, briefly pointed out to him wherein it lacked, and suggested what might be done to improve it.

' If I bring it back to-morrow, will he give me something for it ? I have tasted nothing since yesterday; and I do not know when I shall taste, unless I get something for this.'

He had risen to his feet, and his hand shook as it closed over the sheets that had been written at such

terrible cost. Tears stood in James Bethune's eyes, and
for a moment he could not command himself sufficiently
to speak. That such things should be in great and
Christian London might well make the angels weep. He
took down his hat and opened the door.

'Come with me. You must have something to eat
now. Hush! not a word! What I do is only a duty
from man to man. You dare not refuse. Come.'

Meek, pliable as a child, the stranger followed James
Bethune out of the room and out into the busy street.
The clerks in the lower office looked curiously over the
gauze blinds after them, but James Bethune was equal
to the occasion. He took the stranger by the arm,
fearful lest he should lose him, and led him to a restaurant
in Fleet Street, where he asked to be shown to a private
room, and ordered a substantial repast.

'Why should you show me such kindness?' said the
young man impetuously. 'You know nothing about me;
I have no claim upon you.'

'Save what one fellow-creature has upon another.
Hush! not another word! Eat now, and we can talk
afterwards. You will excuse me; it is only an hour
since I dined.'

So saying, he retired to the window, and picked up a
paper lying on the chair. It was a week-old copy of
the *Times*, but he occupied himself with it, so that the
stranger might not feel himself being watched. It was
a touch of delicacy to be expected in such a nature.
The sight of the tempting food made the poor young
fellow forget all but his hunger, and he ate as those eat
who have kept a long fast. It was well, perhaps, that
James Bethune did not observe him; he could not have
enjoyed the sight of his ravenous appreciation of the food
he had provided. It told a too pitiful tale,

'I have to thank you for the only decent meal I have eaten for many weeks; how many I have lost count of now!' he said at length. 'I feel like a new man. There is hope and strength in me once more.'

'I am glad of it. Come and sit down here and let us talk. But suppose you tell me your name first? Bethune is mine—James Bethune.'

'My name!' The stranger gave a violent start, which was keenly observed by his kind friend. 'Oh, well, if you must have it, it is Lovel—Walter Lovel!'

'Well, Mr. Lovel,' said James Bethune cheerfully, for link by link the chain was growing complete, 'suppose you tell me where you live now. I am a stranger in London, and I live alone. I daresay we can be friends.'

'Friends! Did you say friends with such as I?' repeated Walter Lovel. 'What manner of man are you? There is not another in your position in London who would walk the streets beside an outcast like me.'

'That is a sweeping assertion, which I would not like to believe,' said James Bethune with his rare, kind smile. 'But you have not answered my question. Where do you live?'

'Anywhere,' answered Walter Lovel bitterly. 'I have no home. I sleep where I can—sometimes in a wretched lodging, oftenest in the open air. I have not three feet of space under any roof I can claim as my own. Do you know where I wrote that article?—sitting on one of the seats in St. James's Park.'

'Have you no friends or relatives?'

'No; I have none.'

He rose then, and began to walk up and down the narrow room, as if some haunting memory filled him with restlessness. 'I have a story. I suppose most people have, of one kind or another. You deserve to hear it, but I cannot tell it yet. But you were right in saying that I had been reared in a different atmosphere.'

'It did not require much penetration to discern that. You have the manner and the look of a gentleman. But what are you going to do now?'

'Do? What I have done for many days past—pace the streets till darkness falls, and then creep into some corner and seek the blessed oblivion of sleep. How often have I wished that I should never awake! The wonder to myself is that I have not put an end to it long ago. My life is hardly worth throwing away.'

James Bethune shuddered. Verily, if Willie Lorraine had sinned, he had suffered; he had borne an awful punishment for the waywardness of his youth.

'Will you make me a promise?' he asked presently, fixing his keen, quiet eyes full on the wasted face.

'That depends—but yes, I will. You have a right to such poor promises as I can make.'

'Then you will promise unconditionally to do what I ask?'

'If you wish it—yes. It matters little to me what I do now.'

'Then you will meet me outside the Law Courts to-night at half-past six? I shall be free then—that is three hours hence.'

'Yes; I will.'

'Upon your honour?'

'Upon my honour, if I have any,' said Walter Lovel, and a smile for the first time played about his mouth. James Bethune turned his head quickly aside, lest his face should betray something which might arouse suspicion. For that fleeting smile was the faint but unmistakable reflex of the sunny radiance he had seen upon the face of Beatrice Lorraine. His quest was ended, but there was much to be accomplished before it could be crowned with success. This poor wanderer, embittered and soured with his sufferings, would require very gentle dealing before he could be won back to the better way.

'If I dared take such a name upon my lips, I should say, God bless you,' said Walter Lovel, as they turned to leave the place. A soft and beautiful expression stole into his face as he uttered these words; his eyes swam with tears, all the bitterness was gone. James Bethune felt his heart go out to him, and involuntarily he extended his hand.

'I thank God for the privilege I have had to-day,' was all he said, then they went forth into the street. They parted there, with the renewed promise to meet at the hour and the place James Bethune had appointed, and the latter returned to the office of the *Gazette*. If he was abstracted and uninterested in his work that afternoon, it cannot be wondered at; he had much to occupy his thoughts. Directly Walter Lovel was out of his sight, the fear took possession of him that he had lost him again, and he was feverishly impatient for the appointed hour. Ten minutes before the half-hour he was restlessly pacing the pavements before the Law Courts, and, calm, self-reliant man though he was, he felt himself sick with apprehension lest Walter Lovel should fail him. But no; punctually at the half-hour he saw the poor, shabby figure elbowing his way through the crowd, and he drew a long breath of relief.

'I am thankful to see you!' he exclaimed when they met. 'I was terribly afraid lest I had lost you again.'

'Would it have mattered so much to you?' inquired Walter Lovel with a curious look. 'Why should you take such a deep interest in me?'

'I *am* interested. I want to help you,' answered James Bethune hastily. 'Now, do you put yourself in my hands? You believe I truly want to befriend you?'

'Yes, I do.'

'Then come, promise not to utter a word till I give you permission,' said James Bethune with a smile.

'Well, I will; but I am completely mystified.'

'Never mind,' laughed his friend, and, beckoning to a cabman, motioned Walter to enter, and followed him, after giving the order to drive to Finsbury Square.

'I am lodging there just now. My landlady is a Scotchwoman, and is devoted to me. You will feel quite at home with her.'

'I doubt she will look rather askance at me,' said Walter ruefully, glancing at his miserable attire.

'We'll soon remedy that. We'll hunt up something for you to wear till you can get a suit to fit to-morrow.'

'Am I going home with you, then? How can you trust me so? I might be deceiving you all the time,' said Walter with a strange, boyish wistfulness, which made his face look young and pure and good, like the face in the portrait lying in James Bethune's pocket-book.

'I know you are not deceiving me,' he answered quietly, and there was little more said until they reached the house in Finsbury Square. James Bethune paid and dismissed the cabman, ushered his protégé up to his own sitting-room, and went in search of his landlady. He told her just so much as seemed good to him, and with such effect as to rouse the good woman's sympathies, and overcome her prejudice and caution where strangers were concerned. She would have put herself to the most extraordinary trouble to serve her lodger, and if it was to save a youth from utter ruin she was willing to let Mr. Bethune keep him in the house, if he could give his word that he would not create any disturbance or make her nervous.

James Bethune set her mind quite at ease on that point, and then returned to his strange guest. In about half an hour afterwards, when Mrs. Mackay brought in the tea-tray, the twain were sitting at the fire like old friends.

'This is my friend, Mr. Lovel, Mrs. Mackay. I am sure you will be as good to him as you are to me, won't you?' said James Bethune at once, knowing just how to keep the good woman in the best of humours.

She set down her tray and took a deliberate survey of the stranger. In the interval he had washed and attired himself in a suit belonging to his benefactor, and looked like a different being. As Mrs. Mackay looked at the worn face, the blue-veined brow with the rings of gold lying upon it, at the sad blue eyes and the sweet mouth, her motherly heart filled; and he returned her glance with a hesitating, wistful one, as if fearing her verdict. That look won her completely.

'I'll do that, Mr. Bethune, sir. Come and have your teas now, for your friend, poor young gentleman, looks as if he sair needit it.' So saying, Mrs. Mackay hastily retired, quite overcome.

'But what does this all mean?' asked Walter Lovel in a strange, hurried way. 'May I speak now? Am I to stay here with you till to-morrow?'

'This will be your home in the meantime if you will stay. And we'll get something for you to do very soon perhaps in the *Gazette* office. I'll see about it to-morrow,' said James Bethune hurriedly. 'Come away; no non-sense now! the tea is getting cold.'

'I cannot understand it.   I have no claim upon you. Am I to sleep here all night ?   Is this to be my home ?'

It was indescribably touching to listen to his faltering words, and to see the deep, yearning questioning in his sunken eyes.

'I said so, if you will stay.'

Then Walter Lovel laid his arms on the table, and, bowing his head upon them, burst into tears.

CHAPTER XIX.

SAVED.

'How many hired servants of my father's have bread enough and to spare, and I perish with hunger!'—LUKE xv. 17.

IT was the evening of a fine mild February day. There was promise in the soft clear sky, even as seen above the city; and one could imagine that in country places there would be a sweet unfolding of blade and leaf, and that the air would be full of brooding twitterings, whispering of the spring. I like these mild bright days of the early year, they are so full of hope. It is the season when we can enter with better heart upon any new undertaking, for we feel as if nature, which is a great deal to us, though we may not be conscious of it, is with us in our plannings. It takes a great deal to depress one, I think, in the first joy of the dawning spring.

The West End had filled for the season; Parliament had opened with stirring interest; and great London was busier than ever. The newspapers were

hard put to it to find space for all they were expected
to record; and journalists and their assistants did
not eat the bread of idleness. Towards eight o'clock
that evening two gentlemen were sitting by the open
window of a house in Finsbury Square. That broad-
shouldered, fine-looking man, with the noble head and
the true manly face, inspiring immediate trust and love,
we know of yore: he had changed a trifle perhaps, grown
graver, manlier, as life unfolded before him, and he met
one by one its duties and responsibilities. But he had
preserved in the great and evil city a pure heart and a
noble soul, and had verily kept himself unspotted from
the world. His companion was younger, of slimmer,
more effeminate build. His face was as sweet and
delicately-featured as a woman's, and his hair, worn
somewhat longer than usual, gave him something of a
girlish look. He was well dressed, and had the outward
appearance of a refined gentleman. There was no light
in the room, save that thrown out by the fire, already,
however, burning low in the grate. But the moon was
up, and there was light sufficient for these two, for they
were only talking in a somewhat desultory fashion, both
enjoying the hour of well-earned leisure after a laborious
day.

'Are you going to stay in all evening, Mr. Bethune?'
asked the younger of the two after an unusually long
silence.

'Don't stay in for me, Walter. I do not care to go
out,' answered the other, stretching himself in his chair.
'I shall read or write for an hour or two if you go.'

'I won't go if you won't. What would I do wandering about alone? I am too thankful I have a place to
stay in,' said the other; and, suddenly leaning forward, he
looked into the dark, kind face of his friend with eyes

brimming with love. 'Do you know there are times when I can hardly bear my own thankfulness, when I could go down on my knees to you for saving me and making me what I am.'

'Hush, Walter!' The firm, strong hand touched his slender fingers with a caressing touch, almost as one might touch the hand of a child. 'You promised, didn't you, to say no more about it? Do you suppose it is no satisfaction or reward to me to see you as you are, eh?'

'That may be, but it makes my deep debt none the less, Mr. Bethune,' said the other in his boyish, impulsive way. 'And the most extraordinary thing of all is, that you should never have asked me for any account of myself; you took me entirely on trust, but I've tried very hard to prove myself worthy of it.'

'You have proved yourself worthy, my boy. Haven't I seen it all? Haven't I watched your earnest striving, your constant watching over self? ay, and loved you for it.'

'I thought you did. I knew from your eyes when I pleased you. I have had struggles with myself often, for the degradation through which I have passed must leave its traces behind; it makes it harder for a man to be good.'

'It must be so, but you have nobly conquered. I held aloof many a time when I could have spoken, just that you might learn to be strong and self-reliant, and independent of any help from without. But your reward is not lacking either. You are making a place for yourself. Mr. Maynard thanked me only yesterday for bringing you to the office. I don't mind telling you now that I had a hard job of it to persuade him to give you a chance; but he is thoroughly satisfied now, and, as you know, a few words from him mean a great deal.'

'I know. But it is your opinion I value, your approval I covet and labour for. But, Mr. Bethune, why did you never ask me about my past history?'

'Because I believed you would tell me some day. But perhaps if you had waited very much longer I might have asked you.'

'I hardly think it. Do you know that I deceived you at the very outset of our acquaintance by giving you a false name?'

'I suspected it.'

'And yet you never hinted at such a thing! Will you let me tell you it all now?'

'If it will not hurt you, I shall be glad to listen, Walter.'

'It will not hurt me to tell you. It will do me good. I ought to have told you long ago, but I wanted to win your confidence first, to show you that even a poor lost wanderer, such as I was when you found me out, could know the meaning of gratitude,' said Walter Lovel with deep fervour. 'But you must not call me Walter any more. My name is Willie—William Lorraine.'

James Bethune put up his hand to his face, and turned his thankful eyes to the quiet sky. What deep fulness of gratitude and joy swelled in his heart at that moment, I cannot tell you. He had had his moments of torturing doubt during the last three months—doubts which had kept him from sending a word of hope or comfort to the heart of Beatrice Lorraine. I believe it was the fear lest certainty should prove his doubts correct, which had kept him from putting a direct question to the fellow-being he had saved.

'I was born in London, Mr. Bethune,' began Willie Lorraine. 'My father was a merchant in Bishopsgate Street. Our house was in Portman Square, I had one sister; her name was Beatrice; she was fifteen months younger than I. Our mother died when she was four years old. My father was a strange man, Mr. Bethune, either passionately fond or passionately stern. We alternately feared and loved him. He was a proud man too, and would not have done a mean or dishonourable thing, I believe, to save his life. The business firm, Lorraine and Co., was solely his own, left him by my grandfather, who built it up, and it was a mine of wealth. But I hated it from the very first. It made me sick to go into the warehouses, and have bales of goods and stuffs pointed out to me as if they were the objects of importance and interest in the world. I don't know how I imbibed such a dislike to the place, and to the calling for which my father, I knew, destined me from my birth. He was always speaking to me about the time when I should enter . the business; but, though I dared not say anything, I told myself I should never enter it. I had other aims, other ambitions, if you could call a boy's wayward imaginings by such a lofty name. I was of a dreamy, queer nature always, fond of books and pictures, and those kind of things, and I read until I believed myself a genius about to be blighted by the stern decrees of a harsh parent. I used to tell Beatrice about it when we were at home together from school, but she used to shake her gentle head, and tell me to be a good boy and do as papa desired. Poor Beatrice! she was an angel when she was a child, only wise and womanly, and deep-thinking far beyond her years. I often wonder what she is like, and what she is doing now. Well, things went on until I left school, and then I openly rebelled. I said if I could not go to college, and follow after books and such pursuits, I would

do nothing else.   I remember yet that scene.   I, a
puny thing, setting up to my resolute father, and poor
Beatrice, pale and trembling, looking on, too terrified
to speak.   She was even more afraid of him than I ; he
kept her at a greater distance.   I don't want to blame
him, for I have no right to judge a man so infinitely
better than I can ever hope to be; only he did treat
his motherless girl very strangely, and she was one who
needed love.   She had a strange, clinging nature, which
could love and suffer deeply.   I know that now, looking
back.   Do I weary you, Mr. Bethune?   Do you care
that I should go on?'

    'Go on,' said James Bethune with the brevity of
intense interest.

    'He paid no more heed to my remonstrating, to my
weak striving, than if I had been an infant crying for
it knew not what.   He bore me down with the weight
of his contempt, he set me aside as if I had been nothing
at all, and made arrangements for my being apprenticed
in another business house, in order, he said, that I might
be taught what it was to serve strangers.   I had no
alternative but to go.   Of course I had the usual fever
of grand resolves, such as enter most boys' heads at
some period or other.   Again and again I made up
my mind to run away, but either Beatrice won me to
better thoughts, or the terrors and hardships of an
unknown future overwhelmed me; for I was by nature
rather cowardly and timid, and I liked the good and
pleasant things of life.   So after all I went quietly to
my irksome labours.   I used to think my father must
have told my employers to be hard on me, for they
treated me with greater severity and harshness than any
of the others.   Every offence was punished, every careless act reported to my father, so my life was very hard.

I was miserable at home, and miserable at business, and so I fell into bad company for solace. I need not enlarge on it; you know how easy it is for a lad to go astray in London, if he has the least inclination. So I learned to idle my time, and drink, and, worst of all, to gamble and bet, and spend the little I had in questionable ways. I was always short of money, and it was to get the wherewithal to pay for forbidden pleasures that I went to the gambling-table first. After that I went rapidly down, and at last committed the crime which ruined my life. I owed a considerable sum of money, which I had borrowed to pay losses at the gambling-table, and they were pressing me for payment. There is not much pity or sympathy among those who lead a man astray. He is far reduced when he has only his evil associates to depend on for aid. So I was tempted. I got hold of a cheque-book belonging to my employers, filled it up for the amount, thirty pounds,—not a deadly sum, but the crime was the same, and as I forged the name I got payment without difficulty, the more readily as I had been often trusted with messages for and with money to the bank before; as I was a Lorraine, they believed me honest. In a day or two the exposure came. I was a novice in these matters, and I had made no provision for the consequences. For my father's sake I was not brought to justice, I was not punished for my crime in a public court. But I was sent forth into the world an outcast and a felon, without character or any means of earning a meal. I cannot look back on that time when the full consequences of my wicked act rushed upon me. It unmans me even yet.'

He paused, for his voice broke, his hands shook, the veins on his forehead stood out like knotted cords.

Again James Bethune's firm hand closed over his, with that infinite touch of pity which could calm him in his wildest moods.

'So I found myself in the streets of London, homeless, friendless, penniless—such was the awful punishment for my sin. I do not blame my father. I had been an annoyance and trouble to him all my life, and I could not expect him to forgive or condone open disgrace. He disowned me, and from that hour to this I have never seen his face. Naturally I went to those who had helped to bring me to such ruin; but they shrugged their shoulders, and would do nothing for me. Now that I was penniless I was of no use or account to them, they could not concern themselves with my fate. One advised me to go and beg my father's pardon, and ask him to take me back. I could have killed him for the suggestion, it so nearly maddened me. Then I would cheerfully have died rather than look upon my father's face. Will you believe that their callousness was my cure? It gave me such a keen, unquenchable disgust at them and their ways, that I never looked at them again; and then and there I made up my mind to redeem myself, to begin a new and a better life, and from the depths arise a new man, who might perhaps one day hold up his head in the world with conscious honour. Oh, there were no noble and high resolutions which did not visit me at that time, but they dwindled away one by one. You know a little of life in cities, of its fearful competition, its overcrowding, its relentless pushing aside of the weak and the incompetent, its cruel crushing of many an earnest effort. Could there be any place in London for such as I? Could any man be found generous or God-like enough to take me as I was, to give me a chance to redeem myself? In all London I found only one, and he is here. Until I met him what was my life? I dare not begin to recount its vicissitudes. I could make you laugh and weep by turns, and I should unman myself. It will rest just now; some day, when the hopeful present has taken the sting from that dark past, I may tell it, but not yet. Only one thing I entreat you to believe, my friend, God-sent in my last extremity: I have toiled, and waited, and prayed, and *starved*, but in these past five years I have done no action which can rise up and condemn me in my dying hour.'

'Thank God for that, my friend, thank God!' fell with deep emotion from James Bethune's lips. Such an assurance was far beyond anything he had dared to hope for. What a glad message to carry across the Border to the faithful woman's heart, hungering even for the bare tidings of life!

' Months after I left my father's house, I ventured back to Portman Square, because my heart was breaking for a sight of Beatrice. It was to find it empty, and on inquiry I learned that my father had relinquished his business, and had bought a place in the south of Scotland, near where my mother was born. For aught I know they may be there yet. Some day, perhaps, when I have established myself more firmly in this blessed way of life, I may journey there, and ask to be forgiven. I feel as if I could kneel down now and kiss my father's feet, remembering only his love and goodness to me. Of Beatrice, my darling, I scarcely dare to think.'

It was a mighty effort for James Bethune to restrain himself, but he did it. Not yet; a little longer before he could reveal himself. But the consummation for which he had longed, and so ardently prayed for, was coming very near.

' Walter,—I like the old name; I think we will keep

it a little longer,—there is no happier man in London than you have made me to-night,' he said when he was able to speak. 'Please God, there is a length of useful and honourable days in store yet, and your deepest heart desires will be fulfilled. Come what may, *we* are friends for life.'

'For life!' repeated Willie Lorraine, as their hands met in the grasp of love and fealty; then there was a long, deep silence. Many thoughts thronged upon the hearts of both—thoughts which could find no utterance. Those of James Bethune were strangely commingled, and for a space he had forgotten his companion. He saw himself leading back the wanderer to his father's house; he pictured that blessed reunion; he saw the glory on the sweet face of Beatrice Lorraine.

'What are you thinking of, Mr. Bethune?' said Willie's voice, breaking in upon his reverie.

'Thinking? I was thinking of Scotland, Walter.'

'Are you home-sick for it? I have heard that the Scotch never forget or grow cold to their own country. Are you longing to be back?'

'Yes, I should like to go. I have not seen my brother for nine months. Possibly I may take a run down some night soon, returning next day. Well, shall we have our stroll now?' he added, hastening to change the subject, lest Willie might ask questions difficult to parry. 'It is a glorious night. Come, we can talk outside as well as here. I want to speak of your future. I wish and expect great things of you, my boy. You must not disappoint me.'

'Whatever you wish me to do, I shall endeavour with my whole heart,' answered the young man, looking up into the face of his friend as a scholar might have looked into the face of a revered and beloved master. The disparity in years between them was very slight, yet in James Bethune's manner towards his friend there was a kind, careful, elder brother touch which made that disparity seem more marked. The influence he had secured over the wayward heart enabled him to mould Willie Lorraine almost as he willed; one day he would reap the reward for his deep anxiety and unselfish, brotherly care.

On the Friday of that week James Bethune went to Scotland. He had prepared Willie for his going, so that he looked upon it as the most natural thing in the world, and did not associate his journey with the story he had unfolded to him. It was with a strange commingling of emotions that James Bethune undertook his mission, for his journey partook of the nature of a mission. His thoughts were almost wholly concentrated on the master of Nethercleugh; for, unless his heart could be touched, the beautiful dream in which he had indulged would prove only a bitter disappointment. But at least he could give relief and joy to her, of whom he dared not now permit himself to think, so intolerable had his unutterable longings become.

It was a fine, clear, bracing afternoon when he arrived at Lockerbie, and though the train for Lochbroom was in waiting, he set out to walk through the fields. He wanted the freshness of the spring air about him; he needed some such draught to cool the fever in his veins. He wondered at his own excitement—at the wild restlessness which possessed him. Thoughts whirled madly through his brain, disdaining to be curbed, or to own any sway but their own fantasies. At the entrance to Lochbroom he hesitated a moment, wavering whether to proceed directly to Nethercleugh, or wait first at the manse. It was only a brief hesitation; in another moment he was striding along the path by the burn into the Nethercleugh woods. He had no eyes for the sweet budding beauty all about him—snowdrop, primrose, and anemone nestling among the cool green were passed un-heeded; the young green leaves, the fresh sturdy blades burst-ing everywhere, were of no account to him. Yet, at another time, all these would have rejoiced his heart, and filled him with deep, quiet satisfaction; he had always ·loved the spring. The way seemed longer than when he had walked it with Sandy that memorable summer evening nearly a year ago, and he was glad when the grey old house came in sight. Yet he approached it with almost hesitating feet, not knowing with what words to tell his errand, now he had arrived at his journey's end. The servant who answered his summons recognised him, and made haste to usher him in. He was shown to the library, and there left for some time alone.

At length the door was quietly opened, and he knew Beatrice Lorraine was in the room. When he turned his eyes towards her, he saw the sudden start, the wavering light in the lustrous eyes, the quick rush of colour to the fair cheek.

'It is *you!*' she said, recovering her composure in a moment, and advancing with outstretched hand. 'Forgive my surprise. Kitty said Mr. Bethune was in the library, and I naturally expected to see your brother.'

He took the slim white hand in his earnest clasp, his eyes down-bent themselves on her face; and that was all. He had no word wherein. to greet her, only his heart beat with a hungry, passionate pain. It was as if part of himself and of his life were at his side, and he dared not claim it.

'When did you come?' she asked, moving a little

away from him, and touching with tender finger the white bloom of a hyacinth in a glass on the table.

'I came to-day. I have walked from Lockerbie,' he answered quickly. 'How are you? I think you are changed.'

'I have had some anxiety of late. Papa has not been well. I am afraid he will not be able to see you to-day.'

His eyes never for a moment left her face; he seemed powerless to help himself. Till this moment I think he had not quite realized what it is to love one woman with a life's love. He was only awakening to its watchfulness, its deep interest, its yearning care, which is half pain, half joy. He knew her changed. Her face was worn a little and sad; there was a listless air about her, as if she had grown weary of hope deferred. She was thinner too; the figure in the plain sweeping blue gown was very slender, and looked different from that day when she had worn the white robe with the violets in her belt.

'I trust there is nothing seriously the matter with Mr. Lorraine?'

'We cannot say. Doctor Clarke gives it no name. It is as if he had lost his hold on life. I think what I told you of has borne him down at last. How have you been in London?'

He felt the wistfulness of her look, he knew what question her deep eyes asked, and he thanked God in his heart for the message he had brought. 'Has he changed, do you think?' he asked abruptly. 'Do you think his heart has grown more tender over the old sorrow? Does he ever speak of your brother?'

'Not to me, but I have heard him call him by his name, and always in accents of tenderness and love. I sometimes think that if it were possible that Willie could ever be restored all would be well, everything would come right. I think papa has grown hopeless too, now that he is sure it is too late. I suppose you have never had any clue? Soon after you went to London I used to live in half expectation of hearing something, but not lately.'

'But you did not think the blame mine—that I was making no effort?'

'No, only London is such a great place; and you have much to do, your brother tells me. Oh no, I never blamed you.'

'I was not idle, I did my best; and when I was getting very hopeless, God helped me. He sent him to me, Miss Lorraine.'

No word fell from the white lips of Beatrice Lorraine, but her great, solemn eyes uplifted to his face were wide and almost anguished in their pleading.

'Oh, tell me! Is he found? I cannot bear suspense! How and where is he? Is he not irredeemably lost?' she whispered at last, and her trembling hand sought the table for support.

'No, he is well, and happy, I was about to add, but he has much to regret, much to long for and desire. But if ever a man strove to redeem the past, to atone for the error of his youth, he is doing it now. He is on the way to make for himself an honourable position in the world.'

Joy, wonder, incredulous surprise were expressed on the face of Beatrice Lorraine, as these words fell upon her ears. 'It is too blessed to be true. I feel as if I dared not believe it.'

'It is true. It is what I came here to-day to say. Will you sit down now and let me tell you as briefly as possible how it happened ?' he said very gently, for he saw that her nerves were highly strung, and that her strength seemed spent. She took the chair he placed for her, and listened with strained ears, while he briefly recounted the events of the last five months. His telling of the story was characteristic of himself. He spared her to the utmost, touching very lightly on the most painful parts, and lightest of all on his own share in his deliverance. But she understood. Her face grew more earnest, her eyes shone as she listened, there was something more in their depths than interest or even gratitude, only he did not see it.

'And you took him home? He is with you now?' she repeated slowly. 'You did all this for an utter stranger? God must reward you—we never can!' Her voice broke, and she covered her face with her hands. He could not bear the sight, though he knew they were not tears of sorrow. He took a step nearer, and then drew back, knowing he would forget himself. Oh, this was a hard thing, to be in the presence of the woman he loved, whose soul answered to his, yet to feel that he dared not speak! Would it always be thus? Must he carry with him to life's end this deep heritage of pain? Would this hunger of the heart embitter existence always, taking the sunshine from every good gift?

'If you would compose yourself,' he said in a low voice, 'I should like to talk this over a little. Willie does not know I am here, he does not even know I am aware of your place of abode. I have as long a tale to tell him as he had to tell me.'

He smiled, and she looked up with an answering smile, so radiant and beautiful and glad that her face seemed to shine.

'I am listening. What would you suggest?'

'If you think Mr. Lorraine would see him, would receive him with joy, I should say, bring him at once. But if you have any doubt, I would rather wait. I would not for worlds that Walter's heart should receive such a blow just now.'

'Oh, I am sure he will take him. I could not tell you why I think so, only I feel sure he will,' she said, clasping her hands together, and beginning to walk up and down the room. 'I cannot be still, Mr. Bethune, my heart is so overcharged. Willie alive and well, and living an upright life! Oh, I did not dream that God would be so good! It is so much more than I ever dared to hope for, even in dreams. Do you think him unchanged to me still ? '

'May I tell you what he said ? I can remember his exact words, because they sank into my heart. He said, " Some day, perhaps, when I have established myself more firmly in this blessed way of life, I may journey there " (to your home he meant), " and ask to be forgiven. I feel as if I could kneel down now and kiss my father's feet, remembering only his love and goodness to me. Of Beatrice, my darling, I scarcely dare to think." May we not hope for great things, when we think of the spirit which prompted such words as these ? '

Beatrice Lorraine was silent a moment, her eyes fixed on the western window, where the sunset glow was reddening with a wondrous light.

If James Bethune had needed or wished for any reward for what he had done, he found it in the expression on her face.

She turned her head, and their eyes met.

'I would thank you if I could,' she said, simply as a child, with a look such as he had seen many times of late on her brother's face.

' I need no thanks,' he said somewhat hurriedly.
' Now, what is to be done? I cannot stay, for I have to
see my brother, and catch the London train to-night.
Are we to risk it or not? Shall I bring him down?'

' Yes.'

' Then you will prepare the way, and if you have any
fear of his reception you will let me know. A harsh
word might undo the good we have seen. We dare not
expose him to it yet. He must be aided in his struggles
after a better life. Poor lad! my heart is wrung for him
often. Those who have lived happy, untempted lives
know nothing of such agonies as he has endured.'

' I will let you know,' she answered quietly.

' And I will let *you* know when he will come,' said
James Bethune, turning to go.

' But *you* will come with him?' Her upward glance
was timid and wistful; he could not bear those speaking
eyes, they robbed him of his self-control and stern
resolve.

' If you wish it,' he said almost coldly.

' I do wish it.'

' Then I will come. Good-bye.'

' Good-bye till then. God bless you!'

He had often heard the phrase, but falling from these
lips it had a double meaning, a double sweetness.

' God bless *you*, Beatrice Lorraine, for ever and ever!'
he said, and wrung her hand like a vice.

The next moment he was gone.

CHAPTER XX.

'A man in all the hidden sense
  That gives the grand old word its might;
A man who finds his recompense,
  In knowing he has done the right.'

'IS anything troubling you, Mr. Bethune?'
'Why do you ask, Walter?'
'Because you have not been like yourself since you went to Scotland.'
'Have I not? I believe you are right. Yes,
something is troubling me very much. How
long is it since I was down. Only a week,
isn't it?'

'Ten days. Couldn't you tell me what it is? I don't
suppose I could help you, only I know by experience
that things never seem so bad when another shares them,'
said Willie Lorraine. 'Don't you know how often you
have relieved my mind of burdening thought? Of
course I could never be to you what you have been
to me; but perhaps the very telling of it would give
relief.'

'I know it would, but I cannot tell you yet. You will trust me a little longer, altogether if need be, Walter?'

'Why should I not? I would go to the utmost ends of the earth if you bade me, without asking a question,' said Willie Lorraine with the eagerness of his great love.

'It is a boundless trust you have given me, Walter,' said James Bethune. 'My boy, I will not betray it. I will never be less to you than I have been, but more as the years go on, knitting us the more closely to each other.'

Willie Lorraine looked earnestly into the dark, true face of his friend, wondering to see him thus moved. He did not know that hope was being slowly quenched in that anxious heart, and that it had made its vow concerning him, to stand in the place of father and brother in one, because the ties of kinship had failed.

At that moment the maid entered the room with a letter, which she handed to James Bethune.

'For you, sir. It came at four o'clock. Sorry it was forgotten,' she said, and made haste to leave the room, as if dreading a reproof. He took it eagerly, glanced at the handwriting and the postmark; then his face flushed, and Willie Lorraine saw the firm hand tremble as he broke the seal. He took a newspaper from the table, and held it before his eyes, so that his friend might read undisturbed. After what seemed a very long time to Willie Lorraine, James Bethune spoke, in a low, tremulous, eager voice, quite unlike his own.

'Walter' (he always called him yet by the old name, the name by which he was known to the world), 'put down your paper now. I have a great deal to tell you. This letter has removed the seal from my lips. Do you know that handwriting?'

Willie Lorraine took the proffered envelope, and looked
at it for a moment with startled eyes. Ay, he knew it.
Even once seen, that firm, clear, characteristic handwriting would be easily remembered.

'What strange mystery is all this?' he asked with
paling lips. 'This is the handwriting of my sister
Beatrice. How did it come here? Do *you* know her?
Why have you hidden so many things from me?'

'You will know soon, Walter,' answered James
Bethune with a rarely beautiful smile. 'Read the letter
now.'

Thus Beatrice Lorraine's letter ran :—

'NETHERCLEUGH, LOCHBROOM,
16*th February* 1881.

'DEAR MR. BETHUNE,—I could not write before to-day,
because I have had no opportunity of broaching the
subject to papa. We spoke of Willie to-day; but I did
not tell him what you told me. But I see his heart is
yearning over him, and that he has given up all hope of
seeing him again. I said to him that if he heard of him
being yet alive, and doing well, would he not ask him to
come back. "Why torture me with such fancies?" he
answered. "There is no possibility of such a thing." I
think you should come down with Willie at once. If
possible, I will prepare papa; but he is very weak, and
his moods are so uncertain, I may have no opportunity.
I believe it might be well and safe to trust all to a
meeting. You can talk it over. Please give Willie the
enclosed, and believe me, yours gratefully and sincerely,

'BEATRICE LORRAINE.'

'I do not understand it yet,' repeated Willie Lorraine
trembling with excitement. 'Please explain it to me,

Mr. Bethune. How do you know my sister Beatrice? How does she know I am here?'

In a few words, but concisely and clearly, James Bethune explained the whole matter, his friend listening with that absorbing interest with which we await some vital issue.

'But how have you kept it so long? Why didn't you tell me? You knew my consuming anxiety about her!' he exclaimed impetuously.

'Don't you understand I wanted to know your father's state of mind? I would not have you go home, Walter, unless a welcome awaited you.'

'Kind, thoughtful, considerate in this as in everything!' exclaimed Walter; and then, opening his sister's letter to him, he quite broke down.

Wisely James Bethune let his emotion have its vent, knowing calmer moments would soon come.

'What is to be done, then?' asked Walter, flinging up his head at length. 'Beatrice prays me to come down, but I will be guided by you.'

'Nay, not now. Let your heart guide you, Walter,' said James Bethune with a sunny smile. 'What does it say?'

'You do not need to ask. I am longing, yet reluctant to go. There is so much to be forgiven. I shall be humbled to the very dust before them. Since I have been with you I have seen my past in a different light. It seems more heinous to me now than it did even when I was struggling in the depths.'

'Ah, but there is a fine hope with it all now, Walter. After this ordeal is over, you will bury the past, and I know they will gladly allow you to do it. There is no good in morbid dwelling on evil days. What you have to do now is to go forward with a strong heart and

a noble purpose in the good way. You are done
with the old, and you must *be* done with it wholly
and for ever.'

'What strength you give me!' exclaimed Willie
Lorraine gratefully. 'With your guidance and love I
feel as if I could truly be and do good. Whatever the
future may hold of what is worthy for me. I shall owe it
to you.'

'Nay, Walter, let us not forget that divine, unseen
Friend who is ever with us, even when we know it not,'
said James Bethune reverently. 'Human ties, human
props, are very sweet, but not all-sufficient, my boy, as
you will learn more and more as the years roll on.
Well, what plan have we? Does not your heart bid
you go at once, to-night, if that were possible? I
thought so. Well, I shall walk over to Mr. Maynard's
residence and tell him. Nay, don't start; I shall be
wary and prudent, being as jealous over your interests as
you could be. If he spares us, we shall go to Scotland
to-morrow.'

'You will let me walk with you to the door? I could
not rest in the house. Oh, Mr. Bethune, this is a
strange unrest which possesses me! I cannot realize
what has happened. I have so long been alone in the
world, I cannot believe that there is a home waiting for
me, where I shall see those I have lost so long.'

'It will be a blessed reality, please God, to-morrow,
Walter. When shall I learn to utter the new name?
I am afraid you will always be Walter Lovel to me.
There is one thing I would ask, that you will not reveal
to them the whole bitterness of these dark years; it
would wring your sister's heart. She broods upon
things, Walter; it would sadden and pain her for very
long.'

'Is there any one for whom you have not care and thought, Mr. Bethune?' asked Willie Lorraine impulsively. 'Do not fear; there is one theme which I shall find so absorbing and exhaustless that I shall scarcely have room to enlarge upon any other.'

'What is that?'

'Your love and goodness!'

'Hush, boy! You make too much of it. I have had my deep reward. If you had seen the look on your sister's face when I told her the good news, you would know I had had my reward.'

'It seems so strange to hear you speak of my sister, to think you have so lately looked upon her face. Is she not beautiful, Mr. Bethune?'

James Bethune did not at once reply. His eyes were fixed on the dancing flames, and it seemed as if he had forgotten his companion. Then slowly a great light dawned upon the mind of Willie Lorraine. But he was silent, not daring to intrude uninvited upon that sacred silence.

Next day these two travelled to Scotland by the morning train. Willie Lorraine was intensely excited, as was natural; alternately full of hope and joy, and then downcast and sorely weighed down by the thought of his unworthy past, and the haunting fear lest he should find them changed. He spoke most of Beatrice, but it was of his father his heart was full. It was against him he had most grievously sinned, and sometimes, when a memory of his old, stern, unrelenting judging swept darkly across his heart, he could almost have wished himself back in London. James Bethune read these thoughts like an open page, but said little, only prayed that all might be well. As they neared their journey's end, it was as if some unseen hand had laid a tender touch on

T

his heart, calming its restlessness, and making him strong, self-reliant, quiet for the coming ordeal.

'We can get a train at Lockerbie in a few minutes, I believe,' said James Bethune, as the train, nearing the junction, slackened pace. 'But I think the walk would do us good; it is scarcely six miles. What do you say?'

'Yes; let us walk. There is no hurry, is there?'

'Are you feeling a trifle reluctant now, Walter?' asked his friend with a smile. 'Never mind, all will be well. I feel strangely at rest now that it is coming so near.'

'Without you I should never have come. My heart would have failed me long ago,' said Walter gratefully, and just then the train steamed into the station. A number of passengers alighted, and they made their way through the throng outside the gates; and there a footman in livery stepped up to James Bethune.

'Mr. Bethune, sir, and friend for Nethercleugh?' he said courteously.

Involuntarily the two looked at each other, then James Bethune nodded and took his companion by the arm. 'They have sent to meet us; a good omen, Walter. Keep up your heart.'

It was a close carriage drawn by a pair of fine high-stepping roans; it was as if the master of Nethercleugh desired to do all honour to the expected guests. Not a word was spoken during the half-hour of their drive; but when they swept through the lodge gates James Bethune turned to his companion with a smile. 'Look up and about you, Walter; this is home.'

'I cannot, Mr. Bethune. See, I am trembling in every limb! I could not bear this much longer. Oh, I wish it was all over! Am I not a terrible coward?'

'I understand and sympathize with you. It *will* be

all over soon,' said James Bethune cheerfully. ' I want to tell you, Walter, how proud I am of you to-day. You look so well. You are a son of whom all Nethercleugh will be proud as well as I.'

So he tried to reassure the faltering heart, to give him confidence in himself ; but he too became silent as they neared the house. The hall door was open, and when they ascended the steps a maid was in waiting to usher them in. She led the way to the library, and said Miss Lorraine would be with them directly, just as if they were ordinary callers.

' I think I had better leave the room, Walter, before your sister comes,' said James Bethune the moment they were left alone.

' Oh no, I cannot be left !' said Willie Lorraine nervously. ' Do stay.'

' If you wish it, but I would rather go,' said James Bethune, and, walking over to the farthest window, he stood within the rich hangings, and watched the yellow sunlight falling aslant the daisied turf. These brief moments were like hours to both. At last the handle of the door was turned, and there was the soft rustle of a woman's dress in the room.

' Willie—oh, Willie, Willie !'

' Beatrice, my darling !'

Then there was the sound of sobbing in the quiet room, and James Bethune drew the hangings close about him, and stood looking out upon the sunshine, trying to think of other things. They had forgotten him, and he was glad of it ; he had hoped they would.

' Come !' he heard Beatrice say at length, in a trembling, eager whisper. ' Papa is waiting. He is not able to be out of his room. Come away.'

' I am afraid, Beatrice. I *dare* not meet him.'

'Oh yes. There is nothing to fear, dear. We had a long, long talk to-day. I do not know .which I love best, papa or you. Oh, he will be kind and loving, I know! He too regrets the past. And when he sees you as you are now! When I look upon your face, my brother, and see all that is written there, my heart is like to break for joy. You look better than even in the best of the old days. But come; these moments are hours for poor papa!'

James Bethune felt that she had laid her gentle hand on her brother's, and was leading him from the room. He waited until they had gone away, until he heard footsteps die away on the stairs, then the shutting of a door. Then in the deep hush which followed, he too left the room, and took his hat from the table. As he entered the hall, a maid came out of the dining-room, where she had been preparing the table for dinner.

'If Mr. or Miss Lorraine inquire for me, say I have gone to the manse, please,' he said, 'and that I shall return later in the evening.'

'But, sir, I think you are expected to dine. Miss Lorraine bade me lay covers för three, and the master is not able to be down-stairs.'

'Never mind, Miss Lorraine will understand,' returned James Bethune with a nod and a smile; 'and I shall be sure to return in the evening.'

So saying, he walked out into the clear, pleasant air, and struck across the park to the burn road to Lochbroom. His mission was accomplished, his work done, and they had no need of him. Now that the tension of the past days was removed, he felt strangely depressed, almost sad. Was it that the voice of Beatrice Lorraine had awakened once more that pain which he knew was the hunger of love? He walked quickly, trying to rid

himself of these burdening thoughts, trying to dwell
rather on the joy he had helped to bring to the home
which sheltered *her*, but he was glad when he reached
the manse. The hands of the church clock were pointing
to six when he opened the garden gate and strode up
the gravelled pathway to the house. The minister was
at home, and at tea, the housekeeper said with a smile,
and he walked straight into the dining-room.

'Well, sir, here I am again!' he said cheerily. 'Is
there any of that cheering brew left for me, eh?'

The minister sprang up, and gripped him by both
hands.

'Jamie, you just come down on a fellow like a clap
of thunder. What are you doing here again?'

'I'll tell you presently. I'm glad of anything that
gives me a chance to see you,' said Jamie heartily.
'You are looking well. I had hardly time to get a good
look at you last time I was here.'

'I am well, thanks. *You* have been working too
hard, that's evident. Are your traps down-stairs? You
will be going to stay over the Sabbath at any rate.'

'No; I'm going off to-morrow morning.'

'What does all this mean? If you would give me
some sort of explanation of these frequent and extraordinary journeys, I should feel greatly obliged.'

Jamie laughed, and threw himself into a chair. For
the time the feeling of loneliness and depression was
gone—melted away in the sunshine of Sandy's presence.

'Well, I'll tell you briefly, just to satisfy your
insatiable curiosity—I've been at Netherclough to-day.'

'Oh, indeed! I'm certainly grateful that you should
deign to honour me with a call at all!' exclaimed the
minister in feigned disdain. 'What does this all mean,
Jamie? You did the very same thing last time.'

'Well, the explanation is simple enough. I came across the lost son of the house of Lorraine in London, and he has been with me all winter. Anxiety to bring about a reconciliation brought me down. It is effected now, I am happy to say. Willie Lorraine travelled with me from London to-day ; his father's carriage met us at Lockerbie, and I left him at Nethercleugh and came up to you. Will that satisfy you?'

For a moment the minister stared in speechless amazement.

'Do you say so? How calmly you speak, as if it were a very small matter. How did it all come about?'

'It is a long story. I'll tell it another time, Sandy. I want to hear something about yourself. I have to go back to Nethercleugh to-night, for I took a species of French leave after I had delivered my charge. We'll have a long talk to-night yet. We can sit up till morning. It is only once in a while we have the chance.'

'It is. I was over at Star last week, Jamie.'

'Were you? Aunt Susan is in her usual, I know, for I had Mary's letter before I left this morning. Did you see Mary, Sandy?'

'No, I did not dare to go up. I *will* go some day, Jamie.'

The words were significant enough, and James Bethune looked straight into his brother's eyes.

'You have got over it all, Sandy. This has been an eventful year for you.'

'I know what you mean. Do you know, Jamie, Beatrice Lorraine's refusal was the best thing which could have happened to me. It showed me a great many things. It opened my eyes. Some day I shall thank her for it. She is my friend now; she knows a little of my strivings; she sympathizes and helps me in my work. What a friend she is for any man to have! The one who may call her wife will be to be envied, but *I* shall not envy him—that is past.'

James Bethune sat silent, his heart overcharged with deep thankfulress, weighed down by a reverent sense of the unspeakable goodness of God. Only His hand could unravel the knotted skein of life, and bring sweetest harmonies out of direst discord. There stole into his mind the verse of Faber's hymn which Doctor Kinross had repeated to him one evening at the manse of St. Giles,—

'All is right that seems most wrong
If it be IIis sweet will.'

IIow true they were he had proved out of the abundance of his own experience of life.

'That is the carriage from Nethercleugh, Mr. Bethune,' said the housekeeper, opening the dining-room door. 'Gray says he has to take the gentlemen back with him.'

The brothers looked at each other, and Sandy shook his head.

'There is no need for me to go. You will not be late, Jamie; I can easily occupy myself till you come back.'

'Nonsense, man! You must come and help me through with the thanks I know Mr. Lorraine will insist on pouring on me. They *will* make so much of what I did. Why shouldn't you share the general joy? Come away.'

Perhaps the minister was not very difficult to persuade, for he smiled, and, following his brother down-stairs, donned his hat and coat, and entered the carriage with him.

'Fancy we two riding in a real carriage and pair, Sandy!' laughed James Bethune as they bowled smoothly along the dry roads. 'Do you mind the time when we ran barefoot together to gump in the Star burn? We've seen a lot since then.'

'Ay, we have. Do you know, I have thought more of these old days of late than I ever did. I wish the old man were yet alive, Jamie. I shall never have the chance to atone to him for the past. What an ungrateful, unfilial son I was to him!'

'Don't dwell on these old sores, Sandy. Don't you suppose he knows all up there? Why, he knows more about us than we know ourselves; and I believe it is a real joy to him to see his laddies getting on. When I think of it, do you know, heaven seems almost as near as earth. He was a splendid man our father, Sandy; *I* have never met his marrow.'

'You could appreciate him more than I, because you came nearer his true nature. There were many things about him I never understood, just because I stood on a lower level.'

'Oh, come now, don't say that. You were so much away from home; you did not know him so well as I, if I may so put it. I think we have reason to thank God for our home and our early training. It taught us self-reliance and independence. Why, here we are already! Do you know, I would rather not go in. I could go away back to London content, now that I know it is all right. The windows seem to be all lighted,' he added, looking out as they swept round the curve in the avenue. 'That looks like rejoicing in earnest.'

As they ascended the steps to the open door, Beatrice came running down the staircase as if in haste to meet them. Both looked at her in silent admiration, struck by the radiant change in her appearance. Her face was aglow; her eyes sparkling with happiness; her every movement seemed to be fraught with the restlessness of joy.

'Why did you run away, Mr. Bethune? I cannot tell you how I felt when I came down to find you gone.'

'It was better, Miss Lorraine,' he answered gently. 'With such joy, you know, no stranger may intermeddle.'

'He will call himself a stranger after all he has done!' she said, turning to the minister. 'Oh, is not this a blessed thing which has happened? Willie is with papa now, and it is all right. Will you come up, please, and see him now?'

'I will remain down-stairs, Miss Lorraine,' said the minister, feeling that he had hardly a place in that upper room. 'Don't mind me; I know my way to the library, and perhaps you will bring your brother by and by to shake hands with me. I hardly need express *my* gladness; I think you know it is sincere.'

'Oh yes,' she answered with a bright, happy smile. 'Come then,' she added to James Bethune. 'Papa has asked so often if you have come. He thinks with me that we can never hope to acknowledge or repay what you have done.'

So saying, she led the way up-stairs, James Bethune following, feeling almost as if it were all a dream. Like a dream, too, was what followed. She opened the door of her father's dressing-room, and they entered it together. The master of Nethercleugh was lying on the sofa in his dressing-gown, Willie sitting by him with his hand fast clasped in his. James Bethune was surprised to see the careworn and haggard look, as if he had passed through some trying illness. But there dwelt upon his pale face a look of deep and quiet joy ; his eyes, so keen and restless of yore, were filled with peace and satisfaction and an indescribable depth of tenderness and love. The face of his son wore that strange tremulous expression born of strong emotion, and his sunny eyes were still wet with tears.

At the entrance of James· Bethune, Mr. Lorraine dropped Willie's hand, and made an effort to rise.

'Nay, sir,' said James Bethune, advancing, a sunny smile irradiating his true face. 'Do not rise, and do not speak, I beg of you. I know all you would say. Allow me only to express my deep satisfaction at this happy ending, and then let there be no more about it.'

'No more about it!' repeated the master of Nether-cleugh with a somewhat sad smile, and he closed his two pale hands over the one offered to him in such sympathy and friendship. 'Sir, I would thank you as a father for what you have done. My son has tried to tell me of all your goodness, but words have failed him, even as they fail me now.'

'If I needed any thanks, any reward, Mr. Lorraine, it is here,' said James Bethune, laying a kind hand on Willie's bowed head. 'I have hoped and prayed for this. I cannot express what it is to me to see him here beside his nearest and dearest.'

He turned slightly towards Beatrice, who stood with that lovely smile on her lips, a smile of joy and hope and tenderness combined in one.

'If I could hope to do something, just to show my gratitude,' repeated Mr. Lorraine with a mingling of dignity and pleading in his tone; but James Bethune once more uplifted a deprecating hand

'Whatever you do for Walter,—for Walter he will be

to me, I fear, to the end of the chapter,—Mr. Lorraine, will be done for me. We shall hear great things of him yet, I prophesy.'

Mr. Lorraine turned his eyes, full of ineffable tenderness, on his boy's bent head. That look told James Bethune that the reconciliation had been complete, and that love had conquered all. He turned aside a little, for his eyes were strangely dim. He need not have been ashamed of these tears, they were no dishonour to his manhood.

'Willie, will you come down-stairs and see Mr. Bethune's brother?' said Beatrice presently. 'Perhaps papa would like a little talk with your friend. Do come.'

Willie rose then, and, as he wound his arm about his sister, there was an air of proud proprietorship, as well as of fond love, which became him well. So they quitted the room together, the father's eyes following them until the door was closed.

'It is like the past come back,' he said with a tender smile. 'Mr. Bethune, will you tell me what induced you to do so much for those who were almost strangers to you? Nay, I must talk of it. I do not want to lay it aside or think lightly of it, if that were possible. To my dying day I shall be grateful; how grateful even you cannot know. You have not only restored my son to me, but you have made a man of him.'

'Nay, I only helped him to make a man of himself,' corrected James Bethune. 'I fear you will not find it easy to spare him to his London life again.'

'We have talked even of that in the short time we have been together. He has made his choice; he will return with you. He wants to push his way just as if we had not any part in his life. I honour him for it.

I am content that it should be so, at least for a time God forbid that I should stand in the way of honest endeavour. I have learned my sharp lesson well. You will not withdraw your love and care for him yet awhile?'

'Never so long as he needs it. I have not so many friends in London that I can afford to lose the one dearest to me,' was the answer, given with a smile which was more than the words.

'And you will come sometimes—often here? You will learn to look upon this as your home?' said the master of Nethercleugh eagerly. 'I would entreat you to believe that you are as welcome in it as if you were my own.'

'I thank you, Mr. Lorraine; but it will be better for me not to come—not to think too much of Nethercleugh,' answered James Bethune unsteadily, moved by a strange impulse to utter the words.

'Why not?'

'Do you not understand?'

'I think I do. My daughter?'

James Bethune nodded, and for a moment there was a strange silence, and these two men looked into each other's eyes with a long, intense look.

'You love her, as a man loves the woman he would make his wife?' said the master of Nethercleugh at length; and a smile began to creep about the corners of his grave, stern mouth.

'I do; so much that I cannot promise myself that I can see her often and hide it. This has come to me without my seeking, Mr. Lorraine,' said James Bethune in his manly, straightforward fashion. 'I have loved her since that night I saw her first at the manse of St. Giles. But I shall not forget the gulf between us.'

' What gulf ? There is none which *you* cannot bridge. There is no man to whom I would more willingly give my daughter.'

' Sir ? '

' I am in earnest. You may be poor as the world estimates poverty, but you have what any king might envy,' said Mr. Lorraine with kindling eye, for his heart went out to this true and noble man with a great yearning. ' If you can win her love, I shall not stand in the way ; nay, I will give her to you with a thankful, happy heart. Your wife, when you take one, will be a blessed woman.'

He stretched out his hand, and the warm, fervent clasp sealed his words. James Bethune had not yet formed his answer, when there was the sound of sweet laughter and the tread of light footsteps on the stairs, and the next moment Beatrice and Willie entered the room, followed by the minister of Lochbroom.

CHAPTER XXI.

ALL'S WELL.

'O love! that makes breath poor
And speech unable!'
SHAKESPEARE.

O N an August evening the two brothers were walking leisurely over the hill from Markinch to the Star. James Bethune had just entered upon a well-earned holiday, which he was to spend chiefly at Lochbroom. He had only arrived from London that morning, and Sandy had met him in Edinburgh in order that they might first pay a visit to Aunt Susan and their early home. They were a goodly pair as they strode together up the familiar way,—a stranger would have found it difficult to say which was the more striking of the two. Jamie towered above his brother, and carried himself perhaps with a manlier grace. His face, if less smooth and refined, had its own deep charm of quiet earnestness and power. There were lines on the broad brow, and grave, thoughtful curves about the firm yet sweet mouth, which told of wrestling with the problems of life. But he had found sweetness and strength in the struggle, for is there not a glorious joy in surmounting the hills of difficulty, in wrestling with the lions in the path until they be overcome ? The idler and the day-dreamer know nothing of the deep satisfaction which crowns the earnest life of the toiler, and which I cannot but think is a foretaste of that heavenlier calm with which each true servant of the King will be rewarded hereafter.

They walked slowly, as was natural, pausing often to look at some familiar landmark, perhaps a bramble bush or a rowan tree, or some hidden nook in the hawthorn hedge, where the mavises were wont to build. When they reached the brow of the hill they stood still, and, leaning on the stile, looked at the landscape stretching about their feet. The bonnie waters of the Firth seemed very near; they could see each foamy crest on the blue waves, and the white wings of the pleasure-boats out from the sheltered havens along the coast. The May Island and the Bass stood out clear and well-defined against the sky, with the peak of North Berwick Law and the sunny slopes of the Lammermuirs in the distance. Looking landward, the peak of Largo Law seemed almost within a stone's throw ; and they had to recall a Saturday afternoon when they had set out on a secret pilgrimage from the Star, fired with ambition to climb its summit, but had failed in their purpose before they were half-way to Leven. Then their eyes rested on the little hamlet at their feet, which had still a home-feeling for them both. There were changes there too which saddened them. Looking down, they could see the ruins of many a little cottage, which had each its own history they knew by heart. The weaving trade was done in Star,

killed by the great factories, where machinery had completely superseded hand-labour; and so, there being no
occupation for the young folk, they had to seek their way
to the centres where they could find something to do.

'It's not like the same place,' said Jamie with a half
sigh. 'How strange it is to see the loch yonder in
Carriston fields! Buckhaven folk might have gone else-
where for their water supply.'

'It's rather an improvement to the landscape, I think;
but, as you say, it is all changed. Yonder's a new house
building on the Star burn; whose can it be?'

'Aunt Susan will be able to give us the most minute
particulars, I don't doubt,' said Jamie, laughing. 'Come,
we must be wearing down; it's after four o'clock, and
she'll be wearying on her tea, I know. How would you
like to come back here and live, eh?'

'I can't imagine myself doing it. Neither of us would
relish it much, I'm afraid; but it's pleasant to see the old
place again,' answered the minister, and as his eyes
rested on the clustering roofs of the Knowe, a softened
and beautiful expression filled them. And then there
was a long silence, for each was busy with his own
thoughts. As they strode rapidly down the road, past
the malt barns, many a head was popped out of the
doors, and, when they were out of sight, one ran to
another, asking if 'she had seen John Bethune's sons
gang by.' For though Aunt Susan knew of their coming,
she had discreetly kept her own counsel; even in her
age she retained her rooted dislike to 'clashes.' But
she had grown impatient for their arrival, and directly
they turned the school corner they saw her at the
garden gate, shading her eyes under her white mutch,
and peering anxiously up the road. And in a minute
they had received her warm, hearty welcome, and were

in the old, old home once more. It was not changed.
There were the queer, high box-beds, the wag-at-the-wa',
the plate-rack and the dresser with their shining array;
the quaint old fireplace, whitened with pipeclay, and
the ' swee,' with the big kettle singing merrily above the
' lowin' peats.'

' Eh, laddies, an' ye're here again, thank the Lord!
said Aunt Susan, getting on her spectacles to have a
better look at them. ' My certy! I believe ye're baith
growin' yet. Jamie, bairn, ye're jist by-ordinar' like yer
faither. Is he no' noo, Sandy?'

' He is indeed, Aunt Susan.'

' But *ye* are like yer mither, my man, an' *she* was a
bonnie body,' Aunt Susan made haste to say, lest he
should feel himself left out in the cold.

I may mention that Aunt Susan had of late considerably thawed towards the minister, since he had
shown more signs of grace.

' But come awa' an' tak' yer teas. I'se warrand ye're
ready for't. The cakes an' the scones's mine, an' the
butter an' the cream's the Knowes, an' I wager ye
hinna tastit the like sin' ye were last i' the Star. Fa'
tae, lads, an' dinna mind me. It's meat to me the nicht
jist to look at ye,' said Aunt Susan, her voice a little
unsteady in her great joy, and she hovered about them,
attending to their wants, and heaping up their plates
with far more than they could eat.

' Ye're renewin' your youth, auntie,' said Jamie
merrily, for his heart was as light as a feather to-night.
' I believe I'll get ye up to London yet.'

' There's nae sayin',' answered Aunt Susan with a
twinkle in her eye. ' Maybe, if ye get a by-ordinar
braw English wife, I'll come an' gie her a fricht wi' my
Scotch ways; eh, Sandy?'

u

'I don't think that'll be for a long time, Aunt Susan,' answered the minister, for he had no idea of the hope of his brother's heart.

That one thing Jamie had not revealed, because it was too sacred to himself to be spoken about to another. When tea was over they sat chatting for a while, and then Sandy rose and said he would go out for a stroll. Aunt Susan nodded, and continued nodding, apparently with satisfaction, after he had gone.

'He's awa' tae the Knowe, ye ken. Ay, maybe that'll come richt efter a'. Did I no' aye say he wad rue the day he slichted Mary?' she asked with a species of quiet triumph. 'Did ye ken he wrote a letter tae Dauvit an' Jean no' lang syne?'

'Yes, he told me; but they never answered it.'

'Aweel, maybe he deserved it; an' yet, though I never saw the letter, they tell me it was straichtforit an' weel dune. He owned himsel' in the wrang, an' speered if they wad let him mak' up wi' Mary again.'

'And why didn't they write?'

'It was Jean. Dauvit's heart's saft eneuch, but she's been fell bitter ower't. She says he's ta'en the licht o' day awa' frae Mary for mony a year, an' that he maun bear the brunt o't noo a wee.'

'And what about Mary?'

'Oh, they didna tell her aboot it. It's no' wi' her he'll hae the tussle. She's a lamb, laddie, an' her heart's never swithered an inch frae him. But I'm no' for him takin' her even yet, unless he'll mak' up till her for a' she's borne. The cratur's cairried a sair, sair heart, Jamie, an' grat mony a saut tear, when naebody kent.'

'Aunt Susan, I believe he loves her very dearly. His infatuation for another has been completely cured, and his heart has returned to its old allegiance with a deeper hold. I hope they won't stand in the way.'

'Oh, I dinna think they'll haud oot lang. But Jean 'll gie him a word, I dinna doot,' said Aunt Susan. 'But come, tell me anent yersel'. Hoo's things in Lunnon? Are ye workin' as sair's ever?' As she spoke she sat down fair in front of him, and, folding her arms, waited to hear all the news.

Meanwhile the minister had reached the Knowe. The kitchen door was wide open as usual, but he did not enter as he used to do long ago, without notice or ceremony.

'Come in,' answered the mistress's voice in reply to his knock, and there was nothing for it but to accept the invitation. She was sitting darning at the fire, and, looking up when he entered, said, with the scantiest courtesy,—

'Oh, it's *you!*'

Then she dropped her eyes on the heel of her stocking again, and paid him no further heed.

'May I not sit down, Mrs. Campbell?' asked the minister rather lamely, for his reception was certainly calculated to disconcert him.

'There's chairs in the hoose. Ye didna used to need a biddin',' she answered quite as ungraciously, and another awkward silence ensued.

'Wha is't ye've come to see, Sandy Bethune? I'm no' maisterin' ye, ye see, though ye *be* a minister. Is't me, or Dauvit, or wha is't? If it's me, I'm here. If it's Dauvit, he's openin' the roads on Edom's Laund; ye wad see the barley's ready. He'll be in in the inside o' an hoor.'

'Where is Mary, Mrs. Campbell?'

'Mary's—whaur she is,' answered the mistress stiffly;

then she cut her thread, folded up her stocking, and turned her large keen eyes full upon his face.

'We got yer letter, Sandy Bethune, an' it was me that wadna let the maister answer't. I've aye said that I'd gie ye a word when I got haud o' ye, an' I've gotten the chance noo. But ye look as if ye kent what I think o' ye, so I'll no' say muckle on that heid. I said to Dauvit that if ye were as muckle in earnest as ye said in your letter, ye wad come yersel' to the Knowe. Weel, ye have come, an' afore we gang ony further there are some things I want to ken. Should Mary be willint to forgie ye, are ye prepared to mak' up for't a'? Supposin', noo, that ye mak' her yer wife, wull ye dae weel by her, wull ye try an' mak' her happy? Unless that, ye maun gang yer gate again. Mary disna ken ye are here the day, she disna ken aboot that letter, an' she'll never ken frae me.'

Sandy Bethune sat still, with his face hidden on his hand. These were sharp moments, for Jean Campbell's honest tongue did not spare him. Ay, it was a humbling experience for the popular minister of Lochbroom. But he raised his head presently, and met it with a manly courage.

'Mrs. Campbell, if Mary *will* forgive me, my life will be devoted to her happiness. If she will trust herself with me yet, God will help me to make her a happy woman.'

'Then ye can gang ben to the room, an' I'll set Mary till ye. She's no' faur awa',' said Jean Campbell, and her eyes softened a little, and the sternness about her mouth relaxed. 'Eh, laddie, what way did ye bring sae muckle needless vexation on yersel' an' ither folk?' she added, and the tears started to her eyes. She had had her say, and her heart was touched by the minister's downcast look, and by the earnestness of his whole manner. She pointed him silently to the room, and, shutting the door between, sat down by the fire to relieve her feelings with a good cry.

When the minister crossed the little lobby, and opened the room door, there was Mary at the sewing-machine in the window, her fair head bent low over her seam. When he entered she gave a great start, and the white garment fell from her trembling hands, and she shook from head to foot. Sandy Bethune closed the door and leaned up against it, and these two looked at each other in deep silence.

'Is Aunt Jean not in?' she asked at last in a voiceless whisper. 'Let me go and see; I would rather not stay here.'

'She knows I am here, Mary. She sent me to you,' said the minister hoarsely, and then began to plead his cause with an impassioned earnestness such as she had never seen before. Her colour slowly receded, and she leaned up against the table, and listened in a strange, dazed way, as if she could hardly comprehend it. Even while he was speaking, he took keen note of her fragile appearance; he saw how white and blue-veined the little hands were; the wan, worn cheek, the transparent brow, the shadowed eyes, were not lost upon him; oh no, he saw all these, and they went like arrows to his heart.

'What is it you are saying? Are you asking me to be your wife again?' she whispered faintly. 'I hear your words, but I do not understand. I thought it was past for ever.'

He could have knelt at her feet to pray for her forgiveness, his heart went out in such a rush of yearning love.

'If you will only give me the chance, Mary, to try and atone for the past,' he pleaded. 'Be my wife; I will ask no love until I have won it again. My darling, do not send me away! Unworthy though I am, you loved me once. Let the memory of that old love soften your heart. *I* love you now, with the love of a life. Oh, I pray it has not come too late!'

She stood still, looking with far-away eyes through the little window to the waving corn-fields; it was impossible to tell what were her thoughts.

'If, when it was too late, you should regret, you should find that I am not the wife for you, what then?

'Be merciful, Mary! Don't stab me with the past. I know now that you are far above me. Let me prove to you my sincerity. Don't you see I am terribly in earnest?'

He sat down then and dropped his head on both his hands. For a moment Mary contemplated him as if in wonder, and then slowly the light of a sweet compassion began to dawn upon her face. In another moment she was kneeling by his side, and her arm was about his neck. And the past with its haunting, bitter memories melted away in the deep joy of these moments, and there sprang from its ashes a new and boundless trust, which brought to the hearts of both a soothing and abiding peace.

.   .   .   .   .   .

One evening, a week later, James Bethune walked leisurely along the burn path to Nethercleugh. He had left Sandy at Star, and travelled south alone. If he were to come at all, it was time now, for his brief holiday would end in two days. Had he not been under promise, I believe he would have returned to London without visiting Nethercleugh, for the time had not yet come for him to whisper his passionate hopes to the woman he loved, and he knew that at any moment in her presence he might be tempted to forget the vow he had made, to have some worthy thing to lay at her feet before he asked her to share his life.

But Sandy's happiness had awakened in him all the old, intolerable yearnings, and his heart that autumn evening was out of tune with the beauty and fulness of his surroundings. It had been an exceptionally fine season throughout, and in the early parts of Annandale the harvest was gathered in before a leaf had changed its hue. But now there was a yellowing tinge on the beeches, the brambles were purpling in the hedgerows, and the rowan had taken on its deepest crimson, telling that fruitage-time was wearing past. In the Nethercleugh woods some leaves had softly fluttered to the ground; they rustled under the feet of the solitary stroller, as he walked slowly with his hands clasped behind him and his eyes down-bent upon the ground. So he walked in deep abstraction till he came to the little pathway which would lead him across the park to the house. As he emerged from the darkling shadows of the trees, his eyes were dazzled by the blaze of splendour with which the setting sun had gilded the many windows of the old house until it looked like a dream of fairyland. He stood until the glory gradually dimmed and faded away, until the grey turrets were left to the gentle shadows of the gathering night. The hall door was wide open as usual, and the casements of the drawing-room were ajar, the lace curtains swaying gently in the up-springing breeze. His ring at the bell sent the clear, rich echo rebounding through the quiet house, and startled a bird in the ivy into a sleepy chirp of expostulation.

'Oh, Mr. Bethune, sir!' exclaimed Kitty when she came across the hall. 'Mr. Lorraine has been in Edinburgh to-day, and will not return till the late train. Please come in, and I'll look for Miss Lorraine.'

'Has Miss Lorraine gone out, Kitty?'

'Yes, sir. I saw her away across the park, not half an hour ago. If you'll just come in, I'll soon find her.'

'Across the park, did you say? I'll take a walk through the wood, Kitty. Never mind, thank you,' said James Bethune with a nod and a smile. 'If I miss her, she will probably return before me.'

So he crossed the park again, and, re-entering the woods, turned along the path to the wishing-well. How long ago it seemed since he had walked that way with Beatrice Lorraine! Looking back, he could almost have fancied the experience of that night a dream. He was thinking of it, recalling how she had looked and spoken, for he had never been so near her as then, when suddenly he caught the gleam of something white through the trees. Two more steps, and he saw the slight figure of Beatrice Lorraine standing by the wishing-well, with her arm leaning on the mossy ledge of rock which overhung it, her head down-bent, as if her eyes sought to fathom the dusky depths of the water bubbling and sparkling over its basin into the burn below. The crackling of the underbrush beneath his tread startled her, and she took a hurried step forward, and peered through the shadows, until she discerned the tall figure approaching with no reluctant step.

'I hope I have not startled you, Miss Lorraine,' he said, raising his hat. 'I have been to the house, and Kitty thought you had come this way. If I do not intrude, will you allow me to accompany you back?'

'It is no intrusion,' she said, and her white lids drooped over the eyes under his earnest gaze. 'Why have you been so long? We have looked for you every day. Willie wrote that you had left London more than a week ago.'

'Yes, I have been in Fife with my brother,' he said briefly, for his heart was beating, his pulses thrilling, so that he could scarcely control himself. 'And how are you? Well, I hope.'

'Yes, thank you. I am afraid I greeted you rather unceremoniously,' she said, smiling now, and giving him her hand. 'You see you startled me. It is not often I am disturbed at the wishing-well.'

'Then you come often here?'

'Yes. It is a quiet spot. I like it,' she said quickly. 'Have you enjoyed your holiday? You were in need of it, Willie said.'

'Yes. It has been a hot, trying summer, and I have been working hard.'

'In what way? For the *Gazette*, or have you been writing on your own account?'

'Very little of that; I have had other work. Willie will tell you of it. We have been trying what we can for toilers less blessed than ourselves: God has given us some fruit already. But I made up my mind to leave the story for Willie to tell. He will be down whenever I go back.'

'Willie has told us something of it in his letters, and it made my heart burn. Oh, I could share such work, I am sure. My sympathies and prayers have always been with those who have tried to reclaim the lost.' She spoke simply, but with a deep earnestness, and her eyes grew dim with tears.

'I should not like to see you exposed to a tithe of the risks we have run,' he said quickly.

'Why not? Do you think I should not meet them fearlessly? Do you know I grow very weary at times of this sweet, quiet, monotonous life. I wonder if it is wrong to long for the strife of battle rather than the ease of peace? I cannot but think that such a life as mine is must foster selfishness and narrow prejudices. Indeed, I sometimes feel myself shirking unpleasant duties, and then I grow afraid. Papa needs me yet. He is not getting strong very fast; but I sometimes think if he were strong he would leave Nethercleugh. London has a deep attraction for him now.'

James Bethune stood in silence, watching the ripple of the burn, listening to its musical murmur as it danced and leaped joyously in its rocky bed. His whole heart was stirred. Dared he ask this woman, whom he loved and reverenced with all the strength of his true manhood, to share the struggle with him? Dared he offer her such things as he had, asking her for love's sake to come and make a home for herself and for him?—dared he do it?

'How dark it grows here; let us go,' she said presently with a slight shiver, and drew her white shawl more closely about her shoulders. He looked at her then; his eyes, deep-searching and keen, dwelt yearningly upon her sweet face until once more its colour rose. He took a step towards her; he touched her arm, his face dark with passionate pain.

'Beatrice! I have little to offer but my love. Of that you must know something; I cannot hide it! Will you come?'

She looked at him, her breath came quick and fast, but her eyes did not falter in their gaze. It was a moment of painful tension, almost of agony, when the weal of two lives was trembling in the balance.

'Above and beyond any other, for all time,' she said brokenly at last. 'I will try to be worthy. I'—

She said no more, but the folds of her dress touched him; she laid her hand on his. And so he took her,— the woman whom God had given him for his wife, whose heart had awakened to his, who loved him even as he loved her. I think there are moments still when men and women touch the gatès of Eden; when life seems to be a grander, nobler, heavenlier thing than they have yet imagined it to be. So was it with these two.

'It is dark now, my darling, and I must take you home,' said James Bethune at length. 'I cannot realize that I *dare* call you my darling without reproof.'

'And I cannot realize that I am so blessed,' she said, with her head upon his breast; for she had given herself to him wholly, not seeking to hide or to make little of the love which had grown in her heart. Her self-surrender was characteristic of the woman who had been earnest and true in all things since life's deeper meanings had dawned upon her soul. It is not love, but only one of its many counterfeits, which has its questions to ask, its conditions to make, its reservations depending upon the treatment it receives. No; love, thank God! is something infinitely higher than that.

. . . . . .

James Bethune's book is not yet finished; I know not, indeed, whether a line of it is written; but I do know that the largeness of life is preparing him to give to the world something which will live in the hearts and bear fruit in the lives of his fellow-men. He has probed to the heart of things; he has been content with no surface knowledge; he has examined for himself almost every phase of human life. He is known for his keen insight and unerring perceptions, as he is noted for his wideness of sympathy and greatness of heart. It is not for me to say here aught of his work. Who can estimate the good even one earnest soul, following God's leading, can do ? Its influence cannot be recorded in figures or words. His wife is with him in his work. The one is indispensable to the other ; in such marriage there can be no separate life, scarcely a separate thought. It being so, I need not enlarge upon the happiness of their home. The pity is that such types of what the Creator wishes and intends human homes to be, should be so few.

We will leave them here, saying, ' God bless them both ! '

Willie Lorraine, the one son, dwells with his father at Nethercleugh, but does not live an idle life. He is pushing his way forward as a popular writer, and you will find him always on the side of truth and honour and right, condemning with relentless force all opposed to these three. So, beyond a doubt, these dark years which cast a shadow sometimes yet, had their purpose to fulfil in him. The master of Nethercleugh, though in declining health, finds life sweetened by his family ties, which ought never to have had their broken links.

Sandy Bethune is not now the minister of Lochbroom, but has found a heavy city charge. But Mary had her first experience of the duties of a minister's wife in her husband's first parish, where she won the love of all. His only wonder now is, how he could ever have dared to be ashamed of her; and that humbling memory makes his care for her very tender and very encompassing in every way. And they are very happy, and doing a good work where they now dwell.

As for Aunt Susan, she is still hale and hearty in the cottage in the Lang Raw, and seems likely to live as long as those worthies whose longevity so provoked Peter Bethune on his death-bed. It is a pardonable boast with her that at seventy-seven she went to London, and lived to set foot in the Star again; for Jamie himself, soon after his marriage, came to fetch her; and she came back just overflowing with her sight-seeing, and full of the praises of her nephew's wife, whom she speaks of with reverential love as 'Mistress Jeems.'

THE END.

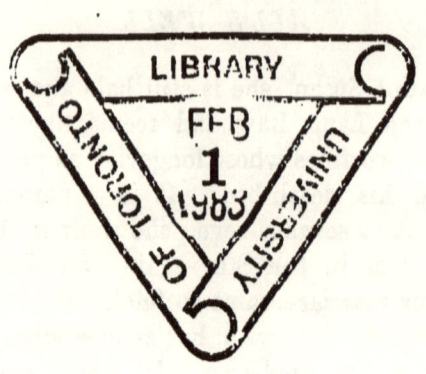

Large crown 8vo, cloth extra, price 3s. 6d.,

Comrades True. By ELLINOR DAVENPORT ADAMS

With Six Original Illustrations by EDITH SCANNELL.

'This is a very charming and original story, and one likely to please old and young. Children will enjoy the adventures of Miss "Tommy" and Conrad, both youngsters being boldly drawn, with natures as frank and loving, and intellects as bright as the most ardent lover of children could desire. The quaint humour of Tommy and the boyish courtesy of Conrad are admirably contrasted, while the narrative of their roamings in wild glens, their country sports and mutual concessions, deepens in interest as Conrad develops into the brave, generous ally of his surly protector. Some incidental sketches of character are drawn with no uncertain hand, one of the best and most amusing being the German violinist, who fails to frighten Conrad, and is subdued by Tommy's aptitude for the study of electricity. The book has a thoroughly refined tone; the "plot" is fresh, and the elements of humour, pathos, adventure, and dramatic incident are deftly combined. It is no narrative of commonplace mischief or schoolroom joking, but sets forth the history of a boy and girl of fine dispositions and active brains, and shows their influence upon each other. The author has observed and sympathised with the fuller needs of children in our fuller day, and her story has an interest of its own for adult readers, since there are but few writers who write equally well for and about children. Her children are real children, but original children, and the system of education which she advocates should have numerous adherents if it turns out many such bright, entertaining, helpful young folk as Conrad and Tommy. The volume is prettily got up.'—*Hearth and Home.*

EDINBURGH & LONDON:

OLIPHANT ANDERSON & FERRIER.

NEW BOOK OF ADVENTURE FOR BOYS.

Large crown 8vo, cloth extra, with Sixteen Original Illustrations,
price 3s. 6d.,

Richard Tregellas. A Memoir of his Adventures in the West Indies in the Year of Grace 1781. By DAVID LAWSON JOHNSTONE.

'I have not met with Mr. David Lawson Johnstone before, but I can heartily say that if he can do anything more as good as "Richard Tregellas" I shall be glad to meet him again. In this Memoir of Adventures in the West Indies in the Year 1781, Mr. Johnstone has produced almost, if not quite, the best boys' book of the season, and although the youngsters are loyal to the old hacks who have supplied them with literary excitement in the past, they will turn with eager interest to the production of this new hand. A story-book like this, daintily bound and beautifully illustrated as it is withal, will insure many an hour's blissful peace in the household when the children romp home for the holidays. *Verbum sap.*'—*English Mail.*

'A model book for boys.'—*Dundee Advertiser.*

EDINBURGH & LONDON:
OLIPHANT ANDERSON & FERRIER.

www.ingramcontent.com/pod-product-compliance
Lightning Source LLC
Chambersburg PA
CBHW060529030726
47498CB00004B/1134